CHOOSE ME

CHOOSE ME

XENIA RUIZ

West Bloomfield, Michigan

WARNER BOOKS

NEW YORK   BOSTON

Published by Warner Books with Walk Worthy Press™

Warner Books

Time Warner Book Group
1271 Avenue of the Americas, New York, NY 10020

Walk Worthy Press
33290 West Fourteen Mile Road, #482, West Bloomfield, MI 48322

Visit our Web sites at www.twbookmark.com and www.walkworthypress.net.

Printed in the United States of America

First Edition: June 2005
10 9 8 7 6 5 4 3 2 1

Library of Congress Cataloging-in-Publication Data
Ruiz, Xenia.
    Choose me / Xenia Ruiz. — 1st ed.
        p. cm.
    Summary: "Told in alternating voices, the story of a Puerto Rican woman and an African American man who find love through a stronger relationship with God"—Provided by the publisher.
    ISBN 0-446-57670-0
    1. Puerto Rican women—Fiction. 2. African American men—Fiction. I. Title.
    PS3618.U56C47 2005
    813'.6—dc22   2004026693

For Elad Demivi, the Adam to my Eve

CHOOSE
ME

You did not choose me, but I chose you and appointed you to go and bear fruit—fruit that will last. Then the Father will give you whatever you ask in my name.

—John 15:16

PROLOGUE

IN THE BEGINNING, *you think you know what love is.*

With the help of the Creator, you are conceived out of love between a man and a woman, your mother and father, who planned you—in some instances—and if not, you'd like to think so. You are born of your mother, who carries you for nine months, protects you in her womb, and then gives birth to you in pain, a pain that dissipates as soon as she sees you are intact, with ten fingers, ten toes. Love is a blessing.

As you grow, you slowly learn what love is because you are helpless and your parents are there to provide for your every need. They love you, no matter what you do, even when you don't deserve it. Love is unconditional.

Later, you think you really know what love is because even though your parents don't understand you, there's someone who does. You hear and see love mentioned over and over in songs, books, and films. You use gifts, flowers, and cards to express love. Love is commercialism and materialism.

As you get older, and presumably wiser, love becomes a deeper emotion that you express with feelings, words, your hands, your lips, your body, your heart, and your soul over and over and over again. Love is desire, passion, and sex.

As the years go by, your definition of love narrows. You start to notice you are running out of time and you must find your true love. Or you start to believe that the one you are with is your soul mate and even if you do not love him—or her—it no longer matters anymore because love is about needing and wanting. Love is about not being alone.

And then one day, you realize that the things that mattered before— the physical, the material, and the sexual—no longer apply and what really matters is that you have someone to talk to, someone to listen to you, someone who gives you peace. Love is companionship, friendship, trust, and commitment.

Finally, in the end, you know that the true meaning of love is the biggest example of selfless love, the greatest love of all. You know that love, real love, is about sacrifice.

In the end, as in the beginning, love is a blessing.

PART
ONE

CHAPTER 1

EVA

LEAD US NOT into temptation . . .

Most days I truly believe that prayer is a very powerful thing. I am a staunch believer that prayer has the ability to heal wounds, grant blessings, and rescue a person from the deepest, darkest troubles in a way that defies earthly logic.

. . . but deliver us from evil . . .

The line from the Lord's Prayer was running through my mind because at the moment, I could not take my eyes off an almost perfect image of one of God's finer creations standing a few feet away from me in the Native American book section. I was farther down the aisle, in the Latin American section where Border's Bookstore had decided it belonged, along with the various "others"—African American, Asian American, and Women's Studies.

Just then, the man looked up and I looked away to where a couple was busy groping each other as if they were in the corner of some dark club instead of a bright bookstore chain that sold a variety of books, coffee, and biscotti. Lately it seemed couples such as these were taunting me wherever I went.

Please Lord, lead ME not into temptation . . . I prayed. A big part of me deeply believed in the power of these words. I believed that if I kept repeating them over and over, I could cast away the temptation, will this man away from me. But another part of me wanted him to stay right where he was. I wanted him to try to give me his best line so I could shoot him down, to prove once again how powerful was my endurance. But what I really wanted was to have an intelligent conversation with a man, something I hadn't had in a while.

That other part of me, the carnal side, the part that wasn't dead, couldn't help but steal looks at him, taking inventory—one peek at a time. He was about five-nine, not very tall, with a pleasant chiseled face, like it had been sculpted by a surgeon's knife, and probably was. I've heard of people who have their cheek fat sucked out, or their back molars removed so they can obtain such statuesque definition. His curly, close-cropped hair glistened in the sun that blazed through the plate-glass windows. Even though he was dressed in blue sweatpants and a fitted T-shirt—his biceps, forearms, and back fighting for space—he looked debonair. *Bam-Bam,* my sister, Maya, would coin him, referring to a man's muscled physique bursting at the seams.

I have always been attracted to Black men. Perhaps because to me they resemble the *café con leche* to coffee-colored cousins and uncles in my Afro-Latin family. Or maybe because they were the first ones to notice me when the Latin boys in high school had passed me by. And it wasn't that I had a preference for Black men as some men and women had accused. Back when I was in the world and it came to men, I didn't discriminate as far as their ethnicity. But I felt a special connection when it came to Black men that went beyond the physical—something along the lines of kinship, something I didn't feel instantaneously with Latinos or men of other nationalities.

This man, although not exactly cover-model fine, had an attractive quality about him. Or maybe I was getting so desperate that any man would do it for me. After all, it had been five years since I had been with a man.

I wondered why he was in the Native American section, then I realized my hidden prejudices that came from living in America all my life were showing their true colors. Maybe he found out he had a Native American grandparent. Or perhaps he was one of those people obsessed with Native Americans, as if they were some kind of extinct species. As I wrestled with my carnal nature, I knew I should take my behind straight to the Spirituality-Religion section and nourish my soul. But my feet were not listening to reason and I could not move.

The next time I glanced up, he was looking right at me and I knew my cover was blown. Having gone directly from work to my boxing class, I was still clad in my Lycra capris and tank shirt with my warm-up jacket tied around my waist. My hair was pulled back and up into the usual hasty ponytail I used when exercising or when I was in between touch-ups. I felt exposed. Losing my courage, I started to slowly inch farther away, scanning the shelves like I was searching for a specific book. When I looked up again, he was walking away and I thought that I had never seen a back as beautiful as his. The shoulders were slightly hunched, the blades poking out, enticing me. I wondered why God had made men's bodies so appealing, but yet expected women to practice restraint. I had hoped for some supernatural courage to overtake me that would allow me to engage the man in conversation over a book, or on the topic of God, or perhaps invite him for a cup of coffee, but it was too late. He was about to turn the corner, headed toward the exit. I felt disappointment, but at the same time, relief.

"Excuse me, sir? Can I ask you a question?"

I whipped around to find my best, and soon-to-be-dead, friend, Simone, going after Bam-Bam like she had no shame. I grabbed her T-shirt, which was tied in a knot at the back of her waist, and tried to usher her in the opposite direction. But she resisted and, having several inches of height and toned muscle on me, I lost the tug-of-war.

"I'm going to hurt you," I whispered viciously, knowing eyes were upon us from all directions.

"Shut up, here he comes."

When I turned around, Bam-Bam was sauntering toward us, so I pulled out the nearest book, *The Latina's Bible*.

"My friend and I are collecting data for our class on human sexuality," Simone lied matter-of-factly, clutching her legal pad and pen. "We were wondering if you could answer a few questions." I couldn't believe her. We were getting too old for this stuff.

The man looked curiously at us—first at Simone, who at just under six feet with heels stood several inches taller than he, then down at me, trying to hide my humiliated face in the thick paperback book.

"What are you, grad students?" he finally asked.

"Undergrad."

"You don't look like undergrads."

"We go to night school, okay?" Simone retorted. The one thing Simone disliked was when people assumed she was older than she was. With her svelte figure and chin-length hair in a curly natural, she looked at least fifteen years younger. No one could wear an Afro like Simone. She was the kind of woman who could make a potato sack look good, the kind of girl others had hated because boys were drawn to her; the kind of woman other women envied but for all the wrong, petty reasons, because she stole the spotlight the minute she entered a room.

"Now, do you want to participate or not?" she chided him in that teasing, reprimanding way she used on men when flirting.

"Sure, why not?"

"Shall we?" She pointed toward an unoccupied table with four chairs. They sat down, but I remained standing.

"Eva, come on, this is your project, too," Simone insisted so innocently I almost believed her myself. I debated whether to ignore her and just walk out, pretend I didn't know her, leave her hanging. But knowing Simone, she could always embarrass me worse than I ever could her and she wouldn't even care about the unwanted attention. There was no shame in her game.

"Okay, um . . . What's your name?" she started.

"Don. Hey, you're not going to use my name?"

"No, we're using numbers. But you don't want me to call you by a number, do you?" Simone looked up at me. "Eva. Are you going to sit down or what?" she said in her most impatient tone, the one she would use on her child—if she had one.

"Yeah, come on, Eva," Don said, smiling, taking me in from head to toe in one sweep. My attraction to him was slowly fading.

I smiled feebly and sat in the chair nearest to me, but at the other end of the table, browsing through my book like I was seriously interested. I realized that *The Latina's Bible* was not a bible at all but a resource book of love, spirituality, and family.

"I'm Simone," she introduced herself, pronouncing her name "See-mo-NAY," the stage name she had created for her new modeling/acting career. I rolled my eyes and held back from saying, *Your name is "Seh-MOAN" from the northwest side of Chicago.* Ever since she had turned forty a couple of months ago, she had undergone a midlife crisis of sorts, getting a leopard tattoo on the small of her back and a navel ring, in addition to legally changing the spelling of her name to "S'Monée," including puncutation marks. I told her I didn't care if she had court papers, she would always be "Simone" to me.

"This is Eva," she added.

"So I heard."

I glanced up from my book and saw him leering at her chest, recently purchased with her last few modeling jobs.

"Okay, Don, pay attention, sweetie. I'm up here. Question number one . . . What do you think of celibacy?" Simone asked, reading from a fictitious list of questions.

"I . . . I don't know."

"Do you think it's natural, normal?"

"For some people, I guess it's natural, like priests, or nuns."

"But what about normal, everyday people? Like, say, a woman who hasn't had sex in five years."

I knew that if I made any movement, any facial expression, any noise, he would know she was talking about me. Giving her dirty looks was almost routine for me so it was hard to keep a straight face, but I kept my cool and kept my head down as I slowly turned the pages.

"I guess if she's happy not having sex, well, I say go for it. But I mean, I can't see how, for five years . . . unless she was like, unattractive, you know, or really fat."

I could keep quiet no longer. "That's a really nasty thing to say," I said, looking straight into his mocha-colored eyes for the first time.

During my teenage years, I had fought anorexia when I wasn't even overweight, before it had become a popular women's problem, before I knew it was a disease with a scientific name. Then years later, when I did gain weight, I went on yo-yo diets, losing and gaining the same thirty pounds over and over. The only good thing that came out of my last relationship with a man was that he helped me lose the weight that had been dogging me, and I had succeeded in keeping it off after the breakup. Still, I carried a sore spot for overweight people and took it personally if I saw or heard anyone criticizing them. Inside, I was still like them.

"I mean . . . I just don't think it's normal for an attractive, healthy woman to deny her sexuality," he continued, not really apologizing at all. "Unless she has some leftover issues from her childhood."

Jerk! I wanted to yell. I got up, ready to go, and then I heard Simone go too far. "Well, Eva's celibate."

I shook my head in disbelief even though she had done this to me many times before, when we partied long ago before I got saved, but back then we were usually drinking and I was able to laugh it off. I dropped the book on the table and spun around and walked away. She called me but this time, I didn't look back.

Being celibate has its advantages. First of all, I had cleansed my body of what I considered to be unclean, germ-carrying men—the men I had slept with in my past without using latex protection, men who had been with countless other anonymous women. Even before the AIDS hysteria, before I found a reliable birth control method that gave me a false sense of protection—from pregnancy but not from STDs—I thought celibacy made sense. Second, celibacy gave me control over my body, which in turn, gave me power over my emotions and my life. I was free from the drama that came with sex. I didn't miss the games, waiting for calls that never came, and the taking for granted that happened once a woman gave herself to a man. But most important of all, being celibate had spiritual advantages. The knowledge that being intimate with a man outside of marriage was wrong went back to my religious upbringing and was reinforced by my mother's warnings. To know that I was pure once again in God's eyes was the biggest reward of all.

So I was proud to be celibate and even wore the T-shirt—"Celebrate Celibacy!"—which Simone had specially made for me on my first anniversary. As one of the leaders of my church's youth ministry, I counseled preteens and teenagers to lead lives of abstinence. I felt blessed when Maya would tell me of her never-ending drama with Alex, her husband, or when I saw how depressed Simone became after men dropped her once they realized they were being used. So why was I so angry with her?

"You were the one who said you wanted to have stimulating conversations with educated men, with similar tastes. Were we not in a bookstore? Is that not where educated men go? I was just trying to help a sister out. I love you, you know I love you, but I hate to see you denying yourself what is fundamentally a human right A basic human right that should be covered in the Constitution. Life, liberty, the pursuit of happiness, *and* getting your groove on. I mean, why does it have to mean anything? Why can't you just have sex and stop attaching so much baggage to it?"

I had forgotten Simone was in the car. When she followed me out of the bookstore, I refused to talk to her, and realizing she had crossed the line this time, she sat in the backseat instead of next to me in the front. She knew my anger was the one thing over which I hadn't gained control. Because of my unpredictable temper and because Simone and Maya thought I hated men, they called me "Evileen." Most of the time, it didn't bother me because I knew I didn't hate men, I just didn't have much patience for the majority of them. However, the nickname still stung when I wasn't in the mood.

"Are you going to stay mad at me all day?" she asked when I didn't comment on her tirade.

We didn't speak for the next couple of miles, ignoring each other: me driving in contemplation, her thumbing through her latest movie script. She was currently starring in an independent film about a woman who couldn't decide between the two men in her life, a role that was written for her by one of her two lovers, an amateur screenwriter-producer-director eight years her junior. The other man, an older man, was the owner of the salon where she worked, her day job.

At the next light, I braked extra hard, jerking her forward.

"That was totally unnecessary. And childish," she said.

"Put your stupid seat belt on," I told her.

A car pulled up next to us at the light and I looked over casually at a late-model Mercedes, then at the brother with a bald head, wearing a business suit and drumming his fingers on the steering wheel to a Ramsey Lewis tune on his radio.

"Unfortunately, Don was involved with someone," Simone continued.

The brother bopped his head over in our direction and nodded in acknowledgment. Still upset, I ignored him.

"Hello," I heard Simone call from the backseat.

"Hello," he answered, smiling over his shoulder at Simone. "Why are *you* in the backseat?"

"My friend likes to pretend she's my chauffeur."

The light changed and I hit the accelerator, jerking her back.

"Do you have to speak to every man you come in contact with?" I said, disgusted.

"Why does it bother you so much?"

"It doesn't bother me. I just don't understand why you have to flirt with every man who speaks or smiles at you."

"It's basic human nature. I am woman, I like men; ergo, I flirt." She explained this with her expressive, salon-manicured hands and her slow, clipped English. "I can't help it if you don't like men. Miss Evileen."

I decided to let that one go. "Just because I don't screw men as often as I go to the bathroom doesn't mean I don't like men," I told her, hoping my words would hit their mark and shut her up. "Just because sex is basic human nature doesn't mean you have to act upon every desire. You're not an animal."

"For your information, I don't screw men as often as I go to the bathroom—which is a tasteless analogy, by the way. You need to stop being so self-righteous just because you have a low sex drive. I can't help it if I'm high-natured." Through the rearview mirror, I could see her glaring at me, furiously snapping the pages of her script.

"How many men *have* you been with?" I asked her.

No response except the flipping of pages.

"Are you ashamed? I mean, if you're so high-natured, and it's such a basic human need, why can't you tell me?" I pressed.

"Because it's too personal. And no, I'm not ashamed."

"You know my sexual history. I have nothing to hide."

"I don't either, but that doesn't mean I'm going to confess the intimate details of my life to you."

"Is it that you don't know or you can't remember?"

Her eyes narrowed like a snake's and when she spoke, her voice was not her own. "My sexual life is between me, my men, and the Creator, and no one else."

"I only asked to prove a point. Women want to be equal to men when it comes to sex, but the truth is, we can't brag about our conquests like they can, because *we* are the spoils, we are the ones who get soiled. And it's not just because of societal stigmas. It's because of the way we're made biologically. It's the way of the world."

"I'm not ashamed," she repeated. "I just don't think it's any of your business."

I shook my head, exasperated. We had had the same argument many times and it always ended the same. She accused me of being a man-hater; I accused her of being a man-teaser. Back in high school, Simone wasn't very popular because many of the other Black girls didn't like that she spoke so-called proper English and had long hair. Back then, she wasn't tuned in to her Afrocentric side and wore her hair relaxed. The same Black girls didn't like me because even though I looked Black, I spoke with an accent. The Hispanic girls stayed away from me because even though I was Hispanic, my skin was too dark, my hair too curly, bordering on kinky. Unlike the other girls, Simone never questioned why I read *Essence* or books by Black authors, nor did she ask me to teach her Spanish curse words. The teasing and our exclusion from the popular cliques made us best friends. One would think she would remember those earlier days, before she pulled a stunt like the one in the bookstore.

I approached Simone's apartment building and braked, switching into park abruptly and bringing the car to a jolting stop. Still looking at me in the rearview mirror, Simone gathered her bags from her earlier shopping spree, her fashion magazines, and her script.

"So are you coming to the screening party this weekend or what?" she asked quietly.

"I don't know. I'll let you know."

"Maya's coming." She leaned on the passenger headrest, suddenly trying to make up. "I need you guys there. You know I love you, right, *chica*?"

"I told you, Puerto Ricans don't say *chica*, they say *mija*."

"Well, I like *chica*. *Mija* sounds like 'hee-haw.'"

Simone, who had been my girl for over twenty years, was finally learning Spanish, but like everything that took time and patience, she wasn't trying too hard and wanted to write her own rules.

"You forgive me?"

"Yeah, yeah, get out."

She blew me a kiss and exited. "BYOB!" she yelled as I drove away. The second "B" referred to not only "beverage," but to "boy"—the latter of which I didn't indulge.

Home at last, I kicked off my shoes and absentmindedly browsed through the mail on the sofa, petting King, my sons' rottweiler, as he snuggled his head on my lap. When they were little, I promised my boys, Tony and Eli, that they could have the dog of their choice once we got a house. When they asked for a rottweiler, however, I hesitated, given the bad reputation the breed had in the media and the public's mind. They tried to convince me that we needed a big dog to protect us since we didn't have a man in the house. After talking to a dog breeder who insisted that it was the owners who made the dog, I caved in. The boys took the last part of their grandfather's name, my father, Joaquin, and named the dog King. As everyone predicted, I ended up taking care of King after they left for college. At first, I threatened to give the dog away, but eventually I fell in love with the vicious-looking, yet noble, animal whose bark and appearance were worse than his bite.

I reached over to the phone table and checked the voice mail. I had six calls: Maya called twice and my aunt, Titi, called the other four times, from Puerto Rico. I didn't feel like talking to anyone, not even my sister, who was closer to me than anyone else would ever be. I felt the beginning of a headache, which could mean one of three things: my monthly cycle, a barometric pressure drop, or stress. Since it wasn't that time of the month, and Simone's childish prank, while not stressful, had thrown my good mood out of whack, I attributed it to a storm front that the weatherman had been threatening for days. Sometimes I thought it was denying my "basic human right" that made me so moody. But other times, I knew it wasn't just that; I had been moody since I was a kid.

I fed King and let him out into the backyard. After changing out of my workout clothes and into a top and sarong, I reclined on the sofa, pressing the remote connected to the stereo and TV. On the stereo, I had Yolanda Adams and Táta Vega's CDs from the day before. On the TV, I pressed the mute and closed-captioning buttons because I preferred to read the news rather than listen to the broadcaster's scripted commentary.

The best part about my being single was the peace and solace. There were people who always needed to be with someone—like Simone—and then, there were people like me who longed for oneness. I had never been alone, going from my father's house, to my aunt's house, then straight into an early marriage and premature motherhood. After my divorce, I raised Tony and Eli, who were, at last, both away at college. The things I enjoyed doing in my spare time—reading, listening to music, and writing essays and articles—were all things that didn't require another person. I was only just beginning to enjoy being alone.

I glanced periodically at the TV screen with a combination of disbelief and dismay. The images of the latest murders, political corruption, and terrorism had become all too familiar so that the reporters' straight-faced presence seemed trivial. By the time the newscast closed with the feel-good story about a toddler calling 9–1–1 and saving her mother's life, it was too little, too late.

The phone rang, but I didn't move to answer it right away. After spending the majority of my day on the phone at work, it was the last thing I wanted to do at home. I debated whether to let the voice mail pick up, but I knew if it was my sister or aunt, they would think something was wrong. Ever since my children left home, they constantly checked up on me, worried that I was at the mercy of the psychos who roamed the streets of Chicago. I reached over to the phone table, just out of reach, and ended up on the floor with a thud.

"What?!" I answered, irritated.

"What's wrong with you?" Maya asked.

"Nothing. I fell reaching for the phone," I said, getting up.

"Dummy. Listen, you're still going to Simone's party, right?"

I sighed. "I don't know. She made me mad today."

"What did she do now?"

"It's not even worth talking about."

Simone had been my best friend first before I introduced her to Maya, who was a year younger than us. Over the years, they became closer because they always had the topic of men in common. Maya had Alex and Simone was never without male companionship. Things changed when Maya started cheating on Alex—although Maya didn't consider it cheating because she had not slept with her "friend"—yet. Simone thought what Maya was doing was her God-given right since Alex had cheated first. I told Maya she should divorce Alex if she didn't want to be married anymore. After all, she had religious grounds and just as she had done when she first got saved, I quoted the scripture she cited to me after my own ex-husband cheated: Matthew 19:9, which justified divorce on the grounds of adultery. Although it refers to a husband divorcing his wife, it applies to husbands also, she had insisted. She and Simone thought I was crazy to suggest that Maya divorce. *Who is going to pay the mortgage and car notes?* Simone asked. *Who is going to raise our two sons, Marcos and Lucas?* Maya demanded. Maya thought divorce was the easy way out for husbands; Simone believed staying married while doing your own thing was the best revenge. What Maya objected to was Simone's insinuations that her relationships with her two lovers were similar to Maya's relationship with the two men in her life.

"L's coming," Maya whispered. Maya referred to Luciano, her friend, as "L" or in feminine pronouns just in case Alex was within listening range.

"Do you really think that's smart?"

"*She* said *she's* tired of meeting in dark places."

"Whatever." I was temporarily distracted by Yolanda Adams singing "The Battle Is The Lord's" juxtaposed by the TV clips of the latest suicide bombing in the Middle East.

"What's wrong with you?"

"Nothing. I have a headache." I began to sort my bills in one pile, junk mail in another, and the latest issues of *Hispanic, Black Enterprise,* and *Diaspora,* a new Christian lifestyle publication, in a third.

"You'll be better by Saturday, won't you? I want you to get to know *her*."

"I don't want to get to know him." So far, all I knew about Luciano was that he was half-Cuban and half-Black. I vaguely remembered Luciano from high school when they first met, before Maya started dating Alex in her sophomore year. Years later they met again at a school where Maya was a teacher and he was a security guard. But by then, she was married to Alex and Luciano had married the first of his three wives. Maya said he treated her like a queen. I told her all men did—in the beginning. But she insisted he was different, as all women who were in love believed. There was no reasoning with her; her rationality was gone.

It wasn't that I sided with my brother-in-law, or that I felt sorry for him, I just didn't like being an accomplice in Maya's tangled web of deceit. After getting over the fact that Alex had seduced my fifteen-year-old sister when he was eighteen, I thought he was a good man, the kind of guy who would be good to her. But then he cheated, and it was almost like he had deceived me also. Initially, I took it personally, but I eventually forgave him, partly because it was the Christian thing to do, partly because he was a good father, but mostly because I didn't have to live with him.

"If you're mad at Simone, I better not tell you what she has planned."

She got my attention. "You better tell me."

"I can't—" she said, then stopped and her voice faded away as she turned to speak to someone in the house. "What? I don't know where it is. Just look for it, sweetie. That's what I do when I can't find stuff." She turned her attention back to me. "She told me not to tell."

"Maya, I am not kidding," I warned. "Blood is thicker than water."

We had all married in our teens, within months of each other. Simone and me were nineteen, Maya was eighteen. None of us had been counseled about going on to higher education since we had worked from the time we were fifteen. We were all anxious to be on our own, so we made plans to get an apartment together. But at the time, we all had boyfriends we loved, and marriage seemed like the next best thing.

Although the youngest, Maya married first. While Alex worked at City Hall, she got her bachelor's and master's in education. They were married almost nine years when their twin boys were born. After teaching for several years, she became one of the youngest principals in the Chicago public school system while Alex became an alderman.

A few months after Maya wed, Simone married her high school sweetheart, Bruce—not because he asked her, but because she wanted out of her parents' house. The marriage lasted a year before she decided she wasn't cut out to be anybody's wife. Instead, she decided to pursue a modeling and acting career. Over the years, she appeared in several magazine ads and acted in a few local plays, even worked as an extra in a couple of big-name movies. In between modeling and acting jobs, she worked as a manager at an upscale hair salon. She lived rent-free in her father's apartment building, and always had men who provided her with almost everything else she needed.

"Okay, okay. She's going to set you up with a guy at the party."

"Ooh. She is so dead." The throbbing got worse in my temple and I began applying pressure with my thumb.

"You're not supposed to know, so don't call her, please? She's just looking out for you." Again her voice faded away. "Alex, honey, I'm on the phone," she said, condescendingly. "I swear every time I get on the phone . . ."

"What's his name? Where did she meet him? Give me details or else. I mean it, Maya."

"I don't know. All I know is she seems to think you have a lot in common with him."

I closed my eyes trying to squelch my anger at Simone while wondering whether my own sister knew more than she was disclosing. The last time Maya introduced me to a man with whom she thought I had a lot in common, he turned out to be an ex-con who had found Jesus while incarcerated. Not that I don't believe in the power of God to transform criminals, but after he beat up a guy who took his parking spot on our second date, I decided he still needed some more Jesus.

"You never know," Maya continued, "this could be your Mr. Righteous."

"Riiigght," I said cynically.

CHAPTER 2

ADAM

THERE IS NOTHING like a good old-fashioned STD to clear a man's head. After I got one three years ago, I vowed to be more careful with my choice of ladies and to wear condoms more consistently. I abstained the required six weeks—which was torture—and thereafter I did the condom thing—more torture, but the alternative, another STD or a child, would have been worse. After that, I dated sporadically, never spending the night, or sending the woman I bedded home rather than waking up next to her with lies or excuses. Not that I had been with that many women. If I thought about it, I could probably count them on the digits of all my extremities and still have fingers and toes left over. I could even remember their names—well, with the exception of two.

Sondra was the first and last woman who broke my heart. We had met at an African arts festival, and truth be told, I was attracted to her looks and body at first. But she manifested into something more, the kind of woman who made a man want to do everything to defy male stereotypes. We talked about moving in together, but after my first live-in disaster, I was still cautious and held her at bay. I couldn't handle the fact that I was falling in love, so we broke up.

A few weeks later, I slipped and slept with a one-night stand without protection. As sadistic as it sounded, having an STD the second time around was a blessing. Thanks to an overzealous resident who insisted I have an ultrasound, a mass was discovered on my testicle and eventually diagnosed as cancerous. Subsequently, I was referred to a specialist. Even though the doctors all assured me it wasn't related to my sexual partners or the STDs, I became scared enough to put women on the back burner. The first specialist recommended surgery, but I refused and sought a second opinion. The second urologist also stated he couldn't treat me without surgery. The fact that the specialists were men who didn't seem to understand my refusal to part with a vital part of my manhood made me search for a third opinion. After doing some research on the Internet, I found a doctor, a woman, who was conducting a study that involved removing the tumor without surgery, using an ultrasound-guided needle. I agreed to this procedure, which was followed by multiple courses of radiation and chemotherapy, then months of observation and tests. During the treatments, I was too weak and sick to care about sex, let alone think about it.

After the doctor declared that the cancer was in remission, I also went into an emotional remission. I no longer viewed women as beautiful creatures or Venuses, nor were they Delilahs or Jezebels. They were just mortals from another dimension to be treated with extreme caution. Now, whenever I saw a hot lady teasing me with her short skirt or low top, I saw warning lights blinking on and off: *Danger, Danger! Proceed with Caution!* All I had to do was envision the humiliating examinations, or the life-draining radiation and chemo treatments, and that would be all she wrote. Most times it wasn't that hard, since some women were turned off by my grungy appearance and saw me as a poor brother who wouldn't be able to wine and dine them like a gentleman should; I let them think that way. There were some women who thought my clothes and hair were eccentric, but these women bothered me too. I concluded that if a woman judged me by my outward appearance, in the long run, I was better off without her.

Then in a moment of weakness, I called Sondra and she came back. I professed my love for her; she confessed that she had been miserable without me. Our attempt to pick up where we left off ended in disaster. I never thought I would hear the words, *"It's okay, it happens."* It never happened, not to me. From that point on, the

relationship went downhill. Instead of admitting that she was seeing someone else, she let me catch them together. Nothing dramatic
like having sex in my bed, just walking in the rain and holding
hands. Just like the old Oran "Juice" Jones song.

Afterward many of my perspectives about women changed. I had
always thought women cheated in retaliation for being cheated on,
but I realized like a lot of misconceptions about women, that one
isn't true. It had happened to me twice—two times too many.

As I turned my attention to the blurry words on my laptop where
I was working on my latest screenplay-in-progress, I tried to delete
Sondra from my mind. The library behind me was full of unfinished
scripts, and for the last week I had been working on a script about
two friends on a road trip in search of their fathers. But twenty pages
into the manuscript, my characters still had yet to leave Chicago. I
had serious writer's block. Ever since I had sold my first screenplay,
which had won a college screenwriting competition, to a producer
who had in turn totally revised the script, I was determined to make
my next one a success. By the time my screenplay, which had started
out as a drama about four Brothers in college, made its appearance
on screen, it had become a comedy about the antics of three friends,
with one token Black friend.

"Yo, Ad-*dam*!"

I turned from my computer screen just as Luciano, my closest
partner, poked his head over the Japanese room divider that separated the living room and my office. Last night, after a typical boys'
night out of shooting pool and the bull, I drove him to his house
where he discovered his wife had finally changed the locks, something I had been warning him would happen soon enough if he kept
acting like he was still a bachelor. He pounded on the door of his
house yelling Lisa's name the way Stanley Kowalski yelled "Stella"
in *A Streetcar Named Desire,* until his next-door neighbor threatened
to call the cops. The last thing I wanted was to spend the night in
jail, a place I had never been and never wanted to be. I had no
choice but to offer the man my sofa bed.

"Don't lean on that, man," I told him absentmindedly.

"Man, how come you ain't got no food up in this mug?" Luciano

Reed was, for the most part, an articulate, somewhat educated man, a disciplinarian at an all-boys' private school, but when we were together, he often lapsed into the old street lingua. And it was infectious.

"I ain't been grocery-shopping this month."

"So, when you going?"

"Don't worry about it. You won't be here long enough to find out." As I looked up at his dejected face, I knew I shouldn't have been so hard on him, but it was fun.

He leaned against the divider, then pulled away quickly when he saw my harsh look. "Lisa's not answering the phone; she turned off her cell. She won't even let me in my own house to get some clothes." Technically, since Lisa got the house in the divorce settlement from her first husband, it was her house. But I didn't bring up this fact.

"She better 'cause you 'cain't' stay here too long," I half-teased.

He ran a hand through his unkempt black hair and dragged himself to the kitchen. I turned back to the computer.

Three years ago, Luciano had married Lisa, a woman with a ready-made family, which included two kids and two dogs. Ever since his first wife had disappeared with his only son, he had become obsessed with finding another wife and starting a new family. Lisa was his third wife. He also had a lady on the side, a woman named Maya. He had wanted to marry Maya a long time ago, but, unfortunately for him, she had married someone else, and, also unfortunately according to him, was still married. I didn't approve of his relationship with Maya, although I could understand his attraction to her. She was sexy, intelligent, and funny. He tried to explain his predicament to me many times, but nothing he said ever convinced me that there was anything right with what he was doing. Once he told me, *I love Lisa, but I'm in love with Maya.* To which I answered, *What does that mean?*

The first time he introduced me to Maya, I knew immediately something was amiss between them. You could smell the sexuality in the air, in the way they looked at each other, the way they didn't look at each other. He might as well have said: *This is Maya, my mistress.*

I got up and went into the kitchen where Luciano was brewing coffee and toasting bread.

"I see you found something to eat."

"Some of your bread's moldy, but I found a couple of decent slices."

I opened the fridge and took out the half-gallon of milk. Without bothering to smell it, I could tell by its consistency that it was bad. I decided to clean out the fridge, something I had been meaning to do for the past few months.

"You want to take my car Saturday?" Luciano asked, scraping the mayonnaise jar for enough mayo to spread on his toast.

"I don't think so. We're taking separate cars. Just in case I need to make a quick getaway." I opened a jar of spaghetti sauce and found thick balls of mold resembling a scientific experiment, so I tossed it out.

"I told you the woman looks like Maya," Luciano said unconvincingly. "Her hair's longer, and she's a little darker, a little shorter."

"A little homelier . . ." I added.

I peeled away the top layers of a head of lettuce, but it was soggy and smelly all the way through. Despite my initial protests, and against my better judgment, Luciano and Maya had insisted on having me meet Maya's sister, who so far had remained a mystery. They wouldn't tell me much about her, not even her name, which was kind of strange and made me suspicious.

In spite of her infidelity, I liked Maya. After all, who was I to judge her? But if her sister was anything like her, she wasn't the kind of woman I wanted to know. I was no prude, but I figured if Maya and Luciano were so much in love, they should both divorce their respective spouses and get together. Not like my old man who had kept two families on opposite sides of Chicago until I discovered my half sister and half brother at his funeral. Every day a woman didn't come into my life was another day without drama like that. But I didn't put up too much of a fight with the whole blind-date thing since I had to admit, I had been craving the company of a woman for some time.

"What was her name again?" I asked, hoping he'd slip up.

Luciano straddled a stool and got busy eating. I slam-dunked a couple of wrinkled, shrunken tomatoes into the trash can. "She doesn't look *exactly* like Maya, just a little," he said with his mouth full of food as if I hadn't spoken.

"You've never met her," I accused him.

"You've never had a *Latina*, have you?" he asked, changing the subject, which intensified my apprehension. Despite his being half-Cuban, and inheriting his mother's Latin physical traits, Luciano rarely acknowledged that part of him, and spoke Spanish only when it was necessary, such as when he wanted to impress a woman. Like lately, whenever he spoke with Maya on the phone, he'd slip into Spanish so I wouldn't know what he was saying.

The first girl I ever kissed was a Spanish girl, Nilsa Ortiz. We didn't really date since we were only ten years old; she was just a girl who let me kiss her. She taught me a few Spanish words, most of which I've forgotten, except *besame*, "kiss me." The first thing she said whenever she saw me was, "*Besame*, Adam," before she said "hello." And I always complied.

I had dated women of other nationalities: a Brazilian, a Trinidadian, even a White girl—though she had been French-Canadian, not American, so technically for me, she didn't count as a White girl. For the most part, my romantic interests had been Black, cultured women. When it came down to it, women were different in some ways, but they were the same in many others. However, when I thought of my future wife, I saw a Black woman in the picture, a woman like my mother and sister.

"Marti was Brazilian," I reminded him.

"She spoke Portuguese, so technically, she wasn't Latin."

"Brazil's in Latin America, ain't it?"

"It's different with Latinas," he said dismissively. "They're cool and tough like Black women, but sophisticated like White girls."

I couldn't believe what he was saying. "Are you saying Black women aren't sophisticated?"

"You know what I mean. Black women are . . . melodramatic. And less forgiving. "

"You mean, when you cheat? And Latin girls have fiery tempers, right? Stop with the stereotypes." Luciano's first and third wives were Black, the second one Hispanic, and each time Luciano had started the new relationship before ending the old one.

"Man, you act like you never cheated in your life." At any attack on his reputation, he would get defensive.

"I haven't," I said proudly, but without conceit. "Whenever I get tired of a relationship, I break it off. If I meet someone new, I end the old one. I don't string women along."

"That's why you haven't been with one in what . . . a year?"

"That's a choice." I had told Luciano it had been a year, but it was more like eighteen months.

"No, that's 'cause of that mop on yo' head," he joked.

He was referring to my dreadlocks; I had started growing them since my cancer's remission and they were now down to my shoulder blades. I know a lot of people have a problem with locks because they aren't as neat as fades or bald heads. But because it had survived the chemo treatments, I vowed never to cut my hair. I felt a connection to Samson in the Bible, whose strength was connected to his hair.

"When are you going to cut that mess?" Luciano asked, rumpling my locks with a slap of his hand.

I punched him. "Yo' mama likes to hold on to them," I joked, reverting to old college insults. He had to laugh at that one.

I knew one thing, if he had some dream about us double-dating with the Latina sisters, he was about to get his matchmaking, Cupid-butt disappointed.

The worst part about having cancer is that it drains you of your strength and robs you of the control and overall attitude you once had over your life. Subsequently, I became obsessed with exercise, running and weight lifting several times a week, not to look good but to gain back that power.

After cleaning the fridge, I changed into a sleeveless T-shirt and jersey shorts, popped a Mozart CD into the joggable CD player hooked to my belt, and went for a run. Classical music gives me a sense that I am floating through a surreal world, making the confusion of the real world disappear if only for just a short time.

I lived several miles from Chicago's Gold Coast neighborhood, in a rehabbed building that was once a rubber glove factory. Sometimes, during really hot summer nights, the smell of rubber seeped through the vents and I imagined the generations of working class who once toiled at the machines. With the money I had received from my first screenplay, I invested in the loft at a time when gentrification was in its infancy and White folks were still pessimistic about moving inland. Eventually I wanted a townhouse in the city, not a house in the suburbs. I was a city boy through and through. I had no problem living across the El tracks from the projects. One good thing about surviving cancer, nothing much scared me anymore, not even thugs carrying guns. I figured in this day and age of mistaken identity and Driving (or Running) While Black, I had more to fear from the cops.

The run from my loft to the lakefront was a rather scenic route that extended from the gentrified blocks of lofts, condos, and townhomes, through the soon-to-be demolished Cabrini-Green housing projects, to the YMCA where the homeless and veterans lived, to the condos of old money and nouveau riche.

A patrol car cruised by and immediately my feelers went up. You would think that by now I would have been used to the increased presence of cops since the upwardly mobile population had surpassed that of the old public housing residents. But I was always on guard. The cruiser turned the corner I was approaching and stopped at the curb just as I reached it. Two uniforms got out, surrounding me like the cavalry, one in the front, one in back. The one in the front was a veteran, White; the one behind was younger and a brown Latino, but he could have passed for Filipino or American Indian. As I slowly removed my headphones, a name ran through my mind: Amadou Diallo, the African brother who had been shot at forty-one times by NYPD cops who claimed his cell phone was a gun. In this age of high-tech terrorism, I didn't want them to mistake my headphones for some kind of New Age bomb.

"You live around here?" the White cop asked.

"A couple of blocks down. On Larrabee."

"Can we see some ID?"

If they could have seen my eyes behind the shades, they'd have seen nothing but innate contempt. With exaggerated caution, I reached into my pocket and brought out my billfold, extending my license using two fingers. I turned to glare at the Latin-Indian-Pacific Islander cop who wasn't saying a word, standing at ease, surveying the perimeter like he was ready for anything that might jump out.

"Mr. Black. We're just checking on a call about a purse snatching on Halsted."

"Let me guess. I fit the description. Black male running."

The White cop smirked; the other one wouldn't meet my eyes. I was handed back my license.

People were strolling by, breaking their necks to catch a glimpse of the commotion, of which there was none, except for the one broiling inside of me. I recognized a couple from my building watching, and when they saw the stone-cold look on my face, they averted their eyes.

It had happened a few times before, just as the demographics were beginning to shift from Black to White. Soon after, the patrols were stepped up as the newcomers complained about the established residents who had yet to be dispersed to scattered-site housing around the city. One time, a searchlight was blazed in my face from a slow-moving paddy wagon; another time, I had been thrust against a cruiser after I insisted I didn't know what "assume the position" meant. After that incident, I stopped running at night, or even dusk for that matter. Now they were hassling me in the daylight.

"Sorry to bother you," White cop muttered insincerely. "Have a good one, now."

I glowered at them as they swaggered around their car, climbing in like they were gangsters who owned the hood. My chest heaving with hostility, I turned around to go back home and take out my frustration on the bench press, but then I decided they weren't going to ruin my day.

At the El station on Franklin and Chicago Avenue, the light changed and I ran in place. A brown-haired White girl who was also running pulled up next to me and flashed me a sweaty grin. I smiled back, concentrating on Mozart's Piano Sonata no. 16 in D Major blasting in my ears, trying to forget the encounter with the cops. When I took a second glance, I noticed she wasn't White but an attractive light-skinned Black woman with a tan, dressed in a white Tommy Girl running outfit. *Definitely not a serious runner,* I thought. She was more about looking cute than getting sweaty. I saw her lips moving so I removed my headphones.

"I'm sorry?" I said, still running in place.

"I said, 'how are you?' " she asked in the affected speech characteristic of the Gold Coast.

"Alright. How 'bout you?"

"Good. Mind if I run with you?"

Running was a solitary activity. Though I'd seen people running together, it wasn't for me. Not to mention that the run-in with the cops had all but killed my usual sociable nature.

"If you can keep up."

When the light changed, I checked the traffic before taking off. She kept up for the most part, but only because I was holding back. I let her get ahead of me once so I could check her out from the back, but then I pulled ahead because I was starting to get behind my time. If Luciano were around, he'd tell me there was definitely something wrong with me when I didn't seize an opportunity to holler at a beautiful sister.

We didn't stop for another light until we reached Loyola University, at which time she stooped over with her hands on her knees and waved me on. I smiled pompously and moved on.

I reached the lakefront in forty-five minutes, behind my usual time and more winded than usual. I attributed it to the woman's interruption, disregarding the fact that I had started smoking again, and vowed not to let anything interfere the next time.

It was a blistering summer day, furiously hot even for August, the kind of day that brought lots of people to compete for the cool breezes of Lake Michigan's shores. All up and down the outer paths, people were running, biking, and Rollerblading. There was no sand on this portion of beach but there were still plenty of half-clad sun-bathers lounging on the cemented shore. *Future cancer patients*, I called them. I always wore shades, a visor, and sunblock; I didn't play. Clouds were moving in, periodically obscuring the sun, and I waited in anticipation for the impending thunderstorm that had been predicted earlier. There was nothing like watching people run-ning away from a little rain. Another good thing about having can-cer—you learn to appreciate the simple things you took for granted before.

I removed my headphones and sat down on the nearest bench and leaned back, soaking in the rays and breathing in the fresh air—as fresh as city air could be.

In the murky distance, I could make out Navy Pier like some mi-rage, the super-sized Ferris wheel barely moving. I remembered the day my father had taken me there before the pier had been turned into a tourist attraction. He told me that during World War II, it was used as a pilot-training base, and now there were about two hun-dred planes resting at the bottom of Lake Michigan as a result of training accidents. Then he told me he was dying of cancer.

Unlike my father, I had defied the odds in so many ways. After my last chemo course, when my blood tests, CT scan, and chest X-rays all came back negative, the doctors were so stunned that the cancer was in remission without surgery, they presented my case at a medical teaching conference. The fact that the kind of cancer I had was rare in Black men made me an even bigger anomaly. I attributed my recovery to God and a rededication to prayer. But sometime in the last year, I had drifted away. And like all sinners who called on God only in times of need, I felt kind of bad about it—but not bad enough to believe I needed to go to church on a regular basis. I was a biannual Christian, the kind who went to church on Christmas and Easter—the Lord's birth and resurrection. I was going on the notion that by attending church on these two holiest-of-holy days, the eternal fires would remain out of reach.

Two cops on bike patrol pedaled by and almost immediately my anger returned. A few years back, a cop wouldn't be caught dead riding anything that didn't run on gas, but as tourism increased, the mayor decided the city could not risk losing the growing revenue. Thus began the recruitment of younger, trimmer cops to patrol the city's parks and beaches. It amazed me how quickly crime fighting became a priority when economics was involved and especially when it came to certain segments of the population.

"If I didn't know any better, I'd think you were trying to lose me."

I looked up and saw the woman runner I had left in the dust several blocks back. She was breathing hard, her chest heaving, and I realized just how young she was, probably in her early twenties.

"I was timing myself," I told her, tapping my stopwatch.

She nodded and straddled the back of the bench, her thighs within inches of my face. "I'm Zina," she said, holding out her hand.

"Adam." I took her hand.

We talked a little about running and as I speculated, she was quite young, only twenty, in her last year at DePaul. At one point, she picked up one of my locks and said, "I just love dreadlocks." I found that usually it was White women who made false adulation comments, but I didn't take it as a compliment. Women like her thought being with a man with dreadlocks was something unique, like it was supposed to be different from being with a man with a conventional hairstyle. They would ask foolish questions like, "Do you wash it?" or "Is it real?" But cancer had made my senses more acute and I was able to smell superficiality and bull that I might have otherwise ignored. The warning lights started going off in my head: *Danger, Danger!* I knew she was flirting with me, but after a while, we ran out of conversation. She got up and stretched, causing her crop top to ride up and reveal a tight belly and a Winnie the Pooh tattoo. I tried not to let the desire in my eyes show, but judging by the smile on her face, I didn't think I was successful.

"Well, since you haven't asked for my number, I'm going to assume you're involved or not interested."

I didn't want to seem rude or like I was scared off by her age. "Neither," I said truthfully. "I don't have a pen or anything."

She pulled a pen out of her fanny pack, took my hand, and wrote her number in my palm. Then she smiled and turned. I watched her walk away until she was a gold-and-white dot in the horizon.

The drops came softly and slowly at first, but people were already packing up and hurrying for cover as if bombs were dropping from the sky. Lightning flashed above, followed by crashing thunder. A woman screamed as she ran over the grass. I shook my head. *It's not that serious*, I thought. The sudden shower fell quickly in layers, soaking everything within minutes, including me. I leaned back and let the rainfall cleanse me.

CHAPTER 3

EVA

I WAS IN the garden pruning my rosebushes near the wooden privacy fence when I believed I was truly losing my mind. I had sensed a presence behind me, so I turned to the spot where the huge oak tree stood in the middle of the yard; I saw a man instead. I thought my eyes were playing tricks on me and I did a double take. There stood a muscular man with a chiseled torso and two brawny arms holding up a huge, magnificent Afro made of leaves, like Mr. Universe holding up the globe. He seemed to be calling me, thrusting his chest out, tempting me like a forbidden tree. It seemed like a sign from God, a preview of the man who was waiting for me. For a moment, I escaped my body and floated toward him, dropping the shears along the way and collapsing at the man's feet. I couldn't see his face for all the hair tumbling from his head, so I began grabbing at the leaves, tearing at the branches left and right. However, the more I pulled, the more obscure the man's face became.

"Ow!"

Awakened from my trance, I looked down at my hand where a thorn had pierced my gloveless finger. Instinctively, I brought it to my mouth and sucked at the blood. I knew it was God who had interfered with my licentious daydream, slapping me back to the reality of working in my garden on a beautiful summer day, not lusting after a man who wasn't really there.

Still sucking my finger, I turned back to the object of my brief desire and saw that it was a tree once again and not a man. No muscles, no Afro, just an illusion of bark and leaves.

I walked around the yard, picking up loose twigs and branches that had snapped in the turbulent summer storm the night before. Judging by the clouds, it looked like it was going to rain again. Lately, since the boys left for school, I couldn't help but think about how quickly the last twenty years of my life had flown by.

After graduation, when I was nineteen, I ran into my first and only high school boyfriend. He had put his hand on my behind on our first date, making that our last. After we reminisced and laughed about the incident that had broken us up, we got reacquainted and soon fell in love. Anthony had joined the army after graduation and was about to leave for boot camp. Whether I was feeling left out because of my younger sister's and best friend's marriages, I couldn't say, but I married him nonetheless and followed him to North Carolina and joined the Reserves to earn money for college. When I became pregnant a year later, quite unexpectedly, I was thrilled; Anthony was not. He thought it was too soon. Then Eli followed just before Tony's first birthday and I was forced to quit college. That and Anthony's numerous affairs put a strain on the marriage, but we held on for six years before we ended it for good and I returned to Chicago.

After my divorce from Mr. Anthony Prince, I found myself juggling a full-time job, going to school part-time while raising our two young sons. I tried to stay away from men after my divorce, but like many women, it was hard for me to be without male companionship. My relationships with men became more guarded after Anthony. I established a six-month rule before I engaged in sex. Condoms were a must, but of course, like always, there were times when they were inconvenient. As long as I didn't get pregnant, I was secure. I found myself bouncing from one relationship to the next. One man seemed satisfied with my six-month rule, but when he realized I was serious, he left. His departing words stung for a long time: *"I can't believe I wasted three months of my life with you."*

And then I met Victor.

He was an English college instructor of Venezuelan descent

whose pastime was volunteering at homeless shelters. Divorced, with no children, he was the most romantic man I had ever known, always surprising me with flowers and silly gifts before the typical traditional holidays. A patient, sensitive man, he became an instant father to Tony and Eli, who were teenagers in need of discipline. With his encouragement and assistance, I re-enrolled in college and finished my bachelor's. Victor introduced me to the benefits of boxing and healthy eating, and he helped me slim down. I thought he was too perfect, anticipating the day I would find out some ugly secret, or he would cheat on me. But other than his obsession with his motorcycle, and his bad habit of gratuitous swearing, there didn't seem to be anything I couldn't live with. I became convinced that he was "the one." We got engaged, moved in together, and set a wedding date.

Then everything fell apart.

While addressing the wedding invitations, a woman called to tell me she was having an affair with my almost-perfect fiancé. I was stunned and humiliated, but I was more hurt than anything. When I confronted Victor, he accused *me* of being unfaithful. Prior experience told me that when men did that, it was to appease their own guilt. He finally admitted that the affair had lasted only a month and when he tried to break it off, the woman became obsessive and threatened to call me. What made it even worse was why he did it. "It just happened," he said, the dumbest, weakest excuse known to man. We tried counseling and I tried to forgive him, but it didn't happen.

My sister urged me not to lose faith in men. *Not all men cheat,* was her motto. After all, I wasn't perfect. *No,* I told her, *but I was faithful.* Trust had always, would always, be a big thing with me. And then one day Maya saw her minivan in the parking lot of a Metra station and found Alex inside having sex with another woman. In the aftermath of his infidelity, she became my one true comrade. *All men cheat—eventually,* was her revised motto. Simone was more optimistic; she believed there were men who didn't, though she had not found him yet and had had her fair share of married and involved men. Deep down, she truly believed she

would one day find her soul mate. Maya was already convinced she
had found him in Luciano. While I shared Simone's belief that there
were men who didn't cheat, I didn't necessarily believe in the concept of soul mates.

That was five years ago. Soon after, my self-imposed celibacy
began. I succeeded in making myself happy and busy, suppressing
my desire for the one thing I felt was missing from my life. In the
past five years, I had come a long way, accomplishing more in my
life than most people seemed to take half a lifetime to do.

During those years, I searched for my spirituality and found it in
the kind of church I had sought all my life. The Community Church
of Christ was a place of worship that stressed community outreach
more than the collection of offerings, which was done via mail once
a month instead of during Sunday service. After giving my life to
Christ, I began to rely more on asking and waiting rather than wishing and hoping. For almost everything I prayed, I received. What I
didn't receive, I believed I didn't need. I prayed for help in getting
my master's degree in administration and, after applying for several
scholarships, I won one that paid everything. When I asked for
guidance in my future endeavors, my prayers were answered after I
interviewed for a position at Chicago University as a student advisor. In a few years, I rose through the ranks and became the first female director of Latino Student Recruitment.

For now, I was fulfilled with my life and the challenge of working in the garden of my new home. My dream had been to own a
home where my sons could play in a big yard instead of on city
sidewalks, but they were sixteen and seventeen by the time I was
able to purchase a house. My recent goal was to have my garden
completed before the summer's end. So far I had completed the
landscaping along the sides of the yard by bricking the edges, plant-
ing hostas, and enclosing them with whitewashed marble chips.
Near the newly constructed deck, I had planted tulips, which had
bloomed earlier in the year, along with roses, mums, and other
perennials. At the end of the yard where other neighbors had
garages, I had cemented a portion for the boys' mini–basketball
court, although now they were rarely home to use it. My last proj-

ect was a miniature greenhouse, which would house the tropical plants of my mother's birthplace.

I tried to convince myself that the reason I had devoted so much time to my garden was not because I wanted to take my mind away from turning forty a couple of weeks before, or from the fact that I was about to enter my fifth year of celibacy, but because gardens always reminded me of my mother. On the tree stump in one corner of the basketball court, I stopped and read the inscription: *"Eva's Garden of Eden—Dedicated to Amarylis Clemente."*

My mother, Amarylis, had been an amateur horticulturist and was appropriately named after a flower. Although we had lived in apartments, my mother always grew plants and flowers everywhere, with a garden on every porch, open or enclosed. In the last apartment we had lived in before her death, a garden apartment, the landlord had allowed her to have a garden in the small yard. My mother had turned it into a paradise of colorful and vibrant flora. The beauty and intricacy of that last garden the summer I was fifteen was overshadowed by my mother's untimely death caused by a brain aneurysm. As always when I thought of my mother, I could not help but think of my father, who, distraught over his wife's death, pawned my sister and me off to my mother's sister, Titi. In the three years before I became of legal age, Joaquin Clemente came to visit us sporadically like a divorced father, never speaking of our mother and becoming more and more distant as the years went by.

A part of me surmised that if I mended the frayed pieces of my relationship with my father, I could resolve my predicament with men. Over the years I tried to reestablish a relationship with my father who seemed content to live year after year without speaking to his daughters or grandsons unless contacted first. But the father I had known as a child had yet to resurface.

I heard the phone ringing inside, but I didn't move to answer it. I didn't like being disturbed when I was in the garden, so I waited for the voice mail to kick in.

It was only in the last year that everything seemed to fall into place after I was finally able to convince Eli, who wanted to join the air force, to follow in his older brother's footsteps at Illinois South

University. For the first time in my life, I found myself alone and at peace.

Just then, King barked and momentarily startled me out of my introspection, as if to remind me that I wasn't alone. A car zoomed down the alley and King bounded after it to the length of the wrought-iron fence, barking as if his jaws could penetrate it if only I would let him.

"King!" I commanded. *"¡Callate!"* Immediately, King stopped barking and sprang toward me and circled my legs meekly. I patted his smooth coat until he relaxed at my feet. My finger was still bleeding, and I walked to the hose and stuck it under the water flow.

Yes, God had been good to me. He had answered all my prayers—except one. While I had taken charge of many aspects of my life, I had never stopped asking for a man of God to come into my life. Maya and Simone tried to set me up several times, sometimes with Christian men, sometimes not. None held my interest. Either they were too much like siblings or I discerned something in their spirit that told me to run in the opposite direction—fast. I had been in church long enough to know that God answered prayers on His own time and not anyone else's, so I tried to be patient. Then again, maybe He had already sent a man in the form of one of the brothers in the church and I had spurned him before they could reveal themselves. Maybe I had run into "him" in the past few years, at the post office or walking down the street. For all I knew it could be Johnny Estevez, the co-leader in the Youth Ministry, who had asked me out for the third time at the last youth meeting. And for the third time, I had turned him down. Not only because he was eight years younger, but mostly because I wasn't attracted to him. And whoever heard of a grown man going by his childhood nickname anyway?

Then I thought of Rashid Ali, the director of African American admissions at the university.

Rashid was a divorced father of two preteen girls, a man I had been attracted to since he first arrived at CU six months ago. He had a great sense of humor and kept me laughing through all the academic bureaucracy and pettiness of office politics. During staff meetings, we would pass notes back and forth as if we were in high school. A few months after he started, I agreed to go to a staff party with him, even though I knew we were of different faiths. Whether it was the festive atmosphere or a mutual lack of companionship, sparks flew. As we were dancing, he asked me if I would be willing to convert to Islam and I replied, "Only if you convert to Christianity." We laughed and resolved to be friends after that. Every once in a while, however, I sensed something more than friendship toward him, which made me wonder if I was meant to come into his life and convert him.

When the phone rang again a few minutes later, I reluctantly walked inside and answered it just before the voice mail could kick in.

"Mother, where were you?" Tony demanded. Over the years, I had gone from Mama to Mommy to Ma. Only when they were angry or condescending did my children refer to me as Mother.

"In the garden." I hunted the kitchen drawers for a bandage.

"Why don't you take the phone with you?" he chastised me, as if I were the child. "It's cordless. It reaches out there." Tony had appointed himself my protector, taking over the man-of-the-house role after his father left, a role he refused to relinquish when Victor moved in, then resumed after we broke up.

"Don't speak to me like I'm not up on technology," I admonished him. "You know I don't like talking on the phone outside. It's so uncouth."

"Oh, brother."

"Speaking of which, have you seen him?"

"Eli? Once, at the bookstore. You know we're on opposite sides of the campus."

It gave me a sense of relief that my children were together, even though they were miles away downstate in Carter, Illinois. When they were little, they were never really close, although they were almost a year apart like Maya and I. They fought constantly, verbally and physically, into their teenage years. Ironically, it wasn't until Tony went away for his freshman year that they began to form a bond.

"What's all that noise?" Tony asked.

"I'm looking for a bandage," I said, opening another drawer. "I pricked my finger." I finally found a Band-Aid with a deteriorated wrapping, but the bandage itself was still fresh. "Please keep an eye on your brother," I reminded him. "I don't want him messing with those college girls, interfering with his studies. You know how he is."

"Ma, I told you. He's an adult. I can't watch him every day."

Eli had inherited his father's good looks and flirtatious nature. During high school, he had had many girlfriends and my biggest fear was that I would be a grandmother before I was forty. Sometimes I wondered if he would have been better off joining the air force despite the imminence of war instead of a college campus crawling with hot-blooded females.

"Tony, just talk to him, counsel him. He still needs guidance."

"Am I my brother's keeper?" This was his usual line of defense.

"Yes, you are," I told him sternly.

"Okay, okay," Tony said quickly, knowing he had gone too far with his comment. "I spoke to your ex-husband."

"How *is* your father?"

"He's fine. He has a new girlfriend."

"That's nice." Anthony's personal life had ceased to concern me long ago. Of course I cared about him, for example, if he got seriously sick or hurt, but the details of his private life were of little significance. The only thing I had asked of him when we split up was that he stay involved in his sons' lives, unlike my own father.

"Have you talked to Grandpop?" he asked.

"No."

"What do you tell us? 'Just because he doesn't call you doesn't mean you shouldn't call him.'"

"Hmmm." I hated it when my words came back to haunt me, especially when they came from the children I raised.

"I hope you're using this time wisely, like to finally find yourself a man," Tony commented. "Now that we're not in your hair, you can concentrate on making yourself happy."

"I am happy," I said defensively. "You know what Titi used to say: 'Don't count on anyone—'"

"'To make you happy,' I know," he finished for me. "But you've got to admit, it might make life a little less lonely."

"Sometimes. Sometimes you can be with someone and still be lonely."

"True."

I smiled, and thought proudly of how my eldest son had grown in the past few years. Our relationship had changed since his early turbulent teenage years, when he was fifteen and I had discovered he was dating a twenty-year-old woman. I promptly called the young woman's mother—because she was still living at home—and told her that I would call the police if her daughter ever came around my son again. Tony accused me of ruining his life shouting, *"You're just jealous 'cause you don't have a man!"* Now, at nineteen, he had been saved for over a year, seriously concentrating on his education, with little time for love.

"Have you been to church down there?" I asked.

"Yes, Mother."

"Are *you* staying away from those college girls?" He didn't answer right away and for a moment I panicked. I knew Tony was a serious and sensitive soul. The year before, a girl from church had broken his heart and it had taken him several months to recover. Until then, I never realized that men suffered from rejection just as much as women. My fear was that he would fall in love again too quickly and drop out and get married before graduating. "Tony?"

"Ma, I don't have time for women. I have a full course load, and my job."

"How're your classes?"

I listened as he talked about his classes and his professors before closing with our usual, "God bless you. I love you."

Before I could reach the back door, the phone rang again.

"Hey, Ma! Miss me?" It was Eli.

"Who is this?" I kidded, sitting down again.

"Ha-ha. You've become a comedian in your old age."

"Don't make me go down there, boy."

Eli was the comic relief in the family. He was the one who kept me laughing whenever I thought I was going to fall apart. Nothing seemed to faze his good humor. When his father and I divorced, Eli, at three years old, asked, *"Is Daddy taking the big TV?"* After Victor moved out, thirteen-year-old Eli had matter-of-factly said, *"Now we'll have more food left over."*

"How do you like college so far?"

"It's raw! I've been to three parties since I've been down here. And the females? Girls, girls every night. I think you should know, I'm not a virgin anymore."

"Elias!" I warned as he cackled into the phone.

"I'm kidding, Ma. I haven't been a virgin for years."

I ignored his little confession. "Have you been to church?"

"Maybe next week."

"Maybe, nothing. You better go."

"Si, Madre," he said sarcastically in his phonetic gringo Spanish.

"Ready to come home?"

"Like you want me back. You know you want to have that man over."

"What man?"

"The one you been hiding."

"Yeah, right."

After we said our good-byes, I decided I had had enough gardening for the day. I had plenty of paperwork to do, but working at the computer at home did not appeal to me after staring at one most of the workweek. I printed out hard copies of the college brochure I was editing and an editorial I had started a week ago to the *Tribune* regarding the inappropriate transferring of students with behavior problems, then packed a bag for the lakefront. I changed out of my overall shorts and T-shirt and into my weekend incognito attire: an Indian sari made of bronze gauze with a matching scarf, which I used as a headband to hold back my hair. Wooden bangles, amber shell earrings, and leather sandals completed my ensemble. If I had my choice, and if the ground wasn't so polluted, I would go barefoot.

I drove to Montrose Harbor, my favorite spot. Before my mother died, my parents would take us here for picnics to escape the suffocating city air. About twenty-five feet above the lake, there were man-made limestone revetments arranged to resemble steps. Maya and I used to call them cliffs, chasing each other up and down the steps, pretending we were orphans who lived on the beach while our parents cuddled at the very top. Swimming and diving was forbidden because of the rocks below the water's surface, but every year, inevitably there were news reports about some foolish teenager or drunken adult who thought they were invulnerable and ended up with a crushed spine or fatal injury.

The lakefront was filled with people walking, running, sunbathing, and playing sand games. Farther down the coast, boats of every size and model were cruising back to the marina as the skies darkened. As I settled on one of the available stepstones, reviewing and proofreading my work, I couldn't help but get distracted by the magnificence of the horizon in the distance. Right after the divorce, the lakefront was the first place I brought the boys after returning to Chicago from North Carolina, to contemplate my future without Anthony. Tony took one look at the horizon and asked, *"Is that heaven, Mommy? Is that where we go when we die?"* Ever since then, the lakefront was where I escaped when I needed to talk to God. If I closed my eyes and concentrated really hard, all the noises around me would wither away: traffic, voices, barking, and momentarily, the world would be as God had originally intended, and would one day return—peaceful, like paradise.

My reverie was interrupted by the sound of drumming coming from the dog beach, which had just opened up. Regretfully, I thought about King and wished I had brought him. Shoving my papers into my shoulder messenger bag, I made my way in the direction of the familiar Afro-Caribbean beat. A small crowd was forming a semicircle around the three percussionists playing two congas and a bongo. Instinctively, my head began to bop in appreciation and nostalgia, though I didn't dare move the rest of my body.

"Muevete, Morena!" called one of the conga players. I realized he was speaking to me since I was the only dark-skinned person in the crowd. He was bare chested, his shirt tied around his head like a turban. I knew if Maya or Simone were around, they would have no

problem dancing in public. The conga player kept grinning in my direction, urging me to move, tempting me with his hands as they banged furiously on his conga. He was a handsome Hispanic, brown like me, and too young, but still I could not help but feel a connection, even a slight attraction. I glanced hesitantly at the off-beat dance moves on the part of some of the onlookers and I thought, *These people don't know me.* I had my shades on and my weekend outfit so no one would recognize me.

As I moved into the circle, swaying my hips and shoulders, I recalled an old Puerto Rican dance my mother had taught me as a young girl called *bomba*, a dance with strong African roots. During the days of slavery in Puerto Rico, bomba dancers would form a circle and take turns challenging the drums with their raised skirts to ridicule the fancy attire worn by plantation ladies and to poke fun at the slave owners.

At first I felt embarrassed, wondering if the onlookers were thinking, *Minorities sure know how to dance,* but then I didn't care. It had been so long since I had danced to the music of my youth. I lifted my skirt just above my knees, shaking it in the direction of the copper-colored *congero,* who laughed and whistled, shouting the call-and-response phrases that are the style of the bomba dance.

Just as I was getting into the beat, and the drummers were taking turns banging out solos, lightning lit up the sky, followed by thunder. Then the rain fell. The musicians stopped, protecting their instruments with their shirts.

When I stopped dancing, a couple of the onlookers complimented me as they dispersed. I took my time walking to my car, not caring that my hair would soon frizz up.

"You made it rain, *Negrita*!" the conga player yelled, running past me, his shoulder-length braids slapping his face.

I smiled. It had been a long time since anyone had called me Negrita, a term of endearment my mother used for me because I was the darkest in the family. For one brief moment, I felt liberated, free from the mundane worries in my everyday life: work, irrational thoughts, men. In my car, I closed my eyes and leaned back against the headrest, listening to the rain slapping the car's exterior like a car wash.

A tapping at the window startled me and I looked up to find the conga player grinning at me as the rain drenched him. Cautiously, I manually cracked the car window.

"You wanna go dancin'?" he asked in a thick Chicago accent that reminded me of the first Mayor Daley.

His question caught me completely off guard, and I was temporarily speechless. I looked at his wet, goateed face, at the beads of rain clumping his eyelashes, then down at his bare tattooed torso, reed-thin without an ounce of body fat. Raindrops were splashing through the crack and hitting my face. Five years ago, the old Eva would have taken him up on his offer. Five years ago, I would not have given the consequences of my actions a second thought. The new Eva knew dancing was the last thing on his mind. And the new Eva blamed me for encouraging him with my dance moves.

"I'm Christian," I replied, hoping to scare him away.

"*Yo tambien,*" he said, lifting the gold crucifix from his neck toward me.

"*Estoy casada,*" I told him, using my old lie that I was married to keep unwanted men away.

He held up his left hand to show me a ring and grinned. "Hey, me too."

"Go home to your wife," I told him disgustedly, and rolled up the window.

He pretended to look dejected, holding his hands together in a begging gesture, the grin never leaving his face. I started the car and backed out of the parking space, glancing in the rearview mirror as he ran toward a waiting van.

There were some days when I felt I could wait for a man of God as long as He wanted me to wait. I would remember my mother's favorite proverb: *Be careful what you ask for, you might just get it,* and back off in fear of what might come my way. I would tell myself I didn't necessarily need a man to complete my life, just to complement it. Because marriage wasn't something I was ready to commit to again, and because I had no intentions of becoming intimate without marriage, my predicament was even more complicated. I had yet to date a man who hadn't eventually expected sex as part of the package.

There were other days when I could keep my craving at bay by imagining the worst that marriage had to offer—the never-ending housework, the disproportionate compromising, usually on the part of the woman, the whole patriarchal institution of it all. In the end, I would resolve that I was better off single.

But then, there were the days when the emptiness in me was so intense, the pain so acute, it cut like a razor blade and all I wanted to do was cry. I would feel the need to pray continuously and intensely, attending every service at TCCC until I felt rejuvenated by His awesome presence. I would think, *Okay, Lord, if you command me to wait some more, then Thy will be done.* I would be invigorated for the next few days, enough to get me through the nights, a week. But then, my spirit, which was very willing, was overwhelmed by my weakened and fervent flesh.

And I could feel myself growing weaker every day.

CHAPTER 4

ADAM

IT WAS FRIDAY and I had been thanking God literally from the moment I woke up that morning. Most days I loved my job, but sometimes when I saw kid after kid coming in and out of my office, day after day, week after week, year after year, I wondered how much difference I was really making.

Ronnie was fifteen years old in a six-foot-one-inch, two-hundred-pound body full of misplaced hate. He wouldn't even look at me when I spoke to him, just stared out the window like he couldn't wait to brag to his partners that he had beaten the rap—no juvey, just probation. I was used to being yelled at, cursed at, even attacked, so being ignored didn't bother me much. I had read somewhere that even though teenagers appeared not to be listening, they always were.

"Ronnie, are you hearing me?" I asked the boy sternly.

He turned up his lip, still staring out the window. He was just one of many and although they all basically had the same history—products of single mothers–absent fathers, poor schools–rough neighborhoods—I saw them as individuals. The critics would say that thousands of kids were brought up under similar conditions but didn't end up in trouble. But those kids didn't concern me; I wanted to help the ones that slipped through the cracks. I didn't dwell on the fact that the parents were partly responsible for the way their children turned out. Out there somewhere were fathers who, for whatever reasons, had no contact with their sons, forcing the boys to choose between the street and the rest of the world. I couldn't do anything about that. I had long since given up assigning blame. I was more about finding solutions.

Like them, I was still angry at my father, so I could relate. I knew what it was like to be dismissed and abandoned, to be an after-thought in a parent's selfish life. I didn't want to be their fathers, or a father figure, but I wanted them to see that there were good men in the world, that it was possible for them to be worthy men despite their circumstances.

"Three years' probation ain't no joke. You got to keep your nose and your urine clean, stay away from your crew, those so-called knot-head friends of yours, finish school, get a part-time job, and re-port to me once a week," I ran down the list of rules.

When I met with my clients, I usually took off my suit jacket so I didn't come off as too authoritarian, but as soon as I got acquainted with them, I rolled up my sleeves to show them I meant business. With Ronnie, I knew I had to bring out the big guns. I unbuttoned my shirt and stripped down to my T-shirt. I could see him turning his head slightly, watching me. He had a couple of inches on me, but I had muscles and years on him and if necessary, I would show him I wasn't about to take any mess from him. Inside, I was harder than he was.

Walking around my desk, I came around and sat on the edge. I scratched my upper arm, pushing my short sleeve up just far enough so he could see my barbed-wire tattoo. I kept the tattoo of the Star of David on my other arm hidden.

"I know you think you got an easy sentence but let me tell you something. Staying straight is harder than serving time, man. Pro-bation is worse than juvey. You know why? 'Cause you got to report to me."

Through all the pretense, I could see he was just a scared kid trapped inside the body of a man. He had probably cried himself to sleep upon hearing his sentence, probably wet himself. Knowing that made my heart soften for him.

"Look, man, I ain't trying to be yo' buddy," I said taking it down a notch, but regressing to street talk. "I ain't trying to be yo' daddy. You just do what you got to do, and I'll do what I go to do. It's as simple as that." I crossed my arms so that my chest expanded. "You understand?"

Ronnie finally turned away from the window slowly and cocked his head at me, his lip still curled. "We thu?"

"Yeah, man, we're through. Get outta here."

He jumped up, the first proof of life. I held out my arm to stop him. "You need anything, you call me, you hear?"

In his eyes, I saw the slightest hint of docility as he barely nodded his head, before the hard look returned almost as quickly.

"See you next week, man."

As he rushed out, he bumped into Derek Cote, a fellow probation officer, in the hallway. Ronnie tried to walk around him, but Derek was built like a fullback, not to mention he was bald, Black, and intimidating. It didn't help that his wife had recently died of breast cancer and he was still angry at the world. He reached out a huge beefy arm and blocked Ronnie's way.

"Hey, young man, the word is 'excuse me.' Use it," Derek said in his baritone voice.

I couldn't hear Ronnie's voice but I knew he had complied.

"Knucklehead," Derek muttered as he walked into my office. "We still on for lunch?"

"Yeah, yeah," I said putting my shirt back on and sitting at my desk. "How you doing? You doing okay?"

"I'm alright, I'm cool," he said dismissing me with a wave of his hand, ready to talk about business.

Derek and I had known each other for five years, ever since I started working at the agency. He took over most of my cases when I was out on medical leave, and I in turn, covered his when he took a family leave to deal with his wife's death. I hadn't seen too many men cry in my lifetime, and the first time Derek broke down in my office, I was stunned. Before his wife died, he would talk about her like she was someone special, made out of rare diamonds. The way he used to romance her, even after twenty years of marriage, amazed me. Sometimes he'd talk about her like she was still alive, in the present tense. *Teresa likes it when I wear this shirt,* he'd say. It made me wonder if loving a woman with that much intensity was possible.

After work I drove toward home with thoughts of relaxation and working on my screenplay, listening to the soulful sounds of Floetry, Common, or Abdullah Ibrahim in the background; then I remembered I had something to do. As part of the Big Brothers Big Sisters program, I mentored two brothers and I had promised the mother, Nikki Miller, that I would stop by and talk to the eldest, Justin. Since his high school graduation a couple of months ago, she didn't like the changes he was undergoing in his quest for independence. She didn't like that he had started locking his hair, even if he *was* emulating me, or that he wasn't coming straight home after his part-time job, or that he was dating a girl she didn't particularly like. Lately, his attitude was getting worse, so she had called earlier to tell me that she couldn't be held responsible for whatever she might do to him if he continued. Reluctantly, but resolutely, I made a U-turn and drove to the West Side.

Ms. Miller came to the door with a scowl on her face, but it quickly disappeared when she saw me through the glass security door. Grinning, she fixed her hair with her hands and promptly unlocked the door. Dressed in her office work clothes—a form-fitting skirt and a low-cut blouse—she looked way too young to have a seventeen-year-old son, and I had to remind myself of her displaced attraction to me because of my relationship with her sons. I had promised myself I would avoid going into the house if possible, careful what I said to her, or the way I looked at her, at all times.

"How you doin', Ms. Miller?" I asked civilly.

"I told you, you can call me Nikki, Mr. Black."

I ignored her reprimand politely by changing the subject. "Where's Justin?"

"Justin!" she yelled irritably over her shoulder, then smiled back at me. "Come in. Sit down, sit down. I just finished cooking. Meat loaf, mashed potatoes, corn. I know you must be hungry after working all day."

"No thanks. I'm supposed to have dinner at my sister's." I wasn't

going but it was the truth, and I could tell from the look on her face
that she didn't believe me. Ever since my sister, Jade, had moved out
to the suburb of Carol Stream, I visited her less and less. I sat on the
edge of the sofa and waited.

Ricky, the nine-year-old, came charging down the hall. He
plopped down next to me and leaned against my arm. I palmed his
close-shaven head.

"Didn't I tell you to stop running through my house?" Ms. Miller
scolded.

"How you doin'? You been doing okay?" I asked him.

He nodded in a frenzied manner.

"Stop lying," Ms. Miller interjected. "You know you were almost
suspended this week. Tell Mr. Black what you did."

Ricky shook his head.

"He spit on the floor in the middle of class," she answered for
him.

"'Cause teacher wouldn't let me go to the bathroom," Ricky
cried out in his defense. "I told her I had to spit, but she wouldn't
let me go." Ricky had been diagnosed with what a lot of boys were
being labeled with recently: ADD—attention deficit disorder. He
was an intelligent boy, but the lack of resources at his neighborhood
school and the impatience of school officials dictated the quickest
solution: transferring him to a different school, into Special Ed, then
putting him on the newest antistimulant medication.

Justin came sauntering down the carpeted stairs, a sullen look on
his face. He leaned against the wall, running his hand over the baby
locks on his head. Unlike the semi-hard-core young men I saw at
work, he was a good kid who missed his deceased father and re-
sented the fact that his mother was still trying to run his life. He had
come a long way from when I first met him, graduating with honors while juggling a part-time job and volunteering as a tutor for
grade school kids. I liked to think that I had something to do with
his success, that my influence had so far kept him from becoming a
statistic.

"Hey, man, what's up?" I asked.

"'Sup."

"Speak coherently, boy," his mother scolded, glaring at him. Justin cut his eyes at her. "You see how he looks at me. You better talk to him."

"You want to go for a ride?" I asked Justin.

"You can talk here," Ms. Miller said, getting up. "I'll leave the room."

I stood up. "That's okay. I have some errands to run. C'mon, man." Justin's face brightened up as he dashed out the door like a pet who had been chained up all day.

"You sure you don't want to eat? I made enough for you. For all of us," Ms. Miller said eagerly.

"Thanks. Maybe some other time."

As she smiled, I realized I made a mistake implying there would be a future dinner.

"I swear I'ma explode if I don't move out," Justin told me, as we drove down the street. "She's gettin' on my nerves!"

"Where you gonna go, huh? You're seventeen, you got a high school education and a part-time job at Old Navy," I reminded him calmly.

"I'll be eighteen in two months. I'll go to the army, the Job Corps, anywhere."

"I thought you wanted to go to college. I thought you were going to work for six months to save some money and then you were going to college."

He shrugged. "My counselor said I wasn't college material. He said my SAT scores weren't high enough."

"But your GPA is good. You had a three-point-three, didn't you? Do you want to go to college?"

"Yeah, I want to go."

"Then you're going. There are some schools that'll take your scores. They'll accept you as a 'special admissions' student for the first year. You got to take advantage of this opportunity now. The government's trying to get rid of affirmative action. I can't believe that counselor said that."

"They don't care about us at that school. They try to push us into the trades and food service, or community college."

I shook my head in disbelief. "If you want to go to college, away to a university, you can do it. As long as you're willing to work hard, you can do it. I'll see what I can do."

Justin looked out the window quietly. I couldn't tell if he was thinking about what I had said or just ignoring me.

"In the meantime, you got to stop giving your mama a hard time," I told him, getting to the matter at hand. "You know she loves you and she only wants what's best for you. It's not easy raising two boys by herself."

"I know, but she's always in my business."

"That's what mamas do. If you go away to college, at least she'll be out of your business for most of the year."

"She's just mad 'cause she caught me alone in the house with Diane."

"And what were you doing in the house with Diane?"

"Nothing. Just kissing. And stuff." I looked at him doubtfully and he smirked. "I swear. We were just kissing. I'm not a virgin but she is. I like her. A lot."

"Don't do anything to mess up your future."

"I'm not. I know how to take care of business."

"You do know no birth control is one hundred percent effective?"

He made a dismissive sucking-of-the-teeth noise. "Man, please don't tell me abstinence is the only effective birth control. I already hear that at church. Do *you* practice abstinence?"

"We're not talking about me, we're talking about you."

"Ahhh!" he whooped. "Double standard."

Again, he got quiet and stared out the window. I debated whether to tell him that I hadn't been with a woman in over a year, without giving him the extenuating circumstances. But I remembered what I was like when I was his age and I knew he probably thought I was too old to care about sex.

"Hey, Adam?"

"Yeah, man?"

"Do you believe in God?"

"Of course," I said without hesitation.

" 'Cause I don't think I do."

"Why is that?"

"I don't know. I just think about all the things going on in this city, you know. People killing each other, drug dealing. If there was a God, why doesn't He stop it?"

"Well, He gave man free will. Everybody has the power to decide between right and wrong. God doesn't interfere with that."

"My mama said He does. She said when you think about doing good, that's God; when you get bad thoughts, it's the devil. You think that's true?"

"Yeah, I believe that. To some extent." I started to head back toward his house.

"Hey, Adam?"

"Yeah, man?"

"Can we go to Burger King?"

"Your mom cooked dinner," I reminded him, amused at how suddenly he switched subjects.

"Man, I can *not* eat her meat loaf."

"You shouldn't talk about your mom's cooking like that," I said, trying not to laugh.

He laughed. "You know you want to laugh. I'm serious, Dawg. I love her and everything but her meat loaf is *too* dry. It gets all stuck in your throat and stuff."

I couldn't remember when I decided I didn't want children. Growing up, there always seemed to be an exorbitant number of kids on my block, many without fathers at home. It always seemed to me that there were just too many children in the world as a whole. Maybe it was meeting my father's children nineteen years ago at his funeral when I was seventeen. Or perhaps when the doctor diagnosed my cancer and I learned I was sterile and couldn't have kids, rather than I didn't want them. But Justin and Ricky, and the boys I came in contact with at work, not to mention my niece and nephew whom I adored, were all like my children. I enjoyed going to their parties and school plays and graduations just like I was their father. They were enough for me.

When I got home, the loft was quiet and I was grateful Luciano wasn't there yet. Lately he had been beating me home and I'd find him sitting in my favorite chair, simultaneously listening to my Afro-Cuban jazz records and watching ESPN. Without his constant interruptions, I would at least be able to get some writing done. I changed out of my suit and into Bermuda shorts, then briefly shuffled through my CD collection before settling on a mix of Parliament-Funkadelic and Frankie Beverly and Maze.

The idea of writing my latest screenplay grew out of my estrangement from my father. For the past nineteen years, I had been trying to come to terms with his betrayal. I never got a chance to tell him how I felt since his secrets didn't come to light until after his death. I spent my last two teenaged years lashing out at everyone because he wasn't around to take my blows. Then, in my twenties, I pretended he had never existed, acting like a boy who had never known his father. In college, whenever I had to write a sociology research paper, or an assignment for my elective creative writing classes, I would always focus on Black children without fathers, even though I had never been one of those children. My father had been the kind of father who had tossed the ball in the backyard and taught me how to fix cars. He had been the kind of clichéd father who seemed to exist only in sitcoms, not to the extreme of *The Cosby Show,* but pretty close. By my early thirties, my attitude had become somewhat ambiguous; I couldn't decide what he had meant to me. Writing was the only way I could sort it out. But even in my writing, I couldn't be truly honest. Unable to write a nonfiction piece, I gravitated toward fiction, in the form of a screenplay, a film that would eventually be glamorized with Hollywood lights, cameras, and special effects because all good fiction contained some truth.

CHAPTER 5

EVA

SIMONE'S SCREENING PARTY for her film, *Two Many Men*, was in her apartment, which she referred to as "the Penthouse." It was really two one-bedroom apartments combined into one, located on the top floor of her father's four-story, multi-unit apartment building. It had double the number of rooms, including two bathrooms, and every inch was occupied with the cast and crew of the film, including Zephyr—her filmmaker-director-producer lover—and a bunch of her model friends as well as some mutual friends. The plastic people—the models and actors—stayed in the front end of the first apartment, which included the balcony, while the real people—everyone else—kept to the back apartment, which extended to the porch.

It had been a bad week for me and I almost didn't come. My headaches had been so severe that I called my doctor to request a new medication. The old one didn't alleviate my nausea and had too many side effects, including hallucinations, the most recent being the Oak Tree Man in my backyard. In addition, I called my pastor who offered me a healing prayer. The new medication, combined with a cold towel on my forehead and a nap in the dark, had worked on the latest headache that I had had earlier that morning.

"Come on, guys, you're supposed to mingle," Simone begged Maya and me and the rest of the group on the porch. Simone was decked out in seventies' wear that included a Cleopatra Afro wig over her own 'fro, bell-bottom slacks, and platforms. *Two Many Men* was set in the 1970s, so she had asked everyone to come dressed as their favorite pop-culture character from that decade. Not everyone complied, including me, with the exception of my bell sleeves and flared slacks. The seventies was not my favorite decade for fashion. I could have used a wig though. Because of the earlier humidity, it had taken more than the usual amount of water and gel to quell my frizzy hair.

"They don't want to mingle with us," Maya said, patting her nurse's hat. She had come as "Julia," and with her recent pixie haircut, she didn't require a wig. "Their *ca-ca* doesn't stink, ours does." Maya struck a model's pouty face and strolled across the porch in her best imitation of a supermodel's walk. We all laughed.

"Stop it. They're nice people," Simone insisted.

"Then you go hang out with them," I told her.

Simone clicked her tongue and left the porch, walking away in her trademark supermodel walk. The porch crowd burst out laughing. When people first met Simone, they thought she was phony, but she was really a good person with a lot of displaced love.

Despite Maya's request that I not confront Simone, I had called her anyway and demanded that she come clean about the man she was presumably setting me up with. She denied it so vehemently that I almost believed her. I eyed her suspiciously all night, waiting for the loser to approach me. But no one stepped up or made inquiries. Earlier, when I was waiting in one of the bathroom lines, the guy in front of me offered to let me cut in and struck up a conversation. I thought he was Simone's set-up guy since no one had so much as asked my name. Simone had designated a bathroom for each of the sexes, but no one paid attention to the homemade computer-generated gender signs on the doors.

"So, what's your name?" Mr. Model-Actor asked after I stepped in front of him.

"Eve," I answered, giving the short Anglicized version I had used during my clubbing days.

"Eve, huh? Like the 'Garden of Eden' Eve?" Even heathens knew the story about the fall of man.

I rolled my eyes and didn't bother to acknowledge his comment.

He didn't say anything for a while and as I was surveying the scene around me, I caught him looking down my blouse. Although nothing was showing, I crossed my arms.

"You here alone?" he asked.

"I'm celibate," I told him, a comment that always threw men off.

"Huh?"

I turned toward him. "I'm celibate. I don't have sex."

He held up his hands. "Okay, whatever. I didn't ask."

After that incident, I stopped being so defensive and tried to enjoy myself. Maya and I attempted to mingle with the *Two Many Men* clique but failed, since they were so self-absorbed. We returned to the porch crowd just as it began to drizzle; the temperature was dropping, normal for Chicago's late-summer nights. The gusts of mist that intermittently blew my way felt good after the sweltering summer day.

The front door, located in the middle of the apartment, opened and everyone on the porch glanced curiously through the open kitchen window at the two men who walked in. Maya jumped up excitedly and I knew one of them was the infamous Luciano. I felt nervous, like I was meeting my son's girlfriend for the first time.

"This is Luciano, everybody," Maya said, hanging on to the arm of the dark-haired one. "My *friend*," she stressed. Because some people who knew Maya knew she was married, there were a few awkward glances, and muffled "hellos." He was olive skinned and striking, with wavy black hair slicked back with gel or mousse, and a killer, crooked smile that read: *That's right, we're together and we're both married, and I don't care who knows it.* I was surprised because Luciano did not look like her type, and knowing her all my life, I knew her type. And pale, pretty-boys were not her type. Like me, Maya had always been attracted to Black men. Alex was biracial, but he identified more with his African American side because he had more contact with them.

The other man had been accosted by Simone's co-star, an anorexic woman wearing a feathered Farrah Fawcett wig. Through the window, I saw her slip him a card, which he glanced at briefly before sticking it in his back pants pocket.

"And this is Adam," Maya introduced the other man. "His friend."

Adam stepped onto the porch half smiling, half waving, and squinting through the darkness at all of us from behind amber shades. I guess someone forgot to tell him that the sun had set several hours earlier. Under better light, on another day, he might have been good looking. It was hard to tell what he looked like through his five o'clock shadow and goatee. Long, thin, golden-brown dreadlocks poked out from under a crocheted cap in the colors of the African American flag. He looked like a ganja-smoking Rastafarian, the kind who frequented Rites of Passage, a reggae club where Maya, Simone, and I used to party back in the old days. He wore a shirt, cargo pants, and vest, all in different shades of tan, and all in need of some serious ironing. He looked very ill-at-ease, like he had just been dragged out of bed. Of course, being the person that I am, I tried to guess his ethnicity. African American and Irish. Or some kind of Afro-Caribbean, old-world mix. In another time, when I was in the world, I might have been interested in someone like him.

Everyone introduced themselves all the way around, but before I could say my name, Maya interjected, rather ecstatically, "That's my sister . . ." She paused for dramatic effect, then continued, "Eva."

Adam looked straight at me, and I at him, and it must have hit us at the same time—Adam and Eve. For one momentary impulse, I contemplated that the best way to hurt Maya was to call Alex up and tell him her little secret, confess her sin for her. Of course I would never do anything that lowdown to my sister. So it wasn't Simone who was playing matchmaker after all, but my own flesh and blood. Why didn't they both stay out of my life? Why was it so hard for them to understand that I was waiting for a special man, a Christian man, not some Rastafarian-looking slacker? There was no way this man was a Christian.

Adam kind of smiled helplessly, uncomfortably rubbing the back of his neck. I looked away first, over at Maya; I was ready to attack her with my eyes, but she was conveniently engaged in a conversation with Luciano.

Then "Dazz" by Brick began to play and some of the couples jumped up to go inside and dance. In one corner of the porch, a loud debate distracted me from Maya and Luciano just as I overheard a woman make a comment against affirmative action in college admissions, a topic that was headed toward the Supreme Court.

"I heard about this study where Hispanics who scored 130 and 180 points lower than Whites and Asians were admitted ahead of more qualified candidates. *That* is totally unfair."

"You want to know what's unfair?" I challenged. "Getting into an Ivy League college when you're a C-average student just because your daddy went there."

A few hoots rippled through the group. Someone imitated a cat's shrieking sound.

"Well, I don't think it's fair for us minorities to think we deserve special treatment just because of our ethnicity. It demeans who we are," the young woman insisted, her eyes piercing through me. The woman looked like she might have been biracial and perhaps thought she needed to prove something to the White side. There were several Whites in the discussion group and I knew this kind of comment coming from an African American, even if she was half, could be construed as retrogressive.

"I don't think they're asking for preferential treatment because of their ethnicity as much as they're asking for a chance to compete. The playing field's got to be leveled somehow," I stressed. "If the government doesn't equalize public education with private education at the primary and high school level, then some concessions have to be made at a higher level."

"All I'm saying is that minorities need to step up to the challenge and compete with the rest of society and stop holding on to the notion that the world owes us something."

I looked around for backup, but Maya, my most staunch supporter, had disappeared with Luciano. Simone was busy heading up a Soul Train line in the front room.

"There are a lot of worse things going on in our government that are unfair. So what if college admission criteria benefits a few Blacks and Latinos. In the long run, our society as a whole is going to benefit from a more educated population," someone commented. I looked up at Adam straddling the porch railing raising a bottle of some obscure juice in my direction in support. "And I don't know about you but there's nothing 'minor' about being African American."

I smiled my gratitude and returned to the debate, ready to tear my opponent to shreds with statistics and facts. But the woman was already leaving the porch. Soon after, the discussion group got smaller and smaller as people grew bored with the controversial topic and began to get up and dance, or form more intimate liaisons. It started to rain a little harder and I moved away from my spot so I wouldn't get wet. The music was getting louder and I could feel my headache trying to make a comeback. I decided it was time to go. I had had enough stimulation for one night. Just as I headed for the front door, I heard Simone yelling, trying to get everyone's attention.

"Okay, people, the screening's about to begin," she announced, turning off the stereo. I thought about sneaking out but I knew Simone would never forgive me. She already believed I didn't support her career choice, not to mention her promiscuous lifestyle. As everyone gathered around the projection screen, Simone's birthday present from Zephyr, I scanned the crowd for Maya. There weren't enough chairs to go around so most people sat on the floor or stood up. I leaned against the wall nearest to the door.

The film was not bad for a "B" movie, shot in black and white, and reminded me slightly of Spike Lee's *She's Gotta Have It*. The emphasis was not so much on the woman's open sexuality as it was on her determination to be independent from men. I found myself slightly embarrassed during the intimate scenes, which weren't as graphic as Simone had led me to believe, but lent a lot to the imagination. At one point, during an intensely heated kissing scene between Simone and her leading man, I had to look away and found myself looking straight at Adam. I felt the heat rise in my face as he smiled coyly and I quickly looked away.

My eyes settled on Luciano and Maya sitting on the arm of the sofa in spoon fashion, his arms wrapped possessively around her like she belonged to him. He looked up and I held his gaze, hoping he grasped the look of disapproval on my face. Still looking at me, he boldly kissed Maya's neck as if to ask, *What're you going to do about it?* I glared at him before turning back to the screen. Although I had promised I would stay out of her life, I decided then and there I was going to have to tell her what I really thought about Mr. Luciano the next time we were alone.

Despite the film's theme, I was pleasantly surprised at Simone's acting. She was good and had come a long way from the high school plays she had acted in. I only wished she would put it to a more appropriate use. After the applause was over everyone surrounded the cast and Zephyr, complimenting them. I headed toward Maya to tell her I was ready to go, but by the time I stepped over the people sitting on the floor, and squeezed past sweaty bodies, she had disappeared again and so had Luciano. I walked up to Zephyr who was talking to Adam.

"Excuse me. Have you seen my sister?"

They both shook their heads.

Adam said, "I haven't seen Luciano either. What's up?"

"I have to go."

Somebody poked me in the back. I turned to find Pam, a mutual friend, dressed as Thelma from *Good Times*. "I saw Maya going downstairs the back way a little while ago," she offered. "With her friend."

I started for the back porch again just as Adam was about to say something. I held up a finger and mouthed that I'd be back. Down the back porch stairs, I peeked over the railing and there I saw Luciano's tan suit in the dark, Maya's arms around his back.

"I'm leaving," I said, slightly hating her at that moment. Although we rarely fought, when we did, it never lasted very long and we never got to the point where we stopped speaking to each other. But this situation with this Luciano person might have the potential to cause some damage to our relationship.

She pulled one hand away briefly to wave at me, her diamond-studded wedding band glistening in the dark.

"How're you getting home?" I asked, trying not to sound like a mother hen.

She peeked out from around Luciano's arm, grinning like a kid in a toy store. "Don't worry." Luciano looked over his shoulder at me with slight annoyance.

Maya giggled and went back to kissing. I shook my head with resignation and started back up the stairs to go out the front way. I had to remember that even though she was my younger sister—by one year, she always stressed—she was an adult. All I could do was pray for her.

"Eva!" she called out. "Where's Adam?" She came up the stairs looking sheepish, her hair and lipstick a mess. I looked at her critically.

"He's inside, talking to Zephyr," I told her quietly.

"Are you mad at me?" she asked in a tiny voice. "I knew if I told you about Adam before, you wouldn't come. He's kind of nice looking, don't you think? Despite the hair?"

I wanted to grab her by the arm and pull her away from Luciano, protect her, but her face had that dreamy look she got whenever she was in church, deeply absorbed in the sermon. The fact that she had the same reaction with this Luciano guy that she had with God scared me. Part of me wanted to smack some sense into her, remind her that she was a married woman, a saved woman at that, and a principal for God's sake, but I knew anything I said at that moment would fall on deaf ears.

Without responding, I turned my back and went inside before I said something I'd regret. I wove through the costumed plastic bodies and fake hair and found Simone. Sometime in the midst of the evening, I had forgiven her for the bookstore incident.

She screamed over the music, "Don't leave!"

Squinting, I pointed to my temple and waved. Using my migraines as an excuse was becoming a crutch, but sometimes it came in handy. She linked her arm in mine and walked me to the door.

"So, what'd you think?" she asked.

"Definitely better than Pam Grier."

We laughed and hugged, her Cleopatra Jones wig almost falling off. Then, truthfully I added, "You were good, girl."

She walked me to the door. As we stepped into the hallway, I almost ran into another couple wrapped up in each other's arms. Simone snapped the hall light on and glared at the couple who didn't even flinch when I squeezed by. I couldn't wait to hit the bed.

"Call me when you get home, girl," Simone shouted.

Down the three flights of stairs, I passed more couples, talking or kissing. Finally on the ground floor, I yanked open the downstairs door and almost ran into a figure in the vestibule. I jumped. It was Adam.

"Sorry," he said, pulling a cigarette from his lips. "Did I scare you?" I noticed he was holding the cigarette like one would hold a joint, between the thumb and forefinger.

"Uh . . . no, you didn't."

He blew smoke out of the corner of his mouth. It wasn't marijuana, but I screwed up my face in distaste nonetheless. Cigarette smoke always made me think of my father, who I remembered had yet to return my call from a few days ago.

Sensing my aversion, Adam tossed the cigarette on the floor, squashing it. I looked down at the stub, slightly displeased that he was littering the clean vestibule, but I didn't rebuke him.

"I'm trying to quit," he explained as if I asked.

I stepped from the vestibule and stood out under the awning and breathed in the misty air. The rain was really coming down, drowning the grass and forming puddles in every crevice and crack in the walkway.

"Eva, right?" he asked.

"Adam, right?" I countered sarcastically.

He smiled, and I couldn't help but smile back. He said, "I was wondering why Luciano and Maya wouldn't tell me your name. What a coincidence, huh?"

"I guess. So you knew about this?"

"Yeah."

"I didn't. I mean, I thought Simone was responsible but it turned out to be my sister."

"Are you older or younger than Maya?"

"Older."

"You look younger."

"Everybody says that. 'Cause I'm shorter."

"So, you're leaving?"

"Yeah. I have a headache."

"Me, too. Want a Tylenol? I just took two myself."

"That doesn't work for me. I get migraines so I take prescription drugs." I leaned against the brick wall, watching the rain fall, debating whether to run to my car or wait until it let up a bit. I heard him moving behind me and when I turned around, he was leaning against the doorway above me.

"What is that scent?" he asked. "Pineapple?"

"Rose oil."

"Smells nice. Sweet."

I was surprised he could smell anything. "What's that smell? Cancer?"

His face dropped for a hot second, and I thought he was going to curse me out, but then he recovered quickly, letting out a small sarcastic chuckle. "Maya was right. You *are* funny."

"Thanks," I answered even though I knew he was being flippant. He was still wearing his shades, which made me suspicious. "You know, the sun set a long time ago," I said, pointing to my eye.

"Oh," he said, and slowly pulled off his glasses. The first thing I noticed were his black bushy eyebrows, a sharp contrast to his light brown hair. They were so dark, they looked dyed, so thick that the brows almost touched his eyelashes. His eyes were a simple brown, but they were an interesting shape, turned down at the ends like a sad puppy dog. I realized I was staring and veered my sight about-face, to the sky. "You thinking about going out in the rain?" he asked.

"I'm not afraid of a little rain."

"Yeah, you got that Puerto Rican hair going on."

I cocked an eyebrow at him. "I have kinky roots."

This made him smile again, even though my intention was not to amuse him but to convey my disinterest with sarcasm. I was throwing my best stuff at him but he was not deterred. I liked that in him.

The rain was letting up, but lightning still periodically lit up the sky, the thunder following at subdued, prolonged intervals. It was a pleasant evening, in the low sixties, which was pretty good for an August night, even if it was drizzling.

I stepped out from under the awning's protection and started down the walkway. "See you."

I heard his footsteps behind me, so I stopped and turned halfway around, looking at him questionably.

"Hey. Uh . . . Maya says you're not . . . seeing anybody."

Instead of looking at me, he was looking up into the trees like they held something mysterious. He was losing his confidence, and this gave me the upper hand. "What else did she tell you?" I asked, my anger at Maya returning. *How dare she tell some man about me without my permission,* I thought.

"Uh . . . let me see. She said you're divorced. And you have two sons in college. You're the director of Latino recruitment at CU and you're a writer."

"She never mentioned you."

He laughed and shoved his hands in his pockets. "I'm a probation officer for the state. No kids, but I have a niece and a nephew I'm crazy about. I write, too."

I turned around to face him fully. "Did she tell you that I'm celibate?"

He scratched his neck and looked slightly uncomfortable, glancing back up at the trees. "Uh, no, she didn't tell me that."

"Yeah, it's true. I don't have sex. So, I'd be a waste of time."

I crossed my arms, quietly fuming, letting the rain fizzle my anger. He reached into his back pocket and held out a card. "Listen, if you change your mind. Not about the celibacy thing, but you know, if you want to have coffee sometime, give me a call."

What would be the point? I wanted to say. I took the card without reading it. I hated it when people gave out their cards. It was so pretentious. I could understand if we were at a networking dinner or a business meeting. What was so hard about writing his number on a piece of paper. I swore if he pulled out a personal digital accessory and said, *"Let's do lunch,"* I'd scream. I knew if I really wanted to blow him off, I could just say, "No, thanks." But then he'd probably go back and tell Luciano what an evil witch I was and then Maya and Simone would reaffirm that I was going to end up alone for the rest of my life.

I glanced at the card and noticed it read, *Chanel Devereau.*

"I thought your name was Adam?" I handed it back to him.

He looked embarrassed and laughed. "Sorry. Some girl gave me that." I noticed he wasn't throwing it away as he reached into another pocket and brought out another card. I stuck it in my purse without looking at it and gave him a phony smile, which he returned. Then I turned and began walking quickly down the pathway, dodging puddles.

When I heard him following me again, I spun around, this time with irritation. "Where're you going?"

"Walk you to your car? It's kind of late to be walking out by yourself."

"I have mace. And I know Tai Bo." My car was parked almost three blocks away and even though Simone lived in a decent area, there was no such thing as a safe neighborhood anymore. But I always walk with the knowledge that I am covered by the blood of Jesus—and the fact that I box for pleasure.

He laughed. "Oh, you're a tough diva, huh?"

I looked at him surprised, remembering how Anthony used to call me "Tough Diva-Eva," albeit spitefully. But I figured Adam didn't mean anything by it so when I started walking and he fell in step, I didn't dissuade him. He took the outside of the sidewalk like a man who had been raised properly. For the first block, we didn't speak and I told myself that if he didn't say anything until we reached my car, it would be just fine. Maybe he thought I was a snob, which I'm not. I just figured rather than say something mundane, it was better not to say anything at all. And then again, who cared what he thought? The less said, the better.

"So, what kind of stuff do you write?" he asked, disturbing my silence.

"I don't like to talk about my writing. To strangers. No offense."

He shrugged. "That's cool. Just trying to make conversation."

My heel caught in one of the sidewalk cracks obscured by a puddle and I stumbled awkwardly, almost falling on my face, but Adam caught my arm and held me up. An electric charge went up my arm.

"Good thing I was here, huh?" he kidded.

"Yeah, I could've been killed."

He laughed and I gave him my fake smile again, trying to cover up my embarrassment for tripping. I looked at his hand, which was still holding my arm, and he pulled it away quickly like he was afraid I was going to hit him.

"You are mean," he said, but his voice was not serious.

"I am not."

"Yeah, you are. You're one of those females who give men a hard time, busts their nuts before you even let them get the time of day. I bet the boys in grammar school ran away from you," he teased. "And in high school, they were probably too scared to ask you out."

"No, that's not me at all." But in fact, it was the Eva I knew, with slight variations. When boys tried to kiss me in grammar school, I'd beat them up. In high school, I cursed out any guy who tried to make an advance because I knew what was on their minds. I thought of how I had broken up with Anthony after he had touched my behind. I didn't trust boys then and I trusted men even less as an adult.

As we fell silent again, I tried to keep my eyes on the wet sidewalk ahead of me, as the misty rain tickled my face. From the corner of my eye, I saw him pull out another cigarette and light it. I noticed he was left-handed, like me, which was good because he was holding the cigarette and blowing the smoke to his left, away from me. We walked the next half block quietly, the peace interrupted only when a car splashed by.

"So, how do you feel about your sister and Luciano?"

"It's her life. I try not to judge her. And I pray for her."

I saw his eyebrows go up. "I used to do a lot of that."

"What? Pray? Let me guess, something bad happened to you and you stopped believing in God?"

He didn't answer right away and when I glanced over at him, he was staring straight ahead with a serious look on his face. I could only surmise that I had guessed correctly.

"I didn't say I stopped believing. I just said, I used to pray a lot. And now, I don't. Pray as much."

I have always dreaded the day that I would be tested by the Lord to the point where I would stop believing, or deny Him. I prayed that that day would never come. At least he was a believer. Nonbelievers scare me, like murderers and pedophiles.

"Oh, thanks for your input in the discussion earlier," I said, remembering.

"My pleasure. Affirmative action is a sore spot for me. Plus, I hate when people use that term 'minority.' It irritates the crap out of me. Especially when it comes from people of color."

"I know. Like the new phrase they've invented for Latinos, the 'majority-minority,' since we're becoming the largest so-called ethnics."

"I guess we're never going to be just plain old Americans," he said lightheartedly, laughing. I joined in. "How's your head?" he asked.

"My what?"

"Your headache?"

I forgot I had faked one. "Oh, it's better," I said, as we reached my Mustang. "This is me."

Immediately, his face lit up. "Nice car. What is it? An '80?"

I nodded, impressed. "It used to be my father's. He gave it to me for my high school graduation."

"Nice. I like old cars too. I got a '76 Chevy Nova. Got it at a junkyard and fixed it up."

"I hate those SUVs people are so crazy about these days," I said.

"I know. It's like they don't understand the concept of depreciation."

"All in the name of looking good when you're riding down the street," I added.

"I know, I know."

I got into my car. I decided to be cordial despite his being a lit-
terbug and a smoker. "Thanks for walking me."

"You're welcome."

He closed the door for me, leaning against it for a while, the cigarette dangling from his mouth. Maya was right, he *was* kind of nice
looking—if he shaved and changed into some decent clothes and
maybe cut his hair. I started the car and rolled down the window.
"Can I give you a piece of advice?"

"If I say 'no,' you'll probably give it to me anyway, right?"

"Give up the cancer sticks. They're hazardous to your health."

He smiled and spit out the cigarette and made an exaggerated
production out of stepping on it like he was stomping it to death.

Before I could stop myself, a smile spread across my face.

CHAPTER 6

ADAM

IF WOMEN KNEW how much power they possessed, they would probably take over the world—or at least take charge of their lives. Even in high school, it always seemed like the girls had all the power. They had something guys wanted and they had the power to make us wait for it as long as they wished. In the end, the majority of us never got what we were after. Somewhere between the time following high school and early adulthood, women lost that power and the scales tilted in the other direction. They allowed men to gain the power, believing they had lost the battle. So many of them were so anxious to fall in love and live happily-ever-after, believing in a fantasy that didn't really exist, that they gave in too easily. Somewhere down the line, men caught on to women's biggest secret, that they feared ending up alone, so men fed upon this knowledge and surpassed women. They found that many women would put up with bad company, exploitation, even abuse, for the sake of showing everyone that they had someone in their lives. The power of life and death might be on the tongue, but the power of happiness and discontent was in the mind.

Just once, I wanted to meet a courageous sister who drew upon her strength, who knew what she wanted and would settle for nothing less.

Take the Latin sister I met the night before, Eva. Instead of wearing her hair loose or in some crazy or phony hairstyle, she had it up in a simple, curly ponytail. Where most of the women at the party, the ones who hadn't worn costumes, had been decked out in short revealing dresses or low-cut tops, trying too hard to draw men's attentions, she had worn a long-sleeved black blouse with black slacks. Plain, natural, but very chic.

However, she was definitely high-maintenance, but not in the way that required weekly trips to the beauty and nail salons. She was the kind of woman you didn't mess with if you wanted to live a quiet, uncomplicated life, without the drama that followed the romantic stage in a relationship. I mean, to actually admit she was celibate to a total stranger, I knew her whole persona was about shocking people just to get a reaction. If people couldn't handle it, that was their problem. Usually, I took women's numbers so that I could decide whether to call them. I gave Eva my card to give her the power. The ball was in her court. I already let my intentions be known: coffee, conversation—nothing more, nothing less. The next step was up to her.

Through the balcony's plate-glass doors, I glanced at Luciano in my living room, flicking through the cable, bored because Maya was unreachable at a picnic with her family.

I was lounging on a patio chair, reading over the twenty pages of new scenes on my laptop that I had typed earlier that morning. After last night's rain, the day was starting off humid and hot, just the way I liked it. Talking to Zephyr, the filmmaker-director-producer at Simone's party, had gotten my creative juices pumped and I had been up for the last three hours creating, hoping Luciano would sleep late. However, depressed people didn't sleep much so he was up with the sun. Intermittently, he attempted to start a conversation, but I kept brushing him off. I didn't want to talk to him or do anything for that matter but write. I loved him like I would my own brother, if I had one, but I couldn't wait until he left. I valued my privacy. I decided I wouldn't panic until I saw him bringing in the big guns—suitcases and furniture. Then I would have to act. I couldn't live with anybody.

What I remembered most about Eva, what stuck in my mind, was that there was no obvious attraction on her part when we were introduced. Either she really wasn't interested or she was really good at hiding it. Luciano was right on one count; she did resemble Maya. They had the same large dark eyes, the same facial structure, but Eva's skin was darker, the color of chestnut, and her hair was black, longer and with a tighter curl. Neither resembled the typical Hispanic girls I had seen, or the Latinas in mainstream media, the ones that looked like Salma Hayek or Jennifer Lopez, and other Hollywood tokens. I supposed that it was the same with other ethnic groups: When it came to beauty, the closer to the ideal, the more acceptable they were.

Not that Eva wasn't attractive. She was pretty in a subtle way, like women who were good looking but didn't make a big deal about it. The kind that would catch your eye standing on the opposite side of the El platform or walking past a plate-glass window as you sat in a restaurant. She reminded me of mixed Black girls, the ones who were part this, part that, with African being the dominant factor in the equation. If I had seen her walking down the street, I would think she was a "sistah." However, I saw nothing but distrust in her huge brown eyes, and that crease in the middle of her forehead, perhaps from too much frowning, made her look mean, almost evil. But then again, maybe it was the headache she claimed she had.

However, when she started debating with that other woman, I saw the fire in her eyes. I thought, now here is a woman who fights battles with her tongue, a sister who would march for justice were marching still in vogue. Here is a woman who would command, demand respect from a man—and get it. The problem was, women like her frightened men, and I was no exception. In talking to her, I got a sense that she had a lot of unnecessary attitude she could do without, which was a little intimidating, but as I said, my post-cancer radar saw right through her veneer and I knew it was a defense mechanism. Even if she was interested, she wasn't going to show it. Like any man, I liked a good challenge now and then, but she was a little too much. Like I said, high-maintenance.

I thought of Chanel, the sister who handed me her card as soon as I walked into Simone's place and whispered, "Call me." And then I remembered Zina, whom I had never called. I knew both of them would definitely be low-maintenance, no mystery there.

After leaving the party, I drove Luciano to his home again, but Lisa still wouldn't let him in. She did come out of the house to talk to him while I sat in the car praying she would take him back. When they were done, she went inside and he came to the car with an overnight bag. I didn't make any snide remarks about him moving in since I had made my position on sharing my living space very clear on many occasions.

Before Sondra, I lived with Monica, a beautiful shapely paralegal who loved to walk around the house nude. Don't get me wrong, there was nothing wrong with walking around naked, especially since she had a beautiful body. I did it myself occasionally, but the woman streaked every single minute of the day. From the moment she woke up in the morning, or walked into the house, until she went to bed, off went the clothes. Her nudity was only part of the problem. She also never wore underwear—ever. I had a problem picturing her at work with nothing underneath her skirt, working side by side with male coworkers. The kicker was when she rolled over and went to sleep right after sex, which again, I did also. But since I used condoms, I had to get up and clean up. When we were just dating, she used to jump in the shower with me; after she moved in, she hardly took showers. Not that she smelled, but because I was raised to wash up as soon as you woke up, I found the whole skipping baths thing unsettling. *Europeans don't bathe every day,* she used to argue. *You ain't European, honey! You're Black!* I finally yelled one day.

Anyway, that arrangement lasted three months and I considered myself a martyr for tolerating her that long. When I began to smell another man on her, an overwhelming European musk cologne masking body odor, I thought, oh heck naw, this madness had to end.

I also lived with a male roommate at one time, a guy I had known from college. He had women calling the house all day and night long, coming in and out of his bedroom like a revolving door. I finally confronted him and told him it had to stop. I needed my sleep and privacy and my steady girlfriend at the time was suspicious that his womanizing would rub off on me. He accused me of being jealous of his Casanova status and refused to move out. I finally packed my stuff and left him with the lease. That was four years ago, before I bought the loft.

"Hey, what'd you think of Eva?" Luciano called out, interrupting my train of thought.

"I don't know," I mumbled.

"You talked to her, didn't you?"

"Yeah, I gave her my card."

"What'd you think?" Luciano prodded.

"She's celibate."

"What do you mean, she's celibate? How do you know?"

"She told me."

"And you believed her?"

"Either it's true, or she doesn't want to be bothered. Either way, she wasn't interested in me."

"Why don't you call her? Or do you want me to ask Maya to ask *her* what she thought of you like we're in high school?"

"I'm not going to call her and no, I don't want you to call your mistress to get the four-one-one. Just leave it alone."

"She's not my mistress," he retorted. "I don't pay to keep her. I knew her long before I married Lisa. We were friends before we . . . fell in love."

"Secret lovers . . ." I sang under my breath.

"Man, shut up. You're just jealous 'cause you ain't got nobody to love, bruh."

"Yeah, that's it. You hit it right on the head, bruh." I could've added something really crude, but I had matured in the last year and no longer felt a need to one-up him.

He got up and went to the fridge. "I can't believe you haven't gone grocery shopping. How do you get nourishment?"

"Man, do I look like your wife? Oh, yeah, that's right. She kicked you out." I hoped he would take my quips seriously and shut up.

"I told you. She just wants to take a little break."

"Mm-hmm."

It was obvious I wasn't going to get any more work done. I saved my document and closed the laptop. Without bothering to smell the pants and shirt from the night before, I quickly dressed.

"You going shopping?" he asked, perking up.

I grabbed my keys and laptop and headed for the door. "I'm going to buy a few things."

"Yo, get some steaks and I'll grill 'em."

I hate grocery shopping, which was why I waited until I was down to the bare minimum before I went. I loved kids, I did. But one place kids did not belong was the grocery store. I glanced at two rug rats in the cereal aisle tearing coupon after coupon out of the dispenser and letting them litter the floor as their mother examined the price on a box of instant potatoes, totally oblivious.

After leaving the loft, I had driven to the neighborhood park and in a half hour typed up ten more pages before finally dragging myself to the store.

Absentmindedly, I pitched a couple of boxes of cereal into my cart, not really caring what brand they were. Farther down the aisle, I heard a young girl whining. I could feel my eye beginning to twitch as her voice squeaked higher and higher.

"Please, Mama, can I have this one? You promised. Please, *please*. You said I could. Yes, you did. *Please*." I cringed and slowly looked over at the little girl begging her mother for a box of Cookie Crisp.

"That one has too much sugar," the mother said calmly.

They all have too much sugar, I thought. *Just give it to her.*

"You said if I did my homework early and cleaned my room, I could. Please, Mama, *pleeease*."

The twitching in my eye quickened and I pressed my finger to steady it. The mother smiled weakly at me as she allowed the girl to put the box of cereal in the cart. *Thank you!*

I steered my cart out of the aisle and quickly went to the fruit and vegetable section. All I needed were oranges, lettuce, and some milk and I'd be done. I had already filled half the cart with meat for the days I felt like cooking and frozen pizzas and dinners for the days I didn't.

Amid the cilantro, collard, and mustard greens, I thought I recognized the woman scrutinizing the avocados, pressing her thumb into their bottoms. It was Ms. Celibate-with-an-Attitude from the night before. She was wearing white pajama pants and a buttoned-down man's shirt with big turned-up cuffs. A red chiffon scarf was tied on her head, her hair flowing loose, frizzy and thick. I picked up the first head of lettuce I touched and tried to sneak away. Halfway down the aisle, I realized it was a cabbage. I wheeled my cart back around to exchange it and, from the corner of my eye I saw her glance over at me, then turn casually away, pretending she didn't know me. *She* was ignoring *me*?

It was then that I began to wonder what was wrong with me. Maybe my hair threw her off. Not all women appreciated natural hair, particularly light-colored kinky locks. A girl once told me she could never marry me because she was afraid her kids would be born albino. Considering we weren't even in a committed relationship, the girl's comment was presumptuous as well as ludicrous. Maybe it was my clothes. Because I spent five days a week in a suit, I liked to dress casually on the weekends, even a bit carelessly, by-passing the iron if I could get away with it. I conceded that I was a little wrinkled the night before, but that was because I had fallen asleep waiting for Luciano and Eva's sister to finish kissing, which to date, he claimed was as far as they had gone. Or maybe it was the fact that I was Black. Maybe she had a phobia about Black men, not exactly a bias, but a fear of the unknown. I recalled being turned down by a multiracial woman who told me that she didn't have anything against me, she just did not date Black men. The fact that she was part Black made her comment sting even more, but I got over it.

Then I thought, *hold up*. I couldn't believe I was doubting myself because of this woman. Obviously Chanel and Zina had seen something she was overlooking. There was nothing wrong with me, it was her. *Who did she think she was?* I thought angrily. Determined to make my presence known, I pushed my cart toward her and deliberately bumped hers. She turned to face me slowly like a robot and undressed me over her shades in one sweep. I knew she recognized the clothes from the previous night because women notice things like that, but I didn't care.

"I saw you," she said.

"Oh, you did? Why didn't you speak?"

"Why didn't you?"

"Hi."

"Hello." She glanced into my cart, inspecting my groceries. Likewise I looked into her cart of spices, Caribbean tropical fruits, and vegetables, some of which Luciano had introduced to me, like plantains—*platanos*. They were great fried with white rice and black beans. In the front basket sat a bouquet of fresh-cut flowers.

"Who're the flowers for?" I asked.

"Me," she answered, a little defiantly, sticking out her chin as if daring me to say something. I noticed she had a slight underbite, something I hadn't realized the night before.

"You always buy flowers for yourself?"

"Always."

"Where are the plantains?" I then asked.

"Right behind you," she said, pointing over my shoulder.

I turned around and picked out a few. She looked at me with a distrustful brow. "You know how to cook those?"

"Peel 'em, slice 'em diagonal, and fry 'em up in some oil. They're sweet. I've eaten them at Luciano's mom's house. She's Cuban."

"Yeah, so I heard." She turned up her lip and I gathered there was no love lost between her and Luciano. "But if you want the sweet ones, you have to get the ripe ones," she suggested. Without asking, she returned the green ones I had picked out. "These are *verde*, too green. You can still cook them, but they won't be sweet. You'll have to smash 'em down and add salt. Not as healthy." She picked through the display of plantains and pulled out some yellow-colored ones with a lot of dark spots that looked spoiled. "These are *maduro*, ripe. They'll be nice and sweet." I couldn't help but watch her mouth as she spoke and noted that her bottom lip was wider and thicker than the top one, giving her a pouty appearance. I guess I was staring too hard because she gave me an odd look, her right eyebrow cocked.

I cleared my throat. "So, you like to cook?" I asked.

"I thought my sister told you about me?"

"So, you don't like to cook."

"I *hate* to cook," she said. "I steam and boil as much of my food as possible. That's the extent of my chef abilities."

"A modern woman," I said. I meant it as an affront but she took it as a compliment and smiled. It was a real smile, not the constipated one she had continuously flashed me the night before.

"I take it *you* don't cook," she said.

"I can throw some stuff together on occasion." The truth was all the men in my family knew how to cook. My mama had taught me how to cook when I was ten after warning me that she wasn't always going to be around. The thought of losing her, not just her delicious meals, scared me into devouring all of her recipes. But the real truth was that cooking was too much work. I would rather clean out toilets than cook, so the future Mrs. Black would have to enjoy it as much as my mama once did.

"Huh," she snorted, not believing me.

"Next time we have a barbecue, you can check it out for yourself."

"Barbecue don't count," she chided in that sarcastic humor of hers.

I laughed, but didn't challenge her and divulge the Louisiana cuisine my mom had passed down to me.

"Well, I got to go," I told her, happy I was the first to dismiss her.

"Yeah, me too."

She went left and I went right. We ended up in checkout lanes next to each other. She gave me the fake smile as I picked up the *Chicago Tribune* and she got the *Sun-Times*. She had two people in front of her; I had one, the oblivious woman with the coupon-delinquents. The woman had awakened from her stupor and was engaged in a lively debate with the cashier over the price of dried potato flakes.

"I know what the sign said and it said two-fifty-nine!" she screamed like she was being cheated out of a million dollars.

"I still have to call it in, ma'am," said the teenaged cashier, who I could tell was trying hard not to lose her temper.

I happened to glance over at Eva in exasperation and she raised her eyebrows in empathy.

"Price check on Betty Crocker's thirteen-ounce mashed potatoes," the cashier screeched over the loudspeaker, a little too loudly.

"I'm telling you, it's two-fifty-nine!"

"It's ringing up two-eighty-nine," the girl retorted.

I got out of line and went to the next opened checkout, which contained three customers, but I didn't care. I had no tolerance for ignorant people who showed out in public. I was a consumer advocate's worst nightmare, the kind of shopper who accepted prices as they were scanned, not advertised. Unless of course, we were talking about something important like a DVD player or a stereo.

In a matter of minutes, the two-fifty-nine dispute had turned into an incident as the manager and security were summoned. I had left the line just in time.

In the parking lot, I saw Eva ahead of me unloading her groceries into her blue Mustang. I felt a slight kinship with our distaste for foreign cars. I ended up behind her in the exit of the parking lot. In her rearview mirror, I thought I saw her checking me out, but she could have been checking for clearance. She turned right, I turned left.

Luciano was out on the balcony with his cell phone, and judging by the sleepy smile on his face and his low voice, I figured Maya had found some way to call him. I noticed he had the gas grill going.

I walked out to the balcony and gave him the grocery bag with the steaks. He pulled out the plantains.

"What's this?"

"What does it look like?"

He grinned and spoke into the phone. "Hey Maya, babe. Our boy brought home some *pla-ta-nos*. You know what that means. He got bit by a Puerto Rican ladybug."

I narrowed my eyes and flung the bag with the loaf of bread at him. He caught it before it fell over the balcony. His laughter resonated in my ears as I went in to take a shower.

CHAPTER 7

EVA

I AM NOT the kind of woman who chases men. My mother died at a very crucial time in my life, just when I was becoming interested in boys, but before I started dating. From the time we were little girls, she always told Maya and me that as long as we keep our hands folded and our knees together, we would stay out of trouble. As we got older, she told us that when it was time for us to date, we should always pay for our share so nothing was expected of us, and that we should always, always take cab or bus fare, just in case we were left stranded. But the main thing my mother taught us was that men were the suitors, women were the courted. Throughout my dating years, I never approached men first, no matter how interested I was. It wasn't that I was shy or stuck-up, I just didn't feel comfortable being the initiator. It was just the Latin way, the old-fashioned Southern way, the way God intended it and what had worked for centuries to make marriages last. I thought of my parents, both sets of my grandparents, and my aunts and uncles, who had all been married for decades until death did one of them part.

The day after the party, Maya called to tell me about a dream she had. Both Adam and I were in her dream, though in what capacity she couldn't remember since she had the unfortunate knack of forgetting the details of her dreams as soon as she woke up. But it was enough to convince her that Adam and I were destined to be together, not only because of our namesakes, and because we were both writers, but more inanely, because we were both left-handed. She tried to sell me on what a great guy he was—how he wrote screenplays and poetry, had even published a book of poems, and that back in college, one of his screenplays won first prize in a competition and was later sold to Hollywood. I countered that this was not enough information to make a man great. What did she know about his past, about his intentions, or more important, his relationship with God?

I opened the top drawer of my desk where I had put away the card. *Adam Black—Juvenile Probation Officer.* On the back, he had scribbled his home phone. A couple of times I thought about calling him, but I kept getting mixed feelings and usually I took that as a sign that God was trying to tell me something. Adam seemed like a nice enough guy, but I found myself concentrating on the cons rather than the pros. His hair left something to be desired. It was intriguing but at the same time somewhat radical. Then I thought about his comment that he didn't pray "as much." Even before I was saved, I prayed almost every night. But then again, a man who worked with juvenile offenders couldn't be that bad. In a way, we were in the same field, steering young people in the right direction. And there was something about him, like he was holding something back, some secret I couldn't quite discern. I couldn't shake the nagging feeling that the flags were flapping all over the place. And yet . . . No, I thought resolutely, I could never be with a man who smoked.

For the past week, I thought about the "Adam and Eve" thing, and Maya's intuition that maybe it was fate, God. Especially after seeing Adam in the grocery store. How many times had I been to the same grocery store and never run into him? But then, maybe I just never noticed him since dreadlocked men in wrinkled clothing never turned my head, unless I was drunk, and I had stopped drinking a long time ago. Maybe God *was* trying to tell me something. I kept remembering what I told him, that I would be a waste of time. Maybe he took it to heart.

I picked up the phone, dialed the prefix, but then stopped. I thought, what would I say? *How about that cup of coffee?* I knew coffee would only be the beginning—of what? Another relationship headed nowhere? After all, I wasn't ready to get married again. And if a relationship wasn't headed for marriage, what sense was there in starting one?

Someone knocked on my office door, which was slightly ajar, and I quickly hung up the phone. I snapped myself out of the doubts and possibilities with Adam and concentrated on the present, which was the final proofreading of the bilingual information brochure on my desk for the upcoming college fair.

"Go away. I'm almost finished," I said, knowing it was my assistant, Dana, coming to warn me about the print shop's deadline.

"Bad time?"

I looked up and saw it was Rashid, not Dana. I waved him in. "No, no, I thought you were Dana."

The intercom rang as he stepped in. I pressed the "hands-free" button while motioning Rashid to a seat. "Yes?"

"There's an 'Adam Black' on 84," Dana announced. "He says you know who he is."

I paused, wondering how he had gotten my work number. I picked up the receiver.

"Should I put him through?" Dana asked.

"Uh, yeah . . ." I waited for the click as she connected the call. "Hello?"

"Eva? Eva Clemente?"

My stomach jumped. "Speaking."

"This is Adam Black. I met you about a week ago. At Simone's party? You tried to ignore me at the grocery store?" I smiled as I recalled our encounter but didn't comment. It wasn't so much that I had tried to ignore him, but rather I hadn't been too thrilled about the way I looked, nor by his own disheveled appearance. I had merely been trying to spare us both an uncomfortable moment. "Your sister gave me your number," he continued. "I told her I'd take full responsibility if you went off."

"Yeah. I remember. No, it's okay." Rashid signaled whether he should leave but I shook my head and indicated for him to remain sitting.

"How you been?" he asked.

"I'm alright. Busy. You?"

"Great. Same-o, same-o."

I couldn't think of anything else to say because as I said, I was no good at small talk. I looked at my nails; I really had to stop biting them.

"Listen, the reason I'm calling . . . I have this kid I'm mentoring. I'm with Big Brothers. He just graduated from high school but didn't apply for college 'cause he had a rotten counselor who told him he wasn't college material. But I think he is. Maya said something about a college fair coming up?"

"It's this weekend, the thirtieth, at McCormick Place. It's for kids who missed the fall deadline or want to start college late."

"Hold on. Let me write that down." I gave him the information. "You'll be there?" he asked.

"Of course. But Rashid Ali is the director of African American recruitment."

At the mention of his name, Rashid looked up inquisitively.

"How do you know my little brother is Black?" Adam asked.

"Oh. I just thought . . . I thought they usually paired kids with . . ." I stuttered, slightly embarrassed.

"Actually, he's half African American. His father was Mexican."

"Sorry."

"That's okay. I was just messing with you." He chuckled and I relaxed.

I tried to think of something to say. Rashid was motioning comically for me to wrap up the call. "How did the *platanos* turn out?"

"Oh, you were right. They were sweet. Real good."

"Good."

"Oh, I meant to tell you. I read your editorial in last week's *Tribune*," he said.

"They published it? I picked up the *Times* by mistake."

"I usually buy the *Times*. I don't know why I got the *Trib*. I didn't read the article but the other boy I mentor was one of those transferred kids. I liked what you had to say."

"Thanks. Do you still have the paper? Can you cut it out for me?"

"For your scrapbook?"

I laughed. "Yeah, you got a problem with it?"

"No," he said. "Now I know what you write about."

I noticed Rashid getting antsy, rolling his eyes, so I said, "Listen, I have someone in my office. I got to go."

"Okay. See you Saturday."

I hung up absentmindedly, wondering what to make of the call. His request seemed genuinely business-related. I decided I wouldn't make any more out of it than I should.

"What's up?" I asked Rashid.

"Nada." Rashid stretched out in one of the chairs facing my desk. "Just thought you'd be interested to know that I just came from Dean Vanover's office. He said he received an anonymous e-mail that I was recruiting students to Islam. Can you believe that?"

The atmosphere on the university campus, as well as in the rest of the country, was very uneasy and leery since the events of 9–11 the previous year and every foreign student and faculty member, especially those of the Islamic faith, were suspect. "What did you say?" I asked curiously, knowing Rashid's knack for being outspoken.

"I told him a couple of students *have* asked me some questions about Islam, but I never tried to *recruit* anyone. So he starts telling me how I need to be careful in 'these volatile, sensitive times.'"

"And you said?"

"I said, 'This is still the United States of America, isn't it? First Amendment, freedom of speech, et cetera, et cetera?'"

I looked at him, shocked, open-mouthed.

"I didn't care. I was highly upset to say the least. So he goes into this long speech about this being 'wartime and how unwise it is to share your religious views.' I just wanted to let you know the FBI has probably opened up a file on me, so if I were you, I'd be careful about associating with me."

"They can't be that paranoid, can they?"

"They can." He paused and looked hard at me. "So, are we still on for lunch?"

"Of course," I assured him. "I'm not afraid of Dean Vanover. Or the FBI."

"I like your hair that way," Rashid commented.

My hand flew to my hair. "Really? I didn't do anything different." My hair has a mind all its own, molding itself to the weather or time of day. I never know what it is going to look like. Tomorrow it could look totally different. And then again, I was in need of a touch-up. Sometimes I wasn't sure if Rashid's comments were innocent flirting or if he was just being genuinely nice.

"Can we say 'thanks'?"

I smiled. "Thanks."

"So, who's Adam?"

"Oh, this probation officer. He's got a protégé he wants to bring to the college fair Saturday."

Someone knocked on the door. Without waiting for my answer, Dana opened it.

"The print shop said they need that brochure by one if we want the copies by Friday."

I nodded. "I'm almost finished."

Dana exited, but not before I saw her and Rashid exchange a look and a smile. I glanced curiously at Rashid, who looked meekly back at me.

"I'm thinking of asking her out," he confessed.

"Dana? Dana Duchamps?"

"Why do you sound so surprised?"

"Uh, hello? She's half your age. Plus, she's a student here."

"First of all, she's not my subordinate, she's yours, no conflict of interest. And for your information, she's thirty and a *night* student. I'm forty-seven, hence she is not half my age."

The intercom rang again. "It's your sister."

"Okay, I'm leaving. I see you're busy with *work*." Rashid got up and I shook a warning finger at him. He grinned.

"Hey," Maya said. "I just wanted to warn you. Adam called for your—"

"He just called."

"Sorry, I tried to call you first but I had this crazy parent burst into my office demanding an impromptu meeting."

"How about asking me first before giving out my phone number?"

"I said I was sorry."

"No big deal."

"Why haven't you called him?"

"I told you, I'm not good at calling men."

"He really is a good person. He's letting Luciano crash at his place since his wife put him out. And Luciano told me he hasn't been with a woman in, like, a year."

"So, we're supposed to be right for each other?"

"Well, you're both left-handed. You both write. I mean it, girl, this is your man. *Adán y Eva*. It's like fate—"

"Maya . . ."

"Then there's my dream. Why would I dream about the two of you? My dreams don't lie. C'mon, you yourself said you don't believe in coincidences."

"There's something about him, I don't know. Like he's got some secret."

"We've all got secrets."

I pondered the validity of her statement just as the intercom light started blinking again. "I got to go," I said. "I have to finish this brochure before lunch."

"Hey," she cried out as I was pulling the phone from my ear. "Are we meeting at Café Central after work?"

"Can't. I have Youth Ministry tonight."

"Oh, I forgot. Your nephews will be there."

Youth Ministry Night took place on the first Thursday of each month. Because the church had accepted that kids younger than ever were engaging in sex, the class consisted of children as young as eleven. The group was supervised by the junior pastor, Allen, while Johnny and I took turns heading the curriculum. Both of us had signed a contract of celibacy in order to properly guide the young members in leading lives of abstinence. Johnny was more rigid in his teaching than I was because he didn't like the kids to get out of control, something he claimed happened whenever it was my turn to run the class. I thought it was more important for the kids to be able to express themselves without the rigidity of a classroom setting, where they spent the majority of their day. My latest idea to have a debate was initially met with opposition by Johnny. But a poll taken by kids proved my proposal scored big points.

"What's wrong with soul-kissing?" a boy named Chris asked. "Kissing is normal. Kissing is not a sin. If God hadn't meant for us to kiss, he wouldn't have given us lips. Or tongues." Chris was sixteen, smart, charming as a snake, and very aware that all the teenage girls in church were crazy about him.

The kids were all sitting in the church gymnasium, on oversized pillows and cushions discussing the pros and cons of kissing. Most of the kids who were in favor of soul- or French-kissing were boys, including my nephews, Marcos and Lucas, but some girls favored it too, just as there were some boys on the con side. I saw Marcos and Lucas nudging each other and snickering, and I shook my head with disapproval. Maya had mentioned that they were already getting phone calls from girls and were becoming more secretive, asserting their right to privacy. I remembered how popular Eli had been with the girls at their age and I did not envy Maya.

"What's wrong with it is that it stirs up the soul," Cara Shakir, one of my favorite students, countered, in a slow deep voice that commanded attention. "The guy's spirit enters a girl's and vice-versa. It's like drugs. You start with weed and soon you get bored so you move up to the next drug, and the next. Why do you think they call it *soul*-kissing? It's not 'cause Blacks invented it. It's 'cause of the power it incites in a person's soul to go to the next level."

Cara was the daughter I never had, a girl I had taken under my wing. With my guidance, she had been accepted to one of the city's college prep schools. The product of an African Iranian father and a British Trinidadian mother, Cara was a collage of striking features with mesmerizing gray eyes, olive skin, and a head of thick, wavy red hair a lot of the girls admired. At fourteen, she already knew she wanted to work in the field of teenage pregnancy prevention. When she learned her high school was going to start dispensing birth control, she formed a club called "Students Against Sex."

I caught a momentary unwavering glare pass between Cara and Chris that went beyond their competitiveness. Everyone knew they were seeing each other, "kicking it" as they put it. While dating between the younger church members was discouraged, the church leaders knew there was little they could do about it.

"Alright, people. We're not talking about drugs," Johnny interjected, "so let's stick to the topic at hand. We're talking about Corinthians 6:18. *'Your body is the temple of the Holy Spirit. You are not your own, you were bought at a price. Therefore honor God with your body.'*" He shot a reprimanding glance in my direction, signifying that I was about to lose control again.

I surmised that he was still slightly chagrined that I had spurned his latest invitation to dinner. I shrugged innocently, refusing to feel guilty. Was I supposed to go out with him despite the lack of attraction? Or was it supposed to be like an arranged marriage where love came later?

"I was just making an analogy," Cara defended herself.

Proud of her, I gave her an encouraging smile and she returned the gesture. She reminded me of myself at her age: outspoken, a nonconformist, the kind of girl who didn't care if everyone else was wearing platform shoes, she was going to keep wearing gym shoes. I then looked at Pastor Allen for direction.

"Let's see who was able to find a passage to back up their argument," the junior pastor suggested.

"Judas betrayed Jesus with a kiss on the cheek and look what it cost him," Cara said proudly.

"Very good," I praised her.

"The passage, please," Johnny reiterated.

The enthusiastic rustle of turning pages filled the gym, silencing Johnny. I didn't even need to shoot him a look of self-satisfaction. It would've been the wrong thing to do. Just knowing it was enough.

*   *   *

On the last Saturday of August, when thousands of college-bound kids were into their second week of classes, the college fair was teeming with prospective students and parents. Despite the number of fairs held every year, there always seemed to be too many students who had not been encouraged to attend college and were uninformed about the vast availability of financial aid and scholarships. If I weren't educated, and prone to paranoid tendencies, I would agree with Rashid, an avid conspiracy theorist, who believes that the inequities in education are a deliberate plan by the powers that be to keep the country in its present condition. For this reason, I believe it is my calling to steer young Latinos toward higher education, particularly given the threat against affirmative action.

Adam showed up late in the afternoon with his two "little brothers." If it weren't for his distinctive hair color and style, I wouldn't have recognized him. He wore a casual shirt, tie, and slacks, in varying hues of olive green. With his face freshly shaven, save for a thin mustache and goatee, and his dreadlocks gathered back in a ponytail, he looked less barbaric. Except for his dense eyebrows, which could have used a waxing, he actually looked normal.

"You clean up alright," I complimented him, then I felt self-conscious because it sounded like something Simone would say.

He smoothed down his tie and smiled. "Thanks. I did look kind of raggedy the first couple of times we met, didn't I?"

"You had sort of a slacker thang going on."

"I call it chic-grunge."

"Whatever," I kidded, and we both laughed.

He then introduced me to his two protégés: Ricky, a hyperactive boy of nine, and Justin, a shy teenager who looked young for seventeen. Adam explained that he had been their Big Brother for a year, and had signed on to be their mentor until they graduated from high school. It was evident that they were very close to Adam, particularly Ricky, who hung on to his arm the entire time, bouncing up and down.

I told Adam that Justin would be eligible for both Black and Hispanic scholarships and gave him the brochure and information packet, which included my business card. Then I walked them over to Rashid, who was in a booth across from mine, and introduced them.

"Hey, did you bring my editorial?" I asked Adam, before walking away.

He cringed sheepishly. "I forgot. I'll mail it to you."

"It's no big deal."

"I'll mail it, I promise."

My booth was inundated with parents and students, keeping me, Dana, and the student advisor, Fátima Cruz, very busy. Rashid's booth was just as crowded. The number of visitors didn't dwindle until the very end. When five o'clock rolled around, I sent Dana and Fátima home, thanking them for a job well done. I decided to stay an extra half hour, along with a couple of the other recruiters from CU and other colleges, in case any latecomers showed up. I knew many parents used public transportation and came as far away as the South Side. As I was packing up the surplus brochures in boxes, Adam returned, Ricky still hanging on to his arm and Justin trailing behind, browsing through the material.

"How long are you going to be here?" Adam asked.

"I'm getting ready to leave now."

"You want to get some coffee?" he asked casually. "Or dinner?"

"You said we were going to McDonald's," Ricky whined as he jumped up and down.

"Burger King," Justin interjected.

"McDonald's!" Ricky shouted as he tried to kick his brother.

"Ricky, my eye is twitching," Adam said, squinting down at him. "What does it mean when my eye twitches?"

"Um . . . you're getting irritated?"

"Now, you said you were going to chill, right?"

"Right." He stopped jumping.

I smiled down at the rambunctious boy who didn't smile back. He looked at me like there was no way I was going to deter his Big Brother from taking him to McDonald's, then he stuck out his tongue, which Adam missed. I bit my own tongue to stop myself from sticking it out at the little monster. Actually, I should have been grateful to him since his temper tantrum gave me a reprieve from having to answer Adam right away.

When I looked up, I saw a woman peeking from behind Adam, listening to our interaction with a very impatient look on her face. Next to her stood a surly teenaged girl who looked as if she had been brought against her will.

"What do you say?" Adam asked. "I'll take these guys to Mc-Donald's—"

"Burger King," Justin muttered.

"Justin," Adam warned him, then turned to me. "I'll drop them off, and swing back and pick you up? I'll bring the editorial."

Behind him, the mother cleared her throat loudly. "Jew eh-speak eh-Spanish?" she asked.

I nodded and waved her around Adam. *"Si, señora."* I turned to Adam and said, "Let me take care of this lady." He nodded and led Justin and Ricky to the side.

I turned my attention to the woman, grateful for a diversion. I half listened to her talk about how she couldn't understand why her daughter wasn't eligible for financial aid and demanded an explanation. I regretted sending Fátima home since the government financial aid forms were her area of expertise. As I attempted to translate the forms to the woman, I could feel Adam's eyes on me periodically as he waited with the boys. I had to quickly think of a good excuse. Anything other than the truth—that I didn't want to complicate my life with a man like him—would be a lie.

I offered the mother several options for her daughter: The girl could work for a year and save up, take out a loan, and/or apply for a work-study program. The mother curled her lip at the options, no doubt expecting me to perform some miracle and get her daughter some assistance. She then began explaining her personal situation with her ex-husband, how he had stopped paying child support as soon as the daughter turned eighteen, how he had two other children with his new wife, and how unfair it seemed that she had worked and paid taxes for twenty years and now that her daughter needed assistance, none was available. Nothing I offered seemed to appease her. Over the woman's shoulder, Rashid was demonstrating in pantomime different methods of suicide and I had to look away to keep from laughing. I caught Adam looking at our interaction with a wrinkled brow. All around me, the other college recruiters were packing up their booths and leaving, glancing at me sympathetically, but grateful that it wasn't them. In the end, the woman took the information before walking away, grumbling to her daughter in Spanish something about Latinos refusing to help out their own.

"Sorry," I told Adam, as he came back to the table.

"Look, if you don't want to go, it's no problem. I just thought, you know, I haven't had good company in a while, present company excluded, of course."

My efforts to stall had not gone unnoticed. I felt guilty, desperate to come up with a good explanation.

"No. It's . . . it's just that my car . . . my car is down here. I'll have to go home first." I sounded like a stammering idiot. Okay, I convinced myself, it didn't have to mean anything. Coffee, stimulating conversation, hopefully. I would make sure I paid for my own coffee so there were no expectations.

"I can pick you up at your house," he offered.

"No . . . I don't think . . ." I stammered. I didn't want to sound like some frightened little woman. "How about if we meet at the coffee place?"

He smiled. "Okay, I get it. Just in case I turn out to be a psycho."

I ignored his sarcasm. "How about Starbucks?"

"No. No fast-coffee chains. You know Coffee Will Make You Black on Milwaukee and Paulina?"

"Cool name."

"It's an old African American saying that means—"

"I know what it means. My mother used to say the same thing to me in Spanish 'cause I liked my coffee black."

"Oh, yeah? How do you say it?"

"*Café prieto te pone prieta.*"

"Huh," he said, watching my lips a little too hard. "Anyway, it's a bookstore café. They sell self-published books and sometimes they have singers or an open-mike for poetry."

"I'll find it. How's seven?"

"Seven's good."

He waved as Ricky pulled him away, anxious to get to McDonald's, or Burger King.

As I loaded the boxes of leftover brochures into my luggage rack on wheels, Rashid walked up.

"So that was Adam? Love the uh . . . ," he said, then he gesticulated comically with his hands, "the hairdo."

"They're called locks."

"Is he a Christian?"

"He's not a Muslim," I assured him in jest. "I met him at a party last week. My sister thought we should meet."

"Ah, Adam and Eve-ah. Charming."

"Shut up."

"So you're going on a date?"

"We're going for coffee."

"Good for you. I asked Dana out. We're going to a play tomorrow."

"Nice. Is she going to convert?" I didn't realize my words sounded biting until I heard them out loud.

"Jealous?"

"Muslim, *please*!"

He laughed uproariously, and I joined in, ignoring how suave he looked in his skullcap and trimmed beard.

As soon as I got home, I called Maya to tell her about the editorial, but Alex answered, informing me that she had gone shopping. I couldn't help but wonder if she was off meeting Luciano somewhere, then I decided not to speculate. Maybe she really was shopping. Browsing through the casual side of my closet, I picked a pair of stretch flare jeans and a cotton shirt with French cuffs that didn't need ironing. I added more gel to my ponytail and, without bothering to look at myself in the mirror, set out again.

On my way to the café, I stopped by Simone's to kill some time. I casually mentioned that I was meeting Adam for coffee. She was more excited than I was, embracing me and squealing in my ear, "*Chica*! I'm so proud of you."

"*Calmate*," I told her to calm down. "We're just having coffee."

"First comes coffee, then comes dinner, then comes sex . . . oops, I mean marriage. I'll be your maid of honor, Maya will be the matron of honor . . ."

"My bridesmaids—if I were ever to marry again—are all going to be virgins."

"Forget you, wench," she hissed, then squealed again, "I'm so happy!" She critically scanned my outfit. "I *know* you're not wearing that."

"What's wrong with it?"

She shook her head reproachfully and led me to her closet as I protested along the way. "This is not a date. It's just coffee. I am not changing into one of your hoochie outfits."

"I do not wear hoochie-wear."

I glanced at her body-hugging tank dress skeptically, which clearly revealed she wasn't wearing any underwear.

I didn't like any of the outfits she pulled from her closet until she hung a silk tangerine blouse with long, wide bell sleeves under my chin. I remember when she wore it how heads had turned to look at her, men as well as women. Because she was taller and slimmer, I knew it wouldn't look the same on me.

"The sleeves will be too long on me," I protested.

"Try it on."

I changed into the blouse and looked into the full-length mirror and was pleasantly surprised at what I saw.

"Just don't get any coffee on my blouse," Simone warned, then she added, "Or any other fluids."

I smacked her arm. "Pig."

"Prig," she countered.

Before I could stop her, she pulled the ponytail holder out of my hair.

"Let your hair breathe, girl."

I snatched the elastic band from her and hastily secured my hair back into a ponytail. "It's out of control. I need a touch-up."

"You are crazy. You've got beautiful hair. I don't know why you insist on damaging it with relaxers."

"You used to *damage* your hair with relaxers," I reminded her.

"Emphasis on 'used to.' "

She began searching her drawers wildly, pulling out scarves and hats. "Here." She pulled out an orange paisley-patterned scarf and wrapped it around my hair, rolling the long ends around my puffy tail and into a big knot at the nape of my neck.

We both stood in front of the mirror, admiring the transformation. For just one brief moment, I almost didn't recognize the woman staring back at me.

CHAPTER 8

ADAM

QUITE BY ACCIDENT, after dodging a woman I had to cut loose, I discovered the Coffee Will Make You Black café one day. It had been an insignificant failed romance that had ended very badly. Half a block away, I saw my ex walking, more like charging, toward me with a homicidal look on her face, and for a moment I thought she saw me, but then I remembered that her permanent, mad-at-the-world look had been part of the problem in our relationship. I had ducked into the darkly lit café and stayed for the coffee, reading the selected poems of Haki Madhubuti and listening to a mediocre West Indian rapper. I kept going back because I liked the ambiance and the fact that I could write until closing time without getting kicked out. I liked it because it was owned by a fearless Black couple, Hassan and Caswanna, who despite the lure of attractive offers from greedy real estate moguls, refused to be bought out. I liked that the African American literature dominated the store and was considered mainstream and not a separate section like in the larger bookstore chains. But most of all, I liked the mixed crowds: the Black bohemians, the liberal White college students, and the different dialects and accents that wafted through the air.

When Eva walked into the café, I almost fell from my chair, which I had been leaning against the wall. It wasn't that she was a knockout, though she looked very nice; mostly, I lost my balance. She had changed out of her charcoal-gray fitted pantsuit and was wearing flared jeans and an orange blouse with long flowing sleeves that almost reached her knees. An orange print scarf covered her head, gathered into a large bun at the nape of her neck. The color accentuated flawlessly the red tones in her dark caramel skin.

I had thought about arriving late and letting her wait for me, especially after she looked like she was trying to back out of meeting for coffee. Like she would hurt my feelings if she just came out and said, "No thanks." But then, I didn't want to take a chance that she might look for any excuse to lump me with the other men in her past. Women loved comparing men with their exes. I told myself I was going to be cool and not weak, let her do most of the talking, let her decide what was going to happen next, if anything. But when she looked at me with those big mysterious Latin eyes, I couldn't help but light up.

"You look . . . nice. That's a great outfit," I told her, instinctively standing and pulling out her chair. On the patio-sized, mosaic-top cocktail tables, the rose-shaped candleholders gave the place an intimate vibe, though I hadn't paid too much attention before.

"Thanks. You look nice, too."

"What, this old thing?" I had also changed into relaxed jeans and a black long-sleeved jersey T-shirt, the sleeves pushed up.

As soon as she sat down, I saw her stare at the scars on my arms, but I didn't volunteer an explanation. She would have to wait awhile before she knew me like that.

I remembered the editorial and pulled it out of my pocket and handed it to her.

"Oh, thanks. I completely forgot about it," she said, reading it through.

"Sure you did," I teased. "I bet you can't wait to frame it."

"It's only an editorial. I've had other things published before."

"Like what?"

"Have you ever heard of *Diaspora*?"

I shook my head.

"It's a new magazine. It's a religious-inspirational women's magazine, sort of like *Essence* but it caters to the Christian market."

"Yeah, I don't read too many women's magazines." I smiled, in case she took offense.

"Well, you should read this one. They've published a couple of my articles on parochial schools and Christian colleges, and prayer in schools."

As she ran down the list of her publication credits, we ordered Cuban cappuccinos; they tasted sweet and strong, and vaguely reminiscent of liquor, which I had not had in a long time. She drank hers black, two sugars. I thought of asking her if she liked her men like she liked her coffee, but I decided against it. I didn't know her that well but what little I knew told me she would take it the wrong way. Then I noticed her using her left hand to stir her coffee, and to lift her cup, something I hadn't picked up before.

"You're left-handed," I pointed out.

"You are so perceptive."

I started to snap on her, but her mouth spread in that contagious smile and all I could do was return the same.

On the slightly elevated stage, a woman dressed in what looked like a gypsy outfit, complete with hoop earrings and multicolored scarf, sat on a stool with a guitar, struggling to adjust the mike.

"She thinks she's India.Arie," I kidded.

"I like India.Arie."

"That's my girl too; that's why I don't like impersonators," I quipped.

"It's going to be alright," she said condescendingly, giving me a look of mock empathy. The woman began strumming her guitar, basking in the glow of the votive candles surrounding the stage. She then began half moaning, half singing a ballad about unrequited love. We were far enough away where we could talk and not be rude, but Eva seemed to be enjoying the music so I kept quiet, observing her every now and then. I noticed that she was having a hard time keeping her sleeves out of the way, shaking her arms in the air to keep them from falling into her coffee cup or from catching on fire from the lit candle on the table.

"This is my girlfriend's blouse," she finally explained. "You know, Simone."

"I thought her name was 'S'Moneé.'"

She rolled her eyes. "Long story."

"It's nice."

Periodically, I could feel her eyes on me, glancing at my arms. Finally, I stretched my arms on the table purposely so she could get a real good look. Caught in the act, she pulled back, folded her hands in her lap, and met my eyes.

"My sister said you write poetry?" she asked.

"I dabble. You?"

"Only what I wrote in high school, you know, juvenilia. Everyone thinks they're a poet at that age. Teenage angst and all that."

"My highlight years," I joked, remembering my early attempts at writing Shakespearean sonnets with an Amiri Baraka twist. "Let me hear one of yours."

"I don't think so," she said, flustered. "My stuff is old, *and* morbid. I was in a bad mood for four years in high school. But feel free to share one of yours."

"Maybe some other time."

"We have a spiritual poetry night at our church," she said. "Second Thursday of the month. This Thursday. You should check it out. Some of it is really deep."

"So, is church a big thing for you?"

"What do you mean?"

"Are you one of those people who *have* to go to church every Sunday or else they think they're going to fry forever?"

"No. I go because I need it. Like some people need to smoke because they say it calms their nerves. God calms my nerves."

I took the implication and felt a need to defend myself. "I know smoking is a bad habit. I stopped for a year and a half and then I started up again this year. I'm down to one cigarette a day."

"You smoked two that first night."

I laughed, remembering. "I was nervous."

"Why?"

"I don't like crowds."

The guitar stopped but the woman was still moaning the last line: "Why don't you love me, hate me, love me, hate me, like you used to?"

I looked at Eva, who rolled her eyes as if to say, "Whatever." We clapped politely along with everyone else. I started to tell her she was the first woman I had ever invited here but I caught myself. I had to remind myself this wasn't really a date. After all, I didn't bring her; we had agreed to meet. And it was only coffee.

"Do your little brothers speak Spanish?" she asked.

"Justin used to but after his father died, when he was ten, his mother said he refused to speak it. Some sort of posttraumatic stress event. What about your sons?"

"It's funny. My older one, Tony, can't speak it but he understands it. Although he likes Spanish music. Eli, my youngest, can speak it but he hates Spanish music."

"Weird." Now that I was closer to her, I could detect the slightest lilt of an accent that education and exposure to the business world had sharpened so that it was barely noticeable. But sometimes, when she said certain words, the ones that contained "t's" but she pronounced like "th's," I could tell she hailed from somewhere else.

"So what's on your mind, Eva?" I asked.

I could tell the question surprised her because she kept the coffee cup near her mouth, blowing into it. Without taking a sip, she repeated the question. "What's on my mind?"

"Yeah. What are you looking for?"

"What are *you* looking for?"

"I'm not looking for anything." It only felt like a little lie.

"You called *me*."

"'Cause I needed that information for Justin."

"Yeah, and I gave it to you." She was playing games, waiting for me to lay my cards on the table. I didn't want to play games.

"How old are you?" I asked, changing the subject.

"Forty," she said without hesitation.

I tried not to show my surprise. "You don't look forty."

"I'm sorry, how does forty 'look'?"

"I'm thirty-six."

"You look thirty-six."

I laughed. "Touché." I leaned closer to the table, to her. I could smell the rose body oil as I tried my best to maintain eye contact but her eyes were so intense it was difficult, and a couple of times I had to look away. "Look, I'm going to come out straight 'cause I'm too old for games. I think we're both too old for games. It's been a while since I've had female companionship. And I thought we . . . kind of connected." There I said it.

"So, you want a companion? You want to be friends? Pals? Acquaintances? What?"

Now I was caught off guard, unable to answer.

She continued: "You want to go out to dinner every once in a while, or just coffee? Movies?" She shook her head from side to side and gesticulated with her hands, prompting me for an answer. Why did I have to be the one to bring it up?

But then she smiled, and I had to smile, too. It was a slight, teasing smile, but with those lips it spread across her face. We both laughed, the ice slowly melting.

"You should come to my church," she said.

Back to uncomfortable topics. I scratched my neck. "Church really isn't my scene."

"What does that mean?"

"It's hard for me to sit through three-hour-long services. Plus, I don't like being yelled at and told I'm a sinner."

"You'll like my pastor. He's not a screamer. He's very calming . . . cool. Our church is multicultural but our pastor's Black."

"Oh, so you think I'll like him 'cause he's Black?"

"Stop being so paranoid. I only meant that unlike other churches where the congregation is one extreme or the other, ours is mixed."

"Don't you think it's possible to get spiritual enrichment without attending church?"

"Yes, I guess. But you get so much more from fellowshipping."

"I don't know. All I remember is people debating too much about the meanings of scriptures. It's open to interpretation. Ten preachers could read a passage and you'd get ten different interpretations." She started to speak but I cut her off politely, holding up my hand. "Take our namesakes, Adam and Eve. Correct me if I'm wrong, but there is nothing in Genesis that says God married them, it says he created a 'help mate' for Adam. The vows that are recited at marriage ceremonies are man-made."

"So you don't believe in marriage?"

"No, what I'm saying is, the relationship between the man and the woman should be emphasized, rather than the ritual, the whole reciting-of-the-vows, and how it looks to other people. It just seems to me that people put more into the wedding than they do the marriage. If a man and a woman who, quote, live together in sin, unquote, are committed to each other and they respect, trust each other, why do they need to go through the motions with a minister? Why is their relationship less blessed than a man and a woman who are married in church and aren't committed to each other at all? That's all I'm saying."

"You need to come to Bible class and pose that question to the teacher," she answered. "He can probably answer it better than I can."

"We'll see," I told her, not really committing to anything.

The India.Arie wannabe began strumming her guitar again. This time, I rolled my eyes, and Eva patted my hand. The hairs on my hand stood up, all the way up my arm. "Be nice. She's okay."

"So who is Rashid?" I asked casually, as I recalled their playful interaction at the college fair. I didn't want to sound like it mattered if they had something going.

"I told you. He's the director—"

"No. I mean, to you."

"We're coworkers, work-friends. He's going through a lot now, you know, being Muslim in a Christian world."

"Hmmm. You want another coffee?"

"I'm all coffeed out," she said, opening her purse.

I held up my hand. "I got this."

"I'll pay for mine, thanks."

"You can get it next time. Okay?"

Her right eyebrow went up and I read her look: *Who said there's going to be a next time?* "I'll leave the tip," she insisted.

"Fine," I said, conceding defeat. Then I noticed that the tip she left amounted to the cost of her two cups of coffee. The woman was covering her bases like a seasoned player. Very impressive.

At the counter, I introduced Eva to Caswanna, who ran the coffee and pastry part of the business, and her husband, Hassan, who operated the bookstore. They both gushed on the coincidence of our names. "You're kidding?" Hassan said. "How bizarre!" Caswanna cried. I knew then our being together would be a problem. But then I remembered, this wasn't a date; it was only coffee.

We strolled down Milwaukee to where Eva had parked her car. Even though the sun was setting, the temperature was intolerably hot, but she looked like she wasn't busting a sweat in her outfit. I, on the other hand, was sweating all over. The coffee had only made it worse.

"Can I ask you a personal question without you getting offended?" she asked.

"Sure," I said bravely, knowing she was capable of asking anything.

"Are you . . . were you a drug addict?"

I chuckled. "No."

We walked on and I noticed that she kept looking at me as if she were waiting for an explanation, like she deserved one. For a hot second, I thought about whether she needed to know my personal business. My cancer, like religion, wasn't something I brought up in casual conversation. I wasn't like her, discussing her sexual habits, or lack thereof, with total strangers.

"I don't like talking about my . . . scars. With strangers. No offense."

It took her a couple of seconds to recall that they were the same words she had initially said to me about her writing. She laughed. "Oka-a-ay. Touché."

"Does it matter?" I asked. "Whether I was a drug addict?"

"Uh, yeah."

"Why?"

"I don't like being around people who mess with drugs, or drink."

"But I told you I wasn't."

"Then why . . . how come . . ."

"I had cancer awhile back. Apparently, I have what they call 'bad veins.' They collapse very easily. The scars are from the IVs for chemo," I explained finally, deciding to let her off the hook. I pulled down my shirt collar to reveal the scar near my collar bone. "They put in a central line when my veins kept blowing."

The look on her face should have been enough vindication for me. Her eyes were big with shock as she was embarrassed into silence. It was a lot of information to swallow, especially since I had given it to her matter-of-factly, as if I were describing how to put on a pair of pants.

When she finally spoke, her voice was just above a whisper. "Are you okay now?"

"Oh, sure," I said sarcastically. "Good as new."

She looked down at her hands, which were interlocked in front of her, as we walked the next block without talking. I waited for her to ask me what kind of cancer I had, which was usually the next question.

"I'm sorry. I didn't mean to assume."

"Don't worry about it," I said nonchalantly. "I'm not going to die or anything like that. At least not anytime soon."

We fell silent as we walked past a Burger King and Popeye's Chicken interspersed with an Italian bistro and a tapa bar. She kept nervously locking and unlocking her fingers at waist level, probably trying to decide whether it was appropriate to ask more questions or just keep quiet. I decided for her.

"Anyway, the chemo's supposed to cause your hair to fall out, but I was one of the lucky ones I guess. Kinky roots, ya know. I felt like Samson, like my strength is in my hair. As long as I don't cut my hair, the cancer won't come back."

"So, is that when you stopped praying? When you got cancer?"

"I don't remember when it was, exactly."

"Why do you smoke if you had cancer?"

"Why do people continue to have sex after they've had an STD? Why do people still sin after they've been saved? It's hard to be good. I *am* trying to quit. There are days I don't smoke at all. I'm sure there's something you do that you wish you could stop. Like picking your nose or biting your toenails."

She laughed and I was glad I was able to lighten the mood.

"I do not pick my nose," she said.

"But you bite your toenails."

"No." She held up her hands. "I do bite my fingernails."

"You see?"

"Biting your nails isn't dangerous to your health."

"It could be. You have dirt under your nails and when you put your nails in your mouth, it goes down into your stomach—"

"Okay, you win. But seriously, if you want to quit, I can say a prayer for you."

"Are you serious?" I smiled, and started to laugh, but then I realized she was being earnest.

"Yes, I am." She stopped in the middle of the sidewalk.

"Right here?" I looked around uncomfortably, as people walked around us, glancing over their shoulders to see what we were going to do. But we were in Wicker Park, the home of eccentrics and freaks, so someone praying in the middle of the sidewalk was not an oddity.

She stepped into the nearest doorway and I had no choice but to follow. She slipped her hands into mine and the softness of her touch gave me chills. She closed her eyes, her lips moving as she prayed silently. I tried to be receptive of her intent even though I couldn't hear what she was saying. Feeling slightly dizzy and weak, I tried not to squirm as sweat trickled from my temples, neck, and down my back. I thought maybe it was her touch, maybe it was the prayer, maybe it was just a combination of the heat and coffee. Maybe.

"You can open your eyes," I heard her say.

I didn't realize I had closed them. She still had my hands in hers, but I felt like she was still talking to me with her eyes, calling me closer. She pressed her lips together, perhaps to moisten them, maybe to give me a sign. I wasn't sure. I found myself unable to tear my eyes away from her lips, especially the thick bottom one, which looked swollen.

I cleared my throat. "I didn't hear anything," I said.

"Yeah, but did you feel it?"

I didn't answer. Tentatively, I took a step toward her, but she abruptly released me and leaned back against the doorjamb. I leaned back on my side.

"I can't believe you have two kids in college," I said, and the way she looked at me with that one eyebrow cocked, I knew she was thinking it was a line.

"That's usually what happens when you get married at nineteen."

I waited for her to ask why I didn't have any children, but she didn't. Whether she cared or not, I couldn't tell. Nevertheless, I changed the subject.

"You know, when I used to go to church, and they prayed," I re-called out loud, "they always made a big production out of it, you know. Praying loud, in front of the church. It was never quiet like this, peaceful."

"That's how it used to be in the church I grew up in. Loud and scary," she agreed. "Do you know Matthew six, verses five and six?"

I shook my head, slightly contrite.

"It says, when you pray, don't pray like the hypocrites who do it on street corners so they can be seen by others. It says you should go into a closet and shut the door, pray to God in secret, and that which He sees in secret, will be rewarded in the open."

"Man, you're deep into this Bible thing. Quoting scriptures and whatnot."

"I don't know many of them, but Matthew is my favorite. I think it contains just about everything that God is about." She looked down, slightly embarrassed, like she had said too much.

But she had said just enough.

CHAPTER 9

EVA

A MULTICULTURAL CONGREGATION and an energetic, humorous young pastor made TCCC one of the most popular churches in the Austin area. Because of its proximity to Mt. Carmel University, a Christian college, there were many students, recent graduates, and faculty who had joined the church over the years. Those who moved out of the neighborhood years before were now coming back as gentrification threatened the diversity and spirit of the community. There were the usual elders who had been in church all their lives and the families who had recently moved into the neighborhood, but the majority of its members were young, single or divorced professionals with a commitment to community outreach. The church ran a day care center and an after-school program, had its own Christian elementary school, and offered tutoring for dropouts and English classes for the growing influx of Latino immigrants.

Because of its large number of unattached members and the recently married Pastor Zeke who had just turned forty-five, the church was dubbed the Singles' Church. It was Pastor Zeke's mission to marry as many parishioners as possible, because he believed man and woman were not meant to be single. The problem, of course, was the dilemma that plagued many churches, and society in general—women outnumbered men.

As always, I listened to the pastor's words with my eyes closed because I found that I was able to digest the Word better that way.

Now and then, I nodded or clapped in case Pastor Zeke looked my way and thought I was sleeping. I liked Pastor Zeke because he never raised his voice in order to get his message across. He was like a father who believed he could be more effective when chastising a child with a low, even-tempered voice than when yelling. I remembered going to my mother's church as a child and how the pastor would shout from the pulpit, with accusation and condemnation, as if we were doomed to be sinners forever with no chance for redemption.

Like many of the churchwomen, I had developed a misplaced crush on Pastor Zeke when I first joined the church, much like a misguided student who idolized a teacher who paid her special attention. When I first heard the pastor's Texas accent and watched him pace back and forth on the lectern, his hands gesticulating with passion, I was mesmerized. But it was the pitch of his voice that most captivated me, the way it resonated with the emotion and conviction of the beat poets from the coffeehouses, and how he paused after every two or three words, stretching his syllables and then accelerating without attention to punctuation. It was unlike any preaching I had ever heard. As the months went by, my infatuation was soon replaced by my passion for the message, disregarding the messenger.

The topic for that Sunday's sermon was the pastor's dominant theme: "Single People, Marriage, and God."

"Let's turn to First Corinthians, chapter seven, verses one and two," Pastor Zeke continued. " 'Now for the matters you wrote about: It is good for a man not to marry. But since there is so much immorality, let each man have his own wife, and let each woman her own husband.' Amen?"

A scattering of "Amens" resonated throughout the church.

The Oak Tree Man had come to me in a dream the night before, the branches hanging over his face like imitation dreadlocks. In the dream, I had succeeded in removing the hidden leaves and revealing its face, a face with nondescript features that looked at me in anticipation, as if it wanted to speak but couldn't because the mouth was missing.

"I don't think you heard me. I said, 'Amen'?" Pastor Zeke repeated, briefly interrupting my fantasy. I envisioned the customary unbroken grin on his face.

"Amen," I whispered along with the chorus of Amens.

"It would be a wonderful world if we could be like Paul and refrain from touching the flesh," the pastor surmised. "But we are not like Paul. Amen? Single people, this is not your time to sample this flesh, and sample that flesh, like a child in a candy store. This is your time to get closer to Him. Amen?"

"Amen," I answered again, louder.

"Let's move on. Corinthians seven, eight, *'Now to the unmarried and the widows, I say: It is good for them to stay unmarried, as I am . . .'*"

My mind wandered and I thought back on my dream, how the branches had reached down and stroked my hair, my face, and my neck. Then before I could move, the branches wrapped themselves around my neck, then my chest and waist, twisting tighter and tighter until I couldn't breathe.

"*'BUT,'* Paul says, Corinthians seven, nine—are you still with me, people?" the pastor asked, then paused for effect, waiting for affirmation that everyone was still listening. And here his voice dropped almost to a whisper into the microphone, slowly and with dramatic effort. "*'But . . . if . . . they . . . cannot control themselves, they should marry: for it is better to marry than to burn.'* Let me reiterate that in case you missed it: *'It is BETTER to marry than to BURN.'*"

I felt a nudge at my right side, and then at my left, which forced me to open my eyes, slightly startled. I knew Simone and Maya were referring to my abstinence, but their teasing couldn't touch me. When I was listening to the Word, their mockery rolled off my back.

On my right, Simone smiled at me. I had finally convinced the little heathen to come to church. She had yet to officially join and accept salvation, but each time she appeared, I liked to think she was one step closer.

To my left, Maya was looking intently at the pastor, as if she hadn't touched me. On her other side sat Marcos and Lucas, and then Alex, who looked like he was losing the battle to stay awake.

The boys were fraternal twins, and though they each favored one parent more than the other, they looked enough alike that people often asked if they were twins, even though they never dressed the same. Sometimes when I looked at Maya with her nuclear family, intact and happy, I wished I had never divorced and had worked things out with Anthony. But I knew the portrait of a happy family was a façade that involved a lot of hard work and tolerance behind the scenes. I knew what my sister had endured, was still enduring, and I knew that everything I had been through—dealing with infidelity, divorce, single motherhood—had to come to pass in order for me to get where I was currently.

I closed my eyes again and returned to my meditative state.

"Now, people ask me what 'burn' means in this context. King James says 'burn' and leaves it at that; NIV says 'burn with passion.'" Again, the pastor paused for effect. "I'ma let ya'll figger that one out for yourselves," he said, switching to slang for the sake of the teenagers in the audience. Laughter echoed throughout the church.

I had awakened at dawn with a start, my heart pounding like my head during a migraine, searching blindly for my new medication. My doctor had said it would take at least a month before the hallucinations stopped. I found myself thinking about Adam, about his cancer, how I had held his hands, not really giving a second thought to my touching him until afterward. I remembered him leaning in closer and how I panicked because I thought he was going to kiss me. As always when I was unable to sleep due to anxiety or worry, I began praying. It took a while before I was able to drift back to sleep.

"They say women *want* to be married, but men *need* to be married." Laughter rippled up and down the pews. "But I tell you, there is a difference between needing and wanting. And God gives you what you need, not what you want. The way I see it, men, ya'll *need* marriage more than the women *want* it."

I felt the poke again, harder this time, from Maya's side and my eyes flew open, just in time to see some women glancing with reproach at their husbands and nodding in agreement. With her head,

Maya gestured toward Alex who had drool sliding from his mouth in his slumber. Maya shook her head in disgust. The boys giggled.

"Uh-oh, I done started a revolution up in here." Pastor Zeke chuckled at his own words, an intoxicating laugh that made people respond with more laughter. "A spiritual revolution. Amen? Amen.

"Just remember, when you're struggling to stay faithful. Remember His awesome power. Remember His ultimate sacrifice. God said that He would, and He will. He said that He could, and He can. Now, all you have to do is believe that He is and it shall be." At his trademark closing remarks, the congregation began clapping in a steady rhythm until it broke into all-out applause and praises. My eyes still closed, I whispered, "Amen, Amen, Amen," my hands coming together like they had a mind of their own, still throbbing from the earlier praise and worship.

After altar call, I got up, following Maya, greeting and embracing fellow parishioners as we walked down the aisle. As we neared the last pew, a red, green, and black cap caught my attention as it streamed through the doors. I strained to get a better look, but there were too many people blocking my view. I thought maybe it was Adam taking me up on my invitation and though I didn't know every single member of the congregation, I knew who wasn't. Outside, I glanced around the parking lot, but the cap and its owner were gone.

Once a month after Sunday services, Maya, Simone, and I took turns having brunch at each other's homes. It was Maya's turn so she went ahead with Alex and the boys to prepare the meal. Simone hitched a ride with me and in the backseat began changing out of her confining "church clothes."

"Why don't you just wear decent clothing? That way you won't have to change," I teased.

"Hush, peasant," she grunted, struggling out of her pantyhose and into some shorts. "You guys know I can't stay long. I have that radio interview on V103 with Zephyr. Then I'm meeting Ian for an early dinner."

I shook my head silently; I had resolved to ease up passing judgment on her.

"What?" she challenged, removing her blouse to reveal a tiny T-shirt that looked like it had shrunk in the dryer.

"I didn't say anything."

"Yeah, but you want to. I can see right through your Oil of Olay."

"You're being paranoid," I chanted.

"No, I'm not," she chanted back.

Maya still wore her calf-length sundress but was barefoot, padding back and forth around her newly remodeled kitchen, making coffee, sandwiches, and Caesar salads. Alex and the boys, she said, had eaten the first round.

"How was coffee with Adam?" she asked.

"Yeah, how *was* the Rastafarian?" Simone asked, suddenly remembering.

"He's not a Rastafarian," I said.

"You know that's a religion," Maya said, as she sliced some romaine lettuce like it took too much effort. I could tell by the frustrated look on her face and her inability to stay still that she had had another fight with Alex. Their fights had become almost routine since Alex began attending church less frequently—and when he did he'd fall asleep. "They believe some Egyptian leader was a prophet. Celeste, somebody."

"Haile Selassie," Simone corrected her, pouring coffee into three cups.

Maya and I looked at her quizzically.

"I dated a Jamaican a couple of years ago. Remember Ty? Remember I used to say 'me like heem'?"

Maya and I shook our heads because neither one of us could keep her men's names straight.

"Maybe he's a convert," Maya suggested.

"He's not Rastafarian," I assured them. "He's Christian. He had cancer and he thinks if he cuts his hair, the cancer might come back."

"Can't he, like, comb it into some cornrows or something instead of those . . . dreads?" Maya asked spitefully. "They look so dread . . . ful."

"He had cancer?" Simone asked, shocked. "What kind?"

"I kind of like his hair," I answered Maya first. Then I immediately regretted it as they both looked at me like I had said something cute. "I mean, when he pulls it back into a ponytail, it looks nice, you know, neater . . ." I stuttered.

Just then, Alex and the boys came into the kitchen. They had changed into tennis outfits and carried tennis racket bags over their shoulders. Alex, a part-time instructor, was convinced his sons were going to be the next Williams tennis champs. He liked to joke that they already had the famous last name. He came up to Maya and said, "We're gone. See you later."

Simone and I watched as he pecked Maya's cheek. It was a basic, run-of-the-mill kiss, but I watched longingly. Simone crossed her eyes in mock disgust. I wondered how Maya could be with Luciano, no matter how platonic she claimed their relationship was, and then come home to Alex. Although I believed her when she said she had not slept with Luciano, I knew that the more time she spent with him, the closer she was to temptation. I realized I had yet to talk seriously to her about my reservations with Luciano.

"Bye, Ma!" Marcos and Lucas cried as they kissed Maya with more emotion than their father had. They then kissed Simone and me before hurrying after their father.

More than anything, what I missed most about being with a man was kissing. I tried hard to remember what it was like, being held by a man, his hands in my hair, around my waist, as he sampled my lips. After leaving Adam, all I could think about was what it would have been like to kiss him. Whether I desired to kiss any man, or specifically Adam, was debatable. I quickly felt convicted, especially after having just come from church. More than once, the pastor had warned that the enemy always attacked just when one was trying to get closer to God. It was certainly the case with me as I thought back to my dream with the Oak Tree Man in the middle of Pastor Zeke's sermon. The dream had been related to the medication, I reasoned. However, the first time I had experienced the hallucinations, the tree didn't have dreadlocks. Already Adam was creeping into my subconscious. *Forgive me, Lord,* I thought. *Remove this man from my mind.*

After Alex's car left the driveway, Simone and I watched as Maya neurotically cleaned the table, swept the floor, and washed the dishes. Then she started in on the sautéed chicken breasts for the Caesar salads, hacking them up.

"Would you stop with the OCD housekeeping?" Simone asked, snatching the bowl of butchered breasts from Maya, insinuating Maya suffered from an obsessive-compulsive disorder. "Remember, I can't stay long. I have to meet Zephyr in an hour and I got a date with Ian later."

Maya finally sat down. I blessed the food and we began to eat. She turned to Simone. "I love you, my sister. But you need to stop dating all these men."

"What do you mean, 'all'? There are only two men in my life." Then she held up two fingers and in Spanish said, *"Uno, dos."*

"This time, it's two. Last year, it was three," Maya said, as if she hadn't spoken. "God did not intend for woman to have a bunch of men."

"Then *He* should have made men more multidimensional. I'm sorry but one man cannot fulfill my every need. And look who's throwing stones?"

"For the last time, Luciano is my *friend*. We are not lovers," Maya insisted. She poured French vanilla creamer into her coffee and took a sip. I thought back to Simone's party, how Maya sat with Luciano on the sofa's arm and, later, kissed him on the back porch stairs. If they were friends, I'd hate to see what her version of "lovers" looked like. But I didn't say anything. "Remind me to say a special prayer for you tonight."

"You need to say one for your husband," Simone countered.

"Oh, I always pray for my husband, sweetie. Always."

Although they constantly got into it whenever the topic of their men came up, I believed that secretly, they envied each other. In a way, Simone wanted what Maya had: the successful husband, big house in a nice neighborhood, the kids—well, maybe not the kids.

And Maya wanted Simone's life, which was basically the freedom she never had because she had been married half her life. However, neither would ever admit it.

"What is *your* problem with *her* husband anyway?" I finally asked Simone.

"My problem is this," Simone began, standing up so she could pontificate as if she were on stage. "Man is supposed to be made in the image of Christ. He's supposed to love his wife like Christ loves the church and all that. He's supposed to be the head of household and lead his family by example. But I don't see your husband doing that. He doesn't go to church all the time—you either go by yourself or with the kids. It's almost like *you're* the head of household and he's a bachelor."

"You don't understand; this isn't about him," Maya explained. "It's about *my* personal relationship with the Lord. I leave my husband in His hands. His salvation is not up to me. I'm doing what I'm supposed to be doing."

"What's the use in being married to a man when he's not doing what *he's* supposed to be doing?"

"Men change," Maya said, almost sadly.

"And women don't?" I asked.

"Women change due to hormonal changes, childbirth, motherhood, the stress of being *slaves* to their husbands, especially working women," Simone cut in, sitting down to eat her salad. "Men change because they think their wives are supposed to pick up where their mothers left off." One would think Simone had been married forever instead of the one year she sacrificed to what she called "the world's oldest form of slavery." Married women, she always said, were still in bondage. While I disagreed with her, I had my own issues with marriage.

"That's why I'm afraid of getting married again," I said. "Take Anthony. When we were living together, he used to help me with the housework. As soon as we got married, I swear not a month later, he just stopped."

"I'm not going to take that chance," Simone said. "I *know* I'm never getting married again. Marriage is overrated."

"With God, you're not taking a chance. God is about faith, not luck, not chance. Just as He did not intend woman to have a multitude of men, He also did not intend woman to be alone. You don't put your trust in Man, you put your trust, your faith in God. Man will disappoint, but God never will."

"So what are you doing with Luciano?" Simone asked pointedly.

"I'm trying to keep myself from dying of boredom," Maya said without skipping a beat. "Even though we're just friends, I know I shouldn't be with him. It's one thing to sin and acknowledge it, but it's worse when you sin and don't care. Meanwhile, I'm praying for a sign from God 'cause I don't know how much longer I can stay married to my husband."

"What exactly did you pray for?" I asked.

"What do you mean?"

"Did you pray for your marriage to work or did you pray that Alex wants a divorce so you can be with Luciano? I mean, you have to know what you want before you ask for it."

"I prayed for patience, for guidance. All I know is, I want my husband to kiss me with passion, like he used to. I want to be loved like I deserve to be loved. I like the attention Luciano gives me, I don't know if I want to be with him."

"I would rather kiss a man than have sex any day," I announced. They gave me that collective look of adoration once again, so I jammed a forkful of lettuce and chicken into my mouth.

"Check her out. She isn't dead after all," Simone said, smiling.

"Get out," Maya said in disbelief.

"I'm serious. I've always thought kissing was much more intense," I said quietly.

"Okay, now I know it's been a long time for you," Simone joked. Then she chanted, "Some-body's sweat-*ting* the Rasta-mun."

"It's sweat-*in*," I corrected her mispronunciation of the slang term.

"Oh, hush. Me? I don't particularly like kissing. All that sharing of saliva," Simone said, shuttering, her face recoiling.

"Oh, and sharing other body fluids is better?" I countered.

"When you wear condoms you don't share body fluids," she said shamelessly with a sly smile. "I believe a man cannot truly possess you until fluids are exchanged."

"Simone!" Maya admonished.

"It's S'Monée," she corrected. "If you call me Simone, I'm not going to answer."

"Keep fooling yourself," I told her, ignoring her request. "Every time you have sex with a man, he takes possession of you. You lose a little of your soul, piece by piece."

"Listen to you," Maya said looking at me with a look of pride.

As I was saying the words to Simone, I hoped my sister was taking heed, and then I thought I should probably remember them myself as a precautionary measure.

CHAPTER 10

ADAM

MY MOTHER IS a very spiritual woman, fiercely devout and ardently dedicated to my father, her husband—and, simultaneously, another woman's—for twenty years. My mother found out about the other woman years before my sister and I did. When I confronted her, demanding to know why she never said anything, she replied rather calmly, "One day you'll understand what love is about."

I could not understand why she would knowingly put up with sharing her man with another woman. I could not perceive how she forgave my father and continued to sleep with him, knowing the only thing that separated her from this woman was a hot shower. I could not comprehend how she embraced this other woman at the funeral, and still kept in contact with my half siblings, who were close enough to my and my sister's ages to have put our mothers pregnant at the same time. My incomprehension was so entrenched that I still could not bring myself to visit my father's grave almost twenty years later. So I guess I had yet to learn what love was.

My mother lived in a senior citizen condo building; she moved there after selling the house I had lived in until I went away to college. She acquired two cats to keep her company and took up acoustic guitar and stained glass art, which she sold at seasonal arts and crafts shows. She stopped cooking large Sunday meals and became a vegan who believed in holistic healing. Essentially, my mother became a hippie in her old age.

As I arrived at my mother's floor, I saw a rather distinguished looking man in a suit emerging from her condo. I thought he was perhaps the landlord, or some other kind of businessman, but then I watched as my mother stepped into the hallway and kissed the man on the cheek. I froze, hoping I would blend into the tan carpet unseen.

"Oh, there's my son," my mother exclaimed when she saw me. I walked slowly down the hallway with my mouth half hanging open. "Jameson Stevens, this is my son, Adam. I call him Love." I was dumbfounded. I could not believe she had shared something as personal as my nickname with this stranger. When I was born she'd wanted to give me "Love" as a middle name but my old man put his foot down. From the time I was little, she had called me Love.

The man stuck his hand out toward me, smiling like he wanted to be my friend or something. I reluctantly, and automatically, shook his hand.

"Nice to meet you, Adam," Mr. Jameson Stevens said before strolling to the elevator, whistling. "I'll see you later, Naomi."

I could not speak as I watched my mother walk toward me. She was dressed elegantly in a floral print dress that accentuated her slimmed-down figure, her pecan face flawless and glowing. Her hair was in a high French roll, giving her the appearance that she was wearing an African headdress. A retired hairstylist, my mother always kept her hair coiffed.

"Love, close your mouth," she said, kissing me on the cheek with the same lips she had used on the stranger. I forced myself not to wipe my face like I used to do when she kissed me in front of my boys when I was young.

"Who . . . who was that?" I asked when I found my voice.

"Jameson Stevens," she said matter-of-factly, turning to go inside.

"I know his *name*. Who *is* he?" I followed her into the condo and closed the door.

"He's my friend."

"Boyfriend?"

She laughed boisterously and gave me a patronizing look. "Boyfriends are for young girls, Love. He's my companion."

I dreaded thinking what the term "companion" encompassed. I didn't want to know if she was sleeping with him, though I knew it was unlikely. My mother took her Christianity very seriously. I didn't want to know if she loved him or was planning to marry him. I didn't want to know anything, but I needed to know everything. "And?" I asked.

"And none of your business. I'm a grown woman. Now, what did you bring me?"

I handed her the shopping bag of fresh fruit and herbal teas I bought at her favorite organic grocery store, enough for two months. She squealed like they were diamonds. My mother no longer ate sweets, so birthday cakes were useless. "Happy Birthday, Mama," I said dryly.

She kissed me again and I took a seat in the dining room.

"Look at this cantaloupe. Beautiful! Grapes!"

Two new stained glass creations with abstract designs hung in the dining room. Her artwork, along with the numerous stained glass supplies, had taken over the apartment, obscuring family portraits of her children and grandchildren. The cats, Mr. and Mrs. Jones, strolled into the dining room, barely acknowledging my presence. They knew I didn't like them and the feeling was mutual.

I handed her the birthday card, which she quickly opened. In her haste, the money I put in it fell to the floor.

"Adam, what did I tell you about giving me money? When I need it, I'll ask for it."

I picked up the money and tried to hand it to her. "Put it in the bank until you need it."

"No, you put it in the bank and give it to me when I ask for it." She began reading the card. "Oh, you wrote me a poem."

I sighed and stuck the money in my wallet. "Don't read it out loud."

"I'll wait 'til your sister gets here." She put the card aside and began to prepare her infamous fruit salad.

"So, who is this Jameson Stevens?" I asked, inconspicuously ex-amining her apartment for evidence of his stay.

"I told you. He is my companion. He lives in the building. And he accompanies me to book readings, to the museums, all the places your father never wanted to go. We have a good time."

"Not too good a time, I hope," I added, half jokingly.

"Be careful what you're implying, young man. I'm a Christian," she scolded, but then she smiled. "How about you? Have you met anybody? Have you even tried to find a good woman?"

"Mama," I warned.

"Oh, you can ask about my business, but I can't ask about yours?"

"I met a woman," I admitted softly before I could stop myself. "We went out for coffee." I didn't know why I mentioned Eva. Per-haps because I hadn't been able to stop thinking about her. I hardly ever discussed my relationships with my mother. I gave her bits and pieces about certain women I had dated, and over the years, I brought a couple of them to family picnics, barbecues, and other in-formal gatherings, but I never actually brought one home "to meet Mama." Not only because I knew no woman would ever be good enough for me in my mother's eyes, but because despite this, she would probably hear wedding bells if she saw me with one woman more than once. I knew that if I were to introduce Eva to her, they would probably hit it off, given the religion connection, and that made me very uneasy.

"Coffee? Hmmm. What's she like?"

"She's uh . . . she's . . . tough, funny. Smart. And, uh . . . Puerto Rican."

"Puerto Rican?" She said this like I had said she was a Martian.

"Yes."

"Puerto Rican? Does she speak English?"

"Of course she does. She was born here."

My mother, while profoundly spiritual, was adamant about in-terracial or interfaith relationships—not that she was prejudiced, she was always quick to point out. She truly believed that the more people had in common, the more likely the compatibility. She still

believed my sister's marriage broke up, not because of infidelity, but
because she had married a Korean man. The fact that he had been a
Catholic, which my mother considered different from Christian,
was just one more reason why their marriage failed—in Mama's
eyes.

In the past few days since Eva and I had coffee, I thought about
her quite a bit and found myself feeling stupid for doing so. It had
been a long time since I had allowed a woman to creep into my
thoughts so often and for such a minor encounter as having coffee.
One would have thought I had had sex for the first time. Whupped
was not something I have ever been and it did not fit me well.

I had not planned to visit her church, but something woke me
early the previous Sunday and so I went. I tried to remember the last
time I had stepped foot in a church other than the biannual holy
days, and I vaguely remembered going back around the time when
I was sick, when I begged God not to let me die.

The Community Church of Christ was filled to capacity by the
time I arrived and I was forced to stand in the back with the other
latecomers and irregular attendees. I had passed the church many
times on my route to and from work but had never given it a second glance. Churches had become part of the regular urban landscape, as ordinary as storefronts and gas stations. As Eva had
promised, I found the pastor's voice riveting in a subdued sort of
way. Although there seemed to be a lot of emphasis on marriage in
his sermon, his delivery was what captivated me, the way he held
the audience's attention without getting all worked up. From the
back, I could see only the backs of people's heads and I took note of
the varying hair colors and textures reflecting the multicultural congregation, something I had never witnessed. I had attended all-Black
churches all my life, and been to a couple of all-White churches for
the weddings of old college friends and coworkers. This was an eye-
opening experience.

When the pastor announced altar call, one of the ushers turned
to me and asked, *"Do you know Jesus?"* My first impulse was to ask
him, *Does anyone really know Him?* But instead I just nodded
slightly, uncertain what "knowing" Jesus entailed. Did I believe He

existed or was He a constant presence in my life? I felt very self-conscious and out of place, and then I began to panic, afraid someone would discover I was a visitor and drag me to the altar. I was one of the first ones out the door.

"She's a Christian," I added.

"Hmmm. Is she Christian-*Christian*, or Catholic?" she asked suspiciously. "You know a lot of Hispanics are Catholic."

"I think the preferred term is 'Latino.' She's Evangelical, I think."

"Well, that's good," she said approvingly. "Maybe she'll get you to go to church."

As my eyes wandered around my mother's living room, I tried not to look at the framed pictures on the walls and tables, because my father was in almost every single one: my sister and I as children, sitting on his lap; my father and I at my high school graduation, which he attended in a wheelchair; my mother and sister at his hospital bed at home during his last days when he resembled a famine victim. More prominent was the eleven-by-fourteen oil painting my mother had commissioned after his death, a portrait of him when he was young and suave and eerily resembled me. It hung over his old raggedy La-Z-Boy. Every time I looked at his hazel eyes and sly smile, all I could think about was his betrayal and the lie he had lived.

I looked away from the photos and settled my eyes on a pile of magazines on the end table. On top was an issue of *Diaspora*, the magazine Eva had mentioned. I picked it up and saw it was last month's issue and turned to the table of contents; there was Eva's name, next to the article, "Bringing G-O-D Back to Schools After 9–11."

"When did you start reading this?" I asked my mother.

She looked up and shrugged. "They've been sending me free copies. It's pretty good. I might start subscribing."

I turned to the article and started reading to get a feel of Eva's writing style. It was more in depth than the newspaper editorial and emphasized her objectivity, knowledge of politics, and the Bible.

"Are you coming with me next week to visit your father?" I heard my mother ask as I tried to concentrate.

My jaw tightened. "No."

"Why not?"

"I'm trying to read," I replied sternly, trying not to get upset with her. "You know I don't believe in visiting graves."

"Love, at some point, you're going to have to forgive your father."

"He's *dead*. You can't forgive *dead* people," I said, stressing the "dead" each time.

"Sure you can. He's hanging over you like a bad spirit. You're still angry with him and your anger is keeping you from committing yourself in a relationship. You keep bouncing from woman to woman with no plans to settle down just because—"

I looked up at her without bothering to cover up my irritation. "Mama, I haven't been with a woman since— You know what, I'm not having this discussion with you. Not today."

"'Cause you know I'm right—"

The doorbell buzzed and I happily jumped up. It was Jade and the kids. After recently divorcing her husband, Jade would be prime fodder for my mother's nit-picking. It didn't matter that Jade ran a successful catering and wedding coordinator business, or that she was studying for her real estate license; she was a divorced woman and single mother, the equivalence of a fallen woman in my mother's eyes. "Hurry," I whispered into the intercom and buzzed her in.

I opened the door and walked out into the hallway to greet them when they got off the elevator.

"Unc-Adam, Unc-Adam!" Kia and Daelen screamed my name as if it were one word.

I scooped up my niece and nephew in each arm and mimicked their munchkin voices, "Unc-Adam!" At four and three, they were at the age where they were still cute and not yet annoying.

"She starting already?" Jade whispered in my ear, kissing my cheek. I nodded. My baby sister looked like a teenager in her bare midriff top and low-riding, hip-hugging jeans, which she pulled up to hide her exposed bellybutton from our mother. She had recently cut her long hair into a chin-length bob and colored it a very light brown, all of which my mother had criticized. Jade proceeded toward Mama for the obligatory hug and kiss. "I know you don't eat cake, Mama, but I bought one anyway. My kids associate birthdays with cake, not fruit and salad. Sorry." I could see Mama scrutinizing her, ready to attack.

"You're the one who's making your dentist rich," Mama said shrugging, eyeing my sister from bottom to top as she cut up the cantaloupe.

"You look good, baby sister," I commented to get her on my side. I set the kids down so they could divert their grandmother's attention with more hugs and kisses.

Mama stopped cutting in order to bend to her grandbabies' level. In the midst of their affectionate exchange, she looked up at Jade. "What is that on your nose?"

Jade and I looked at each other. I hadn't noticed the tiny stud in her nose. It was barely noticeable but she might as well have had a hoop ring hanging out of her nostril under Mama's radar. *Your turn*, I related telepathically. Jade scowled and shoved a piece of cantaloupe into her mouth. "A nose ring," she mumbled.

Mama shook her head, but said nothing more. This was typical Mama, storing ammunition for surprise assaults. "Your brother's seeing a Puerto Rican woman," she then said.

"Mama . . ." I warned.

"What's a Putta Weeken?" Kia asked.

We all burst out laughing.

"It's someone who's from Puerto Rico, a country," I explained to my precocious niece, picking her up and kissing her cheek.

"Oh," Kia said, nodding with total comprehension.

"Jade, baby. Have you decided to stop dressing like a decent woman now that your husband has left you?" Mama asked, now turning back to Jade. Despite Jade's annoyance, I grinned, happy once again that my mother was off my back.

When I returned home, there was a voice mail message from Ms. Miller asking me to call her back right away. "It's about Justin," she said before hanging up. I sighed, wondering what Justin had done now. Before I called her, I put a couple of Maze and Brian Hughes CDs on the stereo and took a shower. When I was finally relaxing in a T-shirt and boxers, I felt prepared for any drama Ms. Miller would dish out.

"Ms. Miller. What's going on?" I asked authoritatively.

"Justin didn't go to work. I called his job and his boss said he phoned in sick. None of his friends have seen him and his cell phone is turned off," she said quietly. She had called before with the same complaint; the first time she told me Justin hadn't come home from school. I was new to the game and went to her house, only to find her dressed in a short black dress, claiming she had just come in from a date to find Justin gone—Ricky was spending the night at a friend's. She was slightly drunk and crying, upset that a date had stood her up. When she tried to make a move on me, I left. Later, I found out from Justin that she had insisted he spend the night at a cousin's.

"What about the girl? What's her name? Diane?"

"Her phone's disconnected. I'd go to her house if I knew where she lived. She has a car, can you believe it? A sixteen-year-old girl with a car? She has a cell phone, but I don't know the number."

"It's only eight o'clock. It's still early. If he isn't home by ten, call me back."

"I'm getting worried. Can you come over?"

Big Brothers weren't supposed to get emotionally involved in the lives of their charges, I reminded myself every time. And we definitely were not supposed to get involved with the mothers. We were supposed to help with homework, transport the boys to extracurricular activities, be more like big brothers than fathers—hence the name. But it was a difficult task in a society full of divorced and fatherless families. At orientation, the program director told the new recruits a story of a mentor who fell in love with his protégé's mother. When the love affair was over, the mother became angry and began to stalk the mentor, who eventually had to file a restraining order. She then began taking out her frustration on her son and eventually lost custody of him. It was an extreme case but an example of what could happen when bounds were overstepped.

"No, I can't," I told her. "Just call me back at ten, okay?"

When ten o'clock rolled around and Ms. Miller hadn't called, I called her, but the phone was busy. I worked at the computer a bit, checked my e-mails, then searched the Internet for a local screenwriting contest someone at work told me about. I was beginning to take my creative writing more seriously, determined to finish my screenplay by year's end. After I located the website and downloaded the information, I called Ms. Miller again. The phone was still busy so I went to bed.

Just as I had fallen asleep, the phone awoke me.

"Adam—Mr. Black, it's Nikki. Nikki Miller." Her voice sounded shaky.

"What's wrong?" I squinted in the dark at the digital clock radio: 12:05.

"Justin hasn't come home. He hasn't called. His cell phone is still off—"

"Hold on, hold on," I said, still half asleep. I struggled out of bed and snapped on the light.

"I don't know what to do. Should I call the police?"

"I'll be right there."

On the drive over, I tried not to think of the worst-case scenario. Ordinarily, I didn't notice Justin and Ricky's neighborhood, but at twelve-forty-five in the morning it amazed me how alive it was—the young brothers on the corners, the constant flow of traffic, drug deals in plain sight as cop cars drove by blatantly oblivious. It was still a nice neighborhood, predominantly full of hardworking and retired Black folks, and I could only imagine what the poorer neighborhoods were like. I drove slowly, glancing periodically at the young men for a glimpse of Justin's familiar hair, his slightly bow-legged walk, even though I knew he wasn't the hanging-out kind. Times like this made me glad I wasn't a father.

When I got to the Millers' house, I halfway expected another trap—dinner and a bottle of wine, topped off with a lonely single mother in a hot dress. Instead I found Ms. Miller distraught, a scarf tied around her head, wearing what looked like her son's clothes: baggy jeans and a T-shirt.

"He hasn't called. He always calls, even if it's to lie about where he is."

"Did you two have a fight or something?"

"We're always fighting these days. Yesterday, he told me he was going away to college and never coming to visit me."

"He was just angry, he didn't mean it."

"He said he hated me."

It was an ugly thing to hate a parent. It was like hating yourself, like hating God. I knew because this was the disease that lived in me and had been eating at my insides. It was like the cancer that had tried to thrive in my body. However, the hate had been more successful. What I felt for my dead father was immune to forgiveness like radiation and chemotherapy was to terminal cancer.

"Kids say those things just to hurt their parents, but they don't mean what they say." I tried to assure her, though I knew it was indeed possible for kids to hate their parents.

I listened as she talked about how hard it had been to be a single mother after her husband died, how careful she had to be about dating, how hard it was for a woman with needs. I should've taken the hint and bolted, but I wanted to make sure Justin made it home safely.

"Men pretend like they're interested in me, you know. They think I'm desperate because I have two kids and I want to find a daddy for them and that I'll do anything, put up with anything, just to have a man in my life. But I'm waiting for someone special," she went on.

Yeah, so am I, I thought. *But I am not the one.* I could feel her eyes eating away at me, piece by piece, and I scratched the back of my neck out of habit. Even though I was sitting across from her, I was on edge and got up and walked to the window just in time to see Justin exiting a gray car.

"He's here," I announced, a little too happily.

She rushed to the door. "I'm going to kill him!"

I put out my arm and held her back. "That's what he wants. To get a rise out of you. Don't let him. Let me talk to him."

At my father's funeral, almost twenty years ago, I remembered standing at his coffin, fighting back the urge with all my might to keep from pounding on his chest. I wanted to bring him back to life so I could choke it right back out of him. How dare he cheat on my beautiful, God-fearing mother who always saw the good in everyone.

I thought, it would have been easier to understand if she had been a bad wife and mother—no, not even then. On the rare occasions when we dared to talk back or be disobedient, Mama would quote Ephesians 6:2, *Honor thy mother and thy father . . . that thy may enjoy long life on earth.*

When I looked over at the section where the family members were assembled, I saw the other woman, a Caucasian woman, and her two children, sitting directly behind my mother and sister. The combination of my father's long-ago mixed genes and the White woman's had produced almost White children. The girl was about my age—I later learned eight months younger—with long, wavy dishwater blonde hair and pale skin. The boy was even more pallid, almost albino, with lighter, straighter hair. He was closer to Jade's age, by five months. It wasn't until years later, when my cancer was diagnosed, after the doctors told me how rare it was in African Americans, that I thought about my father's great-grandfather, the German immigrant who was rarely mentioned when talk turned to the ancestors. "The German," as he was referred to by the family, was the one who had passed down his light eyes and light skin on to my father, and possibly, his cancerous genes, which in turn, were transmitted to me.

The day of the funeral, I recalled everyone whispering around us, or so it seemed. If pointing were an acceptable thing to do at a funeral, the fingers would have been all over us. As it was, the eyes and chins were doing a good job of indicating the scandal unfolding at the front of the parlor. I heard my mother call me, her voice swollen with grief and exhaustion. She said, *"Adam-Love, come meet your brother and sister."* Jade, at eleven years old, had not grasped the depth of their relationship to us and was talking to them like they were long-lost cousins. I whirled around and looked at my mother with such vehemence that she recoiled as if I had hit her. Then I turned and walked out of the church without delivering the eulogy. In my head was the poem I had written and memorized for my father, about his life as a father, a navy man and my hero. But I laid the words to rest and never resurrected them again. I didn't go to the burial, and at seventeen I swore that I would never visit his grave. Ever.

CHAPTER 11

EVA

FIVE YEARS. I had waited for a man like him for five years. And just when I had decided to give up, there he was, standing in front of me, regal like a Black prince with locks the color of dark sand, eyes the color of night, reciting spiritual poetry like biblical verses. It was Adam. He had to be the one.

At least that's what my heart was telling me as I watched him take the podium with an air of confidence associated with success. The tunic he wore blended with his golden skin tone and clung impeccably to each muscle and hard line on his torso. A long duster and loose slacks, both in black, completed his ensemble, shrouding his lower contours in mystery so that the rest of him had to be quickly reconstructed in the Etch A Sketch of my imagination. It was an outfit an eccentric man would wear, like an artist. He wore it like a king.

Now at the microphone, he adjusted his thin-rimmed, amber-colored glasses, which I could tell were for show because he had no broken refraction along his cheekbones where the bottoms of the lenses rested.

"Uhh," Simone grunted with approval. "He don't look like no Christian."

"Don't judge," I whispered to silence her.

She nudged me hard. "You like 'heem,'" she teased in a fake Jamaican accent.

She was right, Adam did seem out of his element, like he belonged at Words, the coffeehouse in Printer's Row where weekly secular poetry slams were held. And she was right, I did like him. His locks were tied back, cascading down his back like a horse's tail. A few locks spilled from his forehead and strategically covered his eyes as if he were trying to avoid eye contact.

It was Second Thursday, Spiritual Poetry Night at TCCC, when members and visitors shared their inspirational verses. Once, a young man read a poem laced with sexual innuendoes disguised as a spiritual sonnet. Subsequently, a sign-up sheet with prior approval of any poetry being presented was instituted after Sunday service, so that no unsaved souls could wander in off the streets to sample their "worldly" poetry on the sanctified. It was censorship but the church was not a democracy. I concluded that it *was* Adam I saw in church the previous Sunday, and I wondered if he had attended just to sign up for poetry night or if he had stayed to hear the Word.

At the table next to where I sat with Maya and Simone, there were four young women who always hung in a pack and whom I had seen only sporadically in church. I had dubbed them "the Sister-Girlfriends." They were the kind of people who came to church for special functions, musical performances, when there was food, or for the weddings or baptisms of people they knew. I noticed that when men took the mike, the Sister-Girlfriends would make comments behind elaborately manicured hands, or snicker into each other's ears like high school girls even though they looked to be in their mid-twenties.

I watched as Adam closed his eyes briefly, for effect, or so it seemed; he could have been nervous. Then he spoke, and I realized he *was* nervous, for his voice belied his demeanor. It was raspy, like someone recovering from laryngitis, shaky, with just the slightest hint of bravado as he intermittently bit his bottom lip.

"This first piece is entitled 'My Precious Father, Eighty-Three,'" he began.

Despite his earlier self-assurance, I could tell he was a first-timer, a virgin. He made no eye contact, keeping his eyes averted to the back of the darkened church on some distant focal point, much like a pregnant woman in labor would do. He held a battered paperback in his hands, which he kept rolling around and around in a tube shape, but he didn't read from it; I assumed it was a prop to keep his hands occupied. I tried to make him feel at ease by flashing a small smile at him from the sea of expectant, judgmental faces. But it was evident that we in the audience didn't exist to him. He was in his own spiritual realm and lost in the anointing of his words. He spoke slowly, deliberately, drawing out each word dramatically but at the same time with a beatnik flair, pausing at every other syllable so that listeners could envision the poem in stanza formation, line by line. As he went on, his voice became more solemn as if he were reciting a prayer.

The poem, cunningly mixed with phrases from various psalms and proverbs, was in the form of an epic; it told of a boy who sought his father's approval from the time he was little until the father's death. In the end, the narrator forgave his father for never being around and accepted that the only true father in his life was God. The poem hit home for me and I thought about my own father. As he repeated the phrase, *"My precious Father, I love you, for being the only Father of this nation's fatherless children,"* his voice faded away, and I wondered if the poem was autobiographical.

The applause was sporadic until I began clapping with appreciation to get everyone to give him his props; soon others joined in. It wasn't until Simone nudged me hard that I realized I was the only one left clapping.

It got his attention. He finally looked down from his focal point and gazed into the audience for the first time. Even though he seemed to be glancing in my direction, it seemed he was staring right through me. I gave him an encouraging smile, but he had already returned his sight to his point of origin and was beginning his next poem.

"This next one is called 'Choose Me, Ninety-Nine.'"

"Yeah," one of the Sister-Girlfriends muttered.

Another one said boldly and loudly, "I'll choose you alright." This was followed by stifled giggles.

"Shhh," I hushed them, shooting a disapproving look in their direction.

Even after I had turned away from them, I could feel their collective eyes shooting daggers at the back of my head. There were murmurs sweeping the church, and I could see Pastor Allen look apprehensively at the emcee, Sister Erma, perhaps wondering if Adam was about to slip in a risqué poem that hadn't been approved.

Adam read the second one with more passion, less pauses, much louder, sending even the teenagers into a frenzy and onto their feet. With the extra beats, the poem went over the three-minute limit. There were the usual "Amens" from the older set and affirmative "Uhs" and squeals from the women. The Sister-Girlfriends continued whispering comments and giggling, but none of it seemed to faze Adam. When he was done, the audience gave him a standing ovation, the applause drowning out the Sister-Girlfriends, who finally realized perhaps, that the "me" Adam was referring to was God, and not himself. As hard as I tried to remember the poem in its entirety, the only words that stayed on my mind were, *"Choose Me."*

"I'm Adam. Thank you," he said, his mouth so close to the mike that his voice exploded over the acoustics. As he stepped off the stage, one woman, then another, reached out to shake his hand, complimenting him. Adam strutted past them and almost rushed down the aisle, keeping his head down. I turned to see where he was sitting, but he headed straight for the door. Before I knew it, my feet leaped from under me.

"Where are you going?" Simone and Maya both whispered aghast.

I waved them off and slowed down as I got to the end of the aisle, pretending I was just going out for air. It was another freakish Chicago summer night when the temperature dropped suddenly and drastically, catching everyone unprepared. In the foggy chilly night, I looked up and down the street, but Adam had mysteriously disappeared into the night.

As I turned to go back inside, I heard sounds, like heavy breathing, coming from the area between the church and the school, and

I walked cautiously toward the darkened gangway. Recognizing the silhouette of Adam's hair and the duster, I stopped at a safe distance and waited so as not to embarrass him. I watched as he expelled ragged breaths in the cool night air, his head bent and his hands on his knees for support. I didn't know if he was having an asthma attack or an anxiety spell. Or perhaps he had lied about being in remission. Maybe he still had cancer.

"Are you okay?" I asked tentatively.

He turned his head away quickly and nodded, his breathing returning to normal, evident by the steady puffs of air.

"I'm okay. Thanks," he said in his raspy voice. He wouldn't meet my eyes, leaning back against the wall and looking up at the sky.

"Asthma?" I asked.

He shook his head. "I kind of hyperventilate whenever I get nervous. It's kind of embarrassing." He finally looked over at me. "Did anybody notice?"

I shook my head. "I don't think so."

He started walking out of the gangway and I backed up, stepping out of the way as he staggered to the steps and sat down, leaning back against the railing. I followed and sat a couple of steps above him. He reached into his breast pocket, I thought for a cigarette, but instead brought out some gum.

"Can I have one?" I asked, because my throat was dry.

"It's smoking cessation gum. You wouldn't like it."

"The trick to speaking in public is not to look people in the eyes," I told him. "Look at their foreheads, over their heads, anywhere but their eyes. Eventually, you get over the fear." He looked at me skeptically as I continued. "I took a course in public speaking once. There was a time when I couldn't speak in public, but now it doesn't bother me."

"I was fine 'til I looked at you," he said quietly, a slight smile on his face, chewing his gum slowly. I thought he was blaming me for his reaction, but then I realized he meant I had distracted him, but not in a negative way.

"Sorry. I was trying to help. Sometimes if you see a friendly face, it helps."

"So, show me."

"What?"

"Recite one of your poems and let me see you not get nervous."

"I told you I haven't written anything since high school."

"So recite one of those," he insisted, nudging my knee. "Go on, Sister. Lay one on me," he added, slipping into a fake cool slang.

Reluctantly, I stood up and turned to face him, concentrating on his smooth, rounded forehead and at the vein throbbing in his right temple. "They're all morbid, I told you."

"Macabre is the foundation for many great works of art."

I searched my memory banks for one of my old poems, then settled on one that had been published in the school newspaper and had caused controversy because of the negative subject matter. Keeping my eyes on his forehead, I began:

They say it is supposed to be the best time of my life,
a time when I should have no worries, no ugly thoughts or strife,
yet it is just the opposite, full of uncertainty,
of who I am, what to do, and what I want to be.
My mind is plagued with confusion, and blatant suicide;
one day up, many others down, why do I want to die?
To all of those who know so much, I dare not spoil their fun,
for they would laugh and say to me, your life has just begun.

The forehead trick didn't work. I was sweating, rocking from side to side, locking and unlocking my fingers the entire time.

He smiled. "You're right, it is kind of gloomy."

"Okay, so maybe it's different when you're reciting bad poetry," I admitted, taking my seat quickly.

"I didn't say it was bad."

"I wrote it just after my mother died. This teacher, who didn't know, came up to me one day and said, 'Cheer up, your life's just begun.'"

"Hmmm," he muttered sympathetically. "In that case, it's not morbid at all; just goes to your state of mind at the time. I liked it."

"Thanks."

He stood up abruptly. "I got to catch a cab. Luciano dropped me off. My car's in the shop." He staggered to a standing position and then leaned against the railing. "Thanks for the invite. And the poem."

He began to walk sluggishly down the block, toward Austin Avenue, away from me. I started to call out to him but I was hypnotized by his walk, the duster blowing behind him like a gunslinger in a Western. It was a walk that bordered between a street-wise strut and a drunken swagger, or maybe he was unsteady from his attack.

"Adam," I called out, unsure of what I was going to say. *Be cool, be cool,* I thought. *Don't act all juvenile like the Sister-Girlfriends.* I thought about offering him a ride, let Maya take Simone home. "Um . . . cabs don't usually stop around here at night." I stood up and took a couple of steps toward him, then I stopped as a checkered cab approached.

He pulled a hand from his pocket to signal the cab but it zoomed by. He looked at me accusingly, as if I had jinxed him, and I gave him a confirmatory nod.

"You should go back in. It's chilly out here," he told me, leaning against a lamppost.

"It's kind of late to be out here alone," I told him.

He laughed. "I'm a man, remember?" *How could I forget?* I thought. *Watch yourself.* The voices of my conscience geared up for battle. I was glad the weather was cool; it kept my hands busy rubbing my upper arms up and down.

"Your poems were . . . ." I searched for the right word, something that didn't sound like adoration or an exaggeration. "They hit home. Especially the father one," I finally said.

He looked at me sheepishly.

"I really liked them," I added with more conviction.

"Thanks."

"What was that book you were holding?" I asked. Adam reached into his pocket and brought out the paperback and held it out. I didn't move.

"Come here," he said softly, the seduction from his poetry reading returning to his voice. And when I still didn't move, he unglued himself from the post and took a couple of steps forward.

Be careful, the voice was saying in my head where the song "God Is Trying to Tell You Something" had begun to play.

But I walked cautiously toward him, careful not to get too close. At the same time, he walked toward me. As we neared each other, a gush of cold wind ripped through us, sending a chill through my body and lifting his duster behind him like wings. In the fog, he looked ethereal—an angel in the night. I shivered in my rayon blouse and brushed the loose strands of my hair back nervously with one hand, feeling the new growth. I was long overdue for a touch-up.

I got within arm's reach and took the book from him, reading the cover of the battered paperback: *Sinner: Confessions of a Christian-in-Progress. Poems by Adam Black.* Even though I could tell that it was self-published, by the simple cover design and the publisher, which was named after him—"A Black Press"—I was intrigued.

"I'm impressed," I said sincerely.

"Don't be. It's self-published, which means I paid to get it published instead of the other way around."

"The word you're looking for is *'gracias,'*" I said, remembering my own difficulty with accepting compliments.

He smiled. *"Gracias."*

Our eyes locked briefly before I broke first, glancing up at his lion's mane. I wanted to touch it, not because I was curious to see what it felt like, but because it had been so long since I had touched a man's hair. As if he read my mind, he reached up and pushed back the stray woolly strands that hung in his face, only to have them fall down again.

A yellow cab neared and he turned and whistled through his teeth. *Don't go,* I told him in my mind. I wanted to tell him that all I had been thinking about was kissing him, completely disregarding the fact that I hardly knew him. The cab screeched to a stop.

"Were you in church last Sunday?" I asked.

He nodded, walking backward toward the cab. "I was in the back. Way in the back."

"Did you come just to sign up for the poetry reading or for spiritual enlightenment?"

"Both, I guess."

"Are you coming back this Sunday?"

He cleared his throat as he opened the cab door. "I don't know."

I couldn't think of anything more to say so I muttered, "See you." I turned and headed back toward church. Then I remembered I had his book.

"Eva!" he called out, his voice much raspier than before. I turned around, walking back to the cab, holding out the book.

He leaned out the window. "Keep it. I have plenty other copies."

"Thanks."

"I read your article, 'Bringing God Back to Schools After 9–11.' I thought you were pretty harsh on the Harry Potter books, but overall, it was pretty good."

"You don't think there's something wrong with having books about witchcraft in a school library, but not a children's Bible?"

"Separation of church and state."

"When the planes hit the towers, did people call on Uncle Sam or God?"

"That's a topic for another day," he said, smiling widely so his gum was visible between his teeth. "What're you doing Saturday?"

I shrugged. "Cleaning up. Gardening. Doing my touch-up."

"Want me to help you?"

I looked at him sideways. "What? My touch-up? What do you know about relaxers? I thought you were all about going natural."

"If you want to oppress your hair, who am I to judge?" I didn't answer as the cab started to pull off. "Sleep tight, Eva."

It would be difficult.

In bed that night, I began reading his poems, beginning with the two he had recited. When I was finished, I re-read "Choose Me":

Choose Me!
Keep your eye on Me, I have what you need.
Don't look to the left where the devil lies,

Don't look to the right to the ones that tempt you;
Keep your eyes straight above—
Choose Me!
I have something greater than their trickery, I have what you're looking
for.
I will see to it that they don't hurt you or reach you
Choose Me!
I will make you My Kings and Queens,
I will respect you, honor you, and protect you
I will give you the attention you need, I will caress your soul when
you're in need—
Choose Me!
You don't have to beg Me to love you, My love is unconditional.
I will love you no matter what, I will love you 'til the end of time.
I don't have to compete for you because you are Mine.
Choose Me!
For if you stray from the prize, if you choose their lies,
I will take what I have given you;
All your treasures will be lost, until you come back to Me—
Come with Me, be with Me, stay with Me, abide by Me;
Choose Me!

As my body sank into the mattress, the image of Adam at the podium materialized. I knew it was wrong. I knew he was talking about God, but as I struggled against sleep, I couldn't help imagining that he had been talking to me, flirting with me, asking me to choose him. Deep down, I knew I was no better than the Sister-Girlfriends.

Then I began to wonder why he had strayed from God, what had made him stop "praying as much." Maybe Maya was right, maybe Adam and I were meant to meet, maybe I was supposed to lead him back to God. Maybe.

CHAPTER 12

ADAM

PURSUING WOMEN IS not my usual mode of operation. Most of the women I had been with had actually approached me first, slipped me their numbers, like the woman at Simone's party or the girl who had written her number in my palm. The number had faded with the rain and disappeared when I took a shower, before I could copy it onto something more permanent. I never called either one. Even when I had made the first move, I left the next step up to them, and usually, they called. But there was something about Eva that made me want to chase her, some inexplicable force. It didn't seem to me that she was playing hard-to-get as much as it was part of her character. One of us had to compromise and it didn't look like it was going to be her.

The door opened to the sight of Eva with hair relaxer smeared at the roots and a towel wrapped around her neck. Behind her, I could see a big black dog barking threateningly. And not just any big black dog, but a rottweiler. Unlike other boys, I never wanted a dog as a child. I could never understand the so-called love between people and "man's best friend." There was just something demonic about them. I don't know whether it was a horror movie I had seen about killer dogs or if I suffered from some repressed childhood trauma; all I know is I never liked dogs and for the moment, I was grateful for the glass and iron security door still between us.

"You didn't wait for me, huh?" I asked.

"How did you get my address?" she questioned warily, her gloved hands frozen at her sides.

"Maya. I told her I'd take the flack."

"I'm going to have to have a serious talk with her." Unwavering, she stood barefoot in baggy sweatpants and a sleeveless shirt tied at the waist in front, staring at me, surprised that I was at her door. The dog continued to bark until she stomped her foot and yelled something in Spanish, which I assumed was "shut up" because the dog stopped immediately. With the dog now quiet, I could make out the vague sounds of reggae wafting in the background. I liked reggae even though half the time I couldn't understand the words.

"Does he bite?" I asked stupidly.

"What do you think?"

We stared at each other through the glass door. She took a step forward, then stopped as if debating whether to let me in or go kill her sister for giving me her address.

I rubbed my neck. "Are you going to let me in or not?"

Finally, she unlocked the security door.

"Okay, but you'll have to let him smell you," she warned. "And don't make any sudden moves."

I followed her uneasily into the living room where she introduced me to King, like they were equals, like the dog was a person. The killer-looking rottweiler tentatively approached me and sniffed me, including the bag I held in my hand. I knew dogs could smell fear, so I pretended that I liked dogs and hoped the false feeling was conveyed. I attempted a half smile, but the canine eyed me with evil, brown, human-like eyes like he knew I was up to no good. *Don't even think about making a move on my master,* his eyes seemed to convey. I remembered someone telling me never to look a strange dog in the eyes, so I glanced at his forehead briefly, then looked away. I wasn't stupid. "Hey, boy. Hey, King. You the man, you the man," I said nervously.

Eva looked amused as she locked both doors behind me. There was no turning back. She walked through the living room, then down a short hallway. "Come on, boy."

"Are you talking to me or the dog?" I kidded.

"Whatever."

"I brought you something," I said, handing her the bag.

She held out her gloved hands helplessly. "What is it? Could you put it on the table?"

"It's spearmint tea. And mint massage oil. My ma says they're supposed to be good for migraines. She's into homeopathic medicine." I set the bag down on the coffee table.

"Thanks. That was nice of you." She disappeared through an open doorway in the short hall. "Help yourself to some juice or iced tea. It's in the fridge. I'll be out in a little bit."

I scanned the living room slowly, surveying the African and Native American masks and sculptures, reprints by African American artists whose work I was familiar with—Romare Bearden and Annie Lee. The sofa and accessories were color-coordinated in various shades of mocha, black, and cream including several kuba- and mud-cloth throw pillows. Either she had a severe case of Negrophilia or she must have been Black in a former life. A built-in oak bookcase lined one wall and was filled to the rim with books. When I looked closer, I noticed the books were alphabetized and categorized according to fiction and nonfiction. One shelf held several Bibles: a King James version, NIV Women's Devotional Bible, and a Spanish version, *La Santa Biblia*. If she was really celibate, I could see how she occupied her time.

Covering another wall were photos of her sons at various stages in their development, in chronological order from birth to high school. On the last wall hung all their graduation portraits and diplomas, from kindergarten and eighth grade to high school. They were good-looking kids with the golden skin and the curly-wavy hair attributed to Latin and biracial children. There were also several graduation pictures of Eva beginning with her in the eighth grade and ending with graduate school. Near the faux fireplace, a small five-by-seven silver frame caught my eye. It was a picture of Eva in a wedding dress, standing with who I assumed was her ex-husband. She looked like a little girl in the photo, a little girl playing dress up, her hair in ringlets and bangs. He was dark brown and looked very African, but I knew Latinos, like Black folks, were a mixed people. I thought it very odd that a divorcée would display her wedding portrait.

Knickknacks and souvenirs from Puerto Rico adorned the walls in the adjoining dining room. Charcoal drawings of percussion-playing natives and Spanish dancers dressed in white surrounded a square glass-block window. An assortment of bamboo, miniature palm trees, and fresh-cut flowers in various glass vases lined the floors, the oak table, and the window seats, giving the room a tropical feel. The lone picture in this room, a black-and-white framed photo, revealed Eva in a boxing stance. This made me smile as I remembered her saying she knew Tai Bo.

To get to the kitchen, I had to pass King, who was sprawled in front of the door Eva had entered. The dog looked like a Sphinx guarding Egypt and was still sizing me up. Cautiously, I wandered into the small hallway, careful not to make any sudden moves. The door was open and I saw it was the bathroom. Eva was bent over the sink washing her hair.

"Need any help?" I asked, leaning in the doorway where I could still keep an eye on King.

"No, thanks," came her muffled reply.

She looked uncomfortable, bent over the low sink like she was, so I walked around her into the bathroom and took the chair from the vanity table and placed it in front of the sink. "Here, sit down."

She turned her head slightly, looking at me through half-closed eyes and underneath the lather in her hair. "What? What are you doing?"

I rolled up a towel for her and put it under her neck for support. Then I directed her into the chair, with her back to the sink, and guided her head backward, under the water faucet. She didn't protest or question me further as I took over massaging the shampoo into her hair with my fingertips, from the roots to the ends. With her eyes closed, she sighed with appreciation.

"Where did you learn to wash hair?"

"I used to work in my mother's hair shop."

"Really?" She said this like she didn't believe me.

"Yup. From the time I was thirteen to about fifteen. I had to quit 'cause the women kept hitting on me."

"Get out."

"I'm serious. These women used to come on to me. Older women. 'That sure feels goo-ood, baby.'" At my high-pitched, mimicking Southern accent, a smile slowly appeared on Eva's face, so I continued with the entertainment. "'Mmm-mm-mm, I sure wish I could take you home with me, sugar.' Then one day, one of them grabbed my crotch as I was rinsing her hair. *That* was my last day."

The laugh she had been trying to suppress erupted, her eyes still closed. "You know what they say. Washing someone else's hair can be sensual." She pressed her lips together as if to keep any more words from escaping. I rinsed her hair, then began another shampoo, listening as the next reggae track began to play.

"Who is this playing?"

"Danté. It's a reggae band. You like reggae?"

"It's got a good beat—you can dance to it," I joked, paraphrasing the old *American Bandstand* line. "I just can't understand what the he— heck they're saying."

"They're singing about God. It's Christian reggae."

"Christian reggae, huh? I didn't know there was such a thing."

"Christian music comes in all genres. There's Christian rock, Christian *salsa*. It's not just gospel. You like gospel?"

"Why I got to like gospel? 'Cause I'm Black?" I joked.

"I like gospel and I'm not Black."

"You *are* Black. The only thing that separates us is a language and a country. Latins are just as mixed as Blacks."

"Ooh, you sound just like . . ."

"Who? Your ex-husband? Boyfriend?"

"No. Rashid. He says skin color and language and religion are all man-made things created to keep us from concentrating on what's really important—God."

I mulled that over for a moment and conceded that there might be some element of truth to it. All the while she was talking, her eyes were closed, her lips moving independently. I decided to test her, to see if there was any interest.

"How do you say eyes?" I asked her.

"What?"

"How do you say eyes, in Spanish?"

"*Ojos.*"

"Open your *ojos.*"

She blinked several times before squinting up at me. "My, what big nostrils you have," she joked.

"My, what big *ojos* you have," I said, playing right along. Then I said seriously, "Nice big *ojos.*" I had intentionally begun my wooing.

She closed her eyes again. "Not 'o-hoes,' *ojos,*" she corrected my Pidgin Spanish.

"*Ojos,*" I mimicked with an exaggerated breathy accent. She smirked but didn't reply, so I changed the theme of our conversation. "Can I ask why you have your wedding picture on display?"

"For the kids. I wanted them to know that there was a time I loved their father. That it wasn't all bad."

"Seems kind of strange. Your kids aren't little anymore."

"It's just been up there so long, I've forgotten it's there. It's not like I stare at it. But I'll put it away if it bothers you."

I started to protest but then I realized she was just pulling my leg when a smile spread across her face.

"You really box?"

"Yeah, but just for the exercise. Maya took that picture of me, the one in the dining room. I used it for an article I wrote on Latin women in boxing."

"I thought you wrote about education issues."

"Mostly. But every once in a while I write about women's topics, diversity, anything I feel strongly about."

I washed her hair a couple more times before conditioning and rinsing it. Her hair was so soft and thick, it felt like velvet. When I finished, I lifted the towel that hung around her neck and started to dry her hair, but she stood up abruptly, taking over, standing so close to me that I had to take a step backward. She pushed the chair with her foot to make more room, pulling a section of hair around to her nose to sniff it.

"I think it's all out. Do you smell any perm?"

I bent down and took a whiff of her hair but all I could smell was the scent of the strawberries-and-cream leave-in conditioner. It reminded me of the strawberry swirl cone I used to get when the ice cream truck came around on summer days.

"Does it?" I heard her ask from far away. "Smell?"

I hadn't realized that she had lifted her head and was looking up at me. I sensed that her eyes were blinking a sort of Morse code, signaling me to kiss her. But then maybe I was seeing what I wanted to see. Had it been so long that I couldn't tell when a woman was hitting on me?

I took a chance. Before I knew it, my hands were in her damp limp hair and I was kissing her forehead, her eyebrows, then her pug nose. With her hands braced on the sink behind her, she tilted her face and closed her eyes. We both turned our heads to each other's left, our lips meeting simultaneously like we had been thinking the same thing at the same time. It dawned on me then that I had never kissed a left-handed woman. With right-handed women, there had always been that initial head-butt because I always tilted left while they usually tilted right.

I took her full bottom lip softly into my mouth. She in turn seized my top lip. I opened my eyes briefly and saw that her eyes were closed. Holding her face in my hands, I tried to swathe the immensity of her lips in my mouth, turning my head from side to side in an effort to taste every inch of them. I kept my tongue away, using only my lips, because I didn't want to take the chance that my breath was still sour from cigarette residue. It had been one week since my last smoke.

For one brief moment, I had forgotten we were in the bathroom, a place I didn't associate with intimacy unless I was in the shower with a woman. I waited for her to stop me, but she didn't. If anything, she was kissing me harder than I was kissing her, her hands still planted firmly on the sink. At one point, I looked into the mirror at myself and saw a man capable of anything. Then, out of the corner of my eye, I was aware of the beast outside the bathroom sitting on his haunches, tongue hanging out hungrily, blocking me like a jealous man. I closed my eyes, and tried to block *him* out, attempting to concentrate on Eva's sensual lips. But the demon-eyed freak was throwing me off. I pulled away briefly and saw that the top button of her blouse had come undone. She wasn't very large, a C-cup, average, and her skin was flawless, with the exception of a small, dark brown birthmark on the left side of her chest.

"Could you lock him up?"

"Why? Is he scaring you?" she asked.

"Actually, he is."

She rolled her eyes and spoke sharply to the dog. "Get in the back." The dog trotted off, his head bowed in submission.

We resumed kissing. This time, she removed her hands from the sink and I could feel them kneading my back and working their way up to my hair until she held my locks and caressed them between her fingers. Then she started kissing me erratically, one moment steady, the next, hesitant, momentarily pausing like she wasn't sure she should go on, until I would take possession of her lips again. One minute she was Dr. Jekyll, the next Ms. Hyde. Her hesitation began to unnerve me. *Was she really celibate?* She sure didn't kiss like a celibate woman. Or maybe that's what celibate people did—kiss.

I fought back the urge to lift her onto the sink because I didn't think I would be able to stop myself if I got her in that position.

Why was she letting me kiss her if she wasn't going to go any further? Was she waiting to see how far I would go? I wasn't an unbridled teenager with unmanageable hormones, but as a man I could only control myself for so long. I began feeling very uneasy and slightly teased.

Finally, I decided it was time to put an end to our session and I pulled away, sliding my hands down neutrally to her shoulders. I cleared my throat.

"What?" she asked softly, innocently. *Was she kidding?*

I scoffed, unable to resist showing my frustration, and out of habit I pushed my hair back with both hands, forgetting that I had a tied bandana holding it back. She stepped up to me and slipped her hands around my waist. I backed up farther, banging the door against the wall, putting my hands on her wrists as gently as possible and removing them from my waist. As we avoided each other's eyes, she leaned back on the sink and covered her mouth with one hand, pinching her lips. There was a look of surprise on her face, as if she couldn't believe what had just happened, as if something, someone else were responsible. As I looked down, away from her face, I noticed that her birthmark was heart shaped, not the typical Valentine's shape, but the form of a miniature human heart. It almost looked like a tattoo. She noticed me staring at her opened shirt and quickly fastened the button.

"You want something to drink?" she asked abruptly, hurrying out of the bathroom.

"Sure," I answered, though what I wanted to do was leave altogether. She went into the kitchen and I withrew to the living room. I sat in a rattan chair and rubbed my hands together. *What was I doing?* I brought my hands to my face and smelled strawberries and-cream all over again. I wiped my hands on my thighs and looked at her wedding picture.

"Was your husband . . . your ex . . . Puerto Rican?"

"No. He's Black." She entered the living room with two wine glasses.

"I don't drink," I told her.

"It's sparkling white grape juice. Non-alcoholic. It's good."

I took a glass and tasted it, nodding in agreement. "So, you like Black men, huh?"

She gave me the dirtiest look. "I hate when people say that," she said, curling up on the cream-colored pillow-back sofa. "You sound just like my father. Just because I happened to marry a Black man and dated a couple of them doesn't mean I prefer them. I'm attracted to them, just like I'm attracted to Latin men and an occasional Caucasian. My sister's husband is also Black. Well, half Black. You can't help who you like, or fall in love with—or think you love."

I was amused by her defensive stance and played into it to take the edge off my frustration. "It's okay to like the brothers. I'm not mad at you."

"If you saw my cousins, you'd think they were Black. Some of them are darker than you."

"Shoot, *you're* darker than me," I cracked.

"Look—" she started, tilting her head in warning.

"Relax," I said, laughing, holding out my hand because she looked like she was about to take my head off. "I'm just messing with you."

She set her glass on the coffee table and began to section her hair with her fingers and twist it into individual coils. I watched, puzzled.

"You straighten your hair with a relaxer so you can twist it?" I asked, confused.

"Yeah. I don't really like my hair straight. I just relax it to get the kinks out."

"Why don't you lock it?"

She flinched slightly. "Too drastic. I mean, certain hairstyles look better on some people but not on others—"

"You mean it's okay for Blacks?"

"No," she said in a condescending tone. "I've seen a lot of people who aren't Black with locks and locks look good on them. I mean, for me, it would be drastic. I've never colored my hair or cut it or anything like that. Maya's the one who's always experimenting with her hair."

I watched as she continued twisting her hair, wondering if she was going to bring up the kiss we had just shared. I decided to be direct. "Are you really celibate?"

"Yes," she answered without hesitation as she continued twisting.

"For how long?"

"Awhile."

"Months? Years?"

"Why do you want to know?"

"I was just curious . . . Do you go around kissing men, getting them excited just for kicks?"

She stopped twisting her hair and looked directly at me. "No. I guess I should apologize. I shouldn't have kissed you. It was wrong."

"It felt right."

"That's the problem. Not everything that feels right *is* right."

"Are you saying we . . . you and me . . . ?"

"I'm saying I can't . . . how do I say this? I can't start a relationship that involves sex before marriage, or that doesn't lead to marriage. No matter how much I'm attracted to a man. Especially since I don't want to get married anytime soon."

"So you're not going to be with a man 'til you get married?"

"That is my plan." She leaned back into the sofa, interlacing her fingers.

"You do that a lot," I pointed out.

"What?"

"That, with your hands. It reminds me of that kid's game. 'Here's the church, here's the steeple . . .'"

"'Open the door and out come the people,'" she finished, wiggling her fingers.

"I do that with my niece and nephew."

We laughed, and I relaxed for the first time as she finished twisting the last few strands of her hair and I sipped my drink. I tried to think of the best way to say good-bye. I could lie and say I had started seeing the girl whose card I accidentally gave her that first night. Or I could just tell her the truth, that there was no way I could be with a woman whom I couldn't make love with at some point. Marriage was in my future but the future was not anytime soon. I have heard of men who said that when they met the woman of their dreams, their first thought was, *"That's the woman I'm going to marry."* That's what I wanted to feel one day, to know that when I met *the* woman I was going to marry, that I would know it right away, without a shadow of a doubt.

The ice in my glass was melting but I sipped the watery white grape juice anyway to keep from talking. King staggered sedately into the living room, a canine version of John Wayne. That was one scary animal. He nuzzled his oversized head on Eva's lap and I watched with slight envy as she caressed his loose jowls. She didn't look like she needed anybody, least of all a man. All she had to do was kiss that beast or allow him to lick her face, and my decision to bow out would be sealed.

I turned my attention to the words of the current song playing: "*It's because there is someone who's got my back, oh yes, there is someone I'll never lack, the one and only one, yes, the one and only one . . .*"

She broke the quiet first. "It's been a while since I've been with a man that I felt . . . I had any feelings for," she said, still stroking the dog. "So I don't know if I kissed you because you just happened to be here or if it's . . . because it's you."

"Oh." I wasn't sure if I was supposed to be pleased or insulted by her explanation.

She went to the bookcase and pulled out my tattered book and handed it to me.

"I finished reading your poems. I really liked them. I liked the way you titled the poems with numbers, like the chapters in the Bible. Do the numbers have any significance?"

"They relate to a particular date, or year. Like 'Father, Eighty-Three.' My father died in 1983."

"So it's autobiographical, *no*?"

He smiled wryly. "Yeah, you could say that."

"Very clever. You were what, seventeen? My mother died when I was fifteen."

"I guess we have a lot in common." I hoped she didn't ask me anything else about my father; the topic was off-limits.

"Have you tried submitting them to a publishing house?"

"I don't think anyone's interested in my therapeutic verse. I wrote them for me and gave them to my family as gifts, in case I didn't, you know, get through the cancer. Then I found I had more copies than family." I laughed. "I have more copies in storage. I'll send you a newer copy."

"There *are* Christian publishing houses."

"Hmmm," I said vaguely. I leaned back and relaxed, turning my attention back to the CD, enjoying the beat more than the singer who rattled on in what sounded like a foreign language. It was hard to believe he was speaking English. On the last track, I was able to make out some of the words from my favorite Psalm, number 23: *Surely goodness and love will follow me all the days of my life . . .*

" '*And I will dwell in the house of the Lord forever,* ' " I sang along in a fake Jamaican accent.

She smiled. "Do you want to borrow the CD?" she asked when the track finished playing. "It's a copy. My sister has the original."

I thought about that for a second. If I borrowed it, I would have to eventually return it, prolonging the inevitable. "I better not."

She pressed the eject button on the remote control and put the CD in its case, handing it to me. "You let me read your book, I can let you borrow my CD."

When I still hesitated, she sighed with exasperation and said, "I tell you what. You can keep it. As a thank-you for the tea and the oil. I can always burn another one using my sister's. That way, you don't have to worry about returning it."

We talked about writing and music, boxing and God, but we didn't discuss the kiss in the bathroom again. On the tip of my tongue were the kiss-off lines I had used on other women to let them down easily or to get rid of them as quickly and painlessly as possible, depending on who they were. *This isn't working out for me. There's someone else.* Also in the back of my mind were the sweet-nothings and quasi-lies disguised as terms of endearment, which I had used on other women in order to break them down, to move the relationship to the next level. *I'm a one-woman man. I woke up this morning with you on my mind.* Or the most potent of them all, *You know I love you girl,* though I was very, very careful about using that one. But then maybe I wouldn't have to say anything at all. Something told me Eva's resolve would be difficult, if not impossible, to break. She was backed by a powerful force I wasn't sure I wanted to mess with, someone definitely out of my league.

CHAPTER 13

EVA

A KISS IS never just a kiss. As harmless as it might seem, a kiss is never innocent. Especially between a man and a woman. Especially when it is on the mouth. A kiss is only the first step, the beginning of bigger and more complicated things. This was what I constantly reiterated to the students in the Youth Ministry during our rap sessions.

When you've done something wrong, even if it felt right, it is easy to convince yourself that as long as no one got hurt, everything is alright. I knew I never should have allowed Adam into my house. Simone would say the reason I was feeling guilty was that I had been brainwashed to believe premarital sex—or any activity leading up to it—was wrong. But because I had been there before, and knew how bad things could get, I knew I couldn't engage in casual sex anymore. It would be like taking two steps back, regressing to the old days of uncertainty and powerlessness. In the beginning, I could deceive myself into believing everything was fine, but eventually reality would hit.

And yet, after Adam left, I couldn't stop reflecting on our kiss in the bathroom, about what could be, and then about the worse-case scenario if I gave in. Day in and day out, I thought of his hands in my hair, holding my face, caressing my lips. Every time I made a cup of spearmint tea, I thought of him. When I thought of his hair, the long, thin ropes, fuzzy and sturdy between my fingers, I was reminded of my first Black doll. Until I was five, my mother had always bought Maya and me White dolls. Then one day I stood in the middle of a crowded Toys "R" Us store and screamed, "I don't want a White Rub-A-Dub Dolly, I want a brown one!"

I hated myself for losing control, for allowing him to come into my thoughts at any given moment. We had departed with no promises of keeping in touch, no mention of where, if anywhere, our kiss would lead. What did I expect? I couldn't go any further with him without compromising my beliefs. If I pursued him, I would only be leading him on.

In the days following the kiss, I couldn't help wondering how the old anti-smoking ads had exaggerated, proclaiming that kissing a smoker was like kissing an ashtray. There had been no hint of nicotine on his breath, his lips, only the slightest minty taste of chewing gum or mouthwash. Maybe he had made up his mind he was going to make a move. Maybe my prayers that he would be delivered from the addiction of smoking had worked, I thought. Maybe he would come to church more often, get saved, and . . . Periodically, I had to literally shake my head in order to get Adam out of my mind, get out of the flesh and back into the Word.

Times like this I wished I could relive my initial conversion, when I longed for that feeling of rebirth I had experienced when I was first saved, like breathing fresh air or walking in from the cold into a warm kitchen. Back then, reading the Bible was like reading poetry, the words flowing with a rhythm of their own. Back then, I couldn't understand, couldn't fathom, how some people denied God. I couldn't get enough of God then. Every night since Adam's kiss, I prayed for that feeling again.

During the next week, I immersed myself in church: morning and evening service on Sunday; Bible study on Wednesday, which I had been missing lately; ending with Youth Night on Thursday.

When I arrived at Youth Night, Johnny was all business, quickly going over his structured lesson plan of typed questions. I was distracted, thinking about the terms of the celibacy contract I had broken so far, like being alone with a member of the opposite sex and soul-kissing. Adam was also not officially "a man of God." Then I thought, *I'm an adult, not a teenager!* So why was I seeking redemption? *Brainwashing*, Simone would say. *Christian guilt*, Maya would say. Too many voices in my head, too many cooks in the kitchen.

We were supposed to study Galatians and Psalm 141 in preparation for Johnny's lesson and I tried to concentrate, stumbling through my Bible. Silently, I read along as Johnny called on various students to read out loud. Galatians 5, verses 16 and 17 stayed on my mind: *So I say, live by the Spirit, and you will not gratify the desires of the sinful nature. For the sinful nature desires what is contrary to the Spirit, and the Spirit what is contrary to the sinful nature. They are in conflict with each other, so that you do not do what you want.* I allowed the words to sink in and prayed that the spirit would flow through me, filling me inch by inch. *Why did I let down my guard, allow Adam into my spirit?* I thought guiltily, then I shut my eyes tightly to push the reprimand out of my head. I listened as Johnny took over most of the instruction, answering questions from the most outspoken students about the peer pressure they endured with regards to sex and what to do when they were taunted for being virgins. As always, when Johnny was in charge, I noticed that the boys were more vocal than the girls, who shrugged or gave brief answers when called upon.

Cara sat off to the side against a wall, biting her fingernails, an indication that something was up. I scooted over next to her. She looked up and gave me a quick smile. She scribbled a message on my ditto sheet: *Can I get a ride home? My mom's working late.* I wrote back: *Sure. Is everything okay?* Still biting a fingernail, she wrote: *Me and Chris broke up.* I rubbed an affectionate circle on her back. *Sorry,* I wrote, *his loss—big time!* Looking around, I observed that Chris was noticeably absent. I also noticed that my nephews were missing.

Johnny didn't seem to care that I wasn't commenting as much nor did he seem bothered that the girls were subdued. It was his turn to lead the instruction, so I let him do his thing because it wasn't about competition tonight, but receiving the spirit. As the class drew to a close, Pastor Allen, who had been observing, called on me to read from Psalm 141, interrupting my note passing with Cara. "Unless you ladies have something else you want to share with the rest of us?" he asked, causing everyone to laugh, everyone except Johnny.

Flustered, I flipped toward the end of Psalms, which I had yet to finish, and started reading. When I scanned ahead to verses 3 and 4, I paused, reading the words in my mind first, before speaking them out loud, softly, *"Set a guard over my mouth, O Lord; keep watch over the door of my lips, Let not my heart be drawn to what is evil, to take part in wicked deeds with men who are evildoers; let me not eat of their delicacies."* There were some snickers from a few of the mischievous students when I read the last phrase.

I tried to keep my face expressionless and innocent, so as not to draw attention to myself. But internally, the words condemned me. At the same time I took the words to heart. God was definitely trying to tell me something.

As the youth members began to disband, Johnny blocked the exit door and said, "Remember, immediate gratification may seem more powerful than the long-term reward, but the penalty is tremendous. It's what we do when we don't think. It's what we do when we don't wait on the Lord."

He was looking straight at me as he spoke the words, his face disparaging, which made me wonder if he sensed my spirit was in turmoil. I looked away just as Cara came up to me, ready to go.

For the first ten minutes of the drive, Cara didn't talk much, answering my questions about Chris, school, and home with shrugs, nods, and shakes of head. Then as I neared her street in Logan Square, she began talking, in between bites of her fingernails.

"He kept, like, trying to touch me," she said in her low voice. "When I moved his hand from one place, he, like, kept putting it somewhere else. He never did that before, when we were just lip-kissing. Then, we started soul-kissing and he, like, he became this whole other person."

"So you broke it off?"

"Yeah, I had to push him off me. I pushed him so hard he hit his head on the brick wall. He came at me like he was going to hit me but I pushed up on him and he backed off."

"Cara, you have to be careful," I told her, double-parking the car in front of her building.

She sucked her teeth. "I'm not scared of him."

"It's not about being scared. It's about being safe. It's one thing to defend yourself when someone hits you first, but it's another to be the aggressor."

"I *was* defending myself," she insisted. "I was madder at myself than at him. You know how I used to say that I didn't understand how girls let boys talk them into having sex?"

"Yes?" I answered cautiously.

"It's not even about that. It's not about peer pressure. It's about fighting yourself, fighting temptation. It's like you almost have to have your mind in the spirit all the time, like that scripture said, or you'll give in. You know what I mean?"

I sighed. "I do."

I saw myself in her, but differently than I had before. Her teenage hormones were changing her much like Adam's kiss had awakened the sleeping desire in me. My advice to her would be simple because it would be much easier for her to grasp the corporal consequences of sex than the spiritual ones. All she had to do was look around at other girls who had given in to temptation: the ones who had gone through abortions or been infected with diseases, who became single mothers, and whose education would be postponed or abandoned. I, on the other hand, knew that the spiritual consequences of yielding to temptation would be detrimental, and thus, worse. I understood that when it came to boys and men, even the strongest of girls and women lose their willpower. For as long as I could remember, I had witnessed women lose their minds and make unwise decisions when love, or men, were involved. It affects all kinds of women, whether poor and undereducated, intelligent or well off; none are immune. Maybe that's what God meant when he told Eve, *"Your desire will be for your husband, and he will rule over you."* Perhaps that was why women felt pressured to "have a man." It went beyond being innate because it was a mandate from God.

*   *   *

As I headed home, I called Maya from my cell phone. Normally, I wasn't the kind of person who talked on a cell while driving. Most of the time, I failed to turn it on and Maya and Simone would always harass me about not being able to get in touch with me. I reserved my phone for emergencies, like when my car broke down. But I was experiencing a crisis of sorts, which required urgent intervention and additional reinforcement from my sister, who I knew would understand what I was going through.

"Why weren't your sons at Youth Night?" I asked her.

"I was too tired." She sounded preoccupied and I sensed something was amiss, hoping it was with Alex and not Luciano. "What was the topic?"

"Living by the spirit versus the sinful nature."

"Hmm. So, what's up?" she inquired, waiting.

"Nothing, just going home."

"Something's up. You *never* call from your cell phone unless something's up."

She was right. She knew me as well as I knew her. "I kissed Adam."

"*And?*" she prodded.

"It was a mistake."

"How did it feel?"

"How do you think it felt? After five years, a touch on my arm feels like fire."

Maya laughed. "I know the feeling." She turned away and scolded one of the boys. "Marcos, do you see me on the phone? You can use the phone *after* I'm off. Go away."

"I'm calling you because I need some encouragement in the right direction. Away from him. I don't want to compare notes."

"Kissing doesn't always lead to sex. Why can't you kiss him and enjoy it and not analyze it so much?"

"Because we're not twelve and he's not going to be happy just kissing for too long."

" 'L' doesn't have a problem with it."

"How long do you think that's going to last?"

"I don't know. I'm just taking it one day at a time."

"So, you're planning to sleep with him eventually? Is that what you're saying?"

"No, I'm not planning anything. If it happens . . ."

"Things don't 'just happen.' You know that. Step one leads to step two, and so on."

I heard the boys calling her and arguing in the background.

"I don't want to hear it!" Maya shouted away from the mouthpiece, though she might as well have yelled in my ear. "You know what, you guys need to relax! I'm not kidding! *Re-lax!*"

"What *is* the problem?"

"You know how they get when I'm on the phone. All of a sudden, everybody needs attention." She paused as I heard Marcos asking her a question. "I don't know when I'm getting off the phone, okay? You'll know when I hang up." She exhaled. "Sorry. Sometimes I wished I had had them when you had yours, then they'd be gone by now. Listen, why don't you just ask him if he can be in a relationship without the consummation?"

"Because . . ." I started, but then I stopped because I couldn't verbalize the truth. I knew even though Adam appeared to be a good man, he was foremost a man. He was flesh before he was spirit. For him, being in a relationship involved sex. I wasn't ready for another marriage any more than Adam was ready for his first. And if a relationship didn't lead to marriage, what was the purpose of being together? "I just want to be able to go out with a man to the movies or dinner every once in a while."

"You already have someone to do those things with—me and Simone. As much as you protest, you want male companionship, period. You need a man in your life."

"Maybe I do *want* a man, but I don't *need*—" I started to protest.

"I want to believe you're going to find a man who's going to wait until the wedding night, but in this day and age, I don't know if it's possible, hon."

"What happened to 'with God, all things are possible'?"

It was clear that calling Maya was a mistake. When she first got saved, after Alex's infidelity threatened her sanity and their marriage, she was able to find comfort and justification in the scriptures

for staying with him and forgiving him. I found solace in her fearless, selfless example. I concluded that if she could survive something as devastating as finding her husband having sex with another
woman in their minivan, I could endure anything. Now, her salvation was in as much turmoil as mine. She could not counsel me.

And then I realized she had indirectly given me the answer. Why
not call and frankly ask Adam? Whatever answer he gave me would
influence my decision. Even though there was the possibility that he
could lie and tell me what I wanted to hear, I didn't think he would.
At least, I hoped he wouldn't.

"Did you remember to call Pop?" Maya asked. "It's his birthday."

I gasped. "I forgot. I called him a couple of weeks ago and he
never called me back."

"You know he doesn't check his messages. Anyway, it's not like
he called us on our birthdays. If Marcos hadn't mentioned it, I probably would have forgotten, too."

"Did you send him a card?"

"Yeah. Don't worry, I signed your name."

"Thanks. I'll give you half on the card."

"No, you buy the next one. Father's Day." The commotion in the
background started again. "*That's it!* Marc-Luc . . . I've had it! Let
me let you go. I'll talk to you later—NO! Nobody's calling any little
fast girls—" The line went dead.

Once I made up my mind to confront Adam, I tried not to think
about what his answer would be, because deep down part of me
knew that the likelihood he would be willing to have a chaste relationship was next to nil. And the more I tried not to think about our
kiss and the inevitability that I would never touch his lips again, the
more it came into my mind.

After talking with Maya, I started to drive toward the lakefront,
then changed my mind and drove to the gym instead. The gym was
one of the few fitness centers that stayed open twenty-four hours a
day, seven days a week, not only for people who worked unconventional hours or who were exercise freaks, but for people like me who
needed to blow off steam. I was determined to purge the demon of
desire from within me, so I stayed at the punching bag longer than

usual until my body was coated with sweat and I smelled like a man. When I stopped to buy a bottle of water from the vending machine, I noticed how men and women alike looked at me as if I were a crazy woman on a mission. I never sparred with the other women because I didn't like to get hit. Hitting unleashed my aggressions and cleared my mind, but getting hit only made me angrier. As I punched the bag, the words I had read earlier came back to me: *Set a guard over my mouth . . . keep watch over the door of my lips, Let not my heart be drawn to what is evil . . .* I punched the bag harder and faster.

The combination of Youth Night, Maya's suggestion, and boxing made me feel rejuvenated. When I got home, I slipped into a hot, soaking bath, something I hadn't done in a long time. I lay back in the tub, with the phone on the vanity table, so I wouldn't have to get up if it rang. Then I remembered I hadn't called my father. I bit the bullet and dialed his number on the speed dial. As I listened to each ring, I closed my eyes, waiting. My father's answering machine wasn't picking up, so I figured he had probably disconnected it, something he had done before, or he had turned the ringer off so that he wouldn't be disturbed. Sometimes, I believed he was home, just listening to the phone ringing. After the tenth ring, just as I was about to hang up, he answered.

"Happy Birthday, Pop," I said.

"Thank you."

"How are you?"

"Tired." A decorated firefighter until a year ago, my father had refused to retire until the department forced him. Even before his retirement, it seemed like something was missing from his life. Now with no work to keep him occupied for part of the day, his life seemed emptier. He told me he started playing the piano again but besides visiting the older members of our family who still lived in Chicago, I really wasn't sure what he did with his time.

"How are my grandsons?" he asked.

"They're good. You should call them."

"If they need anything, they'll call me. I got a card from Tony."

"Did you get ours? From Maya?" I asked, cringing.

"I did. *Gracias, mija.*"

I leaned into my neck pillow and closed my eyes. Talking to him was like watching TV, a one-sided activity, waiting to see what happened. I was too exhausted to keep the conversation going. Through the phone, I listened to him inhaling and exhaling, a sure sign that he was still smoking. He had promised to quit after his older brother, my uncle, was recently diagnosed with emphysema. But I didn't harass him.

"So, you married yet?" he asked.

I opened my eyes. What a strange question for him to ask. "Wh— Why would you ask that?"

"I don't know. I just think you should consider marriage again. Now that the boys are gone."

"Who says I want to get married?"

"Don't wait too long. Don't wait 'til you're old like me."

I wanted to tell him that he was alone because he wanted to be alone. It was always easier for a man to find a woman willing to marry than for a woman to find a willing man. Not to mention that he was at that age when some men took younger wives. But as always, the things I wanted to tell my father stayed in my mind, unspoken and buried.

"Pop, I don't know if I want to get married again."

"It's not good for women to be alone."

"But it's okay for men?" I challenged.

"It's different for men."

Yes, of course it is, I thought, thinking of all the double standards I had heard all my life. It was okay for men to have sex with many women but not vice versa. It was okay for men to wait until forty to get married, but not women. It was okay for men to be alone, but not for women. Of course, in God's eyes, I knew none of these standards was acceptable for men either since Man had corrupted God's words and His original intentions as man had with many other things. It was the secular world that had set the standards that were deeply ingrained in our society and difficult to eradicate from even the most open-minded thinker.

"Pop, I got to go," I said, suddenly sleepy. "Good night."

*   *   *

The following Sunday, Pastor Zeke, as was his practice, reiterated the preceding Bible study and Youth Night topic with a similar sermon: "Spirit Versus Desire."

I shifted in my seat, my arms, butt, and legs sore from overdoing it at the gym. Maya and her sons sat to my left, but Alex and Simone were no-shows. It was my turn to host the Sunday brunch, but when service ended, Maya said she had something else to do.

"What?" I challenged.

"Uh . . . I'm meeting 'L,'" Maya said cautiously as soon as Marcos and Lucas climbed into the SUV and out of earshot. She knew it was no use lying to me. As part of the reparations for reconciliation, Maya had demanded that Alex replace their minivan with a Lexus sports utility vehicle.

"Maya. I've been meaning to talk to you about . . . 'L.' I don't like this. I don't like him. I'm telling you this because I love you. You need to let him go." I tried to pick my words carefully, not be judgmental and self-righteous.

"We're just having breakfast, that's all," Maya said, looking around desperately as if someone were listening in and could decipher our conversation. She didn't understand that the only One who mattered was everywhere and He heard and saw all. *What you do in the dark shall be revealed in the light.*

"I already know how you feel," she continued. "But I can't help it. Haven't you ever loved someone so much it hurt when you couldn't be with them?" she pleaded.

I looked at the anguish on my sister's face and I tried to understand. "No," I told her honestly.

"How's Adam?" she asked.

Immediately, my face grew hot, but I quickly recovered. "What I feel for Adam is not love. Sure, there's an attraction, but not seeing him doesn't hurt. Maybe it's confusing now that I had a small taste, but it's not painful. Our situations are entirely different."

Each day that Adam didn't call was a confirmation that God was interceding on my behalf, protecting me from whatever "evil" could happen if he did call me, to tempt me to eat of his "delicacies." I was safe as long as I was being enriched by the Word and in the company of others who were struggling spiritually like me. But once I left the sanctuary, I was at the mercy of the world and my own carnal thoughts. And that was not love.

"Eva, I envy your commitment to celibacy; I wish I had that kind of commitment for my marriage. But I'm not strong like you—"

"Yes, you are. You're stronger. Staying with Alex after what he did. Putting your children before yourself and staying in your marriage. That takes more courage than leaving. You are a good person—"

"Stupid is more like it. I should've left when I had the chance. I could have been with 'L' now."

"Sweetie, he'd still be with his wife."

"No, he wouldn't," she retorted, then looked around at the church members walking to their cars, talking, hugging, and blessing each other. It was too noisy for anyone to hear anything. She opened the driver's door, but before she could climb in, I embraced her. "Don't go," I whispered in her ear. "Come over and we'll talk."

She pulled away. "I'm a grown woman."

"I'm your big sister."

"By one year."

CHAPTER 14

ADAM

THE PARTS OF the Bible that have stuck in my mind are the stories that were sensationalized by Hollywood: *The Ten Commandments* and *The Greatest Story Ever Told*, or the phrases that were quoted and misquoted over the years in everyday conversation and popular media: *Dust to dust, ashes to ashes. Pride goeth before the fall.* Although I had witnessed the transformation of people who had found Jesus, I did not fully understand what it meant to be saved, to have a personal relationship with Him. Of course, I was "brought up in the church"—went every Sunday—where I was compelled to memorize passages and scriptures that were indoctrinated into me much the same way as the alphabet was until the Word was as logical as "B" came after "A." When I was twelve, I was asked if I accepted the Lord as my personal savior, and I answered yes, even though I wasn't sure what it meant. All I knew was that Mama and the Sunday school teacher told me I wouldn't go to heaven and that was all I needed to know. When you're twelve, going in the opposite direction is a very scary thought.

But knowing the Word was pretty much meaningless without role models who lived by it. My mama of course set a good example as a God-fearing woman, but she was, after all, a woman, and what I needed was a male role model. Growing up, nobody told me my father wasn't supposed to be perfect, so I believed in the myth that he was infallible, invincible. To me, he was like a god who could do no wrong. I cherished and worshipped him and when he fell from grace, it just about shattered my belief in anything good.

"Today's your father's anniversary," my mother reminded me on the phone. For the past nineteen years, at the same time of the year, we had the same conversation. She would call and remind me it was the anniversary of my father's death, then ask me to come with her to the cemetery. I would decline, she would try to change my mind, I wouldn't, and then she would give up and go with my sister and her kids. "Are you coming to the cemetery?"

"No, ma'am." She knew that when I used that expression it wasn't about being respectful, but facetious.

"You know your father accepted the Lord before he passed."

"Funny how some people do that when they know they're going to die. After they've done all their sinning."

"Some people got to see the light before they see the light. You got to learn to forgive as God forgives."

"Yes, ma'am."

"So, you're not going?"

"No, ma'am."

"Alright, I'll go with your sister."

"Alright. Bye, Mama. Love you."

"I love you, too. Your daddy loved you, and the Lord loves you."

"Yes, ma'am."

After I pressed the "off" button on the phone, I pressed "talk" and began dialing Eva's phone number, then hung up before the last digit. *God, what is wrong with me?* I thought. Lately, I had been doing that off and on, sometimes without thinking. I wanted to call her, but at the same time, I wanted to forget about her.

I went into my office space and tried to pick up where I had left off the weekend before with my screenplay. When I talked with Eva about my writer's block, she suggested I incorporate spirituality into the theme, re-read some Bible passages like that of the Prodigal Son to get some insight into the father-son relationship. I told her I knew more about that particular relationship than I cared to. She said a lot of literature and films, even pop culture, borrowed from the Bible, only they hid the spiritual message underneath rhetoric, action, violence, and sex. When I sat down and thought about it, I realized she was right. As I sang along to *The Best of Kool & the Gang* on the stereo, I began revising the synopsis for my screenplay, writing for several hours.

When the phone rang, it startled me out of a nap on the sofa, where I had moved with my laptop. I prayed it wasn't Luciano. When he told me he was going to give me a break and crash at his brother's for a while, I had to try very hard to hide my elation.

"Hey, favorite-Big-Bruh-wonderful-uncle. Feel like watching your niece and nephew tonight?"

"Where are *you* going?" I asked Jade, yawning.

"To a movie."

"With?"

"This guy."

"I want to meet 'this guy.' What's his name?" It was the third time she had asked me to babysit so she could go out with "this guy."

"Akil McClaren."

"A-kill? What kind of name is that?"

"It's A-*keel*. It's Arabian and no, he's not Arabian. He's Black. Stop acting like my daddy."

"I'm worse than your daddy. I'm your worst nightmare: a brother without a love life."

Jade laughed, whining, *"C'mo-o-on."*

"If I don't meet him, I don't babysit."

Akil was a medium brown–skinned brother sporting the beginnings of an Afro and wearing an earring. He didn't appear nervous to meet me but he didn't overcompensate by trying to impress me. I shook his hand extra hard and kept shooting guarded looks at him to warn him that my sister was very precious to me. He seemed like a decent enough brother, but like any big brother, I was suspicious of any man who dated my sister. I didn't want Jade's heart broken since she was on the rebound, having been through a turbulent marriage and a bitter divorce. Furthermore, I didn't trust a man who went out with a divorced mother of two young children. It is a well-known fact that when a man wants a vulnerable woman, single and divorced mothers make the easiest prey. I had dated a couple of single mothers myself with the same intentions; it wasn't something I was proud of, but like most men, I didn't see the errors of my ways until the tables were turned and it was my sister who was being played.

I thought of Eva and determined that she didn't count as a vulnerable divorced woman since her children were grown. She didn't need a man for the essential things since she had her own career, a house, and possessions, and it appeared she was determined to stay single if she couldn't find a man who shared her beliefs. Based on what I had seen, she didn't look like the lonely type, but a woman who enjoyed having her space, as I did. According to Eva, she wasn't looking for a husband. Then I thought, maybe her celibacy was a cover-up for her ultimate goal: marriage. Maybe marriage *was* her ulterior motive.

Babysitting at night was easy because by the time Jade dropped the kids off, they were usually tired from preschool if it was a weeknight, or from running around with her all day on weekends. Because they watched enough cartoons and videos and didn't get to see their father as often as they should, I always played old-fashioned games with Kia and Daelen, games like Horsey, Tea Party, and Wrestle Mania. Before I knew it, I was carrying them off into the bedroom, one over each shoulder.

Afterward, I searched through my video and DVD collection, looking for a movie I hadn't seen in a while. When the phone rang, I picked it up absentmindedly, answering, "Yeah."

"Hey," was all I heard, but I knew it was Eva.

"What's going on?" I said, trying to sound casual. It had been a couple of weeks since I had gone to her house, washed her hair, and kissed her. The memory made my stomach muscles tense up and I rubbed my torso to ease their tightness.

"Not much. What're you doing?"

"Looking for a movie to watch."

"Hmmm."

I waited for her to speak, to tell me why she was calling. When she didn't, I filled in the empty space. "I was working on my screen-play earlier. I thought about what you said, about adding some spir-ituality into the theme."

"And?"

"And I decided to make one of the characters really religious while the other one is struggling with his spirituality. Both of them are at different stages of fatherhood and they go on this road trip to confront their fathers who abandoned them."

"Sounds good. Much rounder than 'two buddies go on a road trip to visit the fathers who abandoned them.'"

I laughed at her recollection of my one-line, rough-draft blurb. "You want to take a look at the new synopsis? Tell me what you think?"

"Yeah, e-mail it to me. My address is on my card. Have you come up with a title?"

"I was thinking about 'Prodigal Sons,' but I'm still debating."

There was a long pause as I waited for her to get to the reason for her call. She cleared her throat.

"I want to ask you something," she finally said.

"Okay," I said, pulling the leather footrest up to the entertain-ment center and sitting down.

"Do you think you could ever be with a woman, I mean, be in a relationship, and not be intimate?"

I scratched the back of my neck, speechless. My first impulse was to laugh, but I knew it wouldn't be appropriate so I cleared my throat.

"It's not a difficult question," she said. "It's either yes or no."

"Let's just say, the last time I did that, I was, like, fifteen. Maybe fourteen."

"I thought so."

"Why do you ask?" I inquired, even though I knew it was obvi-ous.

"Because before I got saved, I went out with men and, you know, had these empty relationships. Not a lot of men, but enough. And having . . . having sex with men without a purpose, without it lead-ing somewhere, took a lot out of me. Like I said, I don't know if I ever want to get married again, you know. I've been there and al-most got married again. So, since I don't know if I ever want to get married again, and I can't have sex outside marriage, I have this dilemma." She paused and I thought, *Yes, you do,* but I didn't say anything. "I like you and I liked kissing you, but I don't know how long that would last before, you know . . . you want more. Or I want more. You know what I'm saying?"

"Yeah, you want a guarantee up front."

"I don't know if it's so much a guarantee because I know there are no guarantees in life. The only guarantees are when you trust in God."

I had no answer to that.

"And I know that you don't believe in God the same way I do. I don't even know if you believe in salvation. Do you?"

"I used to think that it meant if you believe Jesus is the son of God, you were saved."

"And now?"

I exhaled. "And now, I don't think it's that simple."

"But that's the beauty of it. It *is* that simple. John three, sixteen."

She was quiet then and I didn't know what to say, although I wasn't ready to hang up. I sat up and again started thumbing ab-sentmindedly through the videos and DVDs, not really looking at the titles, waiting for her to continue talking or hang up.

"How did you like Danté?" she asked.

"I liked them. I couldn't follow the words much, but the beats were tight."

"Did you decide on a movie?" she asked.

"Why? You want to come over and watch one?" *Why did I say that?* I thought, mentally kicking myself.

There was another long pause and then she said, "I don't think that's a good idea."

"Relax. I'm babysitting my niece and nephew. They're light sleep-ers."

"What are their names?"

"Kia and Daelen. Kia's four, going on five; Daelen's three."

"That's nice of you."

"What, babysitting?"

"Yeah, I don't know too many men who do that."

"My sister, Jade, just went through a rough divorce and every once in a while she needs a night out. She's seeing this new guy."

"I wish I had had a brother like you," she said. "When I first got divorced."

"You have a sister. You guys seem close."

"We are. But she was going through her own stuff back then. My boys really needed a father figure. I didn't bring any of my dates home because I didn't want them to think that I was trying to replace their father. Until Victor."

"Victor?"

"Victor was the man I was engaged to. About five years ago. We moved in together and . . . it didn't work out."

She didn't go into detail so I didn't press for any. I finally came across a movie I hadn't seen in about a year. "Did you see *The Matrix*?" I asked her.

"Yeah."

"What'd you think of it?"

"Overall I liked it. I thought it was a sensationalized version of the Second Coming. But since Hollywood can't deal with God on a realistic level, it had to emphasize the violence and the action, and then throw in a romance."

"See, I don't agree. I thought it was more about society living in a one-dimensional world, how man has allowed himself to be satisfied with conformity until Neo comes along."

"Don't you think Neo represented a kind of savior? And their use of biblical names: Zion, Nebuchadnezzar, Trinity. I mean, the final fight scene between Neo and the agent in the end—that was symbolic of the ultimate battle between good and evil. Armageddon."

"That's an interesting theory, but I think the writers would probably disagree with you."

"Of course they would. They wouldn't have been able to make all the money they did if they had concentrated on the spiritual subtext."

I put the movie into the VCR and pressed the rewind button. We both listened to the tape rewinding noisily, not saying anything.

"Sooo . . . ? You coming over or what?" I knew she wouldn't take me up on my offer, but part of me hoped she would surprise me.

She didn't answer and I imagined her clasping her hands, debating.

And then I heard the slight interruption of her call-waiting signal. "Thank God for call-waiting," I said in jest. "Or should I say AT&T?"

CHAPTER 15

EVA

WHEN MAYA INVITED me to Adam's house for a barbecue, initially I told her I didn't want to go. Apparently, Luciano was throwing the barbecue as a thank-you to Adam for giving him a place to stay when his wife kicked him out. He had finally moved into his brother's house, or so he said. More and more, I was beginning to dislike the idea of Maya having a life on the side with Luciano like they were a couple, and especially when she included me. Then she said Luciano specifically wanted me to come, that he wished we could get to know each other. I believed the get-together was merely an excuse for him to spend more time with Maya, but I was looking forward to the chance to tell him what I thought of him, in person. If he wanted to get to know me, he was going to find out why they really called me "Evileen."

Adam's loft was located in an old part of the city where my family had once lived years ago, before it became prime real estate. His building, and the ones in the surrounding area, had once been factories that had employed the working class in the sixties and seventies. As I knocked on the door, I could hear India.Arie's album, *Acoustic Soul*, echoing from inside the loft. The door was opened by a miniature and feminine version of Adam, his sister, Jade. Her hair was a lighter shade of brown, bordering on dirty blonde, and she looked more like she was in her early twenties than thirty.

"Are Kia and Daelen here?" I asked her.

She appeared taken aback that I knew her children's names. After recovering from her initial surprise, she said their grandmother had taken them to an arts and crafts show. She then introduced me to her date, Akil, whose name and face looked a little familiar.

"I know you, don't I?" I asked him as we shook hands. Akil was not a common name.

"I don't know. Do you work at U of C?"

"No, Chicago U." Then I recalled from where I remembered him. "You go to TCCC?"

"Used to. I live on the North Side now, so I go to Evangel Church of Christ."

"Okay. What a small world."

We talked a little about Pastor Zeke and which members were still at TCCC, which ones had left. Jade watched our interaction quietly, but not with jealousy, more like amicable curiosity. I remembered Adam saying she had just started seeing Akil, so perhaps it was important to her that everyone liked him.

I held up the covered dish of rice and beans toward Jade. "I brought a dish."

"Great. You can put it in the kitchen. Adam's in there."

Even though there was a smile on her face, I could see her scrutinizing me with her hazel eyes. I had tried not to get too dressed up, picking an off-white sarong and peasant blouse, but under Jade's questioning eyes, I wondered if I looked desperate for her brother's attention.

Adam's place was a typical bachelor's pad, a spacious loft with lots of glass, leather, and art deco furniture. I could see almost every room from the door's entrance, except for the bathroom and bedroom. The loft had pale oak hardwood floors throughout and floor-to-ceiling windows where a faint outline of Chicago's Gold Coast skyline could be seen in the distance. With the exception of a few splashes of red in the throw pillows and scattered rugs, everything was black, white, and gray. There were a few abstract paintings and African sculptures on the exposed brick walls and some framed photos on the coffee and end tables.

On the balcony, I saw Simone with Ian, the owner of the hair salon. She was sitting on his lap like he was Santa Claus. Ian was fifteen years older than Simone and treated her like a daughter; in fact, he called her "Babygirl" and she called him "Daddy." Maya was leaning against Luciano, who was tending to the grill. He saluted me with the barbecue fork. I wasn't ready to interact with them just yet. I waved and continued toward the kitchen.

From the kitchen, Adam looked up slightly where he was bent over the sink, a smile slowly spreading across his face as I got closer. The way he was looking at me, his head down, his liquid eyes peering from under his shaggy raised eyebrows, made me feel suddenly flushed.

"Hey there. You didn't have to bring anything," he said, as he rinsed off two chickens in a bowl of water and vinegar.

"Hello," I said holding out the dish. "It's just rice and beans."

His eyes lit up. "Red beans and rice?"

"We say 'rice and beans.' It's a Puerto Rican staple."

"It's also a New Orleans Creole dish. My ma's people are from there."

"Well, these here beans are from a can, and the rice is from a box, courtesy of *Goya*," I quipped.

"You mean they're not homemade? Oh, you're bogus." He laughed.

"Hey, when you're a single mom, you learn to cut corners. They taste homemade. At least that's what the labels say." I laughed along with him.

I set the dish on the stove and leaned against the granite countertop.

"Cool hat," he said, inspecting my straw Panama hat with an amused look. "Have a seat. There're some drinks in the fridge. Pop, iced tea. Sparkling white grape juice." Seeing my curious look, he smiled and said, "Somebody introduced me to it."

I noticed there was also beer in the fridge and wondered who was drinking, but I didn't ask. "I really like your place," I said, pouring myself a tall glass of iced tea.

"Thanks."

"I love this song," I commented, nodding to India.Arie's "Brown Skin."

"It's one of my favorites, too."

I watched him as he skillfully cut the chickens into quarters, the sinewy muscles taut on his scarred arms. Forcing myself to look away, I glanced around the kitchen: the spotless stainless-steel fridge and stove, white oak cabinets, and bare granite countertops; nothing out of place.

"I haven't bought her new CD yet but I heard it was fierce," I commented.

"I have it. I can burn it for you if you want. Then we'll be even."

"Thanks." When my eyes roamed back around to him, I caught him staring at me as he blindly and expertly excised the chicken's innards. I cleared my throat. "Do you like Tracy Chapman? That's who India reminds me of."

"Ah, the original neo-soul girl," he said favorably. "I haven't played her in a while. I got a few of her albums."

"Did Maya tell you we used to live not far from here? Back in the seventies, our parents had an apartment near Chicago Avenue and Noble."

"The neighborhood was really different then."

"Yeah, I can't believe how it's changed," I said wistfully. "Pretty soon they'll be knocking down the projects and the Y."

We delved into a conversation about the pros and cons of gentrification—though we both agreed there were few pros—and the long history of housing segregation in Chicago. After a while, Jade and Akil, followed by Simone and Ian, wandered into the kitchen and joined the discussion.

It was apparent that Jade was very possessive of her older brother, affectionately punching his arm or hugging him as they teased each other. She touched Adam more than she did her date. It was almost as if she wanted to prove to everyone that no one was closer to him than she was.

Before long, Luciano and Maya came into the kitchen. They were holding hands and it irritated me, more so than watching them kiss that first night.

"I thought the party was on the balcony," Luciano said.

"We were just going out there," Adam told him. "Eva brought some rice and beans."

"Some *Cubano* beans?" he asked.

"No, Puerto Rican beans," I said.

"Puerto Ricans don't know beans about beans."

"What makes you such an expert? You're only half Latino," I blurted out. The silence that followed was thick with discomfort. Maya shot me a venomous look that could've burned a hole through me if she had had super powers. Luckily, India.Arie's cut "I See God in You" began to skip and everyone volunteered to fix it, leaving me and Adam to deal with the uneasiness that still hung in the air. As he meticulously sprinkled seasoned salt and pepper over the chicken, he glanced periodically at me from under his brows, waiting, I guess, for me to say something.

"I'm sorry about that," I said, burying my face behind my glass of tea.

"You don't have to apologize to me."

"Yeah, I do. That was petty. Maybe I should go."

"No, you shouldn't. Luciano isn't the sensitive type. He'll get over it."

"Look, I know he's your boy and all. And I have nothing against him, I just don't like him in my sister's life. I don't trust any man who's unfaithful to his wife."

"I thought you said it was her life and all you could do was pray."

I held his gaze for a few seconds. "You sure have a good memory."

"Besides, your sister is cheating on her husband, isn't she? Do you trust her to make her own decisions? Her own mistakes?"

"No. A woman is . . . A lot of women are different in situations like this. They're vulnerable and fall harder than men. Most of the time they're doing it out of spite but they end up falling harder for the guy. Men can have flings and move on. It's harder for women to recover."

"If Maya's marriage is strong, if she really loves her husband, then she will overcome this. If it breaks up, then maybe it was inevitable. Now, let's go and enjoy ourselves."

Adam grabbed the aluminum pan full of seasoned chicken as I followed him to the balcony, carrying my dish. "And play nice," he added.

"I'll try."

It was an Indian summer day, unseasonably hot for the middle of fall, the wind deceptively warm and breezy. Luciano avoided all eye contact and conversation with me, which was just fine. I saw him devouring the rice and beans though, along with a couple of beers. I tried to catch Maya's reaction to his drinking, but she, too, was dodging my eyes. As much as I regretted being nasty to him in public, I hoped he got the message that we were never going to be friends.

I felt slightly uncomfortable since it appeared everyone was supposed to be paired up and Adam and I were presumably a "couple," even though technically, we weren't. We were the only ones not standing or sitting near each other, or touching. Adam was busy tending the meat on the grill because, according to everyone, his barbecue was legendary, even though Luciano was supposedly the host. There was plenty of conversation going around so that it was more of a fun group affair than an intimate event and for that, I was grateful. Occasionally, our eyes locked and I was thankful for my hat and sunglasses so he couldn't tell when I was watching him. And I couldn't help but watch him: the way his royal blue T-shirt hugged his upper arms; the way his faded relaxed jeans fell loosely below his waist, snug at the hips; the way he attended to his guests, and joked around with his sister, displaying his generosity and affection. And the way he put up with Luciano. Only a true friend would tolerate someone so crass and immature. *God*, I thought, *why not him?*

Somehow I was unofficially appointed the DJ, which gave me a chance to get away from the couples whenever the discs needed changing on the five-disc CD stereo. Adam and I had similar music tastes like seventies' funk and early Prince, but he also had a lot of CDs by jazz artists whom I had never heard of, even though I liked the genre. The only gospel album I saw was Yolanda Adams. I inspected the few framed photos in his entertainment center: a picture of him with his mother and sister at his college graduation; one of his sister and her children against a Christmas background; and one of his two little brothers, Justin and Ricky, taken at Six Flags Great America. There was none of his father.

"You're doin' good, Mizz DJ," Adam commented when he came in to check on me.

"I can't find any of your Chapman's," I told him.

He sat down next to me on the floor and hunted through the racks. "They're in here somewhere. They can't all be missing." He began pulling out handfuls of CD cases, at first skimming through them slowly, then searching like a madman. "I had four or five of them. They can't—"

Then he stopped as if suddenly remembering where they were, or rather, who might have taken them. After Victor and I split up, he took my Celia Cruz CDs, not because he liked her music, but because he knew how much I did and he thought I was going to beg him for them.

"Alphabetical order usually works," I told him.

"Oh, like your library of books," he kidded.

I looked at him puzzled and then remembered that he *had* been in my house. He met my eyes and then we both looked away at the same time. I sensed that he was remembering the same thing: the kiss. When I returned my gaze, he acted as if he wanted to say something but didn't know if he should.

"Hey!" Luciano yelled from the balcony. "Come out here, you lovebirds! I'm about to make a toast."

Adam flashed a vicious look at Luciano who had already turned his back. I got up from the floor slightly self-conscious.

"Sorry," he mumbled, as we walked to the balcony.

"How old did you say he was?" I asked flippantly to lessen Luciano's adolescent remark.

Adam smirked, but I could tell he was just as bothered by the comment.

Luciano threw his arm around Adam's shoulders and shook him as soon as he stepped onto the balcony. "I just wanted to say that this dude, *this* dude, is the best kind of friend anybody can ever have," Luciano said. It was evident by his speech and his narrowed eyes that he was slightly drunk. "Whatever you need, he's always there for you. Except he doesn't keep enough food in the house."

"Enough for me," Adam said sarcastically, looking a little embarrassed and scratching the back of his neck.

"One of these days, this man's going to make some woman a perfect husband, a little *too* perfect, I think. The man even cleans his own place, *and* cooks. But that's the way ladies like 'em. Faithful, affectionate, submissive—just like a dog, right, Dawg?"

Another uncomfortable silence ensued, followed by the clearing of throats and averting of eyes. The music was flowing, so there was no excuse to leave the room this time. I finally met Maya's eyes and I gave her a look that said, *This is the man you want to be with?* When she turned away, I knew she read my mind.

Adam nudged Luciano's arm off his shoulder and shook his head. I squinted at the skyline. I was ready to go home.

"Get away from that railing," Jade said, pulling Luciano away from Adam. "Before Adam pushes you over."

"I'm just messing with you, bruh," Luciano protested over his shoulder, as he was led inside.

"Whatever," Adam said, putting out the embers in the grill. I waited for him to look at me so he could see my empathetic expression, but he didn't glance up for a long time.

For the remainder of the evening, I had succeeded in steering clear of Luciano, then, just as I was about to leave, I went to the bathroom and almost ran into him exiting. As he passed me, he flashed me a forced smile, but I stared straight ahead like he was invisible.

In keeping with the decor of the rest of the apartment, Adam's bathroom was black, white, and gray, with splashes of red in the towels and accessories, and just as immaculate. I wondered if he had a cleaning lady or if he really did his own housekeeping. I couldn't resist peeking into the medicine cabinet, where I found the expected shaving products and equipment, hair oil, and several expired prescription bottles: naproxen sodium, Tylenol with codeine, and Vicodan. From my vast history with analgesics, I knew they were strong pain medications.

When I came out of the bathroom, I was startled to find Luciano leaning against the opposite wall.

"Can I speak to you for a minute?" he asked.

I stood in the bathroom doorway, away from him, and crossed my arms and waited, my face impassive.

"I just wanted to apologize for the crack I made about Ricans and beans. It was out of line. Even though I was kidding."

I wasn't planning to apologize but since he was being civilized, or at least pretending to, I decided to meet him halfway. "I'm sorry, too. I shouldn't have snapped on you." *But I'm glad I did*, I thought wickedly.

"I asked Maya to invite you because I wanted us to get to know each other better. It's important for her that we get along. For some reason. She doesn't want you to hate me."

"I don't hate you," I said, which was the truth. I didn't like the way he added "for some reason." Like he didn't care one way or another if I liked him or not. At least the feeling was mutual.

"You don't like me very much."

"I don't know you."

"Exactly. If you knew me, you'd know that I care a lot about Maya."

"Well, I *love* her. And I don't want her to make a mistake she'll regret just because she wants to get back at her husband."

"Is that what you think she's doing? I knew Maya before she met Alex."

For some reason, hearing my brother-in-law's name coming out of Luciano's mouth really bothered me. He was getting too familiar. "I knew Maya way before she met you."

His eyes narrowed as he looked down at me, breathing hard through his nose like a bull about to charge. I got the feeling that he was the kind of man who would hit a woman if he thought he could get away with it. I reminded myself that he was inebriated and that I didn't really *know* him and those two circumstances together could lead to unpredictable consequences. But I didn't allow him to intimidate me and I held his glaring eyes with my own.

"You know, Adam's a real nice guy. I hope he rubs off on you. Maybe if you start concentrating on your own love life, you can let your sister handle her own."

"Hey, you guys talking about me?" Maya teased, as she slipped behind us and linked her arms into each one of ours, dragging us into the living room area. "Did we make up? Are we getting to know each other?"

"Oh, yeah," Luciano said sarcastically.

"Mm-hmm," I echoed.

It was getting late but everyone else was settling down in the living room to watch a movie on DVD. I didn't know about Adam, but I was not about to sit down among three couples and ignore the sexual energy as they all stole secret looks or touches. I announced that I had to get home and feed King, not to mention I still had some office work to do before Monday rolled around. As I said my farewells, Adam pulled me onto the balcony.

"I saw you and Luciano talking earlier," he said. "He didn't get out of line, did he?"

"No. He apologized, I apologized. We're not friends, but we don't hate each other." I didn't mention Luciano's comment about Adam rubbing off on me or his suggestion that I concentrate on my own love life, since I didn't think anything would be gained from disclosing this information.

"I'm sorry about that. He can be a jerk sometimes. Especially when he's drinking."

"I'm just sorry he's your friend. You deserve better friends."

He handed me a blank envelope, which wasn't sealed. I pulled out two tickets to the Danté concert in a couple of weeks. "Where did you get these?"

"I was scanning *The Reader* last week and I ran across the ad."

"Thanks. Maya heard they were coming to Chicago. She was the one who introduced me to them. She's going to love this. How much do I owe you?"

"Well, I thought we . . ." Adam started, and then I realized that he hadn't bought the tickets for Maya and me.

"Oh, you got these for . . . you and me?" I was embarrassed and I could tell by his look that he was just as uncomfortable.

"No, I mean—if you want to go with your sister . . ."

"No. I want . . . we can go. I just thought you didn't really like the music. You said you couldn't understand the words."

"I like the music. I said I couldn't understand a lot of what they say, but I like it."

"Okay. Let's go. How much were the tickets?"

"Don't worry about it."

"No, I want to pay for mine."

He scoffed. "Do you always have to be so . . . such a feminist? Do you think I expect something in return? I don't. I'm not the kind of man who keeps a tab on the amount of money I spend on a woman."

"I'm not a feminist," I objected. "I just feel better if I pay my share. That's the way my mother raised me."

"Well, my mama taught me that a gentleman always pays."

"That only goes if you're dating. Or in a relationship."

"Fine," he said curtly. "Twenty bucks. It's a fund-raiser."

"You're not mad, are you?"

"No, I'm not," he snapped, but it was obvious he was. "I just saw the ad and I thought this would be something you'd enjoy—"

"And like a typical woman, I ruined a nice gesture."

"I didn't say that."

"Look, I think we just need to establish some rules up front so we know where we stand. So we don't misunderstand each other."

"Like?"

"Like, we have to decide whether we're going to be friends doing things every once in a while, or if we're going to date."

"I think we've gone beyond friendship, don't you? Friends don't kiss like we did. I mean, we obviously feel something more than friendship. Right?"

I clasped my hands together, but he grabbed them apart and held them. Surprised by his sudden touch, I looked quickly toward the balcony's glass doors and saw Jade turn from the TV screen to glance over at us curiously. We were far enough away so we couldn't be heard, but I still felt self-conscious because we were in plain sight.

"Am I right? Eva?"

"I told you, that kiss—"

"I'm not just talking about the kiss," he implored. He took a couple of steps away from the windows so the others couldn't see us, pulling me with him and steering me against the brick wall. My hands started tingling with anxiety and I pressed my fingernails into the palms to stop the feeling. I couldn't meet his eyes so instead I looked at the scar on his chest. I didn't like being so close to him and yet, I could feel my heart quicken. It wasn't like when we were in the bathroom and the kiss happened so suddenly. Then, I didn't know what to expect. Now, I knew exactly what could happen. He placed one hand above me on the wall and swept off my hat with the other hand, flicking it on the table like a Frisbee. Then he took a strand of my hair and began to twirl it. I could smell his musk cologne mixed with charcoal and barbecue sauce. He smelled so good. I bit my top lip, then the bottom, hard, to keep myself in check. *Set a guard over my mouth* . . . He leaned in and I tensed up, pressing my head against the wall. *Keep watch over the door of my lips* . . .

"Adam . . ."

He slipped the shades slowly down my nose and tossed them on the patio table. "The sun set an hour ago."

"If we're going to date, you have to realize . . ." I informed him, slowly losing ground, ". . . that I'm serious about my celibacy."

He bent his head, gently parting my lips with his bottom one, and then he began probing the inner crevices of my mouth like he was searching for something he had lost. When his tongue found mine, a tide of desire washed through my body. Before I had a chance to protest or kiss him back, he pulled back.

"You asked me if I could be with a woman without having a sexual relationship," he began quietly. "The answer is, 'I don't know.' I've never had that kind of a relationship with a woman. Every woman I've been with, I've gone to bed with. You said you can't be in a relationship that may not lead to marriage, but you don't know if you ever want to get married again. I *know* I'm not ready for marriage. Eventually, I do want to get married, but not for a while."

He was still twirling my hair around and around his finger, until his hand reached my scalp. Something told me I should take my hair back before he started to massage my scalp, make me weak like he did before. I reached up and took hold of his wrist, but I didn't push him away.

"I haven't stopped thinking about you since I met you. Those are my honest feelings. Now it's your turn," he continued.

As he spoke, all kinds of thoughts ran through my head. How incredibly smooth he was, how everything he was saying would have made the average woman melt, how he was only telling me what he thought I wanted to hear. My first instinct was to challenge him, to let him know I wasn't the average woman; my second was to believe him and be completely honest with him in return. But how did I know he was telling the truth? I went with my first instinct.

"You say you're being honest, but how do I know for sure—"

"Oh, my God!" He released my hair and slapped the brick wall with his other hand.

I was momentarily taken aback by his anger and his use of the Lord's name in vain, so I ducked under his arm to move away from him, where the balcony's five-foot-high railing and wall met. Even though heights made me dizzy, at that moment, I felt safer being close to the railing four flights above ground level than being near him.

"It amazes me how people use God's name so carelessly but are so afraid to use it in praise as easily," I told him, not caring if I sounded high and mighty.

He slowly stepped in front of me. "Sorry. I'm sorry. It's just that you make me so . . . crazy. Here I am opening myself to you . . . If you think this is a cheap attempt at getting you to change your mind, to get you to have sex with me eventually, let me tell you, I don't have to work this hard. There are women out there I could have, easy."

I looked at him askance. I wasn't sure if I was supposed to feel grateful or jealous by his last statement.

The wind was picking up in intensity, and without my hat to keep my hair in place, it blew wildly all over. He reached out to brush it away from my face, but when I crossed my arms, he stopped. He gripped the railing instead and continued. "But I don't want that. What I'm trying to say is, I'm willing to make an effort to have that kind of relationship with you and whatever happens, happens. But don't assume that you know what's going to happen, 'cause you don't. Nobody knows. You're not a psychic or a prophet."

"You don't have to be a prophet to see the future."

Adam leaned against the railing with weariness and held up his hands as if in surrender. I grappled with my inner voices. *Is this man for me, God? He said he's willing to try. Should I believe him?* I didn't have to wait long, because the answer came in the wind. *Yes, yes, yes.* Or maybe I thought I heard it.

Nervously, I peeled myself away from the corner and stood in front of him. He looked at me with what seemed like tired, lifeless eyes. I reached up and attempted to cup his face with my hands, but this time, it was he who pulled back in defense, as if I were going to hurt him. As I pulled his face down to mine, he still looked suspicious, his thick brows furrowed. With my thumbs, I stroked his eyebrows, taming the wild hairs that were sticking out, easing their tension.

"*Adán*, you've been on my mind, too. A lot."

And then our lips touched.

CHAPTER 16

ADAM

THE DANTÉ CONCERT was in a small club called God Search, a sort of spiritual "Star Search" for religious artists who were looking to succeed in the Christian music industry. Apparently, Danté's drummer was related to the owner of the club, who had arranged for them to play a benefit. The place was jumping just like a real concert, complete with people raising the roof, albeit in praise, and holding up cigarette lighters. The way the crowd was yelling and clapping and dancing gave the impression that they were high on drugs or booze. Maya caught me eyeing them suspiciously and explained that they were high on the spirit. While I was feeling the music, swaying to the reggae beat along with everyone else, I didn't feel the same holy fervor that Eva and Maya seemed to be feeling as they lifted their hands in worship, their eyes closed in reverence. Even with gospel, my main choice of worship music, I had never felt truly "blessed" and I found myself envious of their open devotion.

When Maya heard I was taking Eva to the concert, she bought two more tickets for her and Luciano. But Luciano backed out at the last minute, claiming he had to do something for his mother. He didn't tell Maya the truth, that Lisa had finally called him because she was ready to talk. The night of the barbecue, he had deliberately gotten drunk and made a fool of himself because he couldn't bring himself to tell Maya. Things went according to his plan when Maya left my place angrily, making it easier for him to go back to Lisa. In his place, Maya invited Simone, neglecting to tell her that Danté was a Christian band, evidenced by the skin-tight zebra pantsuit she was wearing. Though Luciano's comments comparing me to a loyal dog at the party angered me, I had dismissed them as the words of a jealous and intoxicated man.

After the concert, I saw Maya grab Eva's arm with desperation, leaning against her as they walked ahead together toward the parking lot. Eva looked back at me helplessly. I had no choice but to walk with Simone who, from the little time I had known her, seemed to be a very self-assured sister in need of much attention. Although she had two men in her life who apparently supplied her needs, she didn't seem happy or satisfied. But since she had been Eva and Maya's friend since high school, something kept their friendship intact.

"How did you like the concert, S'Monée?" I asked, remembering how she had corrected Maya's pronunciation of her name when we were first introduced.

"I could kill Maya for inviting me," Simone said furiously, hugging her jacket around her.

I smiled. "I'm guessing she didn't tell you they played Christian music."

"Did *you* know?"

"Yeah. I heard them before. I like the music."

"Man, it just seems like everywhere I turn these days, somebody's trying to get me saved. I mean, I go to church—every once in a while. I'm a good person—most of the time. I'm happy with my spirituality. Why can't people just let people believe what they want to believe, you know what I'm saying?"

"It must be hard to be the friend of two sisters who are so close," I said, gesturing toward Eva and Maya who were whispering and clinging to each other as if they were privy to a conspiracy.

"Sometimes. I have two sisters but we're not as close. They were always so jealous of me when we were growing up. Maya and Eva are closer to me than they are. The only area we don't see eye-to-eye is this salvation thing. Oh, and Eva and I definitely don't agree on the topic of men."

When I didn't answer, she continued.

"Like I don't think one man can satisfy one woman's needs and vice versa. And I don't believe you necessarily have to love someone to have sex with them. Eva thinks sex outside of marriage is a *sin*." She said the word "sin" like it was a curse word.

I smiled evasively and didn't say anything since she really didn't ask me a direct question.

"What do you think? You think you'll change her mind or will she change yours?"

I took the Fifth once again, knowing how women talk and that anything I said would almost certainly get back to Eva.

She laughed. "Alright, it's none of my business. Did you know we call her Evileen?"

"To her face or behind her back?" I asked, trying not to show my amusement.

"Both. 'Cause she's such a man-hater."

"I don't think she's so much a man-hater as she is selective."

She looked at me skeptically. "Are you one of those saved people?"

"Well, officially, I did accept Jesus as my savior when I was twelve, but I guess they'd say I'm a backslider since I don't go to church regularly and all."

"*Et tu*, Judas?" she asked.

I was surprised with her astuteness at mixing Shakespeare and the New Testament, and I guess it showed on my face because she laughed again and nudged me.

"I'm not just a pretty face and a great body," she teased.

Her coquettishness made me a little uneasy and I was glad when we reached Maya's SUV in the parking lot. Maya hurried somberly into the passenger side of the truck.

"So, what's up for the rest of the night?" Simone asked as Eva walked up.

"Maya wants to go home. She's kind of upset," Eva explained.

"Why?" Simone asked. Eva gave her one of those surreptitious looks women give each other that only they can understand. I looked away pretending I was invisible and waited. Maya had picked up Eva and Simone in her SUV, so I knew either they would all go with Maya and have a therapy session, or Simone was going to draw the short straw and have to play the role of chauffeur and nursemaid. Although I was looking forward to having dinner with Eva, I also knew I was the new guy and could easily be the first casualty.

"I'm not ready to go home," Simone said stubbornly. "I'm hungry."

Eva gave her a harsh look and then pulled Simone's jacket sleeve, dragging her toward the rear of the truck. I could see they were arguing and I decided to do the right thing and make myself scarce. I walked up to them.

"You guys go on ahead. We'll talk later, Eva."

"No. Simone's going to take Maya home," Eva said firmly, looking grimly at Simone. "She's in no condition to drive." I glanced toward the truck and saw Maya's face puffy from crying. I felt slightly guilty but at the same time glad that Eva wanted to be with me as much as I wanted to be with her.

"What is she, drunk?" Simone asked bitterly.

"Good night, Simone," Eva said.

"*S'Monée*. Why can't you respect my wishes and call me by my name? Adam did," Simone demanded, her eyes blazing. She opened the driver's door. Then she turned back around. "Hey, how am *I* supposed to get home?"

"Tell Alex to drop you off. Or spend the night. Figure it out, *S'Monée*," Eva retorted.

As we walked toward my car, I began to wonder if it was a good idea for us to have dinner since Eva seemed so irritated, not to mention that during the concert, I had noticed her wincing and surmised she had one of her headaches, although she didn't complain. I didn't want her to take it out on me. When she had leaned against me during a slow song, I could smell the mint massage oil on her temple combined with her usual rose oil scent.

"We don't have to do this tonight," I offered. "If you want to go with your girls . . ."

"No, I'm fine. I'm just tired of being everyone's therapist. Everybody thinks I'm supposed to be this strong person and I have all the answers. But then they don't like the answers I give them."

My car was parked several spaces away in the lot. I surmised that Maya's meltdown had to do with Luciano, recalling how Maya had excused herself several times to go to the bathroom, clutching her cell phone. I caught the look of exasperation and disgust growing on Eva's face. We both knew she was trying to reach Luciano on *his* cell.

"She finally got hold of Luciano," Eva said after we rode in silence for several blocks. "She knows he wasn't at his mother's." I still wore my poker face but she didn't call me on it. "She could tell by the way he was talking that he was with his wife. You know, cagey, whispering. She thinks he was in bed with her."

"Well, she *is* his wife."

"Yes, she is."

"Is she going to be okay?"

"Of course she is. Maya's strong. As long as she leans on God and stays away from Luciano, she'll be fine."

I didn't respond.

"She'll be okay," Eva said as if trying to convince herself. "I'll call her later."

We had reservations at Buono Dio, one of the many restaurants that were sprouting up in the increasing gentrified areas all over Chicago. The restaurant boasted a neo-Italian-American cuisine. I ordered my staple steak and potatoes with a pesto salad, while Eva ordered whitefish with garlic vegetables, the sauce on the side. She always insisted that all her condiments be served, "on the side," which usually elicited rolled eyes or blank stares from the waitstaff. It was something that would have driven me crazy in any other woman, but not with Eva.

She looked cool and chic in a paisley print pantsuit, the jacket long to her calves and a backward Kangol beret on her head. Her hair was gathered in a relaxed ponytail, loose tendrils hanging from the sides of her temples. In the last two weeks, since the night she confessed her feelings for me, we kept in contact via phone calls and almost daily e-mails. I had kept the compliments and endearments to a minimum, trying to play the cool brother, knowing she would see through my radar. But every once in a while, I slipped. I called her "babe" a couple of times over the phone or inserted rose icons into my e-mail messages.

We had met for lunch or dinner a few times in the weeks before the concert, and went to the movies and cultural events on the weekends, during which I noticed many things about Eva. For example, she wore only Indian or African costume jewelry. She never wore dresses, something I had always thought was characteristic of Christian women. When she wore skirts, they were long, almost to her ankles. Her blouses covered her arms and hid even the slightest cleavage. I was dying to see her legs and arms and I wondered if maybe she was concealing some flaw, or scars, but I refused to dwell on the negative. On one unseasonably warm day, she wore capris with high-heeled sandals, and the sight of her small perfect bare feet with pearl-polished toes and smooth veins distracted me to the point where I lost my train of thought.

The previous Sunday, she had talked me into going to church to hear a visiting pastor. The pastor, who had a thick Brooklyn accent and must have been a former stand-up comedian, told jokes throughout his sermon, and had the whole church in stitches. He had an awesome testimony, which included an abusive childhood, drug addiction, and a prison stint where he found Jesus. I was humbled by his journey, amazed at how far he had come. When altar call was announced, I expected Eva to nudge me or glance my way, but she didn't. I sneaked a peek at her and noticed that she was praying fervently, her eyes closed, and I wondered whether she was praying for me.

"What did you pray about?" I asked her afterward. "Or is it like birthday wishes, it won't come true if you tell someone?"

"I prayed for everything." Then she smiled secretly and added, "And everyone."

"You want me to get saved?" I then asked, knowing I was treading precarious, sacred ground.

"That would be great. But you should come to the Lord for yourself, when you feel the spirit, for the right reason. Not for anyone else."

But sometimes I felt like she was trying to convert me subliminally, on the sly, slipping under my sinner's veneer like a spy, using buzzwords like men used pickup lines to woo women.

I had actually contemplated taking the walk up to the altar, saying the words, wondering if it would make a difference in our relationship. But since I knew I'd be doing it for the wrong reason, it was a little too sacrilegious even for me. To me, her pious world was a whole other culture, a whole other dimension.

Eva convinced me to return on poetry night to read again from *Sinner*. I didn't get sick on this occasion, focusing instead on Eva's forehead the entire time. After the reading, I sold the surplus copies of my book to benefit the local women's abuse shelter. I didn't mind donating part of the proceeds since it was a worthy cause and the books *had* been collecting dust in my self-storage unit.

"Do you know what Buono Dio means in English?" Eva asked, bringing me back to the present while methodically cutting into her fish and gliding a forkful into her mouth.

I tried hard not to leer at her lips as she chewed. "I know 'buono' is good . . . Dio, I'm not sure."

"God. It's means 'Good God.'" She moaned as she chewed her food.

"That good, huh?"

"Mm-hmm." She offered me the next bite.

I accepted the morsel, grabbing hold of the fork as I delicately took the food into my mouth, gazing at her through half-closed eyes. Sometimes I did things like that just to see her reaction. Most of the time she smiled indulgently, as if I were a child in need of patience. This time she held my eyes and she didn't pull the fork back. I couldn't help but think about the kisses we had shared in the last two weeks. While I had enjoyed kissing her and was slightly intrigued by the pseudo foreplay, I didn't know how much longer I was going to be able to keep it up. The power I had envied in women like her was beginning to drive me mad. And yet, I still wanted her. Wanting her was testing my patience. Lately, I was becoming short tempered and irritable—a side effect, I told myself, from wearing the smoking patch. Whoever said absence makes the heart grow fonder was definitely not talking about abstinence.

"Maybe they should have called it 'Good Food,'" I suggested, letting go of the fork, and she laughed, the awkward moment broken.

The food *was* good and we were both hungry, so we resumed eating and I cooled it on the flirting.

"You want to taste this?" I asked, giving her some of my pesto salad.

She shook her head emphatically. "Pesto has eggs. I'm allergic to eggs."

"That's too bad. So you can't eat *anything* with eggs? No cake, cornbread—?"

"Nothing. I don't need the calories anyway."

"You don't look like you have a weight problem."

"Ha!" she laughed, and began telling me about her battle with anorexia and crash diets. Periodically, she winced in between bites and eventually, she excused herself to go to the bathroom—I assumed to take her headache medication.

The night before, I had called Sondra to ask if she had taken my Chapman CDs when she moved out. I figured that it had been more than a year and we were definitely over each other. Of course, I could have let her keep the CDs and just bought new ones, but considering what happened just before we departed, I didn't think she would assume I had a hidden motive for calling. It wasn't even the principle of the matter. More than anything, I hated a thief.

"What makes you think I took them?" Sondra had asked, her voice flowing through the phone smooth and pure like milk and honey.

"They're all missing. And you're the only one I know who liked her as much as I did."

"It could've been one of your other women."

I didn't bite at her attempt to inquire about the state of my present love life.

"So, are you seeing anybody?" she then asked bluntly.

"Are *you*?"

"What do you think?"

"Do you have my CDs or not?"

"Yeah, I have them."

"Can I have them back?"

"Is that what you want? Is that really why you're calling me? Because really, Adam, you can just buy new ones or download them from the Internet."

"That's time consuming and I have better things to do. Anyway, they're mine." I sounded like an insecure immature jerk, but I didn't care.

"You want me to bring them over now?"

I tried not to picture her lounging lazily in bed, in a skimpy T-shirt and underwear, her eyes half closed as she smiled seductively into the phone. I was tempted, man was I tempted, but my insecurities got the best of me. There was no way I was going to risk a repeat of our last encounter. I could see her laughing at me already. And then there was Eva. We were officially going together, even though with past women that included physical consummation, and even though there was a possibility that it might never happen. Any other day . . .

"I don't think my lady would like that."

There was a significant pause on her end and as juvenile as it was, I felt vindicated for that unfortunate incident during our last sexual encounter. For one glorious moment, I felt redeemed.

"I'll mail them to you," she muttered, before hanging up.

After what seemed like an excessive amount of time to use the restroom and take a pill, Eva still had not returned and I began to get worried. I signaled the waiter.

"Can you have one of the waitresses check the ladies' room for my date?"

"I think the lady, she is sick," the waiter said in a heavily accented European English I couldn't quite place. He indicated toward the restroom area. "She say not to bother you."

I got up and hurried toward the restrooms and found Eva sitting in the hallway, in a lounge chair, her head in her hands.

"Eva, are you alright?"

Startled, she looked up quickly, her face twisted in pain and tears brimming her half-closed eyes.

"You have a headache," I stated matter-of-factly. "I'm taking you home."

She waved me away. "It's not bad. I'm supposed to take this new medication as soon as I feel a headache coming on. I waited too long. I'll be fine." It was obvious that she was in terrible, excruciating pain.

I sat down next to her. "Give me your hand."

"What? Why?"

"Give me your hand," I insisted.

She extended it and I firmly pinched the web between her thumb and forefinger.

"Breathe deeply," I told her. She closed her eyes and inhaled, exhaled, then moaned. "How does that feel?"

"I can feel the pain going away, a little." I momentarily stopped applying pressure. "Now it's coming back again," she said.

"It's called 'acupressure.' Something about invisible channels of energy in this part of the hand being connected to the head. My mother used to do this when she got stress headaches during my father's illness."

"I've read about that. Your hands and feet are supposedly related to different organs or something. I always thought that stuff was quack medicine."

"My mother believes in all that mess. She won't take any kind of medicine. She has to be really sick to go to a doctor."

"My mother was the same way. Then one day she had a headache, laid down, and died in her sleep."

"Oh, man."

"She had a brain aneurysm. I was always afraid that my migraines were a symptom and that one day I would have an aneurysm. But the doctor assured me that they're almost always sudden. I get an annual MRI just to be sure."

"And they've never found anything?"

"Yeah, they told me that my symptoms are consistent with migraines," she said dryly. "I was, like, 'thanks for stating the obvious, guys.'"

As I listened, I intermittently pressed and released her hand. "How does your head feel?"

"Better."

"Seriously?"

"Yes. I guess there is some truth to it. Either that or the medication's finally kicking in."

"Because there's a pressure point in your foot that works for headaches, between your first and second toe—"

She smiled wanly. "You are *not* touching my feet."

"You ready to go home?"

"After the coffee."

"I thought doctors said coffee was bad for migraines."

"Are we reading medical journals now?"

"Internet."

We got up and walked back to the table. As we waited for our coffees, I took her hand again and started massaging it between both of mine. Her skin was so soft it made my stomach clench. Perhaps because I had been abstinent so long, every little thought, smell, or touch of her set me off. *God, your skin is so soft,* I thought, wondering what the rest of her body felt like. I wanted to say the words, but I knew she wasn't the type of woman who bought compliments, even well-intended and truthful ones, so I didn't even try to put it out there. And knowing her for the short time I had, she might have taken it as a sexual comment. Judging by the way she broke her stare, however, I knew she must have read the pleasure in my eyes. The waiter brought our coffees and we pulled back. It was getting late and we were almost the last patrons in the restaurant. There was only one other table, where two loud and lively couples remained.

"You talk about your mother a lot, but you don't talk about your father too much," Eva said sipping from her cup.

In all our conversations, I had always managed to evade any discussion of my father. I would give her short answers or conveniently change the subject. Sensing my hesitation, Eva looked apologetic.

"I'm sorry. I didn't mean to pry. I don't like talking about my father too much either. I understand."

But then I started the saga of my father, beginning with the good, going into the bad, and ending with the ugly—meeting my half brother and half sister and their mother at the funeral. I felt as if a weight had been lifted from my chest. It wasn't that I had never talked to anyone about my feelings for him, it had just been so long.

"And you've never visited his grave?" she asked.

I shook my head.

"Why not?"

I shrugged. "No use."

"I think you should visit it. I go every year, on my mother's birthday."

"Yeah, but you loved your mother."

"And you loved your dad, *no*?"

I liked it when she ended her sentences with a Spanish "no" or peppered her dialogue with Spanish words or phrases. It was something else about her that made her so out of the ordinary, and made me feel like this time, things were different. And it wasn't, as Luciano claimed, that I saw her as this exotic woman just because she was of a different ethnicity. When we walked down the street, Black women didn't give me the evil eye like they did when I was dating the French-Canadian female. For all they knew, Eva was one of "them"; a Black woman. Most times, because of her bronze skin and curly hair, I forgot she wasn't a sister. It was only when she spoke Spanish, which she rarely did, that I was reminded.

"Before I found out what kind of a man he really was," I finally answered. "Yes, I guess you could say I loved him."

"After my mother died, my father dropped us off at my Aunt Titi's," Eva said quietly. "He didn't tell us why or anything. He didn't talk about my mother again, never mentioned her name. Then he stopped coming to visit us, and whenever we wanted or needed something, we had to track him down. It was like he had divorced us and stopped being our father."

"And how often do *you* visit him?"

She paused and looked down at her cup, turning it counter-clockwise slowly before looking up at me with a gleam in her eye.

"I told my father about you."

"What did you say about me?"

"I told him I'm seeing this man whom I like very much."

I smiled my gratitude. "And he said?"

"*Otro moreno?*"

"What does that mean?"

"Another Black man?"

That stung. I made a mental note to stay away from Papa Clemente. "He doesn't like you being with a Black man?"

"He would just prefer that I be with a Hispanic man. I mean, he likes Alex. And he liked Anthony—until he cheated."

"Do *you* want to be with a Hispanic man?"

"Remember what I said? You can't help who you fall . . . who you like." She smiled coyly and interlocked her fingers through mine. I remembered what she had said: *You can't help who you like, or fall in love with. Or think you love.* But I didn't correct her. "I want to be with you," she continued.

I thought maybe I should return the same sentiment but she didn't seem to expect it. Although she squeezed my hand, her mind seemed to momentarily wander away.

"I don't think I've ever forgiven my father for what he did back then," she said, then looked into my eyes. "Have you? Forgiven your father?"

"I can't forgive someone who's no longer here."

"Can't you?"

I contemplated the question and thought about my father's infidelity, and although I still felt I didn't owe him anything, I began to wonder for the first time in years whether it was time to start facing my demons.

CHAPTER 17

EVA

HE WAS HOLDING my lips hostage, tightly but tenderly with his teeth. In turn, I was trying to get him to release them by holding his face in my hands, slowly pulling his head away. My body was trying to convince me it was tired of fighting, while my mind was screaming *NO!* One minute we were debating the spiritual connotations of *The Matrix*, the next minute he was asking me how to say his name in Spanish. He was babysitting his niece and nephew again, and this time, he had succeeded in persuading me to come over and watch *The Matrix*. One minute we were sitting on the floor eating popcorn and Raisinettes, and the next we were tasting each other's tongues. Although his arms were neutrally on the small of my back, moving slightly up, at the same time, he was pressing me closer to him. The slight aftertaste of mint coupled with the buttery popcorn and sweet chocolate lingered on his tongue as it tangled with mine. This was a dangerous kiss, more sensual than the others, more urgent. I kept trying to convince myself that as long as we were just kissing, in a sitting position, I would be fine.

His hand moved up to my neck, palming my throat as if he were going to choke me, then he proceeded to caress the back of my neck. Suddenly, he stopped kissing me and I was relieved, able to take a few deep breaths. I slowly opened my eyes. I was ready to end our moment of reckless passion, at least for the night, but his face lingered in my personal space, the air between us sweet, salty, and heavy with expectation.

"How do you say lips?" he whispered into my parted mouth, his voice sensual and full of urging.

I swallowed before answering. *"Labios."*

"I thought it was *'besame'*?"

"That means 'kiss me.'"

He obliged, caressing my lips in his mouth like one would hold something sharp: cautiously and tenderly. *Smooth,* I thought. A Spanish lesson had always been part of the courtship with the non-Spanish-speaking men with whom I had been involved. With Anthony, it had lasted a couple of months; after we married, he refused to learn and actually got angry when I spoke Spanish, especially if we weren't on friendly terms and he overheard me on the phone. With Victor, it was always a competition because he thought Venezuelan Spanish was more refined than that of Puerto Ricans.

Adam's hand slid down my throat to my sternum where my heart was beating like crazy, hastened by his touch. I could feel my flesh getting weaker and my spirit all but withering away. I breathed slowly through my nose but didn't move to stop him, though I knew I should. In between gasps for air, I heard moans—strange, pleasurable sounds I had not heard coming from inside me in a long time. They scared me. I tried to swallow the sounds, but they still escaped. I knew I had to gain control of the situation, soon.

And then he started pushing me back, down to the floor, his loose locks brushing forward obscuring his face, prickling mine. I was reminded of my dream with the Oak Tree Man, the branches stretching down, caressing my face and neck. I recalled how the branches had started to twist around my neck, around my body tighter and tighter until I was suffocating. It was like a premonition.

"Adam," I whispered, struggling to sit up. He was kissing my throat, still pushing me down. I had one hand on his rock-hard chest, the elbow of my other arm anchored to the floor. He was so strong, solid like a wall. He came up again to my mouth, just as I uttered his name again with more gravity. *"Adam."*

"Say it in Spanish," he whispered.

"Adam. Wait. Stop a minute." I pushed his locks back with one hand, away from his face, trying to regain eye contact and get his attention. But he wouldn't open his eyes, hiding his face in my neck and covering it with soft pecks.

"Eva, don't do this," he begged, and I could feel the anguish in his voice.

"The kids might wake up."

He started chuckling, looking down at me with crinkled eyes. "That's funny."

I laughed, glad for the respite. But just as suddenly, his eyes narrowed with lust and he leaned in again.

"I just want to kiss you, I swear," he said seductively, grabbing my lips again, but I turned my head.

"Adam, you know I've been celibate for . . . a long time . . ."

"I know, I know."

I pushed against his chest firmly just as he zeroed in again. "I'm serious. We need to stop," I said, putting a little bass in my voice.

Finally, he leaned back against the sofa, exhaling loudly and pushing his hair back in exasperation. We didn't say anything for a while, each lost in our own thoughts.

We had been seeing each other for a month, getting acquainted during lunch and dinner dates almost every day, and every weekend. One night, I had cooked an old-fashioned Puerto Rican dinner for him; he in turn cooked a down-home Creole-Georgian supper for me. It felt strange, weird, and wonderful—cooking for a man—something I hadn't done in a while. I had actually enjoyed it, but I knew I would feel differently if I was expected to do it on a regular basis. During that time, we had succeeded in keeping things fun and relaxed, just bordering on the romantic and sensual, and ignoring the sexual intensity that was undeniably growing between us. Overall, our hands had remained in neutral zones, though there were times when we both went a little too far, when our bodies got a little too close during our good-byes. His kisses left me breathless and light-headed, like when I used to deliberately starve myself. Back then, I knew starvation wasn't good for my body, just like I knew our passionate kissing wasn't good for my soul now. Each time, our kissing encounters lasted longer and longer, building up, leaving me to wonder if he knew this would happen all along, that sooner or later, he would wear me down until I would break.

"Eva, do you honestly think anyone waits 'til they're married to have sex? Even Christians?" he asked quietly.

"I've heard of people. People who've gotten married in our church. This one couple didn't even kiss for seven years until their wedding day."

"How do you know for sure? Were you with them twenty-four/seven? It's not possible. How do people know if they're compatible?"

"It depends on how important you think sex is in a relationship."

"Very. If it wasn't important, God wouldn't have made our bodies the way He did."

I wanted to tell him that he sounded like Anthony at eighteen, before he touched my behind, when he was still trying to get into my pants. One of his favorite lines had been, *Nothing's going to happen that you don't want to happen.* It reminded me of what my mother used to say: *People can only do to you what you allow them to do.*

"What happens if you get married and on your wedding night, you find out the sex is bad. What do you do then?" he asked.

"I'll work it out with my husband. Sex isn't rocket science. Otherwise, we'd all be geniuses."

He stared out of the floor-to-ceiling living room windows, rubbing the back of his neck, his eyes avoiding mine. I crossed my legs Indian-style and took a deep breath. I knew our relationship was going to end, if not tonight, soon. He was not going to wait.

"You know, nothing about Adam and Eve was about love," he said.

"Why are you always bringing up Adam and Eve? We're not Adam and Eve. I'm Eva Clemente; you're Adam Black."

"Because you insist on making this about your religious beliefs," he retorted, whipping his head around to look at me with tapered eyes. "Celibacy is based on religion, isn't it? The apostles, priests, and nuns. The way I heard it, God's purpose in creating man and woman was about companionship and procreating generations of followers. God didn't say 'man needs someone to love,' He said 'it's not good for man to be alone.' Love was never mentioned. Even having children isn't about love. What's that passage? About bringing children into the world in pain?" He turned away again, and I suspected he didn't want any answers to his questions.

I looked at his profile as he stared out the windows, his arms resting on his upraised knees, his voice even. He knew more about the Word than he let on, but he was the kind of person who dissected every word, argued it too much instead of accepting it as is. The Word was not debatable.

I prayed the phone would ring, anything to keep me from having to make the decision that I knew had to be made. I hated myself for being weak, for not being strong enough to turn to God for strength. And then, I did. *Help me, Lord,* I thought. Then I mouthed the words as Adam's voice continued on in the periphery.

"Look, I'm not trying to sweet-talk you or convince you to have sex with me now, okay? I said I was going to try to have this relationship with you, and I am trying. But, you know, we can't continue kissing . . . we can't continue like this and expect . . . you can't expect me not to feel anything."

Closing my eyes, I waited. *Just say it's over,* I told him in my mind. *Make the decision.* I had been strong all my life: through my mother's death, my father's withdrawal, my failed marriage, my children's tough years, and the bad times in my relationships. I had always made my own decisions without consulting anyone. I didn't begin relying on God for strength until after I got saved, and lately, I hadn't been leaning on Him enough. *Be the strong, independent woman you've always been,* I heard the voice within me say. *Be a woman of God, for God's sake.*

Then there was the other voice. *Why? Why did I always have to be the strong one? Weren't men supposed to be the stronger sex, the heads of households? Why couldn't he practice restraint and wait? Wait for what?* I was tired of being strong. Being strong was too hard. It looked real good to the outside world, a shining example to aspiring superwomen everywhere, but on the inside, it was wearing out its welcome, it was wearing me thin.

For once, I wanted to sit back and let someone else take control. I closed my eyes and folded my hands in my lap face-up and thought back to the previous Sunday's sermon: "Let go and Let God." It was directed toward singles in unhealthy or mismatched relationships. *"Let go of that mate and let God pick your fate,"* Pastor Zeke had declared. Lately, it seemed as if every sermon contained a hidden message specifically aimed at my life. Or maybe it just seemed that way because I was so distrustful of my own decisions that everything appeared to hold a possible answer.

Father God, help me. Give me the wisdom to do the right thing here. Give me a sign.

"What are you thinking?" I heard Adam ask.

I shook my head slowly, breathing deeply, without opening my eyes. The answer had not come to me yet, so I kept quiet. It would have been easy to speak without thinking, but for once I didn't give myself permission to relinquish him the answer he was hoping for.

"Eva . . . Will you look at me?"

I didn't allow him to interrupt my thoughts, and for the next few seconds he didn't say anything. Slowly, the answer came to me. *Let go.* It was then that I realized I had been relying on the wrong person to take command. *It is better to take refuge in the Lord than to trust in man.* I had expected Adam to take command, take control, when I should've been giving that power to God. I opened my eyes and looked down at my hands. He was right; I did do that a lot.

"Unc-Adam." We both looked up at the same time at whom I assumed was Kia, Adam's niece. She was a chubby little girl with a head full of long, black rumpled curls, rubbing her Asiatic eyes.

Immediately, Adam rushed over and picked her up.

"I heard my mommy," she whimpered.

"Mommy's not here yet. That's my . . . my friend, Eva. This is Kia."

"Hi, Kia," I said, waving and getting up from the floor to sit on the sofa, but Kia was half asleep, her head buried in the crook of Adam's neck.

"Mommy should be coming soon," he crooned in her ear. "Go back to sleep."

As Adam rocked Kia, I realized the sign I had asked for was right in front of me. I knew that eventually, if and when he married, he would probably want children. At thirty-six, he was at the prime age for marriage and children. I knew that having children was more than a possibility, and *that* further sealed our fate. I didn't want any more children, I knew that without a doubt. I never regretted having my children in my early twenties. I loved the shock on people's faces when they heard that I had two sons in college. I didn't envy my coworkers who were starting families for the first time in their thirties, even their forties. Raising children was hard and doing it on my own had been even harder. When women told me they wanted a challenging job, I would joke, *"Try being a single mother."* The thought of having another child, even if I had a husband to help me, was not appealing. In five or ten years, whenever my sons decided to marry, I would be a grandmother. I could see myself looking forward to being a grandmother, but not a mother. Adam had said it himself, in introducing me to Jade and even Kia. We were friends and anything more was just not going to happen. Accepting this realization gave me some consolation.

"What?" Adam asked, noticing me watching him.

I shook my head, not realizing I was still staring, and smiled. "She's adorable."

"She takes after her uncle."

He carried Kia back to the bedroom, which was on an elevated platform behind a stationary glass-block partition at the end of the loft. He returned, braiding his front locks back and slumped down on the floor at my feet, as if he were tired—perhaps tired of me. I stayed on the sofa, as far away from him as possible.

"You're right," the voice came quietly from within me.

"What?"

"I was thinking, you were right. I can't kiss you without leading you on."

"I didn't say you were leading me on. I said you can't expect me to feel nothing. I respect your beliefs, I do. I don't always go to bed right away with every woman I meet."

"But you expect it eventually."

"I would be lying if I said no."

"Fornication is a sin," I reminded him, though I knew going a spiritual route was useless at such a physical time.

"Adultery is condemned more in the Bible than fornication."

Not wanting to get into a religious debate, I changed the subject. "This is hard for me, too, you know. I haven't been with a man . . . in a long time. A *long* time."

"What? A year? Two?"

Right then and there, the words flowed from my mouth like water. I began my testimony, telling him about my relationships with Anthony and Victor, and the others. I confessed my promise to God, and told Adam how hard it was to hold on to my beliefs and yet still doubt myself. And finally, I told him that even though I had feelings for him, I was willing to risk losing him if it meant breaking my vow.

"Five years, huh? Man." Then he made a confession of his own. "It's been over a year for me, almost two years. Since the radiation and chemo, I haven't been with a woman. I tried to get back with my ex-girlfriend and . . ."

I waited for him to continue but when he didn't, I went on. "It might sound like a fantasy, but I guess you could say I'm waiting for Mr. Righteous."

"Mr. Who?"

"Righteous. That's what Maya and I call a man of God. A man who's saved."

He looked away, toward the windows again. He had the potential to be a man of God, I reasoned. No, God had given me a sign. He wasn't the one.

"You think maybe we should just be . . . ?"

He groaned and leaned his head back on the sofa. "Please don't say 'friends.' "

It took everything within me not to run my hand over his hair, to reach down and kiss his lips one last time. He was wearing an army shirt, buttoned down to reveal his smooth chest and his scar, ripped jeans, and Doc Martens boots. He might as well have been wearing a Brooks Brothers suit.

"I wasn't going to say 'friends,'" I said. "I was going to say *amistades.*'"

"What's that?"

"'Friends' in Spanish."

"You're a regular stand-up comedienne, you know that?" He reached for me and struggled to get to his feet at the same time, while I tried to evade his grasp. We landed on the sofa, side-by-side awkwardly, laughing, our faces just inches apart. He wrapped his arms around me but I kept my arms at my sides, my eyes lowered.

"Eva, Eva," he whispered with disappointment, as if I were going to regret my decision, like it was all my fault. *Did he have to keep saying my name?* "How do you say 'look at me' in Spanish?"

"Let me up first," I commanded, attempting to free myself.

He held me down. "No. Tell me first."

"Mírame."

"Mee-rah-may?"

"MEE-rrrah-meh, accent on the first syllable, roll the 'r.' *Mírame—*"

Even before he dived in for another kiss, I anticipated him, so I turned my head just in time, glancing down at my watch. "I really got to go. I told Maya I'd drop by before I went home."

He sighed with resignation and finally got up, helping me to my feet. "This late?"

"She's still bummed out about Luciano. I told you, it's harder for women to move on." I walked toward the door, reaching for my calf-length leather on the coat rack.

"You don't look like you're having any difficulties," he said, helping me with my coat, "moving on."

"Well, I'm not like other women," I joked.

"No," he said, leaning against the door as I put my Kangol on my head, "No, you're not." He adjusted my cap so that it was backward. "I like it better that way."

As I dug around my pockets for my car keys, he reached his hands into my pockets and pulled me toward him. "Do you really want to be *'amistades'*?"

His breathless voice in my ear gave me what my mother used to call *calor frio,* roughly translated, a hot-cold feeling from my head to my feet. I shuddered. *Stay strong,* the voice within me encouraged.

"Adam, don't make this harder than it already is. Please," I said, trying to make my voice kind, but instead it sounded like it belonged to a cold-hearted witch, a woman who didn't need anything from anybody—Evileen.

"Okay, Eva, my frrriend," he said in an exaggerated Spanish accent, like Al Pacino whenever he tried to play a Hispanic. "Goo' nigh', my frrriend." He took his hands out of my pockets and unlocked the door.

"Oooh, that's so wrong," I said, pretending to be offended.

He walked me to the elevator, leaving the front door open so he could keep an ear out for his niece and nephew. As we waited, we talked about ordinary things like the changing weather, the upcoming holidays—things strangers talked about when they were stuck waiting in line. When I got on the elevator, he reached in and kissed me lightly and quickly on the cheek, pulling back before I had a chance to kiss him back.

At Maya's house, Alex answered the door just as I knocked. He had a dismal look on his face and it was apparent he couldn't wait to escape.

"I don't know what's wrong with your sister," he said, brushing past me as I walked in. "But I'm tired of trying to figure her out."

"Where is she?"

"In her so-called sanctuary downstairs. She won't talk to me. I'm going to pick up the boys from my brother's. I'll see you later."

I heard Sade's "Love Is Stronger Than Pride" blasting before I reached the basement stairs. During her post-depression days, when she was trying to forgive Alex, Maya had hopped from one home-improvement project to another—tearing down walls, sandpapering, and renovating the entire house in an effort to bury her pain, hurting Alex where it mattered: his wallet.

I found Maya in the refurbished basement, her last and most expensive project, which she had to fight Alex for, tooth and nail. I had envied the stone and brick walls, mosaic floors, and track lighting at its inauguration at their twenty-first anniversary party. But I could see Maya was discovering that no amount of renovation was going to compensate for her pain. Obscured amid the pillows on the sofa, Maya didn't even acknowledge my presence. In her hands, she held a book, *The Power of a Praying Wife*, but she wasn't reading. I turned down the music and sat next to her. As I recounted my evening with Adam, her eyes remained unfocused, as if she hadn't heard a word I said. Ordinarily, I would've been angry that she wasn't paying attention to my plight, but at that moment her mood seemed more important than my relationship with Adam.

"I can't stop thinking about him," she said, when I stopped talking, though I hadn't told her everything—how Adam had mimicked Pacino, how he had kissed me hastily as we departed.

"Forget about him. He's not thinking about you," I told her firmly. "He's with his *wife*. You should be with your husband." I hated that someone like Luciano had such a hold on my sister, and even worse that she was allowing it.

"I don't want to be with my husband," she retorted. "He bores me. And I don't want to be with Luciano. But I can't stop thinking about him."

"Maya," I began, scooting closer to her, wondering what I could say that would make a difference. I had never been with a man long enough to be bored. Six years of marriage did not qualify me to advise her. What was it people called the turning point of marriage? The seven-year itch. At thirty-nine, she had been married more than half her life. I waited for some words of wisdom to come to me, to make her feel better, to offer her some hope.

"Maya, I don't know what it's like to be married for twenty-one years," I told her, as I snuggled against her just like when we were little and one of us had been hurt. "But I think God is trying to tell you something. He's taken Luciano out of the way. He's giving you a chance to make things right. You always say you envy me for being celibate. But I envy you for staying married this long."

She didn't say anything for a while and we listened to Sade's words in silence. *If love was stronger than pride, why was the world so messed up?* I silently asked Sade. When Alex first cheated, Maya first wanted to die, then kill him. After she got saved and forgave him, she said no one would ever make her feel that way. She made me promise that if she ever mentioned suicide or murder again, I was to smack her until she came to her senses. I waited for her to speak so I could gauge her state of mind.

"So?" she said, turning to me. " '*Amistades*'? Think you'll be able to handle that?"

CHAPTER 18

ADAM

ANY MAN WHO has ever tried to become, or remain, friends with a woman he has feelings for, or has been intimate with, knows what an impossible feat it can be. I had never had a woman as a friend and I didn't know if I could now. It just didn't seem to be the nature of things.

But for the next several weeks, Eva kept me in check, determined to prove that being friends with a woman was the most natural thing. She made sure we were never alone, like she was following some protocol for "Celibate Living," or she had attended some motivational relationship seminar. We did platonic, safe things, like couple-dating with Maya and her husband, Alex, who were trying to work things out, or with Simone and Zephyr, or Ian, depending on which one she was in the mood for. We went to an Afro-Caribbean sculpture exhibit, a debate about affirmative action at her university, and musical performances and plays. Every week, Eva invited me to church and/or Bible study, but I begged off each time. I didn't lie or make up excuses, just reminded her that church was not my thing. She didn't persist or make me feel guilty, which made me even more suspicious. Once, she teased me by saying that God still loved me. I replied that that line hadn't worked for my mother so far.

Then the Thanksgiving holiday rolled around and she invited me to her house for dinner. She didn't specifically say it was to meet her family, but I knew her sons would be there; maybe even her father. I wasn't sure if I was ready to meet them, so I deliberated the request carefully, because the implications of such a move meant I had to acknowledge that our relationship was moving toward something serious, way beyond friendship. My feelings for Eva were intensifying, but it was hard to make sense of them all since being in an abstinent relationship was something foreign to me. Things were moving too fast in one direction, but not enough in the other. On the one hand, I was willing to do whatever it took to be a part of her life, but on the other, it was becoming more of a challenge than I thought. But one thing was becoming more apparent, I did not want to be *amistades*. And I was pretty sure Eva didn't either. Why I was so drawn to her and unable to walk away, was a mystery I had been trying to figure out from the start.

Then something my mother said once came back to me. *Men always want what they can't have.*

Jade was seventeen, apparently still a virgin, and in love with an eighteen-year-old piece of crap who, whenever he picked up Jade, according to my mother, walked around the house like he was in the market to buy it. I had long since moved out, but Mama asked me to come by and have a talk with him since my father wasn't around to do it. As Jade was getting ready in her bedroom, I overheard my mother tell her, "You can let him kiss you, you can hold hands, and you can flirt with him, but don't tease him. Just let him get an idea of how good it could be, but under no circumstances, sleep with him. Once you sleep with him, he's got you. Men always want what they can't have."

"But what if he breaks up with me?" Jade cried. "What if he finds some other girl that'll give him what I won't?"

"Then he's not worth it. He doesn't deserve you."

I walked into the living room and sat down real close to the skinny, arrogant lowlife whose short-term goal was to get into my sister's underpants. Without even looking at him, I whispered, "You know, if you mess with my sister, I'm going to have to kill you." At twenty-three, I was a menacing sight with my matted corn-rowed braids and low-budget disheveled clothing style. I looked more like a disturbed street person than a gangbanger, capable of cracking his head in half just for the heck of it.

Years later, Jade confessed that he had been her first. So much for my mother's advice and my paternal tendencies.

Still, there was some element of truth in my mother's statement that men wanted what they couldn't have. The chase, the courtship, was what made it all worth it. Who wanted a meal out of a box, quick and easy, when a home-cooked feast tasted much better? But usually, the reward came at some point. With Eva, I wasn't sure there was ever going to be a reward. And while it was a little crass to think of sex as a "reward," there had to be something more than what we were doing, some middle ground between kissing and marriage.

Secretly, I was smoking again in an attempt to gain some control in one aspect of my life. Afterward, I would go to great lengths to disguise the smell on my breath and my clothes if I knew I was going to see Eva. The last time I bought a pack of cigarettes at the drugstore, I picked up some condoms, something I hadn't purchased in months. It was an impulse buy since I didn't have a definite time frame about moving our relationship to that level. Although I believed Eva when she said she hadn't been with anyone for five years, I wasn't going to take any chances. Whether that uncertainty implied that there was still a question of trust was beside the point. One never knows what was lying dormant within, on either of our parts.

"I don't know if I'll have time to stop by," I initially told Eva over the phone when she called me with the invitation. I was at work, smoking my third cigarette of the day. On my schedule, I had one more client, three home visits to go, and two juvey visits at Merriville, the downstate juvenile detention center—a four-hour round trip. I was in no mood for haggling.

As always, since Mama's journey to veggie-land, we were expected at Jade's for Thanksgiving. "My sister lives in Carol Stream, and she's a slow cook. Her dinners drag on forever," I continued, aware that my explanation sounded over-compensatory. It was the truth; my sister was a meticulous cook, and she especially wanted everything to be perfect with Akil and his parents coming.

"Well, we don't really celebrate the customary American Thanksgiving but 'a day of thanks,'" Eva explained. "We don't watch football games or do any of the so-called traditional things. My boys are home and they're cooking this year."

"What, you need guinea pigs?" Humor was my next delay tactic.

"Silly, it's not their first time cooking. I taught them how to cook when they were young so they could be self-sufficient."

"And 'cause you hate cooking so much."

"I don't really hate it. I just don't like it very much."

"Same thing." We were beginning to know each other well enough so that we were able to decipher lapses in conversation or pick up hidden messages in veiled words. Still, I didn't want to hurt her feelings. "Who's coming?" I asked, still stalling.

"My father and a couple of cousins who still live here, though my father most likely won't show; he's kind of anti-social. I also invited one of my students from my church youth group. Oh, my pastor might drop by, but he received so many invitations, I doubt he'll make it."

"How're your headaches?" I asked, switching topics.

"Better. The doctor put me on a blood pressure medication, which seems to be helping. The only thing is I have to take it every day, which I don't like. I'm not used to taking medication prophylactically. You know, for prevention."

"I know what 'prophylactic' means," I said. "Like condoms."

It was meant to be in jest, but she cleared her throat and didn't reply. Taking a last puff out of my cigarette, I exhaled slowly, waiting.

"Are you smoking?" she asked.

Was the woman psychic or what? "Why?" I asked.

"You sound like my father does over the phone when he's smoking."

Silently, I squashed the butt in the ashtray, without denying or admitting anything. I had run out of excuses, and finally she picked up on my hesitation.

"No pressure. If you get a chance, stop by. I make a mean *arroz con dulce*."

"A-what? What's that?"

"Rice pudding. So if you can't make it, I guess I'll see you . . . Sunday?"

"Uh . . . "

She laughed. "The spirit of the Lord told me to keep inviting you to service, so that's all I'm doing."

It was almost six o'clock when Jade finished cooking, eight by the time we sat down to dinner. I found myself eating Mama's tossed salad and vegetarian turkey—"tofurkey"—which she brought. Mama, of course, loved Akil, especially after he delivered an impassioned grace. His parents were also devout, punctuating every sentence with "Praise God," and "Yes, Lord." They talked about religion before, during, and after dinner, as if Jade and I didn't exist, since Jade was as un-religious as I was.

After dessert—after Akil helped Jade clean up the entire kitchen and put away the leftovers—he turned to Mama and said, "I'd like permission to court your daughter." I choked on my second slice of pecan pie and Jade pounded my back; then, when she realized I was faking, she grabbed a chunk of my back in a pinch. I couldn't believe he actually used the word "court." It was too much for me; I had to get out of there.

At nine-thirty, I called Eva, figuring her guests would be gone. She said only her sons remained but they would soon be leaving to visit with her ex-husband's side of the family. I figured by the time I made the forty-five-minute drive from Jade's, it would be safe to drop by. Jade insisted I bring a sweet potato pie, and I stopped at Walgreen's for chewing gum and a couple of bottles of sparkling white grape juice, my contribution to the dinner.

I recognized Tony from his pictures. He opened the interior oak door and took inventory from behind the glass security one, overtly sizing me up just like the dog, King, had done when we first met. Because it reminded me of my reaction when I met Akil, I had to smile, in spite of his ill manners. He slowly unlocked the door without question, so I assumed Eva described me and told him I might be stopping by. He was about my height, with a very serious sneer on his face that, coupled with his close-cropped hair, bordering on scalped, made him look like a menacing ex-con, a mulatto skinhead. As the oldest, it was apparent that he had been the man of the house for a while and, like any dominant male, probably felt his role was in danger of being usurped. Any minute, I expected him to sniff me and mark his territory. I was glad King was nowhere in sight.

"You must be Tony," I said, being the mature adult and extending my hand.

He took my hand in a traditional handgrip, which was firm and confident, but the sneer never left his face. "Mr. Black. Come in," he said formally. As I walked in, I could see him taking in my locks, army-green cargo pants and cracked leather jacket, with a superior air.

Eli, who stood several inches taller behind his brother, had long hair in cornrows. Grinning, he came around and took my hand in a welcoming, brotherly soul handshake. I could tell Eli and I were going to get along just fine.

"Hey, Adam," he said. "Ma's on the phone. Sit down."

Great, I thought as I sat down in the rattan chair in the living room. *The Spanish Inquisition.*

Almost simultaneously, both brothers sat down a few inches apart on the sofa opposite me. From the kitchen Eva waved, the cordless phone balanced between her ear and shoulder.

"I brought some sweet potato pie my sister made," I said.

Eli jumped up and all but snatched it out of my hands. "Alright!" He lowered his voice and said, "Ma can't make sweet potato pie. You know, her being a Hispanic and all."

I chuckled.

"You know my ma from church?" Tony asked with the slightest suspicion in his voice.

"Anthony Roberto Prince, Junior," Eva interjected, walking into the living room. "I already told you where we met, so stop the cross-examination." For the first time, I noticed Eva was wearing a dress, a knee-length café-au-lait number that embraced her curves and clinched the arc of her lower spine. Although I tried not to be obvious, I couldn't take my eyes off her.

Tony frowned at his mother and Eli punched him, laughing. "Yeah, Anthony Roberto." He dodged out of reach as Tony tried to punch him, then whizzed the pie by Eva's face as they bypassed each other. "Adam's sister sent some pie. I'm gonna max this," he said, hurrying into the kitchen.

"Clean up your mess," Eva warned him. "My eighteen years of servitude are over."

"Hey, Ma, have I told you how much I've missed your wonderful voice?" he yelled from the kitchen.

"Oh, I've missed yours more," Eva said, equally sarcastic. She sat casually on the arm of my chair and placed her arm around the back. I saw Tony eyeing us critically through half-closed eyes as he leaned back on the sofa.

"What did Grandpop say?" Tony asked his mother, his eyes still on me.

"He won't be able to come by. He wants you guys to stop by tomorrow."

"So, what's your major, Tony?" I asked.

"I'm leaning toward adolescent psychology."

"Good field."

"You have any children?"

"Tony," Eva said with a hint of warning in her voice.

"No, I don't," I answered, gripping the neck of one of the bottles of sparkling grape juice.

"He knows you don't. I already told him." Eva was staring Tony down, as if daring him to ask one more intrusive question. When he finally looked away, she turned back to me. "You want me to open one of these?"

I shook my head; I did, but I didn't want to be left alone with Tony, not because I was afraid of his questions, but because I wasn't in the mood to put the little knucklehead in his place. I had to remind myself that he was as overprotective of his mother as I was of my own mother. Mama had invited me to have dinner with her and

Mr. Jameson Stevens twice, and both times I made myself conveniently scarce.

The phone rang and I hoped it was for Tony so he would go away for a while.

Eli came into the living room, putting on a jacket and carrying a considerable slice of pie on a paper plate, a big chunk already packed in one of his cheeks. "That was Daddy. He said he's leaving Grandma's house soon so if we want to see him, we better come now." He turned to me with appreciation and gave me some dap. "Hey, man, this pie is fla-a-ame!"

"Eli, don't talk with your mouth full," Eva said. "And don't come home too late. There are a lot of drunks driving out there."

"*Si*, Mommy." Eli smirked in my direction. "She thinks we're still ten."

"Ma, we're going over to Grandma's house to watch the game," Tony insisted, putting on his own jacket. "You didn't want us watching it here. Daddy taped it."

They both kissed Eva on her cheeks. Tony shook my hand again, mechanically, then muttered something that sounded like, "Good meeting you," but I wasn't feeling it.

"You want me to tell Daddy anything?" Tony then asked Eva.

Eva gave him the evil eye and I knew he had asked that question for my benefit. "No. If I have anything to say to your father, I'll tell him myself," Eva said tersely. "You *can* tell your grandmother I said, 'Happy Thanksgiving.' Wait. Take her a plate of *arroz con dulce*."

She trotted to the kitchen, the dress swishing against her calves, and brought back a cellophane-covered plate of rice pudding. Tony and Eli were halfway out the door.

"I love you," she called out.

"Yeah, yeah," I heard Eli say. He popped his head back in the door as Eva was closing it. "Hey, Tone, you think we should leave them alone?"

"Boy . . ." Eva warned and faked a back-handed slap at him.

Eli ducked and laughed, then turned to me. "It was nice meeting you, Adam. Finally. I thought my ma was making you up."

"Likewise," I told him, smiling.

"Don't come home late, I mean it. If I'm asleep, don't wake me up to braid your hair," Eva warned before closing the door.

Then, we were finally alone. Eva brought two champagne glasses out of the dining room hutch and I poured the sparkling grape juice. She sat on the arm of the chair again, this time with her legs turned toward me. *Friends,* I reminded myself.

"You know how to cornrow?" I asked.

"You sound shocked," she said, then added condescendingly, "I can also jump double-dutch and play tennis like the Williams sisters."

I laughed. "You *wish* you could play like Venus and Serena."

"I bet I can beat them in double-dutch."

"Yeah, okay," I said, sipping from my glass. "Your sons look like good kids. Or adults, I should say."

"I've been blessed. They're good boys. Especially now that they're out of my house." She grinned.

"I don't think Tony Junior likes me much, though."

"It's a front. He pretends to be tough," she assured me. "They both worry about me; I worry about them."

"They're grown up. You shouldn't have to worry about them too much."

"There's still a lot to worry about. Especially when they're back in the city. Did you hear about the college student that was killed on Tuesday?"

"Yeah, I heard about that." Two days before Thanksgiving, a college senior visiting his family in Chicago had been shot and killed while walking with friends in his old neighborhood. It was just one of the many shootings that had taken place that week, but because the young man had been a gifted student at an Ivy League school, the news media had capitalized on the story, overshadowing the other senseless murders that had occurred of ordinary young people. "That was sad."

Eva physically shook and crossed her arms. "Sometimes I get sick thinking of all the things that can happen. I try not to dwell on it, but sometimes I just can't help it."

"They look like they can handle themselves." I knew that "handling themselves" had very little to do with the randomness of being at the wrong place at the wrong time, but I was trying to get her mind off of them. I took her glass and mine and placed them on the end table.

She started to get up. "You want to try my *arroz con dulce*?"

"I sure do." I pulled her down into my lap and embraced her, savoring her lips slowly and hungrily. "Tastes real good."

She responded at first, smiling through the kiss, then stopped, pulling away to look at me with her cocked brow. The smile was gone. "Are you smoking again?"

I released her and stretched out my legs, irked that I hadn't been successful in concealing my secret, irritated that she had interrupted the little pleasure she had allowed me so far. "Do I smell like I've been smoking?"

"Yeah, you do."

"Then I guess I have."

"Don't you care about your health?"

"My health?" I asked incredulously. "Why are you bringing up my health? You've never even asked what kind of cancer I had."

"I figured you would tell me if you wanted me to know. I thought it was something personal."

I stared past her at the fireplace and noticed her wedding picture was gone. I debated whether I should tell her. With a finger, she turned my face toward her. "Tell me. I want to know."

"Testicular," I said simply, watching for her reaction. When she didn't have one, I continued. " 'TC' for short. The doctors wanted to do an orchiectomy, remove one of my . . . testicles, but I refused. I opted for radiation and chemotherapy. They said the risk of reoccurrence is higher without surgery, but I told them I would take that chance." It was then I remembered that I was past due for my last follow-up.

As she listened, she took one of my hands between hers and caressed it, much the same way I had done at Buono Dio. However, the feeling was quite different when she was doing the caressing. I wondered if she was aware of how her touch made me feel, or if she was really that naive.

"I broke up with this woman before the cancer. We got back to-gether afterward, but . . . it didn't work out. Anyway, she started see-ing someone else and one day I followed her, and saw her . . . with him . . . walking in the rain . . . holding hands . . ." I paused to see if she knew the song.

"Cold-busted," she interjected and smiled empathetically.

I didn't say any more, hoping she would let it go. I had confessed more than enough. For now.

"Aren't you worried it's going to come back? Especially if you smoke?"

"If you want me to leave, just say so," I told her brusquely. "Don't try to start a fight about my smoking so I'll get upset and leave."

"I'm not trying to start a fight."

"Okay," I said indifferently. "We're supposed to be friends any-way, right? What are you doing kissing me if we're just friends?" I tried to stand up but she didn't move. "Excuse me."

She stood and let me up. I started for the door, but she pulled me back by my coat and turned me around. "Okay, I admit it, I *was* try-ing to get your mind off of us, so we didn't get caught up in the mo-ment and end up frustrated. I know you don't believe this, but this is hard for me, too. Maybe harder. You don't think premarital sex is wrong so it's easier for you. I know you think it's harder for men to abstain, but it's just as hard for women. At least for me."

I scoffed, refusing to embrace her, though my arms yearned to hold her. Instead I held up my hands as in surrender. "What do you want me to say, Eva? I said I was going to try and I did. But it's get-ting harder and harder. One day, I'm fine with it, and then, I'm not."

"So what are you saying?"

"Just that. It's getting real hard to be with you and . . . not go fur-ther."

"I told you," she said, pointing a critical finger at me. "I told you I was serious about my celibacy. You knew up front. It's not like I changed on you."

"Yeah, well . . ." I started weakly. "I've tried."

She shrugged her shoulders. "So? You want to end it?"

The thought of losing her and her bluntness in suggesting it made me feel spiteful. "Is that what *you* want?" I asked resentfully.

"I don't, but . . ."

"Or maybe you want to get married? Then we can have sex 'the right way.'"

"No! No, I don't want to get married," she said, becoming upset, her head snapping back slightly like she was about to get some west-side attitude. She rubbed her eyebrows with her thumb and forefinger.

"Let me guess, you have a headache," I said with spite. "How convenient."

She glared at me from under her hand. "No, I don't have a headache. I'm trying to think."

"What do you want, Eva? What's it going to be, friendship or a relationship? Make up your mind."

"I don't know . . . what I want, but I definitely don't want to get married."

"So, you're happy with things the way they are? Kissing and hugging like we're in junior high," I said sarcastically. "Teasing me?"

She flashed her eyes indignantly. "Teasing you? How am I teasing you?"

I shook my head and looked away. Now I had unintentionally done what she had harmlessly tried to do: start a fight to kill the mood. And the mood was definitely dying, if it wasn't dead already.

"Do I dress provocatively? Do I make sexual comments? Throw myself at you?" she asked accusingly, challenging me.

"You know what you do." Now that I had started, I couldn't stop. I backed up toward the door, getting ready to leave before I said or did something I would regret.

"What? What do I do?"

"Play that innocent Virgin Mary role. Pretend like you don't have any urges, but you know you want it just as much as I do. And why are you wearing that dress? You *never* wear dresses." There was nothing spectacular about the dress; it had a handkerchief hemline, a V neckline, and the flared sleeves she seemed so fond of. I didn't even know what kind of material it was, only that it danced when she moved. Fact was *she* was in it and it looked fabulous on her, and the painful truth remained that I wanted her and she was telling me I was never going to have her. And it was finally sinking in.

She blinked several times and I thought she was going to cry, but I knew it wasn't her style. When she spoke, her voice was icy and even. "You're right. I have urges just like you. I'm not dead. What you call 'innocence,' I call 'self-control.' We're not animals, Adam, ruled by our instincts. God gave us the power over our *urges*, to think before we act."

She was right and I hated that she was right. She had been up front about her celibacy; she hadn't sprung it on me at the last minute. I had walked in with my eyes and heart wide open. I hated that she had the upper hand, hated that she had more self-control than I did. I hated her tough spirit, and at the same time, I admired her ability to stick to her beliefs. At the moment, however, that admiration only made me more furious at her, and at myself.

"And as far as this *dress* is concerned," she continued, her eyes blazing, "my sons bought it for my last birthday and they asked me to wear it. I'm sorry if it *provoked* you."

When I continued to sulk, she took a couple of steps closer. "Don't allow the enemy to spoil what we have," she then said, her voice taking on a softer tone.

"What *do* we have, Eva? Huh? Break it down for me 'cause I'm confused here."

"I thought we had something different, something beyond physical. Something I've never had with any man before. The way God intended."

Lately, when she talked about God, or religion in general, it made me uneasy. She would say it was because I was being convicted, that her words were hitting their mark. Sometimes she looked at me like she could read my thoughts, like she knew what I was going to say before I did. And it made me nervous. It reminded me of when I was little and I did something wrong. One look from my mother and I was confessing and bringing her the belt before she even commanded me.

"We can talk to the pastor," she suggested. "What do you think?"

I scoffed without restraint. "Why do we have to talk to a pastor about *our* personal feelings?"

"Because he can advise us. Because I don't know what to do."

"I do." Unable to resist her any longer, I closed the short distance between us and pulled her to me. "Do you know how much I want . . . to be with you . . ." Momentarily, I released her as my hands faltered, debating which part of her to touch first.

"Adam, you have to help me be strong," she implored.

"I can't . . ." I told her truthfully.

Her hands slowly slipped from my waist. I took her face in my hands, and she closed her eyes, flinching, as if my touch stung. I kissed her eyes one at a time, the top lip, then the bottom, before seizing her whole mouth as our bodies came together from our chests all the way down to our feet. Slowly, we backed up until we reached the wall next to the front door; she was trapped and unable to move. Briefly, I pulled my face away and gazed at her anxious lips, slightly parted like a baby bird anticipating food from its mother's beak. She wasn't fighting me. *God, when did I fall for her?* I wondered, mystified. More bewildering, I didn't know how to tell her without sounding and looking like I was whipped. The words "I love you" were on the tip of my lips but they seemed so banal, so played-out, even though I had used them with only one other woman in my entire life. I wanted to use different words, more reflective of all my feelings, but I just couldn't think of any. My mind was a blank. *A poet at a loss for words,* I thought, *how ironic.*

"Eva . . ."

"What?" she whispered, her eyes still closed, her lips still waiting, trembling.

"I . . . I don't want to break up. I care . . . I want to be with you . . ." I stopped, shutting my eyes tight in frustration, gritting my teeth trying to find the right words. "I care for you . . . like I've never cared for any other woman. Do you understand how I feel?"

She opened her eyes and tightened her arms around my back. "I care for you, too. So much."

Then, before I knew it, something inside of me took over and I lost control. I let my hands wander recklessly where they wanted, and didn't stop my body as it moved with a mind of its own. What a difference a dress made. It made me think of Tina Dinwoody, my first steady girlfriend. I was transported back to the hallway of her apartment building, one watchful eye on the door, fearing her father might yank it open any minute. Eva's hands moved from my back to my chest, at first pushing me away, then grasping my tender pectorals insistently. I winced and groaned, but ignored the dull aching in my nipples, something I had been feeling lately. She wanted me as bad as I wanted her. It was only a matter of time. *What was holding her back?* I was two seconds from falling to my knees and begging, *"Please!"* when the doorbell rang.

She peeled her face away and then tried to squeeze out from under me, as I held her back.

"Adam, don't."

I pinned her back against the wall again, hoping whoever was at the door would go away. She pushed against my chest with a force that surprised me, and I almost cried out when her fingernails dug into my flesh.

"I'm serious, *Adam*. Stop it."

Fuming, I released her and let her look through the peephole. She quickly turned around, her back against the door, her eyes wide with alarm.

"Who is it?" I asked, massaging my sore pecs.

She swallowed hard before answering breathlessly, "My pastor."

CHAPTER 19

EVA

WHENEVER MY BOYS did something wrong, there was no hiding from me; it was all over their faces and in what they did not say. The look on Pastor Zeke's face when Adam emerged from the bathroom, where he had escaped before I opened the door, made me feel like a little girl who had done wrong, guilt scrawled on my face with bright red crayon.

Although the pastor was five years my senior, he was wise beyond his years, my spiritual leader, my mentor. He had taken the place of a parent in my life, a role my father had long forsaken, and he had the ability to still make me feel ashamed. I knew my face was brown-red because my cheeks would not stop burning. If he hadn't shown up when he did, I wasn't sure what would have happened.

He looked from Adam to me with inquisitive eyebrows waiting for an explanation, until I finally met his eyes and tried to appear indifferent.

"Pastor Zeke, you remember Adam Black? He visited our church." My voice was childlike, eager to please, overcompensating for my discomfort.

"When was that?" the pastor asked, standing to take Adam's outstretched hand.

Adam cleared his throat and answered with uncertainty, "Last month?"

"Do you have a home church?"

"No, sir."

"You should come back and join us more often."

Adam nodded hesitantly, looking at me for intervention. "Sure."

I stood up. "Pastor, let me get you some *arroz con dulce*."

"You know that's why I'm here," he said, smiling from ear to ear. He turned to Adam. "This Sister makes the best rice pudding. Have you tasted it?"

The slightest smile crossed Adam's lips, causing me to blush once again. "No. No, I haven't. I was actually on my way—"

"Well, let's have some then. We can visit for a while."

I got up, ignoring Adam's look of desperation, and went into the kitchen. As I pulled out three dessert plates from the refrigerator, I noticed my hands were shaking. *Stop it,* I reprimanded myself. *He's not my father; I'm not a child. I haven't done anything wrong. Not really,* I thought. I hurried back to the dining room, not wanting to leave Adam with the pastor too long.

"So, you don't think attending church is important?" I overheard Pastor Zeke say as I returned with the pudding.

"No, what I'm saying is, I don't think going to church is as important as the kind of person you really are, how you treat others—"

"Here we go," I announced, a little too loudly.

"Alright," the pastor said, anxiously taking his plate. He scooped up a forkful of pudding and ate voraciously. As a hypoglycemic, he could eat like a horse and not gain an ounce. Eating, however, did not interfere with his speaking. "You know, Adam. We're very fond of Sister Eva here. She's a woman of virtue, and a woman of virtue is a very special woman. Proverbs thirty-one."

"'A woman who fears the Lord is to be praised,'" Adam recited, eating slowly. He glanced sideways accusingly at me, as if I had planned the pastor's ill-timed visit.

While I was slightly impressed by his knowledge of the scripture, Pastor Zeke didn't seem at all moved as he continued his lecture. "She's also a child of God and that supersedes what she is to the outside world. One messes with that and you're messing with God."

"No one is *messing* with her," Adam said, looking at the pastor evenly for the first time as he finished his plate. "No disrespect."

"I wish you would stop talking about me as if I wasn't here," I scolded them nervously as I wrapped plastic wrap over a dish for the pastor's wife.

Adam stood up, licking his spoon and handing me the empty plate. "You're right, her rice pudding *is* good. I got to go. Good night."

They shook hands and I walked Adam to the door. He tried to kiss me but I drew back, then regretted it when I saw his eyebrows crease.

"Thank your sister for me," I said, letting him out and closing the door, but not before catching his cold look.

I was anxious to hear what Pastor Zeke thought about Adam, but I also feared he would question me about how far we had gone. I imagined I would be the subject of next Sunday's sermon: *"Eva: Virtuous or Immoral Woman? You Decide."*

The pastor stood up. "I best be on my way. I got two more stops."

"Go ahead. Let me have it," I finally said, handing him the dish for his wife.

"What? Oh, I think you know what I'm going to say, Sister. You are a saved woman; he's not a saved man. You know you shouldn't be seeing an ungodly man, especially alone. When you make a decision to be with an ungodly man, his ungodly spirit cleaves unto you. But I think you already know that. *'Do not be yoked with unbelievers.'*"

I followed him to the door. "He's a believer, Pastor," I said meekly. "He's a good man."

"A good man and a godly man are two different beings." At the door, he turned to me slowly. "A good man is concerned with pleasing himself and others, while a godly man pleases God."

I nodded silently, knowing no defense would be justifiable in his eyes.

Pastor Zeke put his hand on my shoulder. "I know you will do the right thing. Read your Bible, Philippians four, verses eight and

nine. 'Whatsoever things are true, whatsoever things are honest, whatsoever things are just . . .'"

"'If there be any virtue, and if there be any praise, think on these things,'" I finished the verse.

"Amen." He gripped my hand with a reassuring squeeze before going down the steps. "Sister, you have my numbers. My door is always open. Call on me anytime. If you'd rather talk with a Sister, let me know, alright? Alright. God bless you." At the front gate, he exclaimed, "I hope this rice pudding makes it home!"

That night, I laid awake thinking about what the pastor had said, about his definition of a good man and a godly one. I knew God had intervened once again, sending the pastor to the rescue. Everything he had said was true, with the exception that I needed a chaperone. I was an adult, not a teenager who couldn't control herself. But by his admission, Adam was finding it more difficult to control himself. If the pastor had not come along, I wondered if I would have been able to stop Adam. I knew I had to end it with Adam for good, but how and when were the questions.

When the phone rang later that night, I thought it was Adam, but it was Eli, calling to say that he and Tony were crashing at their father's. He promised they would come home the next day in time for the shopping, matinee, and dinner we had planned. After being home only two days, we had barely spent any time together and I missed them. When they were growing up, I couldn't wait for Anthony's weekends so I could enjoy a couple of days of solitude. Back then, the weekends didn't come fast enough. Now, even when they were home, I had to share them with their father, their friends, and the rest of the extended family. Suddenly, being alone was losing its allure.

I spent the next morning doing late-autumn yard work, raking leaves and covering my rosebushes as I listened to my favorite Christian *salsa* group, Querubín, on the portable stereo. Inside the house, I could hear the faint ringing of the phone and I turned up the music, letting it fill the air, allowing the words to sink into my spirit. I didn't check my messages until I was in bed. There were two from Adam.

When Tony and Eli came home, we went to Water Tower Place, saw an independent movie I had been wanting to see, and then had dinner at Shaw's Crab House. Afterward, they went out with friends. Sunday came much too fast and after church, they were packing their weekend bags to go back to school.

"So, Adam seems cool," Eli said, stuffing his clothes carelessly into his bag. "You going to marry him, huh, are ya, Ma, are ya?" He poked me playfully in the side, grinning his infectious smile.

"Of course not," I answered quickly, pulling the clothes out and rolling them properly.

Tony didn't say anything as he packed his toiletries.

"We've only known each other for three months," I added.

Tony shrugged. "It's your life, Mother."

Determined to begin weaning myself of Adam, I didn't return his calls. I knew avoiding him wasn't the solution, but I wanted to say the right words without hurting or judging him. I could sense God was preparing me for Adam's departure, giving me the patience to wait for the right time, the right place to talk with him. Predictably, God tested me as I was in bed trying to read the lessons for the next Bible study class. When Adam called, I was marking Psalm 144 with a highlighter: *He is my loving God and my fortress, my stronghold and my deliverer, my shield, in whom I take refuge.* Instinctively, I picked up the phone, expecting the boys calling to let me know they had arrived safely.

"I called you," Adam said, the annoyance in his voice palpable. "Twice."

"I've been with my sons."

"I just wanted to know if you were still coming to Kia's party next weekend," he said. "My mother wants to meet you."

"I forgot about that." *What was the sense in meeting his mother if it would soon be over,* I thought. There was a weighty pause and I highlighted the passage again. "We haven't talked," I said hesitantly.

"About Thanksgiving? Look, I'm sorry about what I did. Losing control like that."

"It's not just that, Adam. It's the sex issue," I said, relieved I finally got it out. "And your expectations and—"

"Can we not do this now?" he asked gruffly. "Let's have lunch tomorrow. I'm going out for a run. I need to relieve some . . . stress."

I imagined him in his navy blue running suit, the one with the glow-in-the-dark letters that read: "Caution: Running While Black," the one that had become tighter lately. My stomach did a flip as I envisioned him changing his clothes. It wasn't until I hung up that I remembered he said he had stopped running at night.

Carol Stream was about forty-five minutes from the city. It was a nice long drive during which Adam and I listened to music and talked about work, my sons, and his protégés. During the past week, we met for lunch only once because Adam claimed he was busy with work. He briefly brought up Thanksgiving night, but only to apologize once again for his behavior, never touching on the underlying problem of our conflicting expectations. When we parted, he kissed me quickly without holding me in his arms. I found myself not craving more, and surprised I wasn't angry. Yes, God was working in His mysterious way.

Kia's party was well underway in the lower level of Jade's townhouse. I noted that there were more adults than children at the party. It reminded me of the celebrations my family used to have when Maya and I were kids, the kind where the birthday child was usually asleep by the time the cake was cut. From what I could tell, Mrs. Naomi Black was an outspoken woman who carried a lot of weight with her eyes. She was as polite to me as Jade was in the beginning and periodically, I caught her scrutinizing me. As soon as Adam left my side, she appeared suddenly as if she had been waiting for the opportunity to ambush me.

"What church do you attend?" she asked pointedly.

"The Community Church of Christ in Austin. It's on Menard."

She nodded. "Love tells me you have children?"

"Love?" I asked, confused.

"That's what I call Adam. I wanted to make 'Love' his middle name but his father wouldn't have it."

"Oh. I went through that with my ex-husband. He didn't want me to give my sons Spanish middle names, but I did anyway," I said, hoping I didn't sound smug. Wondering how much information Adam had given her about me, I confessed the facts before she could ask: "I have two sons, nineteen and eighteen."

"You must've started *really* young."

I smiled, accustomed to the statement. "I was nineteen when I got married," I explained, making sure she knew I had not been an unwed teenage mother. I could see her trying to do the math in her head, so I helped her out. "I'm forty. I had my first son when I was twenty-one."

"You know Love is thirty-six." She said this like I was robbing the cradle.

"Yes, I know."

"He said you're from Puerto Rico?"

"My parents are. I was born here."

"Interesting. I didn't know there were Black people in Puerto Rico."

"Oh, yeah. We're all over." She gave me a reproachful look, and I realized my words might have come across as sarcastic, or condescending. I felt awful, remembering I was speaking to an elder, not to mention the mother of the man I cared about. Before I could rephrase my statement, Adam came down the stairs carrying a big sheet cake; he was followed by a serious-looking Asian man whom I assumed, judging by the look on Jade's face, must have been Kia and Daelen's father. The man was carrying a huge box in front of him, which he set down at the bottom of the stairs. Recalling how tense things were between Anthony and me following our divorce whenever we happened to be in the same room, I immediately smelled trouble. I prayed Akil would get lost on his way back from getting more ice.

"Look who I found at the front door," Adam announced. Adam placed the cake in the middle of the decorated birthday table and patted the man on the back.

There was silence all around, until Kia and Daelen yelled in unison, "Daddy!"

"Hey, there's my birthday girl!" he said. He scooped both children up in his arms and laughed. "And my little big man."

Adam stood between his mother and me. "Meet the ex-husband, Brandon Cho. He said he'd behave," he whispered.

"You should have closed the door on him," his mother said bitterly.

"Now, is that Christian?" Adam rebuked her good-naturedly.

"Is that my present, Daddy?" Kia asked. "Can I open it now?"

"Of course."

"First, we sing 'Happy Birthday,'" Jade said, with exaggerated sweetness.

"She can open it if she wants," Brandon said, glaring at her.

"After we cut—"

Before she could finish, Kia began tearing at the wrapping paper. She squealed with delight and began jumping up and down when she saw the box photo of a battery-powered miniature terrain vehicle in the quintessential pink. "Mommy, look. It's just what I wanted!"

Jade quietly began lighting the candles, forcing a smile. I felt for her, the embarrassment of losing face in front of her children and family, reduced to nothingness in her ex-husband's presence. But like a good mother, she tried to make the best of an uncomfortable situation.

After that incident, Brandon seemed to settle down, and everyone relaxed. Then Kia showed her father the doll that Akil had given her.

"Who is Akil?" he asked, spitting out the words.

"Mommy's boyfriend," Daelen said, pointing toward the stereo where Jade stood talking and laughing with Akil, who had returned with the ice.

Luckily, Adam overheard the exchange and intercepted Brandon just as he was headed toward them. I felt my stomach tense up as I watched Adam pushing Brandon toward the spiral staircase, talking softly to him and prodding him up the stairs. Initially, Brandon struggled against Adam, but he was shorter and leaner than Adam and he lost the battle. Fortunately, everyone was involved in the kids' dance contest at the opposite end of the room, laughing at their antics. I saw Jade with a worried expression watching the exchange, and, almost simultaneously, we both walked toward the staircase just as we heard loud scuffling and then a couple of thuds that sounded unmistakably like blows.

Jade started up the stairs. "Adam?"

"Everything's okay, Jade," we heard Adam say, though his voice sounded strained. "Stay downstairs. Brandon's going home now."

Jade looked down at me, wide-eyed, on the verge of crying. When we heard the front door slam, we hurried up the stairs. We found Adam washing his face in the bathroom sink, blood dripping from his nose. He half-smiled sheepishly. "He head-butted me."

"Oh, Adam. Are you okay?" Jade cried.

"Is it broken?" I asked.

"I don't think so. It stings a lot, though." He tilted his head back, revealing blood splatters on his shirt.

"Don't do that," I told him. "Pinch your nostrils." I gave him some toilet tissue.

"Ooh, I hate him," Jade said angrily, her eyes teary. "He still manages to ruin everything."

"Adam? Jade?" Mrs. Black called out.

"Go head her off," Adam told Jade. "Don't let her see me. She'll have a fit."

"What do you want me to tell her?"

"Tell her I had to take Eva home. Anything."

As I drove Adam's Nova onto the expressway, he periodically examined his nose in the vanity mirror, groaning. It had stopped bleeding but was swelling up quite a bit and his eyes were turning black.

"Maybe we should go to the ER," I suggested.

"It's not like they're going to put a cast on it. They're just going to pack my nose with cotton. I already did that." He turned his nostrils toward me, showing me the toilet paper he had stuffed into them. It wasn't funny, but he looked silly and I couldn't help but smile.

We were on Lake Shore Drive when I noticed Adam glancing at me, like he had something to say. Finally, I asked, "What?"

"You're driving kind of fast," he said tentatively.

"What?" I glanced at the speedometer. "I'm doing fifty. Fifty-two."

"Speed limit's forty-five on LSD. You know the cops here don't play."

"Stop being a backseat dr—"

Before I could finish, I had to brake suddenly as traffic slowed down for the blue flashing lights of a cop car; it had pulled over a black Mustang on the shoulder. I decelerated and got a glimpse of the driver, a habit of mine, and noted he was Black.

"DWB?" Adam asked.

"Yeah," I replied.

"You notice that too, huh?"

"Can't help it. It happens to my sons." As the traffic slowed to a crawl, I asked Adam about Jade's ex-husband. "Was your sister's ex ever violent?"

"There were some incidents where she had to call the cops."

"He seems to love his kids a lot."

"Yeah, he does. Which is why I let him in."

"You're going to make a great father. Someday."

"I think I make a better uncle."

"But you want to have your own kids some day, *no*?"

He didn't answer, so I didn't press. We were nearing Montrose Harbor so I turned into the next off-ramp, driving down the winding road until we reached the deserted parking lot. There was no one around for miles since the beaches were officially closed, not to mention Chicago was getting an early blast of winter weather.

"Where are we?" he asked, as I parked the car.

"Montrose Beach. My family used to come here when I was little. Me and Maya would pretend we were orphans because our parents would ignore us." I smiled as I recalled the memory. "Then I started bringing my boys. I still come here every once in a while to clear my head." I thought back to that day in August when I had danced and it rained, and I had my brief encounter with the married conga player. I remembered thinking, *Be careful what you ask for, you just might get it.* I wondered if I had willed Adam into my life.

He still hadn't answered my question, and I thought he might be deliberately avoiding the topic, hoping it would go away. I didn't want it to end, but it was obvious that there was no future for us. I had known this for some time but had refused to face it, hoping we could continue the relationship in its current uniform state, which was as much naive as it was impossible.

"I was never one of those men who felt a need to produce a child just for the sake of having someone that looked like him, to carry on his name," he finally answered, squinting through the windshield. He turned to look at me. "I thought I wanted kids, you know. But I think they're too many kids out here. Too many kids without fathers."

"True."

"Plus, I'm sterile," he added quickly and quietly, looking away.

"What?" It was a surprised response; I heard him perfectly clear.

"I can't have kids," he said to the passenger window.

"Because of the cancer?"

"No. A lot of men have kids after TC. I found out before I started treatment, when they did the initial testing. It's funny: I spent so many years worrying about birth control, and all that time, I was sterile."

As I caressed the soft leather steering-wheel cover, I wanted to believe him, but the Evileen who mistrusted everything had heard that line before.

"Look at me. I'm not lying," Adam said, reading through my silence.

I looked at his face, serious and sincere. "I didn't say you were."

"I can show you my test results."

"I believe you," I insisted. It was true, though I didn't know why I believed him. Perhaps because I wanted to believe that a man who had suffered from something as devastating as cancer wouldn't lie about something as serious and personal as infertility. Or maybe I wanted to believe Adam could be the one, that if he couldn't have children, it was one obstacle out of the way.

"Do you?" he asked skeptically.

I scooted across the seat and leaned into his chest. In the vanity mirror, I saw him cringe. I lifted my head and looked at him. "What's the matter?"

"Nothing. My chest has been kind of tender lately."

"Adam, you need to get that checked out. Tender breasts are a sign of TC."

"They're pecs, not breasts," he said defensively. "And how do you know?"

"I read up on it. On the Internet."

"So now you're an expert, Doctor Clemente?" he said facetiously, smirking. "I didn't even have any symptoms the first time. I just happened to go the doctor 'cause I had . . . for something else, and they found the cancer."

"Either way, I think you should call your doctor."

He smiled. "I don't need two mothers."

"I'm serious, Adam."

"*I'm serious, Adam,*" he mimicked.

I poked his nose gently and he winced, laughing. "Okay, okay. I'll make an appointment."

We eyed each other and he leaned in for an instinctive kiss. With his swollen nose and blackened eyes so close to my face, he looked sinister, like a monster. I didn't want to encourage him so I pulled back.

"Remember making out in the backseat?" he whispered. "When you were a teenager?"

"I never made out in the backseat of a car when I was a teenager."

"You lie."

"I'm serious. I was a virgin 'til I was eighteen, then I moved in with my boyfriend who then became my husband, so we didn't have to . . . you know, 'do it' in a car."

"You don't know what you're missing." He leaned back on the headrest with exasperation. "Evileen," he hissed.

"What did you call me?" I asked, surprised.

"Evileen," he said, smiling.

"Who told—?"

"Simone."

I poked his nose again, a little harder than before, and he grabbed me and pulled me to him. "Don't do that," he said, his voice getting deep with desire. "My whole face hurts."

"You're such a baby," I teased. "Love."

He smiled. "I see *you've* been talking to my mother." He released me and opened the car door. "Let's get out and walk," he suggested.

"Are you crazy? It's, like, thirty degrees out there. *Without* the wind chill factor."

He closed the door and started walking backward, taunting me, "Come on, *Evilee-een*."

Reluctantly, I got out of the car and followed. The wind was blowing like a storm was coming, sending huge waves crashing violently against the step-shaped revetments, and forming icy patches in random areas. I had read that plans were under way to replace the old damaged limestone steps with more durable concrete. Soon, the beach would be off-limits.

When I reached Adam, he pulled me to his side, wrapping his arm around my shoulders. As we walked, his opened cracked leather jacket flapped back in the wind while I buttoned the top button of my ankle-length wool coat and pulled my fleece headband down lower over my ears. Ordinarily, I would put my arms around his waist, but under the circumstances, I felt the less I touched him the better.

It was obvious he was not going to bring up the matter of our future, so I would have to. Even if we had both made our positions clear from the beginning about marriage and sex, I knew it was my fault for letting things get as far as they had. Deep down, I suspected he believed I would eventually give in. If he was truly convinced it would never happen, he would've called it quits long ago. Although in my heart I had always known all of this, it made me suddenly angry at Adam, but mostly at myself. *Why couldn't he just be honest and direct? Why couldn't I?* Once again I was looking to the wrong person for answers, for comfort. *He is my loving God and my fortress, my stronghold and my deliverer, my shield, in whom I take refuge,* I thought remembering Psalm 144.

Abruptly, I stopped walking and sat down on the top stepstone. He sat behind me and enveloped his arms and legs around me, shielding me from the wind with his jacket. It felt wonderfully warm in his embrace, like I was shrouded in a cocoon, and temporarily, I felt protected from the imminent and inevitable ending. If only he knew how much I did want him, in every way. If only he could understand how very difficult it was to push him away when I wanted to do the opposite. If only things could stay the way they were, until

"Adam, I'm not going to have sex with you," I finally said bluntly.

"What?" He said this in disbelief, innocently, as if the thought had never even crossed his mind.

"You heard me," I said louder over the wind.

He didn't answer, and his arms and legs loosened their grip on my body, although not completely. In the back of my mind, I knew the main reason why we couldn't stay together, the one reason I had been ignoring. Although he had accompanied me to church a few times, he hadn't made any effort to give his life to Christ, let alone express the least bit of interest. I wasn't sure about a lot of things, but one thing I knew for certain, I could not contemplate anything serious with a man who wasn't saved.

Just then he whispered something in my ear, but because of my hair, my headband, and the wind, I couldn't hear him. "What did you say?" I asked, lifting the headband from one ear.

"*Te quiero,*" he whispered.

"Don't even try—"

"*Te quiero,*" he repeated, louder and clearer, with conviction. I struggled to turn around to face him, to ascertain his true intent, but he hugged me tighter, then burrowed—more like hid—his chin in my neck. "Don't *mirame,*" he added.

If I hadn't been so taken aback at his first declaration, I would have laughed at his novice erroneous attempt to say "don't look at me." As it was, I was too busy trying to make sense of the words, *te quiero*, which, depending on the context, could mean, "I want you," "I care about you," or "I love you." His pronunciation was almost flawless, like he had been practicing it for some time. I knew he must have consulted a dictionary or someone who knew Spanish to know that he didn't need the pronoun *"Yo"* for "I." Someone like Luciano. I imagined him coaching Adam: *Just tell her "Te quiero," and while she's thinking you mean "I love you," you really mean "I want you," and she'll be all yours.* It was much safer, less committed than saying *Te amo*, which solely meant "I love you." Maybe he thought I would be touched that he had learned how to say the words in Spanish. Perhaps he thought I would be stupid enough to conclude that he meant the latter, that I would assume marriage would be the end result and sex would be permissible. And I would fall into his trap, his bed, at last.

God only knew how many women in his past he had said those same words to, in English, just to get them in bed. It wasn't going to work with me. He should know that by now.

PART

TWO

CHAPTER 20

ADAM

IT IS MUCH easier to abstain from sex when you are alone, but it is a little harder when you are involved with a woman. It is more difficult when you find yourself caring for a woman who is celibate and has been for a while—determined to stay that way until marriage or who knows when.

But things really got complicated and confusing when that celibate woman finally gave in.

As my hands roamed over her soft, soft skin, her hands simultaneously and unabashedly explored mine. I cautiously began to unzip her velour jacket, pausing every few centimeters, waiting for her to stop me, because intermittently, I could feel her body tense up, then relax. One moment she would stop my hand, the next her hands traveled up and underneath my sweatshirt, setting off a chain reaction all over. Whether she really wanted me, or she was finally giving in to satisfy me, I wasn't sure. I was usually good about reading body language, but from the beginning I knew Eva was governed by another entity. What's more, I had the strangest feeling there was someone else in the room with us.

"You're so soft," I whispered, unable to stop the words.

I pulled off the silk scarf holding back her hair, and I massaged her scalp, taking my time kissing her face, her lips—relishing the taste of her. Even though my nose was still sore, I could smell the intoxicating scent of her rose oil and the strawberries-and-cream conditioner. The light from the streetlamp seeped through the windows, illuminating her face, but she wasn't looking at me. Outside a storm was raging, the snow blowing sideways in thick panes and making visibility nil. It was the perfect night to stay under the covers, the perfect setting for us to be together at last. I tried to make eye contact in an effort to connect with her, but her eyes were transfixed, staring past me as if someone were standing behind me, causing me to turn and glance over my shoulder. I thought perhaps Luciano had come back, then I remembered he had returned the spare key a long time ago.

At the lakefront, when Eva told me I could forget about having sex with her, she surprised me, especially after she added that if I expected sex, we had come to the end of the road—just as I worked up the nerve to tell her I was in love with her. So what could I say, but simply and indifferently, "Okay, whatever you say." Then, two weeks later, there she was at my place, stating in so many words that she had changed her mind. It took everything within me not to go off on her. *What kind of sick game are you playing?* I wanted to scream at her. But as she stood in the living room, wearing a new velour sweat suit and gym shoes in my favorite color, cobalt blue, I didn't think "easy access"; I thought, "beautiful." I was wearing a sweat suit too, though it was gray fleece and frayed, but clean. I kind of knew she was complying for my sake, to prove that she wanted me as much as I wanted her. But even though most men wouldn't have cared if the sex was unrequited, I felt like garbage, because that's the kind of man I am.

I tried to send her home; I told her not to do me any favors, and at one point I even shoved her gently toward the door, but she persisted. *She was the one who threw herself at me,* I told the little voice of conscience that had been bugging me lately. But I knew I had to acknowledge my role in awakening the dormant craving in her.

Now as I found myself kissing her heart-shaped tattoo-looking birthmark, trying to divert her attention to me, I began to sense her freezing up again. I was losing her.

"You okay?" I asked.

"Yeah," she said, her voice barely audible.

Her voice, so close to my ear, made the hairs all over my body stand at attention. I sprang up, sat on the edge of the bed, and reached hesitantly into the nightstand drawer for a condom before she could change her mind; I couldn't hold back any longer. It had been so long. I wanted to explain that the inability to control myself wasn't something that happened often, but then I remembered what happened with Sondra the last time I was with her, and I began to lose my nerve. I felt awkward and insecure, like I was sixteen again.

With one quick sweep, I pulled off my sweatshirt but kept my back to her and waited. I sensed she was having second thoughts and decided to let her call the shots. If she didn't touch me, I would take it as a sign that she wasn't ready; if she did, she was ready but wanted me to take the lead. At that moment, I closed my eyes and hoped the incident with Sondra wouldn't be repeated. I thought about praying that it didn't, but I felt suddenly guilty for using prayers for such a selfish request. The fear of a reoccurrence of that past event prepared me for the disappointment to come if Eva changed her mind. I wouldn't be mad at her.

I flinched when she began caressing my back, because I had expected the opposite. Then she pulled the elastic band from my hair, freeing my locks. I turned around, and without looking at her, buried my face in her neck and hair, avoiding her lips because I knew if our lips touched, it would be over sooner.

Even though she welcomed me into her embrace, she kept her eyes shut tightly, burrowing her head into my chest. I smoothed back her hair, massaged her temples, and tried to pry her eyes open. Then I kissed her right temple, the site of her tormenting migraines, my lips lingering, wishing I could take away her pain forever. I wanted to tell her I loved her but I knew saying it in bed was forbidden in the unwritten manual of making love. The weekend before we ended things at the lakefront, I had been debating the best way to say the words. Then one night while flicking through the channels, I came upon an old black-and-white Spanish movie in which a woman was resisting a man until he uttered the words, *"Te quiero."* The English captioning had read: *I love you.* In Spanish, it had sounded more dramatic, romantic, less trite than it did in English. As the woman's eyes softened she melted in the man's arms, and despite the melodramatic mannerisms and exaggerated kiss common in old movies, it was effective.

"Open your eyes," I whispered. "Open your *ojos. Mirame.*"

She looked at me timidly, and we stared at each other, our breathing measured, then escalating in sync. Tongue-tied, I tried to convey my devotion with my eyes, hoping she would read me correctly, hoping she could see that it wasn't about lust—that what I was feeling for her was real. *Do you understand what I want to say?* I thought, trying to transmit the words through the air. She reached up and read me with her fingers, tracing my eyebrows, nose, and lips, as if my face were braille. Even if she were blind and deaf, she couldn't deny that I cared about her.

It wasn't long before her gasps and moans took me over the top. I could feel her body trembling beneath me, and soon after, my body's tremor eclipsed and I pressed my face into her hair to smother my own sounds, but it was useless. I wanted to pour out everything inside me, every word I had held back, whisper her name over and over, but I was mute. All I could manage were unintelligible words that sounded like they belonged to an animal, a demon.

It had all happened so fast—we were still partially clothed and drenched in sweat. It wasn't at all the way I had imagined, though it was all I had thought about for weeks. There had been no time to set the mood, no time to fill my place with her favorite flowers—orchids and amaryllises, her mother's namesake. There was no time to play smooth background music, though I had contemplated playing India.Arie's latest, "Talk to Her," or Chapman's classic, "All That You Have Is Your Soul."

As I emerged from her hair, I brushed against her ear, which was wet. At first I thought it was perspiration, but when my lips traveled to her cheek and up to her eyes, I realized they were tears. The trembling I had mistaken for pleasure was actually sobbing.

"Eva, what is it?"

She didn't answer and turned her face away, brushing at her tears quickly.

"What's wrong? Did I hurt you?" As soon as I said the words, I knew they sounded ridiculous and pompous, and I regretted them. The only time a woman had cried in bed was the first time I had sex, but Tina had been a girl of fifteen, a virgin. Eva was far from being a virgin, but maybe after all her years of celibacy she had returned to that stage once again, not only spiritually but emotionally. I began to panic.

She shook her head. "I'm okay." Then she started zipping up her jacket, so I got the message and went to the bathroom. When I returned, she was sitting on the edge of the bed, hunting for her socks and shoes in the dark. I turned on the bedside lamp.

"Don't turn the light on," she cried out.

I turned off the lamp. "What're you doing? What's the matter?"

"This was a mistake. I got to go. I'm sorry." She was whispering as if someone were in the other room listening.

"Eva." I grabbed a sock out of her hand, then the other. She went for her gym shoes. "Don't go. Eva . . ." I pulled the shoes out of her reach. "Will you talk to me? Why are you crying?"

"I'm not crying," she said adamantly, swiping at her eyes. "I'm just . . . upset . . . and confused."

I knelt in front of her and smoothed her hair away from her face, behind her ears. Her jaw was jutting out, and she looked like a little girl who had just lost her favorite doll. She shook her head so that her hair obscured her face again.

"Usually women say they're thrilled after making love with me, or disappointed," I said in jest. "This is the first time I heard upset and confused." It sounded innocent enough in my head, then it hit me that it was the wrong time to mention former conquests. "I'm sorry. I didn't . . . I wasn't thinking. Why don't you stay the night? It's snowing like crazy."

She stood up suddenly. "I got to go, Adam."

"Don't make me beg, Eva." I sounded pathetic, but I didn't care.

"I'm not trying to make . . . I just can't stay . . ."

I surrendered her socks and shoes and she put them on quickly, then she walked around me and out of the bedroom. I followed, slipping into my sweatshirt along the way as she gathered her purse

and coat. At the door, I made another attempt to get her to open up.
I leaned against the door and rubbed my neck.

"You can sleep on the sofa bed," I offered.

Just then the doorbell buzzed and we both jumped. I pressed the
intercom. "Who is it?"

"Luciano."

Eva looked anxiously at me and I put my hand on her arm to assure her I wasn't going to let him in. "What do you want, man?"

"Let me in."

"Can't. I got company."

"No, you don't. C'mon, man. Let me in. It's cold out here."

I hesitated. I concluded that he had imposed on me enough.

"I got Maya with me," Luciano then whispered into the intercom. "She's in the car." I saw Eva close her eyes and lean against the
wall, her lips moving.

"I'm not lying. I got company."

"Serious?"

"Serious."

"You really serious?"

"*Yes.*"

"Alright, man. I'll talk to you tomorrow."

"Alright. Sorry, man."

"No prob, I understand. I'm just glad you finally got s—"

I cut him off just in time and scratched my neck self-consciously.
"Sorry about that."

A tear crept down her cheek and I cautiously reached out to wipe
it away. She covered her eyes with a trembling hand and allowed me
to pull her into my chest. I helped her to the sofa and we sat down
as she sobbed into her scarf. After a little while, she recovered and
wiped her face, sighing loudly. I waited for her to speak and when
she didn't, we sat in silence. One thing I had learned from being
with her was that sometimes not saying anything was better than
talking.

This was the part of a relationship I was never ready for, the emotions that followed. When I initially told Eva I was going to try this
thing with her, I really didn't think it all the way through. Mostly I

didn't want to lose her. I didn't consider what it would mean to allow her into my life. I knew she wasn't like any of the women I had ever been with; I knew she would require exceptional care. I didn't go into this unknown territory as a challenge, confident that she would eventually give herself to me. I was shocked that she had given in, however, and even more confused about my reaction to her giving in. It was a strange feeling. I couldn't quite put my finger on it immediately because the emotion was so unfamiliar. And then it came to me. Shame. I hadn't felt like I had committed a sin in a long time. Somehow I felt like I had interfered between her and God.

"You ready to talk?" I finally asked.

"You wouldn't understand."

"How do you know?"

"I thought I could get into bed with you and not think about anything but you, but I can't. It should feel good and right, but it doesn't."

"I guess it's my fault. I kind of sensed you didn't want to . . ."

"You didn't do anything I didn't want you to do. I *walked* to the bedroom with you."

"Look, I understand that you made this vow to yourself, this promise to God. But we're adults and we don't have to answer to anyone. It's not like we're Luciano and Maya, married to other people. We're free to do what we want with each other. I'm not going to feel guilty for that."

She shook her head exasperated, like I was an idiot and could not, would never, understand. "I *do* feel guilty. Being an adult doesn't mean you're free to do what you feel like. We don't have to answer to just any *one*. We have to answer to Him."

The moment that should have brought us closer together was drawing us further apart. In that instant, I knew I would never possess her. She would always belong to someone else. I couldn't describe the emptiness I felt, but it was like a death. Like a part of me had died, a part of both of us.

*   *   *

I don't remember how long we talked, but I wasn't sure if I said anything that helped ease her mind. I put several instrumental jazz CDs on the stereo, but the music sounded more melancholic than mellow. The snow was not letting up, so we watched the news for an update. White-out conditions had shut down both airports and numerous car accidents were reported on the expressways, including an overturned semi that had killed a family of six. She didn't need further convincing to stay. She refused to let me pull out the bed from the sofa, though, falling asleep on top of the cushions. Just as I was drifting off to sleep, I vaguely heard a reporter talking about a breaking news story, some school shooting somewhere, and absentmindedly, I flicked off the set and went to bed. I had had enough bad news for one night.

When I awoke, it was still dark outside. I walked to the windows and watched the snow, which was beginning to taper off, leaving behind at least a foot on the ground, roofs, and cars. Periodically, I glanced at Eva on the sofa, curled up in a fetal position, hugging her coat like it was a security blanket. I walked to the linen closet and brought out a comforter and covered her. She didn't move a muscle or twitch an eye. Whether she was really that dead asleep or she was pretending just to avoid me, I couldn't tell. *High maintenance,* I remember thinking about her. Despite everything, I felt an overwhelming need to hang on for the long haul. Somehow we would overcome this bump in the road. After all, all relationships were full of highs and lows, ups and downs. It was only the beginning.

The next morning, Eva was still asleep when I got up. I started breakfast: omelets and coffee. I hadn't slept well, not only because I knew she was a few feet away and off-limits, but also because I wasn't feeling very well. A few weeks before, I had discovered a lump, something I didn't have the first time I had cancer. Even before Eva had suggested I see my doctor, I had finally gone in for my past-due checkup, which included blood tests, a chest X-ray, and an ultrasound. Because I had missed my last follow-up appointment, I didn't want to begin fearing the worst, so I tried not to think about it at all.

The phone rang and I glanced at the caller ID and saw it was Dr. Desai's office, but I didn't pick up. It was Saturday; I knew if she was calling on a weekend, the news could not be good.

The phone woke up Eva and she sat up on the sofa, looking around like she had forgotten where she was.

"Morning," I called out.

She mumbled incoherently and hurried to the bathroom. After about fifteen minutes, she walked into the kitchen and stood on the opposite side of the counter, holding her coat and purse.

"Good morning," I repeated, smiling tentatively. I fought back an irresistible urge to reach over and kiss her, but after her reaction last night, I didn't know how she'd respond.

"Morning," she said, almost in a whisper. "Uh . . . I used a new toothbrush in the medicine cabinet. I'll pay you back."

"No need. That's what it's there for. I always buy extra in case . . ." I stuttered. "I mean . . . My niece and nephew sometimes forget to bring theirs . . ." I stopped talking. "Want some breakfast? I made omelets."

"I'm allergic to eggs, remember?"

"That's right. I forgot," I muttered, wondering how I could fail to remember something like that. In the past, I had always fixed omelets for other women the morning after because it was the quickest breakfast to make. I forgot she was not like the others. "I'll make something else."

"Don't bother. Coffee's fine."

"Sit down." I gestured toward a barstool. Eva remained standing, drinking her coffee, still holding her purse and coat in the crook of her arm. I turned off the stove, came around the island, and sat on the stool in front of her. I took her by the waist but she remained immobile, detached. Morning-afters were always uncomfortable, but she seemed exceptionally embarrassed, like I was some one-night stand she had met on the street.

She set the coffee cup down. "Um . . . I think we need to take a break." She rubbed her hands together slowly, interlocking them.

I covered her hands with mine to stop her. I felt my mouth get hard. "What do you mean, 'take a break'?"

"I think I know why I do this," she said, slowly pulling her hands from my grasp and interlocking them again. "My mother used to tell us, Maya and me, that the best way to stay out of trouble was to keep our hands folded."

"What do you mean, 'take a break'?" I repeated sullenly.

"I mean, take some time to think about what we want—"

"I know what *I* want. I want you—"

"And if we don't want the same thing, then—"

I pulled her to me and kissed her. She didn't respond, so I tried to pry open her lips with my tongue, but she turned her head.

"I know you want me, Eva," I said into her hair, "why are you fighting it?"

She pushed against me and backed up, walking toward the door. "Yes, I want you. My body wants you. My mind wants you. But my soul and my spirit are fighting it and I can't . . . think straight and make a decision when my emotions aren't in sync, in control."

"Why do you always have to be in control?" Suddenly I was angry, and I didn't care anymore. I wanted to shake her, push her out. I couldn't wait for her to leave. "You know what? Forget it. I can't compete with your God."

"*My* God?" she asked incredulously, looking at me like I was the devil incarnate.

I turned my face, partly in anger, partly in shame, but I was not about to defend my words. She continued backing up until she got to the door.

"Stupid things happen when you're not in control," she said.

I followed her. "If we take a break . . ." I warned her.

"What?" she said, daring me to give her an ultimatum.

"It's either going to be the beginning of the end or the end, period."

"Why? Why can't it be the beginning?"

"Because we've gone too far to start at the beginning. 'You are flesh of my flesh, bone of my bones . . .'"

She looked at me sharply. "Don't. Don't quote scriptures at a time like this."

"Sorry," I said, more offended at being reprimanded than regretful for what I said.

"Besides, it's 'bone of my bones, flesh . . .'" She stopped and looked down at her hands and said, "Okay, I'm leaving." She turned to unlock the door, but it required the key in order to open, in addition to the dead bolt. I grabbed the keys from the key hook but didn't open the door right away.

"Okay, I guess this is it," I said. I kissed her forehead. "Bye, Eva."

My intention was to kiss her quickly, neutrally. But I found myself squeezing her tightly, forgetting the soreness in my chest, grasping for her lips, and hanging on for as long as she'd let me. I wanted her to remember what she would be missing. She responded to my kiss briefly, but pulled back first. There was no lovelorn look on her face, no tears. Her face was stoic, and, finally, I waved the white flag.

"I'll walk you to the garage," I said, my voice as cool as ice.

"You don't have to."

"I know I don't have to. I want to," I said tersely, and grabbed my leather bomber jacket from the coat rack. The jacket caught on the hook and I pulled on it a little too hard, sending the whole rack crashing to the ground. I yanked the jacket free and shoved my arms inside. I hoped she didn't think I was mad at our breaking up, but mad at her specifically for making things more difficult than necessary.

We didn't say anything as we walked to the elevator, and I was glad. I was tired of talking and debating. I knew I was going to miss her, but I would get over it. At least that's what I kept telling myself. I thought about how long it would be before I found someone new, and it made me weary.

Shoving my hands into my pockets, I found an old cigarette, but since I didn't have a lighter I just let it dangle menacingly out of the corner of my mouth. Eva glanced at me but didn't comment.

There was a couple on the elevator, kissing noisily beneath a sea of down coats and wool outer garments. Eva froze, but after I stepped in, she followed. I recognized the guy. He was a British dude who lived two floors above me, in 6C, and was never at a loss for female company. A couple of months ago, he rang my doorbell in a panic asking to borrow a condom. When I told him I didn't have any, he thought I was lying. *"Dude, I'll pie you bock,"* he cried desperately as if his life depended on it. Judging by the myriad of females he kept, it probably did. Now he glanced at me over his date's head, a bored expression on his face as she began working on a hickey on his neck. Eva busied herself by putting on her coat and hat, searching for her keys, then buttoning her coat, anything to avoid looking at them, or me.

"Are you going to call me?" the woman asked, her voice muffled as she came up for air.

"'Course I'll ring you, love."

"Yeah, like you did last time?"

They looked to be in their mid-twenties. I thought of those days with no regrets. It had been years since I told a woman I would call her but didn't. I had outgrown that phase of my life and thought I was headed for something more significant with Eva.

"You got a light?" I asked the dude from 6C.

The girl looked over her shoulder and inspected us from top to bottom, her eyes heavy-laden with sex, then she leaned into the guy's neck, hanging on for dear life. He held out a lighter. I took a deep drag and exhaled loudly with exasperation, relief, and pleasure all rolled up into one.

"Thanks, man." I could see Eva ignoring all of us, particularly me, staring up at numbers flashing by like she was mesmerized by the complexity of elevator mechanics.

We all got off at the lower-level parking garage and walked toward opposite sections. As soon as I saw Eva to her car, I turned and walked back toward the elevator before the doors closed.

"See you, Adam," she said.

Without turning around, I waved the cigarette in the air. *"Hasta la vista,* baby." It was childish, but I was beyond caring.

As the doors were closing, I heard the guy from 6C shout: "Hey man, hold the lift, will ya?" I stuck my hand in the doors and he jumped on, sighing. "Women. They're all the same, eh?"

"Yeah," I said, even though the thought that we had anything in common made me ill. He didn't know how wrong he was.

CHAPTER 21

EVA

IT HAD BEEN too late to stop. I had gone over the line between right and wrong long before I finally surrendered. Although part of me wanted to stop, the stronger part of me, my powerless flesh, was ready to forge ahead. After Adam and I presumably broke up at the lakefront, I tried to listen to my soul instead of my mind. But the thought of never seeing Adam again had resulted in some emotions I hadn't expected, and I then realized I was no longer in control. I thought if I held out, he would come around and see things my way. I realized I wanted something more with Adam, something permanent. As the days went by and he failed to call, I panicked. I lasted two weeks before I went to his place. I had planned to seduce him, give him what he wanted—what I wanted—and then walk away from him, forever. In my mind a struggle ensued between good and evil, battling for my soul like politicians vying for a vote. *You can stop him. Don't stop him; you want him, too. You care about him; he cares about you.*

The warning signs had been everywhere before I arrived at Adam's loft, and I had ignored them all. First, my car wouldn't start; when it finally did, it stopped twice. Then came the winter storm warnings.

Initially, Adam resisted, claiming he didn't want an unwilling participant. But eventually I was able to convince him, using the old feminine wiles I had learned from my years "in the world," because

I knew that for men, it didn't really matter when it came to sex whether the woman wanted it or not. In the end, I did something I had begun after my mother's death—I made believe it was happening to someone else. I pretended I was a spectator, watching a scene unfolding in a movie. I allowed my body to go numb and let Adam finally do what he had wanted as I went through the motions. It minimized the guilt, the blame, all the mixed feelings I was experiencing. It was a long way from Adam's front door to his bedroom and he hadn't dragged me kicking and screaming, nor had he carried me. I had been a willing participant. When it was over and I came back to reality, the conviction was much worse.

The entire time I was with Adam, something felt wrong inside, though everything on the outside felt so right. And then he gave me his back, his well-defined back of muscled terrain, with his shoulders hunched with tension and doubt. I knew he cared about me, wanted me, maybe even loved me. When he held me in his arms, I could see it in his eyes as they peered intensely from under his dark eyebrows, so full of emotion, they spoke to me. That moment, heavy in silence, had said it all and, briefly, what I was doing seemed right.

But not one part of the night's short-lived passion was enough to suppress my affront to God. He had provided me with several ways to escape temptation and I had gone around them all. I had defied Him and disregarded the judgment to come, which I knew would eventually follow.

When Luciano rang the doorbell, I thought, *Don't do it, Maya,* even though I had. I said a prayer for her, that she wouldn't go to a motel with him, that she would change her mind and go home to Alex. The thought of both of us falling into temptation was too much for me.

Driving home, I couldn't stop the tears, and the more I tried to block them, the more I cried. I hadn't cried in years. When I tried to think of the last time I cried—really cried—I drew a blank. After Anthony and Victor had cheated and moved out, and when the boys left for college, I didn't cry, perhaps because I knew all of their departures were for the best. At one point, I had to park and pull myself together, mentally beating myself up for being so weak.

*   *   *

At home, King was frantic from abandonment and hunger. I had never left him alone at night, and he raced back and forth when I let him out of his kennel, wagging his nub like a wind-up toy.

"I'm sorry, boy. Mommy's sorry."

I ignored the voice mail indicator light, knowing that the usual people were wondering where I had spent the night—I was in no mood to explain myself to anyone. I couldn't even face my only Judge.

I felt too guilty and upset to pray, so I jumped into the shower and scrubbed my body hard with the loofah brush, imagining pieces of my soul going down the drain along with the epidermis of my skin. Unable to look at myself in the mirror, I caught sight of my toothbrush and remembered the extra one in Adam's medicine cabinet. I wondered how many women had been in that same bed, had rolled around in the same sheets; I was probably just one of many. After all these years, how could I have been so stupid? I thought he had probably lied about not being with a woman for almost two years. In one night, my five years of virtue had disintegrated. *How easily we can be deceived when we allow ourselves to be deceived,* I thought.

Unable to stop my racing thoughts, I turned on the computer to check my e-mail. The first message was from the "Verse of the Day" website. Immediately, my eyes widened with shame. I thought twice about deleting it, then clicked on the message and read Psalm 32:4–5: *For day and night your hand was heavy upon me; my strength was sapped as in the heat of summer. Then I acknowledged my sin to you and did not cover my iniquity. I said, "I will confess my transgressions to the Lord"—and you forgave the guilt of my sin.*

Almost automatically, I covered my eyes with both hands and began my confession, asking God for forgiveness. I crawled into bed and pulled my Bible from the bookends on the nightstand and turned to Psalm 32. I read and read until my eyes hurt.

When the phone rang, I awoke to find it was already noon. I was irritable from crying, and from my own anger and guilt. To top it off, my head was killing me, so I knew it was going to be a bad day.

Through my pain and irritation, I squinted at the caller ID and saw it was Maya. If I didn't talk to her, she'd keep calling.

"Where have you been?!" she screamed in my ear. The accusatory tone in her voice made me even angrier.

"Maya, don't start—"

"Did you check your voice mail? Why was your cell phone off? Where were you?!"

"I'm not in the mood. Call me later—"

"Eva!" she said sharply. "Listen to me. Eli and Tony are in the hospital."

"What?" My voice sounded far away, my ears suddenly clogging up.

"They're at Marion Memorial Hospital."

"Where is that?" I asked quietly, not yet understanding, not wanting to.

"In Marion, Illinois, a couple of miles south of Carter. There was a shooting on campus last night. It's all over the news."

I couldn't speak, my voice was trapped somewhere deep in the well of my throat.

"Simone and I are on our way over to pick you up. Get ready so we can drive down there." She quickly gave me the phone number for the hospital.

It took almost half an hour to get through to a nurse who knew what was going on. She was reluctant to give much information over the phone, but admitted that Eli and Tony were in serious and critical condition, respectively. Somewhere between the time I was placed on hold and hung up the phone, a peacefulness shrouded me. My night of sin with Adam was quickly overshadowed by concern for my sons. I tried to think positively, convince myself that they were alright, with only superficial wounds. I packed an overnight bag, trying to forget that the nurse had said they were in serious and critical condition, not wanting to read any more into their meanings.

I turned on the cable news station and before long the screen was filled with images of a SWAT team storming the college with assault rifles, students being carried to ambulances, others crying and holding on to each other. I dropped into the nearest chair, frozen to the TV, unable to move as I heard the reporter's voice-over: *"Another school shooting, this time at a downstate Illinois college campus . . . There have been eight confirmed dead . . . At least ten more students have been taken to two area hospitals . . . The suspect is believed to have taken his own life . . ."*

Like many mothers living in the city, I feared so many things, but it was the senseless violence, the knowledge that any moment your child could be taken from you for no reason, that caused the biggest anxiety. The killing of children while playing in their backyards or sitting in the front window, or walking to the corner store, had become too commonplace. The things I had feared when my boys left for college were what most parents feared: the temptation of drugs and alcohol, the wild parties, the uninhibited, destructive sex. But in addition, I feared the influence of other students who had no moral or spiritual upbringing. More and more, it seemed like there was no escape from the world of terrorism, war and rampant gun violence that seemed to get worse every year. I thought by sending my sons away from Chicago to a small college town, they would be safe. But for a long time, I knew there was no such thing as a safe place anymore.

As I waited for Maya, I reached into the bookcase and pulled out the nearest photo album. I slowly flipped through it, escaping into the happy memories of my boys: what beautiful babies they had been, how happy they looked over the years, how they had tried my patience. I would give anything to deal with breaking up one of their fights, or cutting classes, anything except what was happening. How blessed I had been. In a moment of helplessness, I buried my face in my hands and prayed. *Father God, I will never let another man come before You. Just please, let my babies be alright.*

During the four-hour drive, made longer and slower by snowdrifts and freezing temperatures, Maya brought me up-to-date on all that I had missed while I was with Adam. When the hospital couldn't reach Anthony or me, they called her as the third emergency contact. She was able to contact Anthony, who was traveling in New York. He had given permission for the two surgeries Eli required—one for gunshot wounds and the other, a broken leg. Tony had been shot once in the head, but the bullet could not yet be removed. Apparently, Tony had been visiting someone in Eli's dorm, where the shooting had taken place. Some of the students had been trampled in the stampede that followed the shooting as they ran for their lives. The gravity of the situation was just beginning to sink in. I couldn't trust myself to speak, so I listened as Simone asked the questions I could not utter.

We listened to the radio in silence as more details became available. A freshman, despondent over his failing grades and a cheating girlfriend, had gone on a shooting rampage in Eli's dorm, where the girlfriend was attending a party. A couple of students were interviewed, their voices trembling with fear and tears. *"This isn't supposed to happen here,"* one student said. *It wasn't supposed to happen anywhere,* I thought. It had become an all-too-familiar scene, "a sign of the times," Pastor Zeke would remark whenever a new shooting tragedy or other catastrophe permeated the news, the consequences of an immoral corrupt society. People in church would declare that we were in "the last days," that everything that was happening had been predicted long ago.

After a while, the news got repetitious and Maya turned off the radio.

"When you didn't answer your phones, I knew something had happened," Maya said quietly, after we digested the additional reports. "I went over to your house last night and you weren't there. You don't know how scared I was. Where were you?"

"I spent the night. At Adam's. I was there when Luciano came over."

I stared out the passenger window but I could feel their eyes on me. Because I knew them so well, I imagined their faces: shock on Maya's, surprise on Simone's.

"That was you?" Maya asked. "When he came back to the car and told me Adam had a woman up there, we got into a big fight, right in the garage. I thought he had some other woman up there. I told him, 'I can't believe your partner is seeing someone else while he's seeing my sister.' You know what he had the nerve to say? 'It's

not like they're married.' So I said, 'Hello?! *We* are!' That's when I realized, 'what am I doing with this man?'"

"So, you didn't sleep with him?"

"No. I realized being with him *was* about revenge. It wasn't love."

"I'm glad." At least my prayer for her had been answered.

"That was no one but God, girl. When I got home, Alex had just
gotten the call from the state police."

As we drove in silence, my mind juxtaposed between two different scenes. While I was in Adam's arms, my children were being
shot. While I was in his bed, my children were being carried into
ambulances. And while Adam was kissing me good-bye, my children were lying unconscious, fighting for their lives.

"Did you have sex with him?" Simone finally asked, breaking the
silence.

I nodded, unable to verbally confess. I massaged my right temple as my head threatened to burst.

"Hey-ey," Simone said with approval. "It's about time."

I knew she was trying to liven up the mood and take my mind
off the boys, but her timing was really bad.

Maya sucked her teeth. "Shut up, Simone."

"She doesn't need *you* making her feel worse," Simone snapped.

"I'm not trying to make her feel worse. But she doesn't need you
congratulating her either."

"I'm not—"

"Ladies, ladies," I appealed to them for the sake of my head.

"I knew something was up when I couldn't reach you. Didn't we
promise to always, *always,* let each other know where we are, no
matter what?" Maya returned to berating me.

"Did you tell me you were going with Luciano?" I knew it wasn't
the time to argue, and instantly regretted it. "I'm sorry. You're right,
I should've called you."

"Don't ever let it happen again," she scolded mockingly, trying to
cheer me up, but that was impossible.

"Here I am worried about you falling into temptation with Luciano and I'm the one who falls."

"I'm no better. *'He who has lusted with his eyes has already sinned in his heart.'* "

From the backseat, we heard Simone scoff softly, but she didn't comment.

"I didn't spend the night sleeping in his bed," I said, wanting to clarify my actions, as if it made any difference. "I slept on the sofa, because it was snowing so hard. I realized it was a mistake right away."

"If it's meant to be, between you and Adam, it will be," Maya offered quietly.

"It doesn't matter, anymore. I told him we should take a break and he basically said it was over. We don't want the same things, so what's the point?"

I didn't want to talk about Adam anymore, but I didn't want to think about what was waiting for me at the hospital. I didn't want to think or talk—period. What I wanted was to go back in time or fast-forward to the future, and pretend none of it ever happened. Or just disappear, forever. Adam, for the most part, was history, a part of my past along with everything else that had gone wrong in my life.

"Ms. Clemente, I want to prepare you for what you're going to see," the doctor explained. "Your son Elias was shot twice: once in his chest, fortunately on the right side, so there was no heart damage. He was also shot in the abdomen and his spleen was badly damaged, so we removed it. His left leg was broken in two places in the femur during the stampede. We were able to repair the bone with pins and he's in traction. He was still conscious when they brought him in, but he's been unconscious since surgery; he is responding to pain stimuli. However, your son Anthony—"

I had been listening without interrupting, looking blankly at the doctor's forehead, but now as she paused, my eyes focused to meet her eyes, wondering why she had stopped.

"Anthony is in critical condition. The bullet is lodged in his brain stem," she said, pointing to the base of her neck. Impulsively, I flinched. "This part of the brain controls all the essential functions—breathing, talking, everything. His head is quite swollen, so he may look a little frightening when you first see him. A shunt is draining fluid from his head and we're monitoring him closely with periodic brain scans. There is some activity, but we won't know the extent of brain damage until he wakes up. Ms. Clemente . . ."

"Yes?" I answered, my voice far away. The words "critical," "frightening," and "brain damage" remained suspended in the air like neon signs.

"He's in a coma, on a respirator, which means he's not breathing on his own. We don't know how long it will be before he comes out of it. In time, we can operate, but now, he's too weak. All we can do is wait."

"And pray," Maya added.

I nodded to indicate I understood, though I really didn't. I knew doctors didn't know everything. They thought their skill came from their education and years of practice, but I knew better. God was in control.

I went to see Eli first because I didn't think I could take seeing Tony. But when I walked into Eli's room, I had to cover my mouth to keep from gasping. In addition to the tubes and wires and the machines beeping and clicking, his face was bruised and swollen, like he had been beaten up. The thought of my son prone as feet stomped his body and face made me sick. I prayed that he had been unconscious the entire time. Maya and Simone walked in with me and helped me sit in a chair near his bed. I searched for a bare spot on his face that wasn't covered by black-and-blue bruises, and settled on his nose, kissing him softly.

"You can speak to him. He may be able to hear you," the doctor said.

I cautiously reached for his hand, which was also covered with bruises. "Eli. Elias, it's Ma," I started, my voice breaking. "Maya and Simone are here. Your daddy's on his way back from New York. We'll be right here when you wake up, okay?"

"Do you want me to pray?" Maya asked me.

I nodded. She took my hand and laid her other hand on Eli's cornrows, which were unraveling and in need of rebraiding. Simone placed her hand on top of ours and we all closed our eyes as Maya prayed: "Father God, we come to you in Jesus' name and place Tony and Elias in Your hands, Lord. We are convinced that You alone know what is best for them and You alone know what they need, Lord. Father, we release them into Your anointed hands, to protect and heal them and we ask that You guide the doctors in their work, Lord. Help us not to impose our own will but pray that *Your* will be done in their recovery. In Jesus' name, Amen."

"Amen," Simone and I echoed.

I tried to prepare myself to go to the neuro-intensive care unit one floor above, tried to envision Tony with the same tubes and wires, machines, a bandage wrapped around his head. I prayed silently the entire way on the elevator, down the hall, but when I got to his room, I froze at the glass door. My body began trembling and my knees suddenly buckled. My head was pounding worse than ever. Maya and Simone held me up as we walked into the room.

It was worse than I had imagined, worse than the doctor had described. He was connected to so many machines, he looked like some scientific experiment. My son's handsome face was gone. Someone had replaced it with an ugly monster, a head swollen twice its size. I thought there must have been some mistake.

"That's not my son," I said to no one in particular, even though I could see his shaven head under the bandage, a bandage stained with a yellow substance.

And then everything went black.

When I came to, I was on a gurney in a brightly lit room. Too bright. I squinted, trying to remember what had happened, hoping I was dreaming. But then slowly it all came back to me: I was in a hospital in Marion, Illinois, and my boys had been shot. I sprang up and became lightheaded, falling back again.

"You fainted," Maya said, suddenly appearing by my side.

I had never fainted in my life and for the first time I got a glimpse of what death might be like. You forget about the past, the present. Nothingness.

A nurse appeared at the other side of the bed. "How do you feel, Ms. Clemente?"

"I'm fine." I sat up on the side of the bed, this time slowly, and moaned. "My head is killing me."

"She has horrible migraines," Maya told the nurse. "Can you give her something?"

"I'm fine," I insisted, even though I wasn't. "I have my pills with me."

"Do you want to go back?" Maya asked, handing me my purse.

I nodded. Holding hands like we used to when we were little girls crossing the street, she led me back to the room down the hall. Simone had stayed with Tony, and she quickly wiped her tears when she saw me. This time, I didn't stop at the door, but walked in, my back straight, and sat in the chair that Simone had vacated, next to the bed.

He looked so fragile, I was afraid to touch him, afraid I'd disconnect some vital tube and cause irreparable damage. I touched his scalp where it peeked out of the bandage at the top, and I thought of how he had been teased as a boy because of his "good" hair, how the neighborhood kids used to call him "Whitey." He would beg me to cut his hair close to his scalp where his roots were curlier, kinkier. Later, as a teenager, he hated how his hair was the object of girls' attraction, so he continued getting regular haircuts, opting for the bald look by the time he left for college. Where Eli had used his hair to his advantage with girls, Tony had always tried to repel them.

I slipped my trembling hand under his, my hand disappearing under his big knuckled one so that it looked like he was comforting *me*. He had Anthony's hands, wide flat fingers and box-shaped fingernails. When he was born, Anthony took one look at his hands, placing them both on his cheeks, exclaiming, *"That's my boy alright!"* as if there had been any doubt. From far away, behind me, I could hear Maya praying, non-stop. And then a line from Adam's poem, "Choose Me," came to me: *For if you stray from the prize, if you choose their lies, I will take what I have given to you . . .* In my head, I kept repeating, *Please God, don't take my sons from me.*

*   *   *

I was afraid to sleep, afraid to leave Tony's side, so I asked Maya and Simone to stay with Eli while I stayed with Tony. I didn't eat or drink anything because I didn't want to go to the bathroom. Deep down, I knew if I left, he would slip away. I tried to remember my last words to him, the last time we spoke, but my head was hurting too much. I stroked his arm and told him all the things I would tell him when he woke up: how proud I was of him, how much I missed him every day even if I didn't act like it. A couple of times I thought I saw his eyes flutter, as if he were trying to wake up but it was too hard for him. When I asked one of the nurses if it was a good sign, she informed me that they were only involuntary reflexes, her tone so matter-of-fact I wanted to slap her.

The next day, Eli regained consciousness, and it was then that I reluctantly switched places with Maya.

"Hey, *mijo*," I said, my voice catching in my throat at the sight of my youngest son's opened eyes.

"Don't get mushy, Ma. I'm alright," he said groggily.

I pressed my lips to his cheek, my tears flowing onto his face. He moaned and I pulled away. "I'm sorry. Did I hurt you?"

"How's Tony?"

"He's in critical condition, up in ICU."

"How many people died? They wouldn't tell me anything."

"Eight so far," I said without hesitation, because there was no easy way to say it, and because he would soon find out.

"Who died?"

We all looked at each other, debating whether he needed to know. Simone tried to hide the newspaper she had been reading.

"You might as well tell me. I'm going to see it on TV sooner or later."

Simone read the names from the newspaper. At the mention of a girl named Rain Dandridge, Eli paled.

"Did you know her?" I asked.

Eli swallowed hard and turned his face away. "She lived down the hall from my dorm. She's Tony's fiancée."

"What?" I asked.

"She wasn't the girl the killer was after, was she?" Maya asked.

"No. She and Tony have been going together since last spring." He turned to me. "He didn't tell you 'cause he knew you'd freak out if you found out he was serious about a girl."

Stunned, I couldn't respond. *How could my son have been engaged without my knowing?*

"You told us to stay away from the girls down here and concentrate on school, so he never told you."

"I just didn't want you to get distracted from school, or make a mistake."

He gave me a weak smile. "He was going to bring her when we came up for winter break. He was crazy about her, Ma." His voice cracked and he turned away.

The next couple of days were a blur as family and friends arrived: first Anthony, his parents, and various members of both of our extended families. Pastor Zeke drove down in a church van with some of the church elders. The first thing they did was bless Tony's body with anointed oil, forming a prayer circle around his bed. I noticed the doctors and nurses step aside, making way, some even bowing their heads in respect or perhaps joining in. I felt God's presence multiplying sevenfold, empowering me with strength, the weight of my burden lifted from my shoulders, if only briefly.

Afterward, the church leaders left to help with accommodations for people staying overnight, preparing meals with the help of a nearby church so visitors wouldn't go broke in the hospital cafeteria. They offered to sit with Tony so I could take a break, but I kept my vigil, eating little of whatever people brought and washing up in the sink in his room.

Pastor Zeke stayed behind, sitting in the chair on the other side of Tony's bed.

"Pastor, I broke my contract," I confessed.

"Did you ask for forgiveness?"

"Yes."

He covered my cold hands with his warm ones. "Do you remember what Jesus said to the woman who was about to be stoned?"

" '*Go and sin no more,*' " I answered.

With that, he said nothing more. The paging system announced that visiting hours were over, and with one last prayer, the pastor left. Only the immediate family was allowed to stay overnight. Anthony stayed with Eli while I remained with Tony, reading the Bible to him, hoping the words would find their way to his soul as I simultaneously sought comfort. Periodically, I stroked his arms, his legs, his scalp. Sister Erma had provided a portable stereo from which gospel and worship music had been softly playing non-stop, competing with the beeping, clicking, and whooshing of the multiple machines surrounding him. In the short time that I had been there, I had come to rely on all the sounds together, lulled by their cacophonous rapture. They were a constant reminder that my son was still alive, trying to find his way back from the abyss.

On the fourth day, my father showed up. Even though he had called the hospital a couple of times, I hadn't expected him to come at all. I glanced at him briefly, then turned away as if he were one of the many nameless hospital personnel who streamed in and out of Tony's room around the clock. I hadn't seen him in months, but he hadn't changed.

"What are you doing here?" I asked, surprisingly calm.

"I can't come see my grandsons?" He sounded offended that I would even ask such a question.

"You didn't before," I said, making no attempt to cover my disdain.

"What are you talking about?"

"When was the last time you called them to see how they were doing? They would always have to call you." The words rushed from my mouth before I could stop them. I sounded like a child but I didn't care. Fear and grief had made me bold. I knew it was not the time; I didn't want Tony to hear us arguing. But I couldn't stop myself. It was the closest I had ever come to telling my father how I really felt.

"Why are you saying this now?" He walked to Tony's other side, reached out his hand but uncertain where to set it down, gripped the side guardrail.

Because I can get away with it, I thought bitterly. I turned away from him and turned back to my Bible, but I had lost my place just as I had forgotten my place as the quiet obedient daughter. "We needed you when Ma died. But you just dropped us off at Titi's like you were the only one suffering."

"You girls were teenagers; you needed a woman in your life. I wasn't in any shape to raise two girls."

"We still needed a father."

He didn't respond, nor would he look at me as he sat in the cushioned window seat and stared out the window. We didn't speak for the rest of the evening, which was just fine with me. Ordinary conversation was useless if it had to be forced. I was through trying to make an effort. The only things that mattered at that moment were my sons.

In the middle of the night, as I slept in the bedside chair that converted to a recliner, I heard someone talking. My first thought was that Tony had finally awakened. I leaped out of the chair, throwing the covers off, expecting to see Tony alert, his dry lips parted in speech. But it was my father.

"I fell apart when your ma died. She was my life. Do you know what it is to love someone so much, for so many years, and then lose her like that?" He held up his hands helplessly. "And you girls, you looked so much like her. Looking at you both was like seeing her ghost."

In the semidarkness, I could see him sitting in the window seat, staring into the pitch-black rural night. His lips were barely moving, his voice a monotone. I looked back at Tony and watched as the respirator forced his chest to rise and fall.

"The people you love are yours only temporarily, but in the end, like in the beginning, we all belong to God."

He sounded so distressed, it made my heart clench. I couldn't understand it. My father, who refused to go to church on Sundays and cursed God when my mother died, was acknowledging His supremacy. *Why was he being so philosophical now?* I thought resentfully. *What was he asking of me?* I needed to lean on *him.* Yet something was telling me to go to him, but as I fought it, I could feel my heart shutting down. I had to save my strength for Tony; I had none to spare. As I drifted back to sleep, I tried to shut my father out with my nightly prayer: *Please, Lord, let my son live.*

Out of the blue, the low-pitched howl of a wounded animal startled me awake.

"God, I loved her so much," my father whimpered, his sorrow-filled tone piercing through me.

I forced myself to go to my father, sitting behind him and wrapping my arms around his chest. He clutched my hands, and after so many months—years—his touch felt strange, and at the same time so familiar.

"He's going to be alright, *mija*. He's going to be alright," he assured me. "He's watching over him."

And as we held each other, my faith became like a child's, believing without seeing, without question. I regressed to a motherless child again, trusting him, believing everything he told me.

CHAPTER 22

ADAM

I STARED BLANKLY at Dr. Desai, then looked past her, out the window. It was just beginning to snow. A pigeon sat on the ledge, the dumb city bird that didn't fly south for the winter, content with the scraps it was able to find in the gutters. It reminded me of a story my mother told me one night when I couldn't sleep because I was worried about something. She said birds were never concerned about where their next meal came from; God took care of their every need. Surely, I was more important than a bird, so it was silly for me to fret. Mama told me this story to illustrate the futility of worrying and the significance of God's role as my provider. But at the time I was young and I didn't get it. I told her birds were stupid; they didn't feel concern because they didn't know how to.

Although I had asked Dr. Desai to give me the results without pulling any punches, I was still shocked, unable to speak. Ironically, I was thinking how badly I wanted a cigarette.

"The cancer's back," she repeated. "And you *have* to have the orchiectomy this time—no ifs, ands, or buts. The tumor's grown larger this time. You should've come in sooner. I told you if you opted for no surgery, you'd have to adhere to the surveillance protocol; blood tests and CT scans every four months, chest X-ray, every eight months. You missed your last appointment. What's wrong with you?"

I took my scolding like a condemned man who knew there was

no use pleading innocent. I thought of the symptoms I had had, the soreness in my chest, the nausea, the lump. I wanted to believe that if I ignored them, they would disappear. I had been neglectful and it was hopeless to lie or make excuses.

When I was referred to Dr. Anjali Desai the first time, I protested, suspicious that a female doctor could be as knowledgeable and sympathetic about testicular cancer as a male. Her French and East Indian beauty and accented English initially made me even more uncomfortable. But after two doctors insisted they couldn't treat me without surgery, she believed it could be done. After the preliminary consultation, she was all business and I became a believer.

"After the surgery, depending on the blood test results and the CT scan, you have two options: surveillance, which in your case, I don't recommend since you've been noncompliant; or chemo, no radiation this time."

"Aw, that was the best part," I said sarcastically, finding my voice. I knew the cancer's return in less than two years wasn't good.

She ignored my sarcasm. "The body can't tolerate large amounts of radiation; the damage is cumulative. You may need more cycles of chemo, but that's up to the oncologist. We can schedule you in next Monday. For the surgery."

Things were going too fast. I tried not to think of how I was going to break the news to my mother and Jade. The first time they had taken the diagnosis worse than I did. My attitude had been positive, all about survival. No one could tell me I wasn't going to pull through. Now, I wasn't so sure. From the beginning, Mama had been against the radiation and chemotherapy, insisting they were poisonous and would do me more harm than good. And in a way she was right. Sometimes the treatment is worse than the disease. It weakened my immune system, leaving me more prone to infections and more susceptible to other cancers, like leukemia. She urged me to see her homeopathic doctor and seek alternative nontoxic treatment. Jade, already emotionally distraught over her pending divorce, cried whenever she came to see me. When she wasn't crying, she was smothering me. I knew they would both blame it on my smoking, forgetting that my father had passed his cancerous genes to me.

"Do you have any questions?"

I shook my head like an automaton. My PDA was in my right hand, the stylus pen poised over the calendar menu, but at the moment my left hand was trembling so badly I couldn't use it.

"So Monday, eight a.m., alright?"

The pigeon was bopping its head as it walked back and forth across the ledge, pecking at the air, then down at the concrete ledge. It came up with something in its mouth, some obscure crumb. Three stories up, it had found its lunch. Good thing about being that pigeon; it didn't have cancer.

"Adam?"

The pigeon gobbled its lunch, looking at me through the glass, head bopping, mocking me. Then I watched with envy as it flew away. *Stupid lucky bird.*

"I think I'm available," I answered lightly, trying to sound non-chalant, but my voice betrayed me. It was important to let her know I wasn't intimidated by the news or the pending surgery, because it was partly my fault; I hadn't followed the protocol. Reoccurrence had always been a possibility—I knew that—but I never wanted to believe it would happen to me. Then I remembered, my birthday and Christmas were right around the corner. *Happy Birthday and Merry Christmas to me.*

"She cried?"

Luciano chuckled and nudged me lightly with his fist, nervously eyeing the IV on the back of my swollen hand and my frequent wincing from the pain in my groin. "So either you did a really good job—or a really bad one."

I didn't know why I thought telling him about my night with Eva would provide some insight. But there was no one else I could talk to about my confused feelings. When cancer or serious illness strikes, people usually fall under one of three groups: supporters, drifters, and deniers. The supporters, like my mother and sister, remained loyal and sympathetic, albeit sometimes overwhelmingly.

Then there were those who drifted away and stopped visiting out of fear of the unknown or because they just didn't know what to say or how to act. Luciano fell under the denial category. His objective was to avoid any discussion of cancer at all costs with humor, diversion, whatever. The first time I had undergone treatment, he was living in Phoenix with his second wife, the Tex-Mex one, visiting only when he came to see his Chicago relatives. He hadn't witnessed the majority of what I had gone through.

The surgery had gone "as well as can be expected," considering I had lost part of my manhood. If I wasn't already sterile, the doctors would try to convince me I could still have children, but since I was, there was no consolation. The results of my blood tests and CT scan would not be available for several days to a week, the medical profession's idea of torture. The only good news I got was from the chest X-ray; my lungs were clear of disease.

"I'm trying to have a serious discussion with you, man," I told Luciano. "You think I should call her?"

"Remember what I said about Black women being too much drama? She's in that category," he said callously. "If you ask me, she ain't worth it. You got enough problems."

"I didn't ask you all that. I just asked you if I should call her," I said, suddenly irritated.

The anesthesia was beginning to wear off and I grunted, swallowing hard to keep from groaning. An hour after the surgery, Dr. Desai had encouraged me to get out of bed as soon as possible and walk around the room. If I hadn't been in so much pain, I would've laughed. The sooner I could move, she said, the quicker my recovery, and the sooner I could leave the hospital. But considering how much time I would be spending in and out of the hospital in the next few weeks, I was all for getting discharged "STAT." After mediating the discussion between my body and my mind, I got up with the help of the nurse and hobbled around the room like a ninety-year-old with a walker. The pain was ten times worse than the time Kia had jumped on my lap without warning. I hobbled right back into bed, not caring if I looked like a wimp in front of the nurse.

"If you want the additional drama, call her," he answered, shrugging as he fumbled with his PDA. He had brought my own PDA and laptop but I had no energy or desire to type, not even to check my e-mail. "Need anything else, man?"

I shook my head and closed my eyes. What I needed, he couldn't provide. I pushed the nurse's call button to request more pain medication.

"So she cried, huh?"

I turned my head away to indicate that I didn't want to talk anymore. All I wanted was to return to the numbing comfort of anesthesia, where things were tranquil and pain-free.

"You know Maya dumped me that night. Before we did anything. So I guess we're in the same boat."

I opened my eyes, alert.

"Yeah. That night when I went back and told her you had company, she started screaming at me," Luciano explained, glad he got my attention. "I didn't know it was Eva. She got upset when I told her that it wasn't like you guys were married."

I couldn't help smiling. "That was smart."

"She hasn't called me in a week and I haven't called her."

"Maybe it's better this way. You go back to Lisa; Maya goes back to her husband."

"And we'll all live happily-ever-after," he said cynically.

When I was first diagnosed with cancer, I reviewed my life and wondered where I had gone wrong. Right away, I began making deals with God. I saw the disease as punishment for something bad I had done in the past. I stopped drinking, which wasn't difficult because I had never acquired the taste for it. Then I gave up smoking, a habit I had attempted to break at least once a year since I started at eighteen. I thought of all the women I had been with, and I couldn't think of anything really bad I had done, except that there was never a commitment—emotional or otherwise—no promises, no intentions for future plans; it was always about "the now." But I had respected them, never cheated. I thought of my father and his indiscretions, and remembered what Mama used to say about generational curses, how if you didn't watch out, you were bound to repeat them. *The sins of the father* . . . Then I thought of how I still hadn't forgiven him, even posthumously, but that didn't seem like enough to warrant being cursed with cancer. So I had this conversation with God and I told Him, if He'd let me live, I'd stop having meaningless relationships. Later, I learned that one thing you don't do is make deals with God. As Mama says, God isn't a game show host. *Don't negotiate with God 'cause you'll never win,* she'd said when I told her about my proposal.

The results of my blood tests were not good. My tumor markers, which were elevated before the surgery, had not returned to normal. The CT scan showed one enlarged lymph node, approximately 2.3 centimeters in diameter and another measuring 5 millimeters. The diagnosis was stage one nonseminoma cancer, which meant the cancer had spread to the lymph nodes. The oncologist offered me two choices: radical surgery to remove my lymph nodes or chemotherapy to shrink the tumors. Even if I opted for chemo, there was a chance that I might still need the surgery later. The prognosis was good, 90 percent curable. I decided to take my chances with chemo, which would start in a couple of weeks. I wanted to avoid major surgery at all costs, but I wasn't looking forward to the chemo. Not only because I had been cursed with bad veins, necessitating the re-opening of my central line, but also because it was going to be longer and more grueling. My life as I knew it would soon cease to be.

During my first chemo session, Mama brought my Bible, which she said she found stuffed in a drawer of summer clothes.

"You should always keep your Bible near you. On the nightstand or under your mattress," she told me.

I didn't answer because I knew silence was the only way to keep from arguing with her. I could tell she had been crying even behind her oversized, polarized, multi-focal glasses. She tried to force a smile.

"Your sister's coming by after work, after she drops off the babes at their father's."

I closed my eyes and kept quiet.

"You doing alright, Love?"

I was beginning to feel the effects of the chemo, the icy-cold feeling traveling down the vein in my chest followed by the queasiness. Between the initial saline drip inserted in a vein in my hand, followed by another drip with the antinausea medication, it would take about five to seven hours for the entire treatment. I opened my eyes slightly and patted her hand. "I'm okay, Mama."

"You sure? You look like you're in pain."

"I'm not, Mama. Just tired."

"You want me to read to you?" she asked, reaching for the bedside table.

A volunteer had dropped off the *Trib* during the morning rounds, but I knew she was referring to the Bible on top of the newspaper. To refuse the word of God was tantamount to blasphemy in her book. "If you want."

She picked up the Bible. "Look at that," she said, glancing at the paper. "They done shot up another school. Lord, what is this world coming to."

As with the first time I had cancer, she started with the book of Job to illustrate that what I was going through was nothing compared to what he had endured. *Yeah, that's what I needed, someone who had suffered more than I ever would*, I thought as I closed my eyes. *I felt so much better.*

Jade came by during the last hour of my treatment. She showed me some drawings from the kids, which made me smile. Sitting in a nearby chair, she leaned on the armrest of my chemo chair, interlocking her fingers in mine. Immediately, it reminded me of Eva. Almost as quickly, I pushed the thought of her from my mind.

"How're things with '*Akeel*'?" I asked, emphasizing his name sarcastically because I knew it would amuse her.

She smiled. "Good, I guess. He's a nice, sweet guy and everything . . ."

"But?"

"He's a little *too* nice."

"What do you mean?"

"He's just so *sweet.*"

"I guess it's true what they say. Women like bad boys."

"No. Not bad boys; guys with an edge. With a little excitement."

"Maybe he's what you need right now. The opposite of Brandon."

"I don't know if I can measure up to his standards. He's a church boy and he claims he's celibate."

"That's a good thing, isn't it?" In my eyes, not having to imagine my baby sister having sex was a good thing.

"I don't know, is it? I've never had a relationship that didn't involve sex. Have you?"

I hesitated, then shook my head. *Not anymore*, I thought.

"I don't know. It might be fun to see how long he lasts," she said.

"Don't you go tempting that church boy, Jezebel."

"Shut up."

She climbed into the chemo chair next to me, forcing me to move over as she laid her head on my shoulder. "Adam . . ."

Soon, I heard her sniffling and felt the tears seeping through my hospital-issue gown.

"C'mon, girl. Don't start. You know I got to deal with your mother and *her* tears. I can't take the both of you."

"I'm sorry," she sobbed quietly. "I don't want you to . . . "

"I'm not going anywhere."

" 'Cause I still need you."

"Yeah, to babysit." I chuckled half-heartedly.

"Promise?"

"I swear."

After the chemo session, all my body craved was sleep. When I got home, I didn't even make it to the bedroom, plopping down on the sofa and sleeping for four hours straight. When I woke up, I dragged myself from the sofa to the bedroom, only to fall into bed, fatigued. After another half hour, I had to force myself to get up and drink the required eighty ounces of water needed to flush the drugs out of my system. I was also instructed to exercise despite my weakness. The trips to the bathroom were about as much exercise as I could muster.

Television is never more mundane than when one is sick and stuck watching it for entertainment, or to kill time. Not even cable provided stimulation. Just a couple of weeks before I was up on the latest national and world news, but the outside world had become insignificant as the cancer took precedence. News to me meant negative CT scans and low tumor markers. Half the time I ended up turning off the set and listening to music, going through my entire CD collection from the late seventies until the present, eventually dozing off. Sometimes I woke up humming the last song that was playing just before I fell asleep.

At first, the side effects from the chemo were familiar and tolerable: flu-like symptoms, low-grade fever, mild nausea. The best part was that I had no loss of appetite—in the beginning.

By the end of the first cycle, which included five straight days of chemo, I spent the weekend inside my loft under two comforters curled up like it was winter, with chills, dizziness, lethargy, and non-stop nausea. The nausea was the worst; I almost prayed that I would vomit. Food lost its appeal and I was grateful for the Boost shakes I was able to keep down.

Swallowing my pride, I called Eva a couple of times, but her voice mail at home was full. Her assistant at work told me she had a family emergency, but couldn't give out any more information. I then called Luciano to see if he knew anything, but he wasn't able to reach Maya at work or on her cell phone either. I realized then something was definitely wrong.

Birthdays had never been a big deal for me. December babies always got cheated; the closer to Christmas, the bigger the rip-off. My family tried to make my thirty-seventh birthday special by throwing a surprise party, not a good idea given my situation. I was in my second week of chemo and developing more side effects from the drugs: a pimple-like rash on my back and torso, swelling in my legs called edema, and headaches. The headaches made me think of Eva and I wondered if hers had improved. I was given more medications for these side effects, which in turn had side effects of their own. Needless to say, I made a concerted effort to appear appreciative for the sake of Mama and Jade. I had become very adept at hiding my misery and pain behind false smiles.

After everyone left, just as I was being lulled to sleep by the sibilant sound of the TV, I heard a report about a shooting on a college campus. As I struggled to stay alert, I remembered my mother mentioning something at the hospital about a school shooting, and then I vaguely recalled the news report about a shooting the night of the snowstorm, the night Eva spent on my sofa. A spurned boyfriend had gone on a shooting rampage at ISU, the school Eva's sons attended, killing eight students. Half-dazed and lightheaded, I sat up as the photos of the dead students were flashed on the screen, holding my breath, thankful when her sons weren't among them. I began to put two and two together and presumed she must have gone downstate to check on her sons. Exhaling, I waited to hear how many students had been injured, and after learning six still remained hospitalized, I dialed her cell phone, hoping she had it turned on. I was surprised when it began ringing.

"Hello," I heard her anxious voice.

"Eva?"

"Adam," she said, and I thought I caught the slightest hint of disappointment in her voice.

"I just heard about the shooting. Where are you?"

"I'm down in Marion, near Carter. At the hospital."

"Are your sons okay?"

"They're in the hospital. Eli was shot twice, and he has a broken leg. He's conscious, but Tony's on a respirator. He was shot . . . in the head." Her voice was so deadpan, I figured she must have been numb with grief.

"Eva, I'm so sorry."

"Thanks. Maya and Simone are here. And my father, the pastor, and some church members. Everyone's helping out, praying. I just happened to go outside for some fresh air. They're supposed to call me if Tony wakes up, so I can't stay on the phone too long. I don't have call-waiting on this thing." The connection was so clear she seemed close enough to touch, yet her voice was so distant, distorted.

"Oh, okay, I understand."

"How have you been?"

"Me?" *It's my birthday,* I thought. *I have cancer again, but other than that, life's great.* "I'm fine."

"Yeah? You sound tired."

"You do, too." I wanted to tell her that I wished I was there with her, but I held my tongue. This was not the time. Also, I didn't want to put my heart out there to get shot down. I was too weak for rejection.

"I haven't slept much."

"Me either." I paused, then I took a deep breath and plunged in. "I've been thinking about you. About us." Suddenly, there was static as if she had moved out of range, perhaps deliberately, followed by silence that lasted so long, I thought we were disconnected. "Hello? Eva?"

"I have to go, Adam. I need to check on Tony."

"Okay."

"Thanks for calling. I'll call you, or call me back, whatever—"

There was more static and then we were disconnected for real. "Yeah, whatever," I said to the dead air.

As much as I hated to, I took a medical leave from work and a temporary absence from the Big Brothers program. It bothered me to back out on my obligations to Justin and Ricky, especially with Justin leaving for Midwestern U in the next month and Ricky improving in his new school. I couldn't let them witness my decline in health, though, especially Justin, who had watched his father slowly die from AIDS. At first, I thought about taking them out to dinner at Enchanted Castle, a pizza place with video games and karaoke, the only restaurant they had ever agreed upon. Somewhere I read that whenever parents had to break any bad news, like a divorce, they took their children to eat at a favorite restaurant. This seemed like a terrible idea to me, because the kids would always associate the place with the bad news, like the news of my father's cancer being synonymous with Navy Pier. I didn't want to do it at their house, so I brought them to my place, something I had occasionally done.

Ricky took the news fairly well, perhaps because he was too young to comprehend the complexity of cancer and because his father's illness and death was a family memory he had been told rather than experienced.

"Are they going to give you pills like me?" Ricky asked, his thumbs and forefingers moving lightning-fast on the controller of the PlayStation 2.

Perplexed, I looked at Justin, whose hands were frozen on his controller.

"He's talking about his Ritalin," Justin said quietly.

I chuckled. "No, it's a little more complicated. I have to go to the hospital and get my medicine through an IV. An intravenous line that goes into here," I explained, showing them my central line scar.

"Coo-ool!" Ricky said, taking his eyes off the football video game long enough to crane his neck to look at me. "I wish I had one of those. Then I wouldn't have to swallow those stupid pills."

I laughed and ran my hand over his head.

"Does chemotherapy hurt?" Ricky then asked, his eyes back on the TV screen.

"Not really. It makes me a little sick and really tired, so I won't be able to do a lot of things I used to. Like work and run. Or pick you guys up and take you around. "

"How long before you get better?"

"Not for a few months. Maybe as long as six, it's hard to say."

"Stop asking so many questions," Justin rebuked Ricky.

"That's okay. He can ask me questions."

"Whatever," Justin replied, annoyed.

"Man, I'm kickin' your team's butt," Ricky cried excitedly.

I looked over at Justin, who had set down his controller on the coffee table and was leaning back in the sofa.

"Justin? You want to ask me anything?"

He finally looked solemnly at me. I realized I was his age when my father died, but he looked so much younger. I remembered feeling so old.

"Is your cancer curable or incurable?" he asked.

"It's about ninety percent curable," I told him honestly. "When it's caught early."

"That's like a B."

I laughed quietly. "Yeah, it's like a high B, and a B is better than an F."

"I got a B on my math test," Ricky piped in. "I forgot to tell you—*touchdown!* Ha! I beat you. Bears win the Super Bowl!"

"Like that'll ever happen in real life," Justin said dismally.

I leaned back in the sofa next to Justin. "You know, one day, you're going to be glad you have a brother."

Of course he turned up his lip in revulsion.

"While I'm off getting treatment, I want you to do something for me."

Justin lit up, though he was careful not to show too much enthusiasm and lose his coolness.

"Stop giving your mama such a hard time," I told him seriously, then grabbed him in a half nelson. "If she calls and tells me you're making her cry, you and me are going to go at it like Mortal Kombat."

He scoffed.

"But seriously, when I went away to college, I missed my mama most of all," I said.

"Wimp," he teased.

I wrestled him to the floor, but he got the best of me in a matter of seconds because I had very little strength left.

Later, when I dropped them off back home, Justin turned to me and asked, "Do you still believe in God?"

"Yeah. I do."

"Why?" he asked, a look of bewilderment on his face.

"Because the alternative is worse."

"What's the alternative?"

"To believe in nothing."

He contemplated my answer, bunching his lips to the side, trying to weigh its validity. I couldn't imagine what it was like to believe in nothing.

During the treatment sessions, I passed the time with other men in the neighboring chemo chairs, and we got to know each other very well, sharing cancer war stories and providing encouragement.

We threw around terms like CBC reports, seminomas, teratomas, and the names of chemo drugs like we were doctors in training. There was Dan, a guy five years younger than me, who was a chemo cycle ahead of me. He had gone to my alma mater and was a social worker, so we had a lot in common. Then there was Mark, who made the nurses blush with his incessant flirting and never lost his sense of humor, even after he was told the cancer had spread to his kidneys and would require a transplant. When I told him about my screenplay, he said he had a brother who was an agent, and he offered to put in a good word for me. I was always the only African American, and a couple of times I got the predictable, "I thought Black guys didn't get this kind of cancer." But I learned that when there is a common enemy, race sometimes takes a backseat.

The hardest thing was watching the men who had wives and girlfriends with them. Of course, I wouldn't trade the support of my mother and sister for anything, but sometimes I missed not having someone special by my side, someone who could go home with me, lay with me, and wake up with me to face the next day's battle, and subsequently, the future. But then I tried to convince myself that it would probably be worse having one more female worrying about me, smothering me. And in the beginning, it worked.

I knew Mama and Jade would never complain about driving me to my appointments and being forced to rearrange their lives, but I couldn't help feeling guilty having to depend on them. I knew Mama was seeing Mr. Stevens on a regular basis and that Jade would rather be with Akil despite her protestations that he was not her type. In addition, Jade had the kids and her business to run. On the days my mother did not accompany me, she would go to church, to pray for me while Jade escorted me. The third and final week of the first cycle involved only one course on one day instead of five days. It was only the beginning of three, possibly four, cycles. The apprehension of starting the five-day treatment cycle all over again in another week set me on a collision course of depression and bitterness.

On the last day of my first cycle, it was Jade's turn to come with me. As soon as Rachel, the infusion nurse who was hooking me up, disconnected my central line, I felt sick and threw up, despite having had the antinausea medication. Jade, who had been a nonstop chatterbox about the latest wedding she was planning, gasped and turned her face away. Most of the bile landed on the floor, but some splashed on Rachel's white shoes. I groaned loudly, cursing under my breath.

"That's okay, Adam," Rachel said sympathetically as she began to clean up my mess. "Don't worry about it, okay?" Of all the nurses, Rachel was the best, the most patient. She patted my shoulder but I shook her off and immediately regretted it. I got up and walked to the bathroom to wash up. It was the first time I had thrown up; not a good sign.

By the time I went back into the room to apologize, she was gone.

Jade returned to her seat and began showing me more drawings from Kia and Daelen, her hands shaking. It was hard for me to force a smile, so I didn't try.

"Hey," she said, her voice trembling as she blinked back tears. "What's going on with you and Eva?"

I closed my eyes again and breathed slowly in and out through my nose, wishing she'd go away with the rest of the world. "Me and Eva? There is no me and Eva."

CHAPTER 23

EVA

DURING MY PREGNANCIES, I used to crave hot chocolate with marshmallows. Anthony joked that our babies would be born the color of milk chocolate and covered in marshmallows. On the day Tony died, the day after Christmas, the first day of Kwanzaa, I had gone to the cafeteria for some hot chocolate. The cafeteria had run out of marshmallows and a staff member had to go to the supply room to get more, and, because I couldn't drink hot chocolate without marshmallows, I waited. With the exception of the day Eli regained consciousness, I never left Tony's side for long periods, not even to visit Eli as he got stronger and better every day.

As I walked back to Tony's room, I saw Maya and Simone holding on to each other, and Anthony and my father leaning against opposite walls—all of them crying. The doctor met me at the door as I tried to get through. He explained that Tony had a seizure, and, despite their best exhaustive measures, they weren't able to save him. Then he apologized, but I could tell they were just words, a speech he had rehearsed in medical school while practicing different facial expressions, trying to see which looked the most sincere. A nurse tried to usher me into the hall, telling me I should wait until they cleaned him up. I handed her the cup of hot chocolate with the extra marshmallows and pushed her aside, my face daring her to touch me again. When I took Tony in my arms, he was still warm, and as I held him, his body slowly grew cold, causing my own body to shudder. Even as I felt his spirit leaving, I held him tighter, try-ing to hold it back. My father's words came back to me: *"In the end, like in the beginning, we all belong to God."* Remembering how I used to kiss Tony's soft spot when he was a baby, the pulse beating against my lips, I kissed the top of his head. I willed it to beat once again.

In my heart, I knew there were some things we as mortals weren't supposed to understand and the death of a child was one of them. I would never, nor did I ever want to, understand why that boy killed my son. Why he killed all those students before turning the gun on himself. *Why couldn't he just kill himself?* I thought angrily. Maybe God was testing my faith. Or maybe He was punishing me for Adam. Yes, Tony's death was my payback. God may have forgiven me, but the consequences of my immoral act remained. I played, now I had to pay. Now I had to take my medicine like a good Christian.

The days following Tony's death were shrouded in haziness as I went into automatic pilot, making arrangements to transfer his body to Chicago, for Eli's discharge and subsequent assistance at home, and for the funeral. On the outside, I appeared to be the pic-ture of rationality, the strong woman, a faithful believer who didn't question God. Internally, I was deteriorating slowly, day by day. When Eli broke down and said he couldn't live without his brother, I told him he would. While everyone cried and mourned around me, it was I who comforted *them*.

It gave me a little comfort knowing that Tony was saved the year before, but it wasn't enough to smother the pain of what his loss would mean in my life. Everyone said it would, with time. But I knew my wounds would not be healed with bandages or medicine or time, I didn't care what anyone said. I knew that every time I looked at his pictures, every year on his birthday, whenever I thought of him, I would be reminded that he was dead and he would never graduate or marry or give me grandchildren or grow old. And I knew these things only had merit in this temporary world we called life. I knew they were insignificant things compared to the greater glory, but he was my son and I wanted to hold on to my memories of him, the dear things I would never have, for as long as I could. I knew no matter what, there would always be a hole in my heart.

At the funeral, there were family members I hadn't seen or heard from in years, many of Tony's classmates from college and high school. The church was filled to capacity, and it seemed everyone had only good memories of Tony. I vaguely remembered Johnny, teary-eyed, hugging me, his words of condolence undecipherable. Many of my coworkers came, including Dana, Rashid, and the dean. I was so calm and quiet, I scared Maya and Simone, who tried everything to get me to talk. Through it all, I kept it together, even consoling Anthony's mother when she collapsed at Tony's casket. Tony had always been her favorite.

My Aunt Titi, who comforted me and Maya during the difficult years after our mother's death, came up to me at the burial site, after everyone else had long drifted away. I hadn't seen her in a couple of years since she left for Puerto Rico to care for my sick grandmother. She was booked on a flight back to the island that night.

"*Estoy muy preocupada por ti,*" she said, and at first, I found it difficult to translate the words into English in my muddled mind. It took me a few seconds to interpret the words: *I'm very worried about you.*

"Why?" I answered in English.

"I haven't seen you cry at all," she said, switching to English. "You need to cry, *mija.*"

"I've got the rest of my life to cry," I said. I didn't know why I had yet to cry. Perhaps I was too angry. Perhaps I was afraid if I started, I would never stop.

After the repast, Maya and Simone offered to stay and help me clean the house into the night. I knew the minute I fell asleep, I would dream about Tony, and when I woke up, his death would be more real. Since Eli's room was in the finished basement, we switched my bedroom with his, to make it easier for him to get around in his wheelchair. Thankfully, Tony's room was in the converted attic; I wouldn't have to pass it by since I had no reason to climb the stairs. Eventually, I would have to clean it, but that day would not come for a long time.

"Alex agreed to go to counseling," Maya said, making my bed. "We found this husband and wife team who do marital therapy. They both have Ph.D.'s and they're Christian. *And* they're a biracial couple, which is the main reason Alex agreed."

I was scrubbing down the walls, something I hadn't done since I moved in.

"Eva, did you hear what I said?"

"I heard you, hon. That's nice." Although I had my back to them, I could feel them giving each other looks and gesturing behind my back.

"Did I tell you I've given up Zephyr and Ian?" Simone announced. "Cold turkey. I told them that I had to find out what the Creator had in store for me. They both said I had lost my mind. But I told them, 'on the contrary, I think I just found it.'" She laughed.

"Isn't that great, Eva?" Maya asked. "I think Ms. S'Monée's on her way to getting saved."

"Now, I didn't say all that," Simone said.

I should have been happy. My sister had decided to save her marriage while my best friend was trying to save herself. It had taken my son's death to make them see what was precious and important. Because of my loss, every mother at TCCC would hug her child just a little tighter at night, every father would be less harsh the next time he had to discipline his child. My loss would serve as a lesson to anyone who had taken life for granted. Death had a funny way of scaring people straight.

It was almost midnight when we finished. They tried to spend the night but I pushed them out the door. They knew that when my mind was made up, there was no changing it.

Eli had fallen asleep on the sofa bed, so I didn't disturb him. Still avoiding my own bed, I decided to clean out the drawers of the dining room hutch. In the bottom drawer, I came across the sympathy cards and letters where I had tossed them as they came in, without reading them. I couldn't read the words, "I'm sorry for your loss" without reading, "I'm glad it wasn't my child." I opened them one by one, scanning them quickly. There were cards from neighbors, coworkers, parishioners, Cara and Rashid, even one from Johnny.

And then there was a padded envelope from Adam. Maya had mentioned that she got a call from Adam and I half-expected him at the wake or funeral. When he didn't show, I was disappointed, but at the same time relieved because I wasn't ready to face him. Inside the envelope, there was a gift wrapped in Christmas paper with brown-skinned, curly-haired angels. I didn't have to open it to know it was a CD. There was also a brand new, clean copy of his book of poems. On the title page of the book an inscription read: *Many women do noble things, but you surpass them all. Charm is deceptive, and beauty is fleeting; but a woman who fears the Lord is to be praised.* Below that, he had signed his name in Spanish: *Adán.* On the dedication page, he had written: *I am so sorry about your son. I miss you. Call me.* With a composure that was becoming a typical and normal emotion for me, I placed everything inside the envelope and put it back into the drawer.

Day by day, Eli became morose and distant, and it was evident that he was taking Tony's death especially hard. He barely spoke to the point of muteness, never asked for anything, and responded in grunts or monosyllables whenever I tried to initiate conversation. If some news update or feature about the shooting came on, he would quickly change the channel. He unbraided his hair but wouldn't let me rebraid it, nor would he untangle it. Getting him to bathe and shave was a battle. King sensed that Eli was not the same master who played and teased him. He barked constantly at the wheelchair for the first few days, before settling down at Eli's feet whenever Eli sat listlessly in front of the TV, or followed him as he rolled aimlessly throughout the house.

It was hard to tell if Eli's weekly visits to the therapist were helping since he wasn't speaking. I also had sessions with Kahinde, the therapist, who was a faith-based counselor. Although she couldn't divulge the specifics of their conversations, she assured me that Eli's moods were normal considering what he had been through. She diagnosed Eli with posttraumatic stress disorder and said it could be months before his mood would change or he was back to normal, with God's help, of course. Kahinde insisted on concentrating on my own therapy sessions, but when I told her I had already accepted Tony's death as God's will, she decided I was in denial. Since she was the expert, I didn't disagree with her or argue when she insisted on extending my sessions.

Anthony stopped by more often to visit Eli, which seemed to lift his spirits, especially since Anthony had never visited the house. We talked very little about our past together, concentrating on the topic of Eli's recovery.

The week after Tony's funeral, Anthony and I were having coffee in the dining room, talking quietly while Eli slept, something he was doing a lot of lately. It had been years since we had talked face-to-face. Most of our conversations had always been over the phone or from car windows when dropping off or picking up the boys when they were younger.

"I think he needs to go back to school," Anthony said.

"When he wants to go back, he'll go back. And I doubt he wants to go back there."

"A lot of the students have gone back."

"A lot of the students didn't get shot."

"The sooner he goes back, the better off he'll be."

"I see. He should just pretend nothing happened," I said, my voice rising.

"No, Eva, that's not what I'm saying. But he can't let this incident define his whole life."

His statement made me angry, something I had reserved for my son's killer. As selfish as it sounded, I wanted the world to stop for a while and acknowledge my son's death. It didn't seem fair that everyone was going about their daily lives when Tony no longer could.

"I'm sorry, but I'm not one of those people who thinks life should go on," I told him, abruptly clearing the table. "I think he should be as angry and as sad for as long as he needs to. I'm sick of people acting like getting shot is something we have to live with! Like, oh well, it's a sign of the times." I stopped because my voice was quivering and I didn't want to get hysterical in front of Anthony. "Did you forget his brother was killed?"

Anthony glared at me, his chin sticking out and trembling. "He was my son."

My heart softened for him, but only for a moment. I exhaled and lowered my voice. "He'll go back when he's ready."

Anthony got up and when he moved toward me, I looked at him like he was crazy. "Come here," he said, his voice low and gentle. It had been twenty years since his voice had pacified me and a part of me wanted to collapse against him, find comfort in his embrace. It didn't take much to please me back then.

"No," I said sharply.

When he advanced, I retreated and he backed off, shaking his head. "Still Tough Diva-Eva," he scoffed. He didn't understand; it wasn't his arms I wanted to be in.

I took a family medical leave from work, partly because I didn't want to go on with "business as usual," but mostly because I was afraid Eli would hurt himself, although he never specifically threatened to do anything. For the most part, I continued going to church, but my heart wasn't in it. I sang and clapped during praise and worship, going through the motions. Once, during spiritual emphasis week, I caught my reflection in one of the church's mirrors and I was amazed at how normal I looked, as if nothing had happened. *Tough Diva-Eva.* Eli, who had always viewed church as a social gathering where he could flirt with church girls, refused to go at all.

At the gym, the punching bag became the killer, the NRA, all the senseless, stupid violence that threatened the world on a daily basis, and forever changed my life and that of my sons. Ordinarily, I didn't like to sweat, but as it trickled from every pore, it was as if my body were weeping, compensating for my dry eyes.

New Year's Day came and left. All of the TV channels ran stories about the year in review, featuring the shootings at ISU as one of three major incidents of gun violence that had occurred. I couldn't watch any of it. I couldn't understand how the parents of the murdered students could talk to reporters about their personal pain, crying on camera for all the world to see. It all seemed so sadistic. I turned down all requests for interviews. One reporter was especially persistent, speaking to me in Spanish as if that would make me open up to her. My patience worn, I finally told her in Spanish, "When *your* son is killed, then we can talk." She stopped calling.

After a few weeks, Eli's moods did change—for the worse. He became angry and nasty, prone to sudden outbursts of violence. Whenever King climbed the stairs to Tony's room and whined at the door, Eli yelled or threw objects at him. Out of the blue, he would punch the walls or anything in his way, making dents in the refrigerator, dishwasher, and a hole in the pantry's faux wood door. With his hair turning into untamed dreadlocks, he began to look like a deranged homeless man.

Finally, after he punched yet another dent in the fridge, I confronted him, gripping the armrests of his wheelchair and leaning into his face, his wild, untamed hair hanging in his apathetic eyes. "Look, if you want to hit something, you can come to the gym with me and we'll hit the bag together. But *do not* take your anger out on my house. I know you're angry, but making *me* angry is not going to make your life easier."

"Leave me alone!" he snapped, trying to wheel the chair around me. I held on to it. He screamed louder, "Get out of my face!"

"If you don't want to talk to me, that's fine. But don't scream at me, okay?"

He bit his bottom lip and looked away. I knew he was on the verge of breaking down into tears and he was trying hard not to do it in front of me, so I left him alone.

As I walked away, I heard him mutter under his breath, "I told you I didn't want to go away to school."

I stopped, and turned languidly around to face him.

He was glaring at me through his snarled hair with a hatred in his eyes I had never seen. He had always been the good-natured one, who could make me laugh with his mischievous smile, a smile I hadn't seen in weeks.

"You should've let me join the air force like I wanted. This never would've happened. Tony would still be alive."

I stood paralyzed, as his words sunk in. I couldn't think of a response to defend myself or to console him, so I grabbed my keys and left the house. I thought of driving to Montrose, but with the exception of the day Adam and I broke up, it had been my sanctuary and I was in no mood to feel good.

When I returned later that night after driving around aimlessly, the house was dark and eerily quiet. I had driven by Simone's place, and then Maya's house, but the last thing I wanted to do was talk. I then drove by Adam's building and noticed his windows were dark. I didn't want to talk to him; I just wanted to feel that pang of desire sweep through me once more, to force myself to remember the feelings I could never allow him to ignite again.

As I walked down the hallway, I heard the faint sound of snipping and found Eli in the darkened bathroom. Flipping the light switch, I watched in horror as he haphazardly clipped his hair, his long tangled brown locks floating to the floor. He hadn't cut his hair in five years.

"Elias," I gasped, when I found my voice.

"I was watching the History Channel," he said in dull, flat tone. "Did you know the Indians used to cut their hair when somebody died?"

I watched him wordlessly as he continued clipping, his eyes distant and dazed, recalling the times I had braided his hair, oiled his scalp, some of our most cherished bonding moments. After a while, I gestured for the scissors and he surrendered them silently, remaining immobile as I finished the job. Then I took the electric clippers and gave him a nice fade. I ran my hand over his smooth new cut, remembering his misshapen newborn head, recalling how Tony's head felt, the last part of him I kissed. Realizing that it had been some time since I kissed Eli, I bent to kiss his head, but he saw me leaning in the mirror and flinched away from me. Tears filled my eyes but I held them back.

"Cut it lower," he said. "Like Tony's."

In the empty space in my heart, I felt a stab of pain and I clutched at my chest. It was all I could do to keep from bawling when I heard him say his brother's name.

*   *   *

As the days went by, things improved somewhat for both of us. There were times when I began to feel some semblance of my old life returning, but then I'd remember Tony was forever gone, that things would never be the same.

One evening, just as I was turning off a news program after yet another story regarding the shootings, I caught a clip of the makeshift memorial students had erected in front of the dorm with stuffed animals, flowers, posters with messages, and photos. As the camera panned the memorial, I saw Tony's yearbook photo and I literally got sick, making it to the bathroom just in time. The last thing I wanted was to remember the site where my son had met his fate.

Eli's leg was in a cast for six weeks and as soon as it came off, he seemed to come to life. With a brace on his leg, he was able to get around with more ease. Using a cane, he took King on short walks and began to shoot baskets in the yard.

One day, I caught him standing in front of the full-length mirror in the bathroom, staring at the scars on his bare torso: one in his chest, one in his belly. I leaned in the doorway and he glanced at me in the mirror.

"Ma, look," he said, chuckling, and just as suddenly stopped. "They look funny."

They didn't look funny to me at all, but it was something that the old Eli would have said, so I took it to heart. Eli was back.

Nights were the worst when I would lay wide awake, praying to God to plug the hole in my heart, as I tried to remember Tony's face, tried to forget what the last minutes of his life were like before the shooting. Even though I wasn't there, the image of him dropping to the ground would replay over and over in my mind. It was during the nights that I thought of Adam, how he was also forever gone from my life. I tried not to think about Adam in the same space as Tony's memory, how Adam had looked at me the last time we were together, how he had kissed me with such tenderness, how good it would've been to bury myself in his arms until I fell asleep. One day, I finally opened his gift and found a CD he had burned of Tracy

Chapman and India.Arie's greatest hits. On the disc, in permanent marker, he had written, "To Eva; Love, Adam." I picked up the phone, telling myself I was only going to thank him, but my guilty conscience won over my gratitude and I hung up. Thinking of him made me feel selfish and wicked. Although Kahinde constantly reiterated that it wasn't my fault, I blamed myself. If I hadn't insisted Eli go to ISU, he wouldn't have been shot. If I hadn't constantly nagged Tony to watch out for his brother, he never would have come out of the dorm room to check on him when he heard the shots. If I hadn't given into temptation, God wouldn't have needed to test my faith. And Tony would still be alive.

One night, I awoke with a sensation that something, someone was hovering over me. Even though I don't believe in ghosts, I had heard of people who dreamed of deceased loved ones, so my first thought was that it was Tony. I shot up in bed as my heart fought to jump out of my chest, rubbed my eyes until Eli came into focus. With his newly shaven head, he resembled Tony, but Eli was taller, thinner. Ordinarily, his hobbling gait and cane coming down the basement stairs would have been enough to awaken me, so I must have fallen into a deep sleep.

"What?!" I yelled, frantically.

"Ma . . ." was all he could say.

I snapped on the lamp and looked at his contorted face. He looked like a little boy again, awakened by a thunderstorm or a bad dream. "Eli. What is it? Are you in pain?"

I lifted the covers and he readily crawled into bed next to me. I pulled him to me in spoon fashion just as I had when he was little, although now his body was too long to fit in the cocoon I formed with my body. But I held on to him tightly as his body shook with sobs. It had been so long since he allowed me to hug him.

"Talk to me, *mijo*," I crooned.

He stopped crying long enough to squeeze out, "I can't," before his voice broke again. I held him tighter and let him cry for about a half hour or so.

"Ma . . ." he started again just as I was drifting off to sleep. "I played dead. After he . . . I got shot, I played dead. Tony came out of Rain's room when he heard the shooting. I could've yelled to warn him, but . . . There were all these people . . . bodies on top of me, and somebody started screaming . . . I heard more shooting above me . . . on top . . . Everybody on top of me was dying . . . so I played dead."

"Oh, baby. It's not your fault."

"I should've yelled but I didn't want to get shot any more. I just kept praying that I didn't die instead of yelling for Tony to go back."

He started crying uncontrollably again and all I could do was hold him and repeat over and over, "It wasn't your fault."

As his body shook, my own tears fell onto his back. My heart ached for him, all he had gone through and kept inside, for everything he would always remember.

"I miss him so much," he finally said, his voice congested and shaky.

An avalanche of memories washed over me as I pressed Eli's body closer. I remembered how I used to tell the boys to love each other after pulling them apart from a fight, their chests heaving, their eyes ablaze with contempt. I thought of how Tony had more than once declared, *"Am I my brother's keeper?"* whenever I asked him to keep an eye on Eli. And I remembered them holding hands before pre-adolescence dictated it wasn't cool, how they would laugh covertly at me when I did something old-fashioned or what they considered "Hispanic," like when I dressed in eccentric outfits or started speaking Spanish out of the blue.

"I know, *mijo*. I miss him, too."

Early the next morning, I awoke to find Eli gone from my side. After checking his room, I found him snoring, the covers around his head like a hajib. I drove to Montrose Harbor, parking outside the barricades that now sealed off the closed beach, not caring if I got a ticket. There were a few runners out, a couple walking their dog. A fresh dusting of snow covered everything and the bitter wind quickly cut off the circulation to my bare hands, head, and ears. My car-length leather jacket and fashionable boots were not sufficient protection, more suited for early fall than midwinter and my teeth were involuntarily chattering, but I ignored them. It was so savagely cold, it hurt to breathe. But looking out across the harbor, for one brief moment, I forgot to breathe and overlooked the freezing temperature. The lake was dazzling, awesome in its simplistic beauty, the waves closest to the shore frozen in midmotion, resembling icebergs like fabulous sculptures only God's hand was capable of creating. I stood on the top revetment, watching the horizon in muted fascination, trying hard to clear my mind.

For just a little while, I didn't want to think about anything. Before long, my mind started numbing and I could feel my heartbeat throbbing in my head, which felt too heavy for my neck. I didn't have my migraine medication with me and this suited me fine. More pain. I wanted to feel as much pain as possible, just on the brink of death. I didn't want to die; death was too easy.

Suddenly I felt weak and began to sway on my feet, so I slipped to the ground and sat down. I realized I hadn't eaten the day before and couldn't remember when I had, only that I had drank coffee.

A memory crept into my mind, of the winter when I was ten, playing in the snow with Maya and my father as my mother watched us from the window. I had been so excited about making a snowman with the fresh wet snow that I hadn't bothered to put on my boots. Even when I couldn't feel my feet, I kept playing until my mother had to drag me indoors. When I pulled off my gym shoes and socks, my feet were red and painful, the air making the pain worse. I didn't start crying until my mother placed my feet into a bucket of warm water, which felt like a million pins stabbing me. My parents thought I was exaggerating but they didn't realize I had early frostbite until they took me to the hospital. Later that night, after my mother had safely tucked me into bed, and kissed my bandaged feet, I had a dream that the doctors had cut off my feet. I woke up screaming.

The memory of that night was so vivid, I could still hear my screams. Then I realized that I was screaming. At first, I cried sounds of bilingual frustration, "AHHH!" and "AYYY!" Then I yelled to drown out a plane flying overhead, so I could be heard in the heavens above. I screamed until my voice gave out and my throat

was hoarse and raw. Suddenly, I realized I had forgotten to visit my
mother's grave on her birthday, hadn't thought of her in a long time.
Would Tony also "slip" my mind in a few years? The thought made
me cry out harder.

Looking out across the lake, I remembered the day Tony had
asked, *"Is that heaven, Mommy? Is that where we go when we die?"* I
could hear his animated voice in the wind, could see his cherub
face, too serious for a four-year-old. I tried to remember what my
reply had been. Had I said, *"I think so,"* or *"You're never going to die,
baby"*? I couldn't remember.

I knew my face, hands, and feet were on the verge of frostbite, vi-
brating with hypothermia. But it felt justified, the ultimate punishment for finally succumbing to my temptations while my sons were
under attack. I imagined someone finding me frozen solid in a sitting position like an archaeological discovery.

God never gives you more than you can bear. I had been hearing
that saying all my life.

"I can't bear this, Lord, I can't," I said, my voice inaudible and
ragged.

I didn't want to understand my son's death, or accept it, I just
wanted the pain to be over, once and for all. Maybe one day I would
find peace with the fact that Tony was chosen because he was the
saved one. Perhaps Eli was left behind in order to provide him with
another chance to give his life to the Lord. If it had been the other
way around, if Eli had died, I had to believe Tony's somber demeanor would have made it more difficult to handle his younger
brother's death. And then I heard my Father's voice: *He's going to be
alright. He's with Me.*

"You're going to be alright," I heard the voice say louder, a voice
that was gentle and tranquil, a voice that belonged to a nurse. Dazed
and cold, I couldn't turn around right away. At first I thought I was
hearing voices because I had heard that that's what happened when
one went into shock. Then I knew it was God, that it had to be God
talking to me. I knew many people didn't believe hearing God's
voice was possible, and immediately labeled you crazy, a Jesus freak,
a fanatic. But He talked to people all the time, through others,

through signs. I heard the same voice again, louder, a voice that filled my body with warmth and comfort like a moving gospel song that gave me chills.

"I said, 'are you alright'?" the voice asked, and I realized I had misunderstood the first time.

Shivering, I turned and saw a woman in a sweat suit, running shoes, mittens, and a hat—all in white. The first thing I thought was, *You're not supposed to wear white after Labor Day*.

"Do you need help?" Before I could answer, she crouched down to my level, her strange muted eyes benevolent, full of concern. She handed me her mittens. When I didn't take them, she slipped them on to my hands as I watched like a child who didn't yet know how to tie her shoes. Then she put her skullcap over my head. I felt God's presence in her, His fatherly hands trying to heal my wounds, mend my heart.

"No," I said, finding my voice, though it was barely there. "I'm alright."

Slowly, my body warmed up as heat flowed into my extremities and through my head like new blood from a transfusion. On the outside, I trembled, colder than February, but inside I was warmer than August. With the woman's help, I got up and walked sluggishly back to my car, anxious to turn on the heat. I was eager to get home, to Eli, my son who awaited me.

CHAPTER 24

ADAM

LONG BEFORE MY father got sick, I had accepted the fact that death was as natural as life. When I was eight, my favorite older cousin, Steve, died suddenly on the football field of an undetected congenital heart defect. Four years later, my grandfather was killed in a car accident. And when I was fourteen, my mother's only sister, Violeta, who had been unable to conceive, finally became pregnant at age forty only to die in childbirth, something I thought had gone out with polio and scarlet fever. Death was something that came suddenly, angry like a fist, silent like the night. It could happen to anyone, any time. No one was immune.

It wasn't until my father's death that I was a witness to how calculating and cruel dying could be. I watched my father disintegrate from a two-hundred-pound retired navy man and police sergeant to a one-hundred-twenty-pound skeleton. One day the doctors told my mother there was nothing more they could do for my father and sent him home to die. The rest, my mother said, was up to God.

In a way, I always knew that some day I would make peace with my demons—or rather the one demon that had dogged me for almost twenty years. Only I always thought I would be older, in my fifties or sixties, wiser and docile, the anger finally gone out of me like air from a flat tire. I figured I would be more optimistic, closer to the end of my life, when the things that had mattered when I was young and foolish no longer held any value. I would be able to look back on his memory and see *him*, not as a stereotypical man, aka a dog, but a real man, a human being with faults, born to err. And I would be able to forgive him, finally.

And so, on a very sunny and frigid March day, I walked over the dead grass of St. Michael's Cemetery, past monuments, tombstones, and markers that men erected in honor of the dead, much like the material possessions they coveted in life. Only the stone and marble blocks with all their fancy proverbs and epitaphs meant nothing to the dead, only to the living.

Two years ago, my life was divided into "before" and "after." Before cancer and after cancer. Now, it was "the first time" and "the second time," and I hoped, the last time. I remembered thinking how invincible I felt after surviving the first time, how I feared nothing after enduring cancer. Now, I took it back. I had always feared its return. And now that it had, the possibility of my dying scared me to the point where I found myself praying not only at night, but throughout the day, more times than the most devout Muslim who prayed five times a day. *Did God listen to the prayers of sinners?* I wondered.

That morning when my mother called to ask me if I wanted to visit my father's grave, I gave her the same answer I had given her for the last nineteen years: *No, ma'am.* It wasn't his anniversary and I didn't understand why she was going, but I didn't ask. She was silent for a moment, and I waited for her usual line of questioning, expecting her to plead with me given my current circumstances, but she simply replied, "Alright, Love," and hung up. She went alone, according to my sister.

I followed the directions I had received from the cemetery office and found his gravesite in the veterans' section without any problem. The closer I got, the slower I walked, not only with reluctance, but with fatigue. All morning long and on the drive to the cemetery, I kept reminding myself of all the things I wasn't going to do: talk to him, say a prayer, cry.

But as soon as I saw his name—Nelson Charles Black—followed by his birth and death dates, and the inscription: *Beloved Son, Husband, and Father*, my eyes started tearing and I had to choke back a sob. I tightened my jaw and squeezed the bridge of my nose where a permanent bump now resided, thanks to Brandon Cho, and momentarily regained my composure. Self-consciously, I looked around the cemetery, grateful I was alone. On his grave, there was a small bouquet of carnations, undoubtedly left by my mother. Although we didn't talk about it, I knew Jade visited his grave the most, not only on his death anniversary, but on his birthday, Father's Day, and the patriotic holidays. Quite unexpectedly, I felt guilty for coming empty-handed, but the feeling passed just as quickly as it had appeared.

Squatting down with my elbows on my knees, I tried hard to think of something to say. Mama told me that when the other woman found out about her, she refused to let her children visit my father, their father, in the hospital during his illness. It was Mama who called to tell the woman about his death and the funeral arrangements, and it was Mama who made amends. Now, I wondered if "his other kids," as Jade referred to them, visited his grave. Before that day, I hardly thought of them at all.

There was a time when I didn't hate him, and I tried to concentrate and build on that. I tried to remember the happy times, the family things we did together, the nights I'd wait up for him when he was on second shift, before I knew about his other life. Still no words came. I then tried to think of an appropriate prayer and the only one that came to mind was Psalm 23, which I had memorized for a Sunday school competition years ago.

"The Lord is my Shepard, I shall not want . . ." I began, my voice a monotone.

Before he died, my father accepted Christ as his savior. I was there when it happened, in the living room, which had been converted into his temporary bedroom, complete with hospital bed, IV, and the shark cartilage pills he was convinced were going to cure him. I listened as my mother's pastor asked him to repeat the words that transformed him from sinner to saint, *"Lord Jesus, I repent of my sins. I believe You died for my sins. I ask You to come into my heart. I make You my Lord and Savior."* My father could barely speak, and each syllable was an effort in itself. I had expected some miraculous

vision, some kind of change to come over his face, like peace, something immediate and different. I had expected him to be saved from
death, to live. But afterward, my father looked the same, pallid and
pain-stricken, and a week later, he died.

" *'Yea, though I walk through the valley of the shadow of death, I will
fear no evil, for thou art with me.'* " The words were coming back to
me as a matter of course as if they were something I said every day.
And then before I could get to the end, my voice broke and tears
were blinding me.

"Stop!" I cried out, straightening up quickly and covering my eyes
with the heels of my hands. Incensed and embarrassed, I pressed
down with all my might until I could see the colors of the rainbow in
geometric designs behind my lids, trying to force the tears back from
wherever they came. But they seeped around the edges, forcing me to
acknowledge their existence.

More than anything I wanted to curse him, but what came out of
my mouth was the complete opposite. "God!" I dropped down to
my knees, still shielding my eyes, trying to keep my emotions intact
and hidden inside.

At that moment I began to see things clearly for the first time in
my life, past the black and white, past the shades of gray. For almost
twenty years I had stayed away, determined to prove that the seventeen years he had been my father had meant nothing after learning
about his other family, determined to believe that it didn't matter
whether I ever forgave him. I had awakened that morning with no
intention of coming to the cemetery. And yet, here I was. The only
explanation was one word: God. God had led me to this place on
this day.

As my body shook silently with years of pent-up lamentation, I
uttered the words I had pushed deep within me years ago, the words
my father, my true Father, had been waiting to hear: "I forgive you."

Things were different the second time. It was hard enough recovering from the orchiectomy, but then during my second cycle of
chemotherapy, the unexpected happened. I began to lose my hair,
which had survived the first time. The first time, I had attributed its

endurance to my strong, resilient African roots. This time around, one day while greasing my scalp, I noticed that as I parted my hair, knotted coils began to fall out easily. A couple of days later, a simple touch yielded more strands. I didn't care so much at first because I had plenty of hair to spare, but it physically hurt. It was as if every single hair were attached by a needle into my scalp, and any touch, any contact like laying on the pillow, felt like the needles were pricking my head. The pain convinced me that my hair was connected to the rest of me like a limb; once it was gone, it would never come back. If it couldn't survive, how could I?

By the second weekend, I was able to pull whole locks with a simple tug, leaving sporadic patches on my head like a really bad haircut. Dr. Desai said it was a good sign, proof that the drugs were killing the cancer. Looking in the mirror was agony. When I brushed my teeth, I kept the medicine cabinet open. Dr. Desai gently suggested I shave my head. I refused.

Every few days, my mother experimented with different kinds of oils: olive, coconut, and carrot, which she massaged into my scalp twice a day. Nothing worked. I started wearing a bandana. Luciano brought me a beret, which I wore on top of the bandana, making me look rather cool, like some throwback revolutionary.

Despite this, there were days when I felt like I was actually getting better, overcoming the side effects, winning the battle. As my strength returned and my frame of mind improved, I began to take longer walks, e-mail friends and coworkers, and work on my screenplay. I began incorporating my illness into the screenplay, which kept my mind off the cancer. It was as if by transferring the illness to the protagonist in my future film, I was purging the poison from me.

There were even moments that stretched into hours that stretched into days when I forgot I had cancer—as long as I didn't look in any mirrors. My hair loss was a constant reminder that the cancer was real. And it wasn't a vanity issue, rather my hair had been an act of resistance, one of those never-ending battles with my father who felt that anything longer than a military cut was anti- and counter-everything he stood for. My father had always worn his patriotism like a medal. He hated people who celebrated the Fourth and Memorial Day with barbecues and picnics without giving a thought to the soldiers who had fought and died in past wars.

I remembered seeing pictures of myself as a child with an Afro in the seventies and thinking how rebellious and free I looked. In the eighties when my boys in high school were abusing their hair with the Jeri Curl, I began braiding mine. My father and I fought over my braids like suburban fathers battled with their punk sons who had green-dyed Mohawks. In his last days, my father asked me to do something for him. Anything, I answered. He asked me to cut my hair and I did. After the funeral, I started growing it again. Dreadlocks were not only an expression of my African heritage, but a sign of nonconformity, a last stand against my father, even if he was no longer here. So, yes, losing my hair was very traumatic.

By the end of the second course of chemo, there was no use putting it off and I decided it was time to shave my head. The fact that baldness was in, and even considered sexy according to Derek and popular media, did little to cheer me up. Reluctantly, I let Mama, the ex-beautician, do the honors. She did it in the kitchen, away from any mirrors, and then I washed my head in the sink. When it was time to look at myself, the steps to the nearest mirror were the longest I ever had to take. My head felt weightless without the excess mane, detached from my body. I was alright when Mama embraced me from behind, murmuring gently, "It's only hair, Love. It'll grow back so fast." I even held it together when Jade burst into tears as soon as she saw me. But when Daelen announced, "Unc-Adam don't got no hair no more," I lost it. I went to the bathroom and cried like a kid who was denied candy, swallowing sobs in huge gulps.

The only solace was that my eyebrows and eyelashes had so far been spared, although Luciano joked that my eyebrows could use some thinning. The best part was that I had no razor stubble and I wouldn't have to shave, something I had always found cumbersome.

And then just as I was getting used to my shorn head, Dr. Desai gave me the latest results of my blood tests. My tumor markers were up and the CT scan showed that while one of the lymph nodes had only slightly diminished in size, the other one had grown considerably. In addition, a teratoma was discovered, which, although a noncancerous growth, had the tendency to grow and push other organs out of the way and lead to additional cancerous growths. Surgery was strongly recommended.

"There's no way around it, Adam. The chemo's not shrinking the nodes," she insisted. "You *need* the RPLND."

Retroperitoneal lymph node dissection. I had read about the major surgery required to remove the lymph nodes, followed by a two-week bed rest. The chemo guys referred to it as "ripped" surgery because the doctors literally slashed an eighteen-inch incision from the sternum to below the belly button, then pushed the major organs aside in order to cut out the lymph nodes located deep in the abdomen. The first time, my lymph nodes had been cancer-free.

The news literally knocked the air out of me. When I started breathing again, my breaths came fast and hard, labored and I couldn't control them. Dr. Desai kept asking me if I was alright as she searched her office for a bag. When she couldn't find one, she pushed my head down between my knees until I stopped hyperventilating. Her warm hand felt soothing on the back of my neck.

"What if I don't have the surgery?" I stupidly inquired.

"What, are you kidding me?" she asked in disbelief.

Ever since I received the news, I had taken to rubbing my torso trying to imagine what it was going to be like to have a huge scar, to be without lymph nodes, whose purpose and existence was a mystery until now.

There was no one I could talk to about death, or rather the possibility of my dying. I certainly couldn't talk to my mother, who shunned all negative talk and quoted Proverbs 18:21: *"The tongue has the power of life and death, and those who love it will eat its fruit."* She truly believed in the power of positive thinking and speaking, that if I believed in my heart that I wasn't going to die, and spoke the words, then I wouldn't die. Never mind Jade who cringed at the sight of a needle. And whenever I brought up the topic with Luciano, he brushed me off, repeating, "You ain't gonna die, man," as if him saying so made it so.

I thought about calling Eva, but the last thing she probably wanted to do was talk about death. I could only imagine the pain she was going through, having both her sons shot, and then losing Tony. I couldn't even begin to imagine anything happening to Kia or Daelen. I had wanted to pay my respects but I wasn't sure how I fit in since I wasn't family or a friend. In retrospect, the sympathy card I sent seemed inadequate, but her lack of response in the past few months confirmed that she probably no longer considered me a part of her life. I tried not to think of her at all: her skin, her lips, her touch, and especially that last night, the night that determined the beginning of our end. In an ironic twist, now that sex wouldn't be an issue for me, at least for a while, I was probably the perfect guy for her.

A few weeks before, Jade told me she had run into Eva while shopping at a local department store. She told Eva I was sick and suggested that she call me, but I never heard from her. Sometimes I thought about calling her just to hear her voice, her laugh. I thought about lying to her, tell her I was over her, that I wasn't mad at her, in the "I ain't mad at you" sense of the phrase. Since she never called, I figured she had succeeded in getting me out of her mind. I tried to do the same, but just as I thought she was gone from my memories, the littlest details would come rushing back. Like the way she asked for her condiments on the side whenever we went out to eat. Or the way she cocked one eyebrow when she was about to argue or didn't believe something. And always, there were hands, her soft, silky hands locked in defense, a reminder of her mother's adage that the best way to avoid trouble was to keep her hands together. All these things I thought about when I thought of Eva.

With the surgery postponed until May, I decided to go back to work part-time. Half-days were about all I could muster, as long as I didn't have to do too many home visits or deal with too much stress.

As I tried to catch up on paperwork and phone calls, numerous coworkers dropped by to welcome me back, which took up most of the morning. The first week I was back, Derek was on vacation.

When he strolled past my open door the following week, he let out a joyous shout.

"Hey, man, how's it going?" he greeted me happily and loudly. Grinning, he came in and pumped my hand. "Why didn't you tell me you were coming in, you nut?"

Derek had taken over many of my cases while I was out and had kept in touch via e-mails. His support had been a godsend.

"I wanted to surprise you," I said, getting up as he swallowed me in his running back embrace, patting my back several times.

"I see you decided to emulate your mentor," he joked, stroking his bald head.

I laughed, touching my Kangol. "At least mine'll grow back." Still uncomfortable with my naked head, I kept a cap or hat on at all times. No matter what hat I wore, however, it was impossible to ignore the drastic change.

He sat down and we talked, discussing my treatment and the pending surgery, before he brought me up-to-date on my caseload.

"How are *you*?" I asked him seriously, after we were done with business.

After contemplating my question, he answered, "I'm doing . . . better, what can I say? I miss her, you know. But it's all part of life, right?" He got up and cracked his football-player neck from side to side. "Feel like doing lunch?"

Food still held no appeal for me. "Not today. Maybe Friday?"

"Friday's cool. Good to see you back, man." He left only to pop his head back a few seconds later. "Oh, forgot to tell you. Ronnie Aguire? He's in lock-up."

I leaned back in my chair in frustration. "Aw, man, when did that happen?"

"Yesterday. He got mad at his boss and threw one of those fryer baskets at him. You know the ones they use to fry French fries? Luckily, he hadn't put it in the grease yet. The man wasn't hurt but he's pressing charges—if the boy doesn't apologize."

I shook my head disappointedly. Ronnie had been doing so well. According to Derek's earlier e-mails, he had started attending classes, working at Wendy's, and making all of his probation visits.

"Floremont or Merriville?" I asked, naming the local and downstate juvenile detention centers.

"Floremont. I tried to talk to him when I visited last night, but he tuned me out," Derek said, resolutely. "Maybe he'll listen to you. All the man wants is an apology. "

Floremont, literally translated, meant "flower mountain." The juvenile lock-up, however, was no rose, but it was a mountain of a building, a gloomy behemoth looming on Roosevelt Boulevard, a street that time had seemingly passed by. In an effort to renovate the institution and keep costs down, the city had recently sandblasted it, but now the edifice looked worse, ghostlike.

Ronnie casually strolled into the visitor's room, the permanent sneer on his face as he tried not to look surprised at my appearance, but I had changed too much so that he couldn't play it off.

"What happened to yo' hair, man?" He dropped onto the chair opposite me. "Man, you skinnier than me."

"Chemo."

"Wha-a-a? I didn't know you had cancer. They just said you were sick," he drawled.

"What's going on?" I asked, getting down to business. "You were doing so well."

"Yo, the man insulted me in front of everybody. Called me a lazy bum. I ain't lazy. I been bustin' my back working O-T, he know that."

"You can't go around throwing stuff at people when you get angry. All he wants is an apology."

"He gon' apologize to me?"

"I doubt it."

"Then I ain't apologizing." He slapped the air like he was swatting at a fly.

"Don't be stupid, Ronnie. If he presses charges, you *will* go in this time. You like this place?"

"I don't know. I could get used to it," he said unperturbed, but he wasn't fooling me.

"Yeah, okay. You do that. You get real nice and comfortable," I said indifferently, getting up and heading for the door. I felt myself deteriorating, even though I had been sitting most of the morning. I could feel a fever coming on and congestion in my chest, which meant I was probably getting an upper respiratory infection. From now on, I wasn't going to put any extra effort into people who didn't want to do for themselves.

"Yo, that's it? You gon' give up on me that easy?"

I turned to look at him, my hand still on the door. He was standing up, his arms spread wide, his face hard with bravado.

Normally, I didn't use my disease as an excuse for anything, but I was fed up. "Ronnie, I'm going through some serious stuff right now. In a couple of months, I'm going to have major surgery. In the future you're going to find that this petty stuff is nothing compared to what life's got in store for you. You've got to learn to put things into perspective, decide which battles are worth fighting for. Sometimes you're just going to have to submit."

"I submit to no one but God," he said bitterly.

"Then do that." I knocked on the door to notify the guard I was ready to leave.

"Mr. Black, Mr. Black," Ronnie called out. "Hold up, hold up."

I turned around again, my eyes narrowed from exhaustion, impatience, and the pending fever. "What is it, Ronnie? I got things to do."

"Can I . . . can I just talk to you about something right quick?"

Ordinarily, it was at this point where I would be swelling up inside, proud of myself for getting through to another troubled youth. But the past week had been an emotionally draining one for me and I didn't think I had any more compassion to lend. I couldn't even fake it. Then I looked into Ronnie's pleading eyes, crying loudly for help. I gestured to the guard that I wouldn't be leaving just yet.

After leaving Floremont, I found myself driving toward Montrose Harbor. I parked the car half a block away and walked the rest of the way since the parking lot was closed for the season. Whenever I felt a need to escape for some solitude, I drove to Montrose, secretly hoping that I'd run into Eva. But I never did. She either stopped going or we kept missing each other. In spite of this, I kept going back because being near the water made me feel something I hadn't expected: a sense of invincibility, like I was the last man alive on earth and not even death could touch me.

Most of the time, few people braved the frigid wind-chill factors and the icy winds, which were harsher closer to the lakefront, confirming Chicago's much-deserved nickname. Even though it was March, huge chunks of ice still floated in the lake and the Chicago skyline looked like gray icebergs in the distance.

Today, however, there were city workers walking around, measuring the landscape, taking notes. I had read in the paper that they were going to be renovating many of the lakefront beaches, an estimated billion-dollar project. Ordinarily, the allocation of government funds for beautification purposes rather than for the city's needy social programs would really set me off, but not today. Today, my physical and spiritual health was at stake.

It turned out that Ronnie didn't really want to talk about anything, he just didn't want me to leave. So even though my eyes were beginning to burn from the fever, I sat and talked with him about anything and everything until visiting hours were over. Traveling down Lake Shore Drive, the words I had said to Ronnie kept coming hauntingly back to me: *Sometimes you're just going to have to submit.*

There were many times I felt something pushing me toward God, a gnawing feeling I couldn't quite explain. At first, I thought about re-dedicating my life to Christ to get closer to Eva, to understand her, be a part of her world. Then later, I thought it would bring her back to me. In the end, it was just plain old fear, fear of cancer, fear of death. I had started praying more often, but it wasn't the same as allowing Him in my life, completely. I didn't want to be like my father, on his deathbed when he got saved. *Some people got to see the light before they see the light,* Mama had said about Daddy. *When was the right time to come to God? What was the right reason?* I wondered.

Walking on the bottom stepstone closest to the frozen water's edge, I tried to remember the day I first accepted the Lord, when I was twelve. While I couldn't remember the exact words I had been instructed to say, I remembered being dunked backward into the church's baptismal pool, holding my breath, waiting for Jesus to enter my soul. When I emerged from the water and opened my eyes, my mother was the first person I saw. Seeing her glowing face was like seeing God's light beaming down on me.

With my shoe tips perched on the edge where the stone ended and the ice began, I waited for the words to come to me, wondering if I should be down on my knees. I tried to recall the words my father spoke. *Lord Jesus, I ask You to come into my heart . . .*

"Lord," I started. "God . . ."

"Don't you go jumpin' in 'ere," I heard someone behind me say. "Cuz I ain't gonna save ya."

I turned around slowly to see a city worker lumbering down the steps, his barrel chest leading the way, busting out of his city-issued jacket. He was carrying surveying equipment and he wore a crooked smirk, like he was looking forward to witnessing a suicide.

I gave him a dismissive laugh. "There's only one person who can save me," I told him, surprised by the authority in my voice. The words were not mine; they had come to me seemingly from nowhere. But I knew they came from somewhere, someone else. Someone who had been trying to come inside for the longest time. Someone who had always been there from the beginning, after I had turned away, and was still there, now that I was trying to come back.

The man's sneer disappeared as he walked away, almost slipping on a patch of ice.

I turned back around and got to the matter at hand.

"Lord, I feel like You've been trying to tell me something," I whispered. "If this is what it is, give me the right words."

And He did.

CHAPTER 25

EVA

THE ELEVATOR DOORS opened and I got on, my nose buried in a book about gunshot victims and posttraumatic stress disorder in hope of deterring anyone who wanted to talk. At first, I thought I was alone because the elevator was so wide, since they used it to transport patient gurneys and large equipment. But after I pressed the button for the top floor and walked to the elevator's rear, I looked up from my book and noticed a man leaning against the wall near the number panel on the other side. His head was bowed and his eyes were closed like he, too, was purposely avoiding eye contact, or maybe praying. Then he raised his hands at his waist and folded them, the index fingers and thumbs touching.

He wore a blue bandana, which was tied on the top portion of his head, and I could see that the back of his scalp was bald, but not in the way when men shaved with a razor. There were no razor bumps or hair follicles, and I realized that his baldness was a side effect from disease. I had seen others like him here before, men and women of all ages, children and even babies, with no hair, wearing baseball caps, scarves, and other headwear. Some patients went bareheaded, modeling their baldheads without shame. Usually, they were on their way up from, or down to, the basement, the "lower concourse" as the hospital referred to it, as if the fancier name concealed the hazardous radiation and chemotherapy treatments taking place on that level.

As the elevator stopped on alternating floors letting people on and off, I noticed the man remained in the same position, like a statue, his lips moving silently. People stole curious glances at him, but he didn't look up. His clothes hung off him like the teenagers who had created the oversized, sloppy dress mode that had yet to go out of style: cargo pants sagging, an extra-large plaid shirt with sleeves hanging down past the knuckles. But he wasn't a kid. The higher the elevator went, the less people remained until we were all alone.

I must have made a noise in my throat, or sighed, I can't remember, because he looked up slightly startled. And then I saw the glasses on his face, amber colored and wire rimmed, sliding down his nose as he slowly lifted his head. But it was the shaggy eyebrows that stunned me, still thick and cryptic, more contrasting than before. My heart began pounding uncontrollably, and I touched my chest as if to keep it from pushing through my blouse.

Our eyes met and we both smiled as we walked simultaneously toward each other and hugged, like old friends, my arm around his neck, his around my back. Unable to resist, I reached up and touched the back of his head.

Adam. His name was on the tip of my tongue, but what came out of my mouth was, "Your hair." I thought of Eli when he had chopped off his tresses.

"What are you doing here?" he asked, just as awestruck.

"My son's with his therapist. Then he's got physical therapy, for his leg. You know, because of the shooting."

"Right. I remember. Eli. I was so sorry to hear about Tony."

I didn't reply, just slightly nodded, not wanting to talk about it. Contrary to what everyone said, talking about my pain didn't make it easier. I was tired of saying "thanks," which seemed an inappropriate response to condolences. I knew it was proper etiquette, but decorum was not on my priority list.

"How's Eli doing?"

"Much better. He had a rough time for a while, but he's going back to school in the fall."

"To ISU?"

"No, no. He's transferring to North Carolina. That's where he . . . my sons were born there and we still have family there. The change will be better for him."

"So you're going to be all alone?"

"I still have King."

"Ah, yes. The beast."

"Hey, don't talk about my baby," I said, smiling.

"Baby?" He smiled, and then his face turned serious. "How are *you*?"

"I'm doing good, considering. How about you? I heard about the cancer coming back."

"Yeah. My hair wasn't so lucky this time." He ran his hand over the circumference of his head, pulling off the bandana. His scalp was smooth, a lighter shade of butterscotch. There was now a bump at the bridge of his nose that gave him a Roman or Aztec look, and I recalled the day his ex-brother-in-law had broken it. It still looked painful, but it suited him, complemented his new haggard look.

"You coming or going?" I asked.

He glanced up at the numbers flashing higher and higher. "I was supposed to get off on the second floor. To the parking lot. I was kind of out of it when I got on."

Then I remembered that the last time I had been with him on an elevator, I couldn't even look at him. "I'm going up to the sun deck. Want to come?"

He nodded as he tied the bandana back on his head. We reached the twentieth floor, the sun deck, where I had come many times in an attempt to reconnect with God. It was too warm, a little stuffy, but the sun filled the enclosed deck with glorious light. At the end of the deck, a man sat facing a woman in a wheelchair, the woman's head bent back in laughter. When she brought her head back up, I could see how thin and frail she was, a White Sox baseball cap turned backward on her hairless head. Adam waved at them, and I surmised that she was a cancer patient.

I searched my purse for change to put in the coffee-vending machine, but he reached into his pocket and brought out two quarters.

"Thanks," I said.

He bought a bottle of water and we sat down in the lounge chairs facing east, where we could see the Chicago skyline and Lake Michigan very clearly. I started thinking about Montrose Harbor, about the last time I had been there, when I had my catharsis, and the time before that, when I had been there with Adam.

He tapped my hand. "So, how are you, *really*?"

I shook my head slowly. "It's been hard since, you know . . . But I'm dealing." My eyes swelled with tears and I bit my top lip to keep them from spilling, turned away from him so he couldn't see. It had been five months and I still could not say "Tony" without getting a lump in my throat, still could not look at his photos without getting weepy. Recently, at another college fair, a potential college student introduced himself as "Tony." Instinctively, I replied, "That was my son's name," before bursting into tears. I didn't know if it was just hearing the name or because I had used the past tense in referring to him.

"You've lost weight," Adam commented.

"So have you."

"Grief and disease, guaranteed diet plans," he remarked.

We drank our respective beverages quietly, both of us periodically glancing at the couple talking and laughing.

"Did you get my package?" he then asked.

"I did. Thanks."

"Did you recognize the passage? The last verse in Proverbs; a virtuous woman."

I nodded, and sipped my coffee quietly. It was horrible watered-down coffee, but I drank it anyway. It kept my hands and mouth busy.

"So, did you like the CD?" he prodded.

"Yes. It was all very thoughtful. Thanks." Sometimes I played it, to test myself, to remind myself of the superficial things on which I had placed so much value instead of remembering the important things in life, like keeping God first.

I decided to change the subject before he went down memory lane. "Hey, I heard your screenplay was being opted for a cable movie."

"Yeah. I met this agent at the hospital, of all places. His brother was in for chemo. So we're in negotiations."

"Congratulations. I'm happy for you. Did you finally settle on a title?"

"*In the Absence of Fathers.*" He said it like a movie preview announcer.

"I like it."

"Why are you changing the subject?"

Caught, I didn't reply. I brought the coffee cup to my mouth, but I didn't drink, just used it as a prop to hide part of my face.

"What about you? What have you been working on?" he then asked.

"I wrote a series on school shootings and gun control for *Diaspora*. I didn't think I could ever write about it, but it just came out."

"I read them," he said, and I tried to keep from looking pleased. "My mom's a subscriber. I thought they were very . . . powerful. That part about you feeling Tony's spirit leaving his body, it was . . . deep."

I had been glancing back and forth, from him to the couple whose faces were so close to each other that any minute I thought they'd merge into one another. It was hard to keep my eyes fixed on Adam, the paleness of his skin, his gaunt face naked without the massive mane. He was a ghost of the old Adam. He was still handsome, his facial structure more defined and rugged. But the change was more than physical; there was something else, something deeper. I knew he was probably wrestling with his own demons, but I wasn't ready to share battle wounds, not yet, so I didn't pry. We continued to drink silently.

"I did sort of the same thing, with my screenwriting," he continued. "I found myself transferring the cancer onto my main character and it helped a lot."

"They've made me their staff education writer. *Diaspora*," I added, aware that we were now talking *at* each other rather than *to* each other. Turning my attention to the couple, I saw the man kneeling in front of the woman and palming her skeletal face tenderly in his hands like she was glass. He was speaking and even though I couldn't hear what was being said, the amorous way she looked at him told me she was captivated by his words. I used to say that what I missed most about men was kissing. But now I realized what I missed most was the way Adam had held my face the same way, looked into my eyes. Until then I hadn't realized how much I missed his voice, his eyes, his smile, and his laugh.

"That's great," I heard Adam say. Then I heard him shift in his chair. I could feel his eyes on me as I pretended to be mesmerized by the blueness of the sky. "Eva . . . *Mirame.*"

I turned to face him and tried to make eye contact. "Very good," I praised him, adding a smile to cover up for my discomfort. "You're still not rolling your 'r'—"

"I know I'm not as cute as I used to be," he interrupted, then smiled. "But I'm still me."

"You're still cute," I teased. Then I realized that he might construe the comment as flirtatious, and again I changed the subject. "How's your treatment going?"

"I'm finished with chemo. I'm getting my strength back. I just came in for some tests today. Now I have to have this surgery and then hopefully, I'll be cured."

"I hope so."

"I pray to God that I am." My eyebrows shot up before I could stop them and he chuckled. "Yes, I'm a praying man again."

"Well, praise God," I said automatically, happy for him. Now I knew what I had sensed—his changed spirit.

"All the time." He was smiling broadly, almost proudly, waiting for me to question him, and when I didn't, he filled me in. "I got saved. Again. Baptized in the Holy Spirit and water, joined the church, the whole *enchilada.*"

This time, I had to smile. "You need to stop with the ethnic epithets."

"What?" he said innocently, still smiling.

"So when did this happen? Where?" I asked, intrigued.

"Technically at the lakefront, about a month ago. Officially, on March 10. At TCCC."

"TCCC? You got baptized at *my* church?"

"I didn't know it was *your* church," he said, amused.

"How come I haven't seen you?"

"You know I'm an early bird. I go to the eight o'clock service."

I attended the eleven o'clock service, so that explained why we never bumped into each other. But why would he join my church and not his mother's?

"I figured I pass by it all the time," he said, as if he read my mind. "It's closer than my mama's church on Eighty-ninth." Then he got serious. "What about you? Are you still a praying woman?"

I finished my coffee and set the cup on the table between us. Folding my hands in my lap, I leaned back and looked out the windows. The truth was that since my breakthrough at the lakefront, my faith had gone on mechanical mode. I was still going to church regularly, "religiously," but I wasn't *there*. My prayers were becoming perfunctory, my singing dispassionate; worse, I wasn't feeling God. I remembered the very first night Adam walked me to my car, how I had thought I'd dread the day the Lord would test me and I would stop believing, and prayed that day would never come. But I hadn't stopped believing, not really, and I tried to convince myself of this every day as I became more apathetic. I kept telling myself it was only temporary, but my lackadaisical attitude was beginning to frighten me.

"I still pray," I finally replied briefly.

From the corner of my eye, I saw him lean forward and reach out; for some reason I flinched, not significantly, but enough so that it was obvious. I could only envision his face because I didn't look at him.

"Don't worry. I'm not contagious," he said.

I glanced at him, slightly offended at his suggestion. "I know that. I've just been very jumpy lately."

"You still having those migraines?"

"Not as bad, not as often. Just every once in a while."

"Jade said she saw you in Target a couple of weeks ago," he said.

I knew that was coming. I had seen the children first, at the end of the health and beauty aisle; Daelen sitting in the front basket of the shopping cart, and Kia inside the cart, surrounded by dish-washing liquid, toothpaste, and other sundries.

"Hi, Kia. Hi, Daelen."

They stared at me with their identical almond-shaped eyes, bluntly and warily, as only children could look at strangers and get away with it. Of course, they didn't remember me since it had been months since I last saw them.

"Hello, Eva." I looked up to see Jade peek around the end of the aisle, eyeing me coldly.

"Hi, Jade. How're you?"

"Fine," she said, curtly. "You?"

"Good." I reached over to squeeze one of Daelen's cheeks because they were so irresistibly plump and because they reminded me of my own sons' cheeks when they were little. But the look on Jade's face stopped me, the look of a lioness protecting her cubs. Instead I said, "I used to put my sons in the cart the same way, one in the front, one in the back."

"Oh," she cried out, her face, tone, and demeanor suddenly changing. "I heard . . . I'm sorry about your sons. How are you holding up?"

"Okay. Taking it one day at a time." I hated that people felt they needed to treat me with special care because of Tony, but I was beginning to accept the fact that his death would forever be a part of my identity.

"I don't know if you know, but Adam's sick," she then said. "The cancer came back."

Part of me thought the reason he hadn't called was because he had finally realized I wasn't worth it, that I was a waste of time and we were better off apart, not as friends, but as two people who had departed as was expected with certain relationships, the kind that could bump into each other later down the road and let bygones be bygones. But part of me still thought that perhaps something had happened to prevent him from calling. Something bad. Ever since Maya had broken her ties with Luciano, I hadn't heard anything about him or Adam.

"I was going to stop by . . ." I started. "I was going to call . . ." It was the truth, but it still sounded weak and pathetic, inadequate.

"Why didn't you?" he asked quietly, and I sensed an edge to his voice. He took a long swallow from his water bottle.

"I don't know."

"Yes, you do."

I looked out past the buildings outlining the cloudless sky, at the water so clear and blue, so perfect and so blissful.

"I don't know," I said again. "I just thought it'd be easier if we left things as they were."

"Unresolved?"

"Yes."

"Okay." He finished the rest of his water and sat back.

"No," I then said. "It's not okay. When Jade told me you were sick, I didn't think I could handle it. Seeing you sick after watching my son . . . Tony never regained consciousness. I didn't just lose my son, I lost a part of my life. He had always been the man of the house, my helper, my strength."

"I know. The first time I saw him, I saw how protective he was of you."

"I needed someone to lean on; I was in no condition to offer you support."

"We could've leaned on each other," he suggested. Then he quickly added, "But I understand."

"Do you?"

"I watched my father die, remember? It's a hard thing to watch." He paused and sighed. "I finally went to the cemetery last month."

"You did? How was it?"

"I went there with all these preconceptions, about what I wasn't going to do, what I wasn't going to feel. But I broke down. I guess the cancer has thrown my emotions out of whack."

"Why, because you don't usually cry?"

"No, I don't," he protested a little too adamantly.

I smiled.

"Well, I haven't cried in a long, long, *long* time," he admitted, cracking a smile.

"I used to cry every day. Now I'm down to once a week."

He sat up again, sideways in the chair, and waited until I looked at him. He reached over and unhooked my hands from their habitual position, and pulled me upright, facing him, our knees bumping. His touch was warm and familiar, but still I felt I should pull away before it was too late. I looked into his eyes and tried to determine if lurking in his mind was some veiled attempt to bring up the past. *Don't go there, please,* I thought. But he looked tired and sad, not at all roused by our closeness.

"Are you still boxing?" he asked.

"Yes, why?"

"Hands are getting kind of rough there," he teased, causing me to laugh. He inspected my fingers closely. "Still biting your nails too, I see."

"Shut *up.*" I tried to pull my hands away but he tightened his grip.

"Do you want me to pray for you?" he asked quietly.

"What for?" I replied without thinking, and immediately regretted it. When someone wants to pray for you, you shouldn't question it.

But he didn't flinch. "For your peace of mind. To ease your pain. And Eli's."

A lump formed in my throat as I nodded with contrition and closed my eyes. He recited the King James version of Psalm 23 in a subdued voice. I had always thought it was one of the simplest psalms, but as Adam spoke the words, I began to visualize myself lying in a pasture beside a still river, my head being anointed with oil. When he was finished, I felt him slide his left hand into mine and interlock our fingers like we were about to wrestle. I kept my eyes closed.

"Think a brothah can call you every once in a while? Or maybe a sistah can call a brothah? Or we can e-mail, whatever."

His request seemed casual, like it didn't matter to him one way or another whether we kept in contact. What I had expected him to say was that he wanted to pick up where we left off, to try again now that he was the man I had prayed for: a man of God. I didn't trust myself to respond. Grief had triggered an erosion of my strong woman persona, a sapping of my hard-core strength.

Just then, we heard a whoop. Startled, I looked over at the couple. I had forgotten all about them.

"Hey, my girl said 'yes'!" the man screamed in our direction and then turned toward the glass. "Hey, God, did you hear? She said 'yes'! Whoo!"

"Congratulations," Adam told them, smiling.

"Do you know them?" I asked.

"I've seen them around, talked to them a couple of times, but I don't really *know* them. She has a rare brain cancer."

I felt like crying. "That's so sad. They're getting married and she's going to die."

"Who said she was going to die?" Puzzled, he looked at me as he stood up, still holding my hand. "Listen, I got to get ready to roll."

"I'll call you," I promised.

"Don't say you're going to call me and then not call," he said.

"When I say 'I'll call,' I'll call."

"I heard that before," he said sourly, curling his lip, but then he slipped into a tight smile. He finally released my hand as he started walking away. I couldn't help thinking he was walking away from me for good. That he was giving up, finally. Something told me to call him back. *Don't go,* I thought.

"What'd you say?" he asked, turning around.

I didn't realize I had vocalized the words. I cleared my throat. "I said, 'don't go.'"

He strolled back and stood in front of me, his hands pressed together with his fingers spread like a starfish. "You want to talk now?" he asked.

"I do, but I can't," I said, looking at my watch with regret.

"That's right. Eli."

"No, it's not that. He'll be tied up for another hour and a half. I was supposed to meet Simone and Maya for lunch fifteen minutes ago." I could have rescheduled, but I had already done so twice, and they were giving me grief. "Want to join us?"

"Nah. I'll leave you females to your little hen party."

I reached out to punch him in jest, but at the last minute decided against it and stood up. "I'll ride down with you."

We descended in silence, though it was a more comfortable silence, laced with quiet smiles and coy glances as other patrons entered and exited, impeding any privacy. It seemed as if we reached the second floor too soon, which was connected to the hospital parking garage by a enclosed bridge. As he exited, he held the doors, much to the chagrin of two young women who remained on the elevator.

"I'll call you when I get home," I assured him.

"You remember the number?"

I rattled off his phone number quickly, trying to ignore the sharp looks from the women. One of them sucked her teeth. Adam didn't seem to care that they were getting impatient, refusing to release the doors. "Say hi to Maya and Simone," he said.

"I will."

"And King."

The elevator started buzzing and I admonished him with my eyes. *"Let go,"* I mouthed.

He finally released the doors, and just before they closed, he mouthed, *"God bless you,"* leaving me with my mouth hanging open and his memorable smile fixed in my mind.

Simone and Maya were already at Café Central, a Puerto Rican restaurant we referred to as "our restaurant." However, because of our conflicting schedules, we hadn't eaten there in months. As I anticipated, they pre-ordered my usual *jibarito,* a steak sandwich made with two slices of fried plantains instead of bread.

"Tell her," Maya urged Simone, as I sat down next to Simone.

"What happened?" I asked, not really wanting to hear any bad news.

"I'm going back to school to finish my degree," Simone announced. "I've decided I'm not going to be the only one without a degree."

I leaned over and hugged her around the neck. "I'm so proud of you, *chica.*"

"Yeah, I figured you'd be. I've wasted so much time already."

"It's amazing how your head clears when men are out of the picture," Maya teased.

"Well, they're not totally out of the picture." We looked at her with reproach as she smiled demurely. "We-e-ell, I still work with Ian. I see him every day. But we *are* abstaining. It's actually very exciting."

Maya and I looked at each other with resignation.

"Don't look at each other with that 'she just doesn't get it' look," Simone said. "Anyway, he's really helping me with school. Specifically, tuition."

The waitress arrived with our orders and I said grace. Maya and I listened as Simone talked about her new plans for her life: getting her business degree, then opening up her own spa and salon. She sounded genuinely determined and I prayed she would stick to her plan.

"Adam says 'hi,'" I mentioned when there was a lull in the conversation. They both looked at me questionably. "I ran into him at the hospital."

"What? When?" Maya asked excitedly.

"On the elevator just a little while ago. He's finished with chemo. Oh, and he's saved."

"He's saved?" Maya nodded knowingly. "I *told* you—you and he are not a coincidence." She turned toward Simone. "Didn't I tell you this was her man?"

"Don't start," I begged her.

"No, she's right," Simone said excitedly. "I thought she was *loca* too—"

"Hey," Maya protested.

"Sorry. But seriously, what are the chances that he would be on the same elevator at the same time as you? It's got to be fate."

I ate my sandwich as if I hadn't eaten a good meal in ages, then asked for another 7 UP without acknowledging their statements.

"It's time you loved yourself, do something, *do someone*, for yourself," Simone insisted. "You've neglected your needs long enough. Stop the madness already, girl."

"Why does everything have to be about sex with you?" I snapped.

" 'Cause everything *is* about sex."

" '*It is better to marry than to burn,*' " Maya reminded me.

"I can't think about Adam right now. I made a vow to God—"

"Not to let a man come before Him, I know," Maya interrupted. "And as long as God is first and foremost in your life, a man can't interfere with that."

"What was it Paul said? 'The unmarried are concerned with the Lord's affairs, but the married are concerned with pleasing each other and the world.' "

"Who is this Paul?" Simone asked, irritated. "And what does he have to do with this?"

Maya almost choked on her *empanada* and my 7 UP went down the wrong way as we both burst out laughing.

"Ha-ha, funny," Simone said. "I'm assuming he's one of your biblical characters."

"No, you didn't call Paul a biblical character," Maya said with disbelief. She shook her head at Simone. "I'll get to you later." She turned back to me. "Eva, I don't understand you. Didn't you pray for a man of God? A righteous man? When you first met him, he wasn't one. Now you run into him and he is. I don't care how independent you are or how wonderful you think your life is. You don't want to be old and alone any more than any other woman, or man for that matter. You want this man. You *need* him. I can see it in your face; I can hear it in your voice."

This was where I usually blew up at her, told them both to stay out of my life. A year ago, I would have snapped, defended my independence and my wonderful life, and debated the need for a man. As always, they saw through me. Still, I felt I had to put up a brave front.

" 'Need' is such a *needy* word," I said weakly.

"If you want to have a relationship with Adam, join the couples' ministry. It's not just for married couples."

"We're not a couple," I protested.

"But you want to be," Maya insisted. "You might as well ask the man to marry you." As I started to protest, she lifted a hand to stop me. "Why don't you pray on it? If it's meant to be, it will be."

"Yeah, pray on it, girl," Simone insisted, then shrugged when we looked at her skeptically. "I mean, what can it hurt?"

"You told me once, you have to know what you want before you ask for it," Maya continued. "Do you know what you want?"

I picked at the cold rice and beans on my plate, turning her question over and over in my head. *Did I know what I want? Did I want Adam? Did I?* The question was, did Adam want me?

CHAPTER 26

ADAM

SEEING EVA AGAIN was like getting my last dose of chemo—relief and elation rolled up in one. As promised, she called me the day we ran into each other, then I called her; other times we e-mailed. Sometimes we met in the hospital sunroom during Eli's appointments, or at Coffee Will Make You Black. Sometimes Eli would join us. It was hard to explain our new relationship. I guess the best description was one of an old friendship, something that felt familiar and true, like what I had with Luciano but without the testosterone. Even without the expectation of sex, or even a kiss, the attraction was still there, but of course, because we didn't act on it, couldn't act on it for more reasons than not, the atmosphere was less tense, less tempting.

Whenever we met, we'd bring each other gifts, little things that didn't carry any hidden meaning. Sometimes she would bring me a hat: a crocheted Muslim khufi, a Civil War cap, and a doo-rag to name a few, the latter I liked best because it made me look tough when I didn't particularly feel it. I in turn would give her a jazz or classical CD or a self-published book of poetry. Other times, she brought flowers from her garden, which I had always associated as a gift for women, but they brightened my apartment. Every once in a while, she'd bring plates of food, but she was quick to add that I shouldn't get too comfortable because she still didn't enjoy cooking. When we weren't able to get together, we would exchange long, intimate e-mails about our deepest thoughts and fears. There were

still so many things we didn't know about each other. She would always preface her messages with a biblical verse or famous quote in
the subject line. One of the first messages she sent was currently
running across my laptop screensaver marquee, Psalm 144:1:
*Blessed be the Lord my Rock, who trains my hands for war, my fingers
for battle.* It encouraged me figuratively to keep writing about the
cancer in a journal, and metaphorically to fight the disease with my
mind.

During Easter dinner my sister announced that she and Akil
were getting married. In an effort to fatten me up, Mama had temporarily suspended her cooking strike and prepared one of her infamous New Orleans meals: honey-glazed salmon steaks, red beans
and rice, seafood gumbo, and my favorite, pecan pie à la mode.
Mama was beside herself with happiness, glad that Jade would no
longer be a statistic and a stigma. She was even more thrilled when
Jade announced that she had accepted the Lord, though she wasn't
too pleased that Jade had joined Akil's church and not our family
church. She already felt that I had turned my back on "her" church
by joining TCCC. *"All these years I tried to get you to join my church
and here comes this woman out of the blue and you just up and join her
church,"* Mama criticized. I tried to tell her it was more a matter of
convenience than anything, but she was convinced that Eva was the
culprit. I couldn't very well tell her I preferred Pastor Zeke's mel-
lowness to her old-fashioned hollering preacher.

Jade and Akil's wedding was planned for late June, a year after her
divorce. I thought it was too soon, even if Akil *was* a God-fearing
nice guy.

"You've known him less than a year," I pointed out as I drove her
and the kids to their suburban home.

"What can I say?" Jade said happily. "When you know, you
know."

"Know what?"

"That he's the one."

"How do you know?"

"Because he *shows* me, rather than *tells* me, that he loves me, you
know. And I love the fact that we haven't made love, at least not

physically, but we've made love spiritually. You know what I'm saying?"

"TMI, TMI," I interjected, using Justin's abbreviation for "too much info."

She laughed. "You know what he said?"

"What?" I asked, rolling my eyes theatrically.

"He said the first time he saw me, he told his friend, 'I'm going to marry that girl someday.'"

I pretended to stick my finger down my throat and made a gagging noise. She jabbed me in the side.

"Alright, now," I warned her, pushing her away. "You're going to make me have an accident."

"Mommy, stop. You're gonna make Unc-Adam have a accident," Kia cried, reprimanding her mother.

"See, you're scaring the kids," I said.

Jade turned around. "Okay, Mommy's going to stop."

"So, without giving too many details, how does he 'show' you he loves you?" I asked Jade.

"In a lot of ways. He respects me, he speaks to me with respect, he listens when I talk. He brings me flowers just because. Everything just feels right when I'm with him."

"But don't we all do everything right in the beginning? It's all part of the game in getting the girl, or the guy."

"When I was younger, and dating, yeah. But with Akil, it's genuine. You know how sometimes you see red flags, but you ignore them? They were flapping all over the place when I was with Brandon, but not with Akil."

I glanced over at her as she laid back against the headrest, speaking whimsically about her future husband. Over the past couple of months, I had witnessed a dramatic change in Jade. Gone were the short, tight outfits and her nose ring. She had also stopped asking me to babysit, because Akil didn't mind having the kids around. "Speaking of red flags, have you told Brandon?"

"Of course not. I'll send him an invitation."

"You're kidding, right?"

She laughed. "Of course I am. I was planning to tell him next time I drop off the kids for the weekend."

"You want me to be there? In case he goes off?"

"He'll be alright. He's got a girlfriend now, he doesn't care."

"What about the kids?"

"Akil loves my kids. They love him. And Brandon will always be their father."

"Looks like you've got everything figured out."

"I want you to give me away."

"What, again?"

"Yes," she said laughing. "Uncle Casey can't come. Uncle Ruben is sick. I could ask Uncle Corey, but you know we've never been close. Besides, who better to give me away than the first man who walked me down the aisle?" I recalled the day very clearly. She had been twenty-three, too young to get married, I thought. Now, I felt it was too soon after her divorce.

"Will it be for good this time?"

She punched me and then leaned against my arm. "Are you going to be recovered by June thirtieth?"

"Let me see. After the surgery, I'll be in bed for about two weeks, then I'll have this huge scar running down my chest so I'll be kind of sore for a while. Then I have to have the staples out. Hmmm, I don't know, I'll make a note in my PDA," I said sarcastically.

"When's your surgery?" she asked, ignoring my cynicism.

"May sixteenth." I hadn't thought much about the upcoming surgery, leaving that burden in the hands of the Almighty. When I first got the news, I couldn't stop worrying, unable to sleep. Ultimately, I had no choice but to put my faith in God to pull me through the rest of the way, because I knew doctors were humans—fallible mortals with God complexes who made mistakes all the time. I had to believe the only way I was going to live was through my renewed belief in God. In the days since visiting my father's grave, my faith had made me stronger, braver, and gave me the determination to keep fighting.

"Do you think Eva would want to be a bridesmaid?"

"I'll ask," I said, touched that she would think of Eva in that capacity.

"You know what the best part is?" Jade asked. "He reminds me of you."

"Hold on, I've got to throw up."

"What?" she asked, alarmed, pulling away to look at me. "Are you feeling sick?"

"I'm kidding, I'm kidding." I pulled her back to me and hugged her, maneuvering the car carefully.

She pinched my side, hard, several times. "Ooh, I hate you sometimes. Don't play like that."

I jerked back, away from her, causing the car to swerve slightly.

"Mommy!" Kia yelled.

Just then, flashing blue lights appeared in the rearview mirror. Jade looked chagrined as I glanced accusingly at her.

"Ooh, it's the pah-lice," Daelen said.

"You're in big trou-ouble," Kia said. "We're gonna go to jail."

"Don't worry. Nobody's going to jail," I assured them. "He's probably just going to give me a ticket. Everybody got their seat belts on?"

I pulled over and before the cop reached my window, I had my license and insurance card out of the wallet.

"Everything alright?" the cop asked.

"Yeah," I answered briefly. I had learned from years of experience that you don't volunteer more information than necessary when being questioned by cops, particularly suburban cops. Whatever he said I did, I wouldn't argue with him; I'd just take the ticket and leave. A few months ago, I might have argued just on the matter of principle, but now, DWB stops didn't faze me.

"You were weaving a bit back there," the cop pointed out.

"My hand kind of slipped off the wheel, that's all."

He bent down to look into the passenger side and then into the back. Through the rearview mirror, I could see the kids looked scared. Undoubtedly, they remembered the visits made by the police to their home when their father was around.

The cop smiled and waved at them. "Hey, kiddies." Then he turned to me. "Have you been drinking, sir?"

"No."

"My brother doesn't drink. He has cancer," Jade said curtly.

I looked over at her slowly and gave her a dirty look, but she looked back at me defiantly. She knew I never used cancer as a crutch. I didn't want nor did I expect any special treatment because of it. When I turned back toward the cop, he was skeptically eyeing my head underneath the crocheted skullcap as if he were trying to decide whether to believe Jade or if I was just another bald-headed Black dude. I almost wished I had worn my doo-rag, then I really would've fit the profile.

"License and insurance, please," he said. I handed over both cards. He walked back to the cruiser to check my driving record and verify that I didn't have any outstanding warrants. If I hadn't been so mad at Jade, I would've smiled thinking of his disappointment when he discovered I had never even had a moving violation, just a lot of DWBs, but of course, those weren't a matter of record.

"They make me sick," Jade said bitterly. "Stopping you 'cause you were weaving. With all these drunks driving around."

"Don't say nothing to me," I told her quietly.

"What? What did I do? 'Cause I told him you had cancer?"

I didn't answer her and just shook my head slowly, disappointedly, a characteristic of our father's when he tried to make us feel guilty after we had done something wrong.

"Don't be mad, Big Bruh." When I didn't say anything, she resorted to her old childhood antics of giving me attitude right back. "Fine. Be mad."

The cop returned and handed me back my cards. "I'll let you off with a warning. This time." He didn't leave right away and I guess he was expecting me to thank him, but I just looked at him and dismissed him with a slight nod. "Bye, kids," he added, waving at the kids before walking away.

We drove in silence, the kids falling asleep as I drove farther and farther away from the city. I could see Jade in my peripheral vision, her head turned away from me as she looked out of her window.

Tears would not save her this time. When I reached her house, I got out and helped her carry Kia and Daelen, the bags and leftovers from the car. After putting the kids in their beds, she followed me out. "Adam, wait."

"Bye, Sis," I said, still walking.

She pulled me back by my jacket. "Are you going to walk me down the aisle, or do I have to call somebody else?"

"You know I'll be honored, Babysis."

She clung to my jacket. "Don't be mad at me. I can't stand it when you're mad at me."

When we were younger, I used to give Jade the silent treatment whenever she did something that made me angry. I would make her wait on me hand and foot, make her give me her allowance, and make her cry until she would beg me to be her "friend" again. Once, Mama caught me commanding that Jade get down on her knees and beg for my forgiveness as I impersonated Yul Brynner in *The King and I*: "*When I say kneel, you shall kneel; when I say beg, you shall beg.*" Mama gave me the biggest beating of my life. Afterward she said, "*Don't you ever demean your sister, or any woman, like that again.*" I never forgot that lesson.

I kissed her cheek. "I'm not mad at you. Anymore." It was true; it was hard for me to hold on to my anger these days. That's how I knew God was at work in my life.

There was a certain peace that followed my surrender to the Almighty. Knowing that He had the power over my life and death, and that there was nothing I could do to change that, made me less afraid. Pastor Zeke said it best when he told me, "*When you relinquish the desire to control your future, you obtain peace.*" This was in direct contrast to what I had been taught all my life, in school and work, that I alone controlled my destiny, that I was the architect of my future. By giving me the strength to get through the cancer the "second time," by bringing Eva back into my life, He had given me a second chance.

I wasn't sure what to do with my feelings for Eva, so I wrote a poem. I couldn't bring myself to give it to her though, because it made me feel so vulnerable. I just couldn't take the chance that she wouldn't reciprocate my feelings and so, I put them on hold, pretending they didn't exist. Our conversations centered on our writing, work, and topics such as which version of the Bible was the best. One thing we didn't talk about was the past, or the possibility of any future between us.

Eva had invited me to Eli's birthday celebration, which was to take place in her backyard the day before my surgery. Since she had consented to be a bridesmaid in Jade's wedding, I felt a small obligation to go. Maya and her family were there, as was Simone, surprisingly unescorted. I met Eva's father—a quiet, reserved man—who seemed uncomfortable in a social setting and left after about an hour. He seemed cordial enough, not at all like a man who was prejudiced against Blacks, but then again, Eva may have told him we were now only friends. Eva also introduced me to her ex-husband, Anthony, and I was surprised she had invited him, given his history of marital infidelity, although I knew he was still Eli's father. Anthony bore a remarkable resemblance to Tony, right down to the fixed smirk meant to intimidate. Eli appeared to be extremely close to his father and grandfather, and his spirits had improved dramatically; even his limp was barely noticeable from the last time I saw him at the hospital. A few of Eli's friends from ISU stopped by, including a student who had recently emerged from a coma caused by the shooting. When he first arrived, Eva couldn't take her eyes off him, and I could tell by the way she looked at him, with a combination of envy and sadness, that she was probably wondering why Tony, who had also been in a coma, hadn't been spared.

Eva and I didn't get much of a chance to talk since she was busy grilling and serving. She was wearing her blue velour warm-up suit, the same one she wore that fateful night, our first and last night together. After Eli's friends left, and her small family circle remained, the talk turned toward the future of affirmative action, which was headed toward the Supreme Court.

"What people fail to realize is that affirmative action was designed to make amends," Eva was saying. "A sort of reparations for past discriminatory practices created by the majority. It's not a handout. We didn't ask the University of Michigan to give Black and Hispanic applicants twenty points for their ethnicity. *They* came up with that." I glanced at her periodically as she began to cut the strawberry shortcake.

"A few Blacks and Hispanics get into college, or move into a neighborhood, and they think 'there go our jobs, there goes the neighborhood,'" Alex chimed in.

"But don't you see? That's what they're afraid of," Maya said. "That we're going to take over. That's why they're getting rid of everything. Just when we get wind of all the loopholes they've had access to all these years, they decide to change the rules."

"'They, they, they,'" Anthony jumped in. "Who's 'they'? You guys sound paranoid."

"*They!*" Maya shouted at him as she jokingly grabbed him by the collar. "The government, the Republicans, the powers that be who are so threatened by change—take your pick!"

Alex dabbed Maya's head with a napkin as if she were a boxer coming into her corner. "Calm down, honey," he said.

"Am I the only one who thinks we should go back to the time when *we* didn't rely on *them* to give us *anything*?" Anthony almost pleaded, knowing he was outnumbered. "There was a time when we helped our own with businesses, built our own schools. We have to continue helping our own."

Simone then took the center of the circle. "Look, Mr. Black Republican. That was then, this is now. We can't go back in time," she said, punctuating her words with jabs of her fork in Anthony's chest. "Meanwhile, 'the powers that be' are getting rid of financial aid so our boys—and girls—have to join the military in order to get money for college. Then they end up in some godforsaken country fighting the next Vietnam or Iraq. And I'm not just talking about African and Latin Americans, I'm talking about the working class of this country."

"No one's forcing them to join the military. They can take out loans, work—"

"And be in debt for life?"

"That's the American way."

"What makes me so angry is that the people who originally ben-efited from affirmative action are now its biggest critics," Eva jumped in, eyeing her ex-husband with accusation and vehemence. It reminded me of the first time I had seen her debate, ironically about the same subject, the first time we met that rainy day in August.

"Are there any conservatives in the house? Where's my son?" Anthony spread his arms helplessly. "Adam?"

Up until then, I hadn't contributed much to the discussion and had pretty much kept to myself in a corner of the deck. I had been sipping on tamarind smoothies and stuffing my face with grilled tilapia, *platanos*, and vegetable kabobs since I was supposed to stop eating before midnight in preparation for my surgery. It wasn't that I didn't care about issues like affirmative action. Ever since my fight with cancer, especially with the upcoming surgery, and given that my mind was in a higher place, I had begun to pick my battles more discriminately, placing importance on the things I could handle or change. As with chemotherapy, I was about treating the problem, not wallowing in it. For the time being, discussions regarding affir-mative action, the government, even the red tape involved in my own field had taken a backseat.

Eli was busy playing basketball with his cousins Marcos and Lucas, and their rambunctious shouts, combined with some Christian-Spanish rap music bumping on the stereo, drowned out his father's call for help.

So I spoke up. "I think we can talk about a topic until we're blue in the face, but in the end, if we don't have the power to change the system, what good is talking?"

"Some of the greatest grassroots organizations were started by just talking," Eva said.

Our eyes locked as she continued slicing and serving the cake. The moment that followed was one of those awkward interludes when everyone started looking at their feet or into space, waiting for someone else to save the day. But because Eva and I had acquired a special intimacy since we became reacquainted, we knew our ex-change was less confrontational than everyone assumed. My eyes traveled sheepishly to her warm-up suit and I wondered if she thought of that night whenever she wore it.

It was Eli who came to the rescue, calling for any takers to play him a game of two-on-two, and I was more than happy to oblige.

I hadn't played fifteen minutes before Anthony bulldogged his way in, running the court in his dress slacks and Enzo loafers, trying to show me up and slipping a couple of times in the process. I tried not to make the man look bad in front of his family, particularly his son and nephews, but I was pumped, fueled by my new slim build and outlook on life. I could see Eva watching us apprehensively, her ex-husband and ex-boyfriend, as if she were afraid we would end up rolling around on the court like schoolboys fighting over her. Considering I was not performing at my top game, and I had one of the twelve-year-old twins on my side, Anthony was one pretty bad player. We beat him and Eli in the first game, and turned down his challenge for a rematch, mostly because I was beat. Limping across the court and holding my side, I sat down in the wooden glider under the big oak tree.

Maya walked over, followed by King, who ambled over to me and began nudging my knees, waiting for me to pet him. I did, cautiously, still nervous about being around dogs. On the deck, the group had resumed talking, though on a less serious topic, evident by their voices rising and falling with excitement, then erupting every so often into laughter.

"How are you? I haven't seen you in a while," Maya said, sitting down next to me and rocking the glider.

"I'm good."

"Eva says you're having surgery."

"Yeah. Tomorrow."

"I'll say a prayer for you."

"Thanks. I'll take all the prayers I can get." I smiled my gratitude. Lively laughter exploded from the deck. "What are they talking about now?"

"Our high school days, how mean Eva was to all the guys," she said, smiling up at Eva. "Man, they hated her, but they wanted her. It killed them that they couldn't have her."

"Men always want what they can't have," I said.

"And women, too."

We rocked the glider slightly back and forth, not speaking, as snippets of their conversation floated down toward us.

"Remember David Correa?" Alex asked Eva, elbowing her. "Man, that crazy nut was writing love letters to you after one kiss."

"He was not. It was one poem," Eva protested.

"Yeah, two pages long! On both sides!" Simone interjected.

"More like a manifesto," Alex suggested.

"You kissed David Correa?" Anthony asked. "How come you never told me?"

More laughter followed. All evening, I had noticed Anthony eyeing Eva. It was the way a man looked at a woman who had gotten away, with new eyes. Eva had never talked much about him except to say that he had had several affairs and was always traveling. But I knew they had a long history, being high school sweethearts and all, not to mention having two sons, and sharing a tragedy that had the potential to perhaps bring them together for comfort.

A strong wind shook the leaves above us and I looked up at the oak tree. One of the branches was growing into the wooden nine-foot fence and whenever the wind blew, the fence creaked ominously. It had been a flawless spring day, not quite yet summer, complete with an early morning shower, sunshine, and unseasonably warm temperatures. It was the kind of day when people braced themselves for an imminent storm because the weather was too nice, too soon. With dusk falling, the temperature was dropping, dictating sweaters and jackets, but it was still pleasant enough to remain outdoors.

"Eva doesn't have any feelings for him," Maya said.

"What?" I asked, pretending I hadn't heard her.

"I said, don't worry. Eva doesn't love Anthony. He hurt her too much. She may have forgiven him but she could never forget what he's done to her."

I guess I hadn't done a very good job of hiding my feelings, but I still pretended it had no significance to me.

"How are you and *your* husband doing?" I asked, turning the tables around.

She smiled slyly. "We're doing better. Still working on it. How's Luciano?"

"Do you really want to know?"

"I wouldn't ask."

"He and his wife are renewing their vows," I said cautiously, watching her face for a reaction.

"I'm glad," she said, sounding genuinely pleased.

We heard Eva laugh and we both looked up to see her trying to cover Alex's mouth as he started to divulge a secret. "Don't you dare!" she warned Alex.

"Next week is Tony's birthday," Maya said in a low voice. "He would've been twenty."

"He and Eli were really close in age, huh?" I inquired.

"Yup. One week short of a year. I just hope she doesn't fall apart."

After everyone left, Eva began wrapping up the leftovers, going in and out of the house, moving like a dancer across the stage. I volunteered to clean the grill while Eli wrestled with King. I watched with fascination and alarm as the dog held Eli's forearm in its powerful jaws, growling menacingly, then obediently released him when Eli commanded him to.

"I got my cell phone on speed-dial to 9–1–1, just in case," I told Eli.

Eli smiled and hugged King around his thick, saggy jowls, kissing his snout. "I'm going to bed, Ma. Thanks for the party." Eli trudged up the steps, King on his heels. He planted a quick kiss on her cheek and turned to go, but she held him around the waist and hugged him. "C'mon, Ma," he protested.

"You don't have to go," she said.

"Sure," he quipped, throwing an exaggerated wink my way. Eva swatted his backside with the aluminum foil.

"I'll be in, in a little bit." I watched her as she walked around the deck, blowing out the tiki lights, shoving the patio chairs underneath the table. I was sitting on the bottom step of the deck rinsing off the grill with the hose.

"Leave that alone. Eli'll do it tomorrow," she commanded.

I turned slightly to look up at her, the motion detector lights behind her creating an outline of light around her silhouette. "I'm almost finished. Come down here and keep me company."

She didn't move nor did she reply.

"What—you afraid to be alone with me?" I asked.

"No," she replied, a little too quickly, laughing nervously. "Why should I be afraid?" She walked down the steps and sat sideways on the step above me, propping her feet against the railing.

"Are *you* afraid? About the surgery tomorrow?" she asked.

I scoffed, trying to play it off, but of course, I knew she could see right through me. The truth was I was more than scared, I was downright petrified. I wish I could say prayer had alleviated all my worries, but absolute fearlessness was impossible. It was how God kept us on our toes. It was what made man fallible. What made matters worse, in the last week, a couple of tragedies had occurred. Dan, my chemo chair neighbor who had been one cycle ahead of me, was given an incorrectly mixed chemo dose and died. Another patient, one of the youngest testicular cancer patients, a twenty-year-old college student named Erik, died during his RPLND surgery. Although their deaths were attributed to human error, the 90 percent chance of survival lost its meaning; it killed my positive outlook. Death became very real once again.

But then, I read the story of the ten-year-old boy with spinal cancer who had endured fifteen operations, chemotherapy, radiation, and a stem cell transplant and was finally cancer-free. There were more stories, about younger patients, even babies, who had bravely fought and survived cancer. Every morning, I tried not to feel sorry for myself and began my day with a mantra: *"There are people worse off than I am, there are sicker people than I am."*

"Yeah," I finally answered. "But I'm not scared about dying. I'm more afraid of not seeing the people that I care about. My family . . ." I paused and scrubbed the grill with the wire brush. "And you."

I waited for her to say something, my head bowed, my face growing hotter by the second as I scrubbed harder and harder. All I wanted was an acknowledgment that there was some hope for us later on down the line, a shining light in the distance I couldn't help but go toward. When I felt her hand on my shoulder, I relaxed and straightened up. Cautiously, I leaned my head back on her extended legs; they were slightly trembling but I couldn't tell if it was from the cooler temperature or nervousness. Listening to the crickets, I stared up at the night sky and realized what "midnight blue" meant.

"Everything's going to be fine," she said. "When you wake up, your family's going to be there. And I'll be there. *Si Dios quiere.*"

"If God wants?" I translated, turning to face her.

"God willing."

"I thought *'quiere'* meant 'want,' or 'love.' "

"It depends on the context . . ." she said, her voice fading as she turned to look up at the house. I knew Tony's room was up there, in the attic, still untouched since his death. I wanted to absorb her pain, just for a little while, hold her in my arms all night, and tell her that everything would be alright for her also. Staring at her stretched neck and her protruding chin, I remembered how soft her skin was in that spot, remembered what it was like kissing her there, like falling into a deep sleep. When she turned back around, a faraway look shrouded her face and she reached out to me. I closed my eyes, waiting for her touch. Her hand hovered over my head, then down to my eyebrows, a stroke of a finger and then, nothing. When I opened my eyes, she was looking away, into the blackness of the yard, her hands safely cradled in her lap.

CHAPTER 27

EVA

"WHO SO FINDETH a wife findeth a good thing and obtaineth favour of the Lord." As Akil read the passage from Proverbs 18:22, many of the wedding guests, the women mostly, whooped and clapped. I had heard the passage recited at other weddings and it always elicited the same response. I used to think the passage meant that a wife was "a good thing" for a man because he was getting the convenience of a housekeeper, sexual partner, and cook all in one. Now, I acknowledged its meaning in the spiritual context, that a man who got married was making a covenant with the Lord, because it was assumed he was forsaking all other women.

The passage was part of the wedding vows Akil had chosen from different scriptures of the Bible, excerpts from Corinthians and Proverbs 31. When it was Jade's turn, she began with selections from Genesis, Ecclesiastes, and ended with Ephesians. Before she could finish, she started weeping and Akil had to complete the last few verses before he, too, choked up.

I glanced over at Adam who was standing with the other groomsmen after walking Jade down the aisle, beaming like a proud brother. His eyes were closed but he was smiling since it was his suggestion to use scriptures in lieu of the traditional wedding vows. The fluttering in the pit of my stomach that usually occurred whenever I looked at him or he was near me resurfaced. He looked so noble in his black Nehru tux, which hugged him like a custom-made suit. A black-and-white mud-cloth–patterned bow tie completed his outfit. His hair had grown quite a bit so that he was sporting a modest, updated Afro, a combination of twists and finger-combed locks.

Over the last couple of months Adam and I had grown closer, like very good friends. Watching him recover from his major surgery was difficult, but because I had seen post-op pictures on the Internet, I was prepared when I visited him in the hospital. Through his recovery, I learned to cope with my own grief. My pain was still palpable; I felt it in the numbness in my chest, the lump in my throat, the knot in my stomach, but I was slowly recovering. I gained strength from watching his positive outlook and silent determination. Even though he was in pain for several weeks, and was still taking drugs for occasional discomfort, his attitude remained upbeat. When his mother or Jade couldn't tend to him, I stepped in to help with meals and make sure he didn't exert himself. The one thing I didn't do was change his dressing, not only because I felt a nurse was better equipped, but it seemed inappropriate for me to see him shirtless, given our past. Not that I didn't trust myself around him, but I knew my weaknesses and I didn't feel the need to test myself anymore. I found I was falling for him all over again, but I kept these feelings suppressed.

The week before the wedding, I accompanied Adam to the tuxedo shop for his final fitting. Since his first fitting, he had gained some weight and had to have the tuxedo altered a little. I walked over to where he stood in front of the three-way mirror as the tailor stuck pins around the shoulder area.

"What do you think, ma'am? Your groom looks good, huh?" the tailor asked.

"Oh, no, he's not—" I answered automatically, blushing slightly.

"We're not—" Adam said almost as quickly.

The tailor realized he was mistaken and smiled sheepishly. "Well, you make a nice couple anyway."

As the pastor blessed the new couple, I felt someone watching me. It was Luciano, who had been assigned as my partner, something Adam claimed was not his doing. But since he was no longer involved with Maya, it didn't bother me much. He seemed to have matured a little since his wife filed for divorce, despite recently renewing their vows. We were even able to have a civil conversation about our respective jobs. Only once did he ask how Maya was doing. When I told him that she was "still married," he took the cue and changed the subject.

I turned my attention back to Jade and Akil. Ordinarily, when I attended weddings, I had a tendency to look beyond the pretty dress-up clothes, the elaborate decorations, and the sentimental words and tears. As a marriage veteran, and a realist, I knew marriage was a job, a career in itself that involved a lot of compromising and a lot of taking for granted. Because I had been married so briefly and divorced so young, because I had spent half of my life raising my children alone, I didn't have a romantic view of marriage. I didn't believe in the fantasy of it, the knight in shining armor on a white horse riding me off into the sunset to live happily-ever-after. After the clothes were stored away, the decorations discarded, and the words and tears were spent, reality was waiting like a bucket of freezing water.

For the moment, however, I set aside my cynical thoughts and concentrated on the lovely aesthetics around me. Jade looked radiant in her gold African-inspired dress and headwrap; Akil, elegant in his coat and tails. The bridesmaids' dresses were in gold-and-black mud-cloth crepe de chine, styled according to each bridesmaid's preference. Of course, I had mine designed in the style of a sari and had received many compliments. Jade had commented that I was stealing her spotlight, and I apologized before realizing she was joking. Nothing could spoil her day.

My eyes drifted back toward Adam. He looked at me like when we first met, strangers across a room, smiling tentatively. I returned the smile and for the first time, I began to imagine what it would be like to be married to him. Not in the wedding-day-fantasy-honeymoon scenario, but in the day-to-day marital setting. I could see Adam watching ESPN as I cooked dinner and cleaned the house; Adam and I arguing over the toilet seat being left up, or the tube of toothpaste being squeezed in the middle; Adam coming home late at night while I lay in bed wondering where he'd been. Then I realized I was reliving my marriage with Anthony. It would be different with Adam, wouldn't it? I was not the same woman I was at nineteen, naive and headstrong, and Adam was not Anthony. We were older, more responsible, committed to our relationships with God, with a friendship that was stronger than it had been in the beginning. There was something about marriage, about living under the same roof, that ruined all that. Then it dawned on me that Adam and I had never really discussed marriage, at least not in depth, except to say that neither one of us wanted it. So why was I even thinking about him in that context?

Just as the pastor was about to present the new Mr. and Mrs. McClaren to the guests, a loud yawn was heard. Everyone laughed as all eyes turned toward Daelen, the ring bearer, who was stretching his body in his miniature tux. Kia, the flower girl, put her gloved finger to her lips. "Shush, boy!" she scolded him loudly. This was followed by more laughter.

The wedding ceremony was followed by a long session of photography and videotaping. The photographer was a petite older woman of about sixty, an independent, never-married aunt of Adam and Jade's on their father's side who had owned her own photography studio for thirty-five years. She had a salt-and-pepper mini Afro and was dressed in a cream-colored fitted pantsuit that accentuated her extra-small figure. The two cameras she alternately used looked like they weighed more than she did.

"The ceremony was nice," I told Adam when we had a sit-down break between poses. "The vows, especially." My gold-dyed shoes were killing me, so I slipped them off and lifted my feet onto the pew.

Adam shook his head. "They should've memorized them. They didn't sound natural."

"They sounded alright. It's the words that count, not the presentation. We can't all be poets."

"It would've sounded more ro . . . dramatic, if they had recited the words, instead of reading them," he said critically, but not harshly. Then he began reciting the words in his lyrical voice, *"Love is kind and patient, never jealous or boastful, proud, or rude . . . It doesn't keep a record of wrongs that others do . . ."* His voice dwindled as he momentarily closed his eyes and massaged his torso underneath his tux. Although he was officially recovered from the surgery and was in remission, I knew he still had pain management issues and was seeing a specialist who kept trying different medications. Some of the drugs sapped his energy, and there were times when he would doze off when we were together, other times when he seemed preoccupied.

"Show-off," I said. "When *you* get married, *you* can say it the way *you* want."

He opened his eyes and looked at me with mock scorn and I held his gaze as a camera went off, startling us.

"I just love your dress, honey," Mattie, the photographer, cried. "An Indian sari out of African print. I love it, absolutely *love* it."

"Thank you."

"Let me get a picture of you two."

"You just did, Aunt Mattie," Adam protested.

"Don't argue with me, boy. I want another one over there." She gestured toward the rostrum where two columns were decorated with an arrangement of lilies, foliage, and baby's breath.

"Did she just call me 'boy'?" Adam asked loudly of no one.

Adam pulled himself up with effort, pulling me with him as I struggled to step back into my shoes. We posed in a classical bridesmaid-groomsman pose: turned slightly toward each other, holding on to the bouquet.

"I don't like that. You look staged," Mattie said, shaking her head. "Put your hands down. Look at each other like you were looking at each other a little while ago."

With everyone looking at us, I felt self-conscious and hesitantly looked up at Adam as he looked down at me. The flash went off and I rubbed my eyes, pretending the bulb had blinded me.

As we walked off the lectern, Mattie held my arm and pulled me back. "What did you say your name was, sweetheart?" she asked in a low voice.

"Eva."

"Um-hmm. I've been watching you two eyeing each other all afternoon."

Before I could tell her that Adam and I were just friends, she called up the rest of the wedding party for final pictures. We were directed to gather around Jade and Akil, joining hands in what Mattie called "a circle of love and blessings." Adam leaned over to me.

"I'm ready to go," he whispered in my ear.

"You can't leave your sister's wedding," I whispered back.

"Watch me."

He looked at me in that way he had been lately, like there was something on his mind, something he wanted to say but didn't know if he should. This confused me because I thought we had reached a point where we could tell each other anything.

The reception was held in Akil's parents' home, a Victorian three-story mansion with a wrap-around porch. It sat on a double lot in Hyde Park. A beautiful rose garden and gazebo in the backyard created a ready-made decorated effect. The band, comprised of college students from the nearby University of Chicago, played a variety of neo-soul and R & B love songs from the eighties and nineties. Adam and I danced to a couple of ballads during which we held each other like junior high kids who were forced to dance together at their first dance. Several times, his lips brushed my forehead, but whenever I looked up, his eyes were closed as if it had been unintentional. We also participated in the usual group dances: the bus stop, the electric slide, the cha-cha slide, dances I was familiar with, and which I infused with my own salsa moves. Adam ran out of steam after the first two numbers and after I finally sat down, he commented that he didn't know I could move "like a sistah." It dawned on me that we had never gone dancing.

The food was supplied by Jade's catering business and included many of her family's traditional Creole dishes, and an orange-wine wedding cake. Jade took my advice and served sparkling white grape juice, which when slightly frozen tasted like bubbly champagne. I noticed that Adam wasn't eating much of anything, just drinking water and juice. When I questioned him, he claimed to have an upset stomach.

As the afternoon wore on, I was a little overwhelmed by Adam's and Akil's extended families, even though I had gotten to know many of them during the rehearsals and on the dance floor. Whenever I got the chance, I stole away for some quiet time, exploring the mansion or some corner of the expansive yard. My solitude was interrupted every time by Adam, who would come hunting for me, wondering why I kept disappearing. He still didn't understand that sometimes I just wanted to be alone for the sake of being alone. It didn't necessarily have to mean anything. When the band started calling for a conga line to the tune of "Feeling Hot, Hot, Hot," I disappeared from the reception once again. I had noticed the small greenhouse at the far end of the yard, and finding the door unlocked, I went in. Akil's mother had a variety of breathtaking orchids and tropical plants. My first thought was of my mother, how she had always dreamed of having a greenhouse. Then I remembered that I had never gotten around to building my own.

From inside the greenhouse, I could hear the band begin to play the Chicken Dance, and despite being alone, I rolled my eyes as I imagined the antics of the guests.

Just before Eli's birthday party, I had taken Pastor Zeke's advice and continued praying, rising early and doing my daily devotion, falling to my knees at night, things I hadn't done in a long time. Slowly but surely, I was beginning to feel God's presence in my life again, to participate fully in church once again, and in the Youth Ministry. I was beginning to let go of the anger at the man who had murdered my child, let go of the helplessness I felt when I tried to make sense of Tony's death. Although no explanation was plausible, I was beginning to accept it, in spite of my efforts not to. When his birthday rolled around, I was busy helping Adam convalesce, which kept me from getting depressed. It was still a horrible time, but somehow I got through it. Next year, it would be easier, I told myself, a promising, yet somber thought.

The night after the party, after everyone was gone and I was finally alone, I sat in the backyard glider for what seemed like hours, listening to the night sounds: the crickets chirping, the wind whispering through the leaves.

For some people, there was usually some event that triggered their reconnection with God. For some, it was a specific song they heard, for others, a particular sermon that touched them. For me, it was being alone, in the middle of my backyard, the night of my son's birthday. That night, surrounded by God's nature, I began my nightly prayer, waiting for His guidance. I could have easily continued being complacent, letting the days slip by, going through the motions of life. But Eli, although grown, still needed not only me, but God. I realized that even though my relationship with my father was far from ideal, it was better than it had been. And I had finally begun to forgive and love myself, my life, once again. I was at peace in my solitude, only this time I wasn't wanting for anything, or anyone.

Even when Adam came back into my life and started making his way into the crevices of my mind, I remained steadfast and blocked him out. When we were together, I didn't allow him in my personal space and anything I felt, I kept to myself. In our e-mails and phone calls, we shared so much more than we ever had before, about our deepest fears, our relationships with our fathers. We were able to talk about anything—except the way we were, what we had meant to each other, and what, if anything, we would be in the future. He respected my boundaries, never attempting anything. Had I been as strong in the beginning, that first time I let him into my house, the kiss in the bathroom never would have happened, nor would've any of the events that followed. Our attraction to each other was still quite obvious, at times tangible in the air between us, but because of other important issues—his surgery and recovery, my ambivalent relationship with God, his rededication—we didn't cross the line. And always in the back of my mind was the promise I had made to God, when I feared my children would be taken from me: *I will never let another man come before You . . .*

In the distance, I heard someone at the microphone announcing the throwing of the bouquet and garter. Although I had no intention of participating, I always enjoyed watching the unmarried guests clamoring for the trinkets that promised future matrimony. As I strolled back to the reception, Adam headed toward me.

"I've been looking all over for you," he said impatiently, taking my hand. He steered me in the opposite direction, away from the party. "Let's go for a drive."

"What? Now? They're getting ready—"

"Come on."

Adam headed straight for the lakefront, past Montrose Harbor, which was already under construction and fenced off, and on to the next beach—Wilson. The lakefront was crowded and people turned and stared at our wedding attire like we were wearing spacesuits. All around us, blankets were flying up, and picnic gear and garbage were being tossed about. He led me by my hand as an impatient adult pulled a tired child, my heels sinking into the sand. Finally, he stopped at an unoccupied spot and faced the water, his eyes closed tightly. He released me and I waited for him to speak, but he didn't.

Despite his efforts to appear happy for his sister's sake, I had sensed that something was going on. I started to ask him what was wrong, but the grave look on his face stopped me. His lips were pressed against his teeth, his dense eyebrows furrowed, like he had a headache or there was some kind of war going on in his mind. His hands were hidden in the pockets of his pants, his long jacket open and blowing back from the muggy blasts of wind. Momentarily, I was reminded of that day, after the poetry reading, when he hyperventilated, that foggy day I first fell in love with him. I panicked, fearing he was going to give me some bad news about his health, and I thought the worst: that perhaps he was, after all, dying.

"Adam, are you alright?" At the sound of my voice, his body swayed back and his eyes flew open, as if he had forgotten I was there.

"Wait," he said, holding out his hand. "I want to tell you something."

"What? Can't we talk in the car?" Not only was the sun scorching down on us, but people were staring and pointing, some even laughing, or maybe it seemed that way since we were definitely overdressed for the beach.

"I have something to say." He wouldn't look at me so I finally walked in front of him and tugged at his jacket. "A couple of months ago, I thought I was going to die," he continued.

I cautiously grabbed the hemline of his Nehru jacket, afraid of what was coming next, prepared for whatever he was going to say, even if he said he had only so many months to live. What did one say to that? "But you didn't," I assured him.

"You . . . I want you to know I appreciate everything you did. For being there . . . your prayers. You renewed my faith in God and that's something I didn't think would ever happen."

I had renewed *his* faith in God? How was that possible when a few months ago, my own faith had gone stagnant? I turned around with my back to him, not too close so that we were touching, but close enough so that I could feel the heat from his body. It was overpowering, but at the same time soothing, and I wanted to stay there, stop time and bask in his solace. "What are friends for?" I asked lightly, rubbing my burning arms.

"You're more than a friend, Eva."

"Okay. Ex-girlfriend," I replied, still trying to make light of the situation.

"I want you to be more than that."

I didn't speak. I couldn't trust myself to say anything. Did he know how hard it had been for me these past few months, watching him suffer, wanting to hold him, love him.

"Are you listening?" He whispered in my ear: "I want us to be more than friends, more than what we've been."

It was his survivor's gratitude talking, I knew this. I had read about it. It was like making promises to God when you want to get out of a bad situation, when all hope is gone.

"I brought you here because this is where I felt alive when I was sick. Out here, when nobody was around because it was too cold, I felt the most alive. I felt like I was the only one in the world and it was just me and God. Remember the first time you brought me out here?"

He brought his hands out of his pockets and turned me around to face him, but I could only look at his chin, where tiny hairs were beginning to grow. He held my face in his hands, forced me to look at him. The warmth from his hands sent tiny prickles of heat through me.

"I want you to know that when it's cold, I want to be the one to keep you warm. When you're scared, I want to be the one to make you safe. When it feels like the end of the world, I want to be there with you. I want you to know . . . I have no problem being number two in your life—"

"Adam, you're just . . ." I started, trying to remove his hands from my face. "You're feeling this way because you were sick and—"

"Can I finish?" he interrupted, irritated, but he tenderly stroked my cheeks with his thumbs. "What I'm trying to say is . . . what did you think? About being together? You and me?"

His hands were making my face sweat. I put my arms on his waist and gently pushed him away from me, but he wouldn't let go. I could feel his bottom ribs, jutting out underneath his shirt. He still had a lot of weight to gain in order to reach his precancerous weight. It had been so long since I touched him.

"What do you think?" he repeated.

I looked up at him, meeting his eyes. "What do I think? I think you probably think you owe me something for being there for you. You don't owe me anything. I would've done the same thing for my sister or Simone, or my children. God brought you through, not me. I was just on the sidelines."

"Spiritually speaking, yes, He did. But emotionally, you were the one."

"That's no reason to get back together again."

"I'm not just talking about us getting back together. I'm talking about getting married."

I was so astonished, I couldn't speak, and it was too late to stop the stunned look that took over my face.

"I want us to get married," he repeated. "I want to marry you."

"You want to marry *me*? Why?"

Immediately, I found myself analyzing his unorthodox proposal. Compared to what I had experienced in the past, and what I had witnessed and heard about in my family, it was unconventional. There had been no proposal with Anthony, we had mutually agreed to get married, shopped for our rings together, and paid for our own wedding. Victor, on the other hand was a hopeless romantic, and took me to the restaurant where we had our first date and arranged to hide the ring on the dessert tray. When the waiter came around with the tray, Victor got down on one knee and said, *"Chocolate mousse, flan, or me?"* But the element of surprise was never a part of my previous proposals; they had been expected. Adam's was not.

He half-scoffed, half-laughed, finally removing his hands from my face. Predictably, he rubbed the back of his neck. "Man, this isn't at all what I expected. On TV, women scream, or cry, or throw their arms around the man."

"This ain't TV," I said seriously, but without malice.

"Why do I want to marry you? For that reason right there. Because other women would scream, cry, or throw their arms around a man who asked for their hand, but not you. You've got to give me a hard time."

"You want to marry me 'cause I give you a hard time?" I asked, confused.

He exhaled, exasperated. "I want to marry you because you are *you*. Because you are a good woman, *woman*. Because you're a woman of God. Because we were good together. I've been missing you since the day we broke up."

I thought, that day was so long ago—the day after we had sex when I believed I had made the biggest mistake of my life.

"Why now?" I asked him.

"It's something I've been thinking about."

"You said you didn't want to get married for a long time. What's changed since then?"

"You have to ask me that?"

He reached into his pocket and I panicked, thinking he was going to produce a ring. Why was he doing this in front of all these strangers?

"So what do you say?" he asked.

"What do I say?"

"Could you stop repeating my questions?" he said impatiently. "Look, I know it may be hard for you to believe, but I'm a faithful man. Cheating is not my style. I'm not Anthony or Victor. I will never cheat on you."

It took everything within me not to say *I've heard that before*. How could anyone promise something like that?

When I didn't respond, he dropped down to his knees and clasped my hands in his. People, who at first had looked at us curiously but eventually turned away, were now staring more expectantly. A few were smiling, comprehending what was happening, although I was having a problem grasping the gravity of the situation. In the presence of so many witnesses, I felt deeply embarrassed, knowing anything other than the affirmative would be emasculating and humiliating to Adam.

"Can we talk in the car? Everybody's looking," I whispered through my teeth.

"I don't care about these people," he said, without breaking his gaze. "Eva. *'Come with me, be with me, stay with me. Choose me.'*"

I could feel myself losing strength, my resolve depleting as the words from his poem sunk in and touched the deepest part of me where I had stored my love for him. *That* part of me wanted to say "yes," but I was sweating and becoming irritable, and I was stalling for time. I didn't want to tell him the painkillers were probably affecting his judgment, that in a couple of months when he was back to normal, he might feel totally different. In the car with the air conditioning on, he could think more clearly. But more important, I could turn him down in private. Then another thought came to mind. What if he *was* dying and he wanted to get married because it would be his last chance? Before, marriage had been a distant concept, something he, like many men, put off until after they had sown their wild oats, until they came face-to-face with their mortality, as I suspected Adam had. All of sudden, he was ready?

"Are you dying?" I finally asked, not wanting to know the answer.

"What? Why are you asking me that?"

"I don't think you're thinking clearly—"

"You think I'd ask you to marry me if I was dying?" He was incredulous, shaking his head in disbelief, and he was getting loud, oblivious to the people around us. He stood up, loosening his tie frustratingly. "Don't you want to marry me?"

"I've been there."

"Not with me."

"Do you know how hard marriage is? How hard it is to live with another person when you've been single for so long?"

"Are you trying to convince me or yourself?"

"You've never been married before, I have. I'm not a traditional wife; I cook when I feel like it, I don't like cleaning up after anyone."

"I don't plan on being a traditional husband. I cook when *I* feel like it, and I don't like cleaning up after anyone either."

"Men start off saying they'll share the housework, but they always change," I told him matter-of-factly. "Plus, I don't think I want to change my name."

Adam looked up and spoke to the sky, but loud enough for me and our spectators to hear. "I cannot believe this woman." Any minute, I expected him to turn to the audience and say, *"Can you believe she turned me down?"*

When he looked back at me, his face was hard, his eyes steely. I could hear someone giggling behind him. "I can't believe you're talking about petty things like housework and not changing your name. What was it you said when I asked you what you would do if the sex was bad on your wedding night? 'We'll work it out. It's not rocket science.' Well, *we* can work it out. Housework isn't rocket science. I'm not so backward that I think a woman should do it all. *Especially* if she works. As far as your name is concerned, keep it if it's so important to you. It's just a name."

"Fine, fine," I finally said, because I didn't want to argue anymore, and I was ready to leave. "We'll get married."

"Wha—?" he said, then he held up his hands in aggravation. "Nah, nah. I don't want to marry you if you're going to be like that. Like you're deciding on an entrée. I want you to *want* to marry me."

I thought about his request, about what it would mean to be a wife, to be his wife. I could see Adam cooking dinner as I cleaned the house, listening to the news in the background; solving the toilet seat dilemma by putting both the seat and lid down; dismissing the toothpaste problem as trivial; calling to let me know he'd be home late so I didn't worry. I thought of coming home to him after a bad day at the university, listening to him talk about his charges at work, being with him finally as God had originally mandated, reaching the ultimate passionate connection. *It is better to marry than to burn.* But it wasn't even about that anymore.

"Can I think about it?" I asked quietly.

He shook his head in disbelief, massaging the back of his neck, then he spun around, his shoes sinking in the sand as he hurried toward the car. He didn't look back once to see if I was following him. After I had gathered my dignity, and the hem of my dress, I started walking slowly over the sand, staring straight ahead and ignoring our audience who were like nosy witnesses to an ugly car accident, wanting to look away yet needing to see the carnage.

CHAPTER 28

ADAM

WHEN A MAN decides to love a woman, he takes all kinds of chances with his emotions, his way of life, even his future. He begins to understand that loving a woman isn't something that happens overnight, at first sight. He begins to recognize that love is equivalent to a baptism. At first, the water is sudden, a splash of light, an awakening. But conversion isn't instantaneous. It takes a while before the blood washes out the old soul, gives birth to the new. One day he wakes up and there he is, a new man.

I didn't know when the thought of marrying Eva entered my mind. Perhaps when I saw her on the hospital elevator. Or the night of Eli's birthday when we were alone and I wanted to ease her fears. Or when I woke up after surgery and saw her by my bed, before I saw my mother, before I saw Jade. For days, I had mulled over several scenarios for the proposal. The first one involved waiting for a light rainy day, reminiscent of the night we met, then casually popping the question as we strolled through the rain. But my timing was always off; either it rained too hard or we could never get together. The second involved taking her to Coffee Will Make You Black and reciting the poem I had composed, but each time I read it, it didn't seem adequate, or good enough, or romantic enough. Then I thought, doing it in front of a crowd seemed pretentious. It should be a private thing. The last setting involved learning how to say *"Will you marry me?"* in Spanish and asking her at Montrose

Harbor, but construction was already in progress and the beach was closed to the public.

And then at Jade's wedding, I looked at Eva sitting on the pew next to me in her stocking feet, as we took a break in between pictures, and something just told me that that was the day I would ask her, no frills, no preparation. I figured we could pick out the ring later.

But there were so many things I left out of the proposal. I wanted to tell her I no longer believed in coincidences, that it was fate that had brought us together, not Luciano and Maya. It was God who separated us and brought us together again, that day on the elevator, and everything that happened in between.

Can I think about it?

Eva's answer dogged me relentlessly in the days following my proposal, until I saw the words suspended in the air around me, on my computer screens at home, and at work. Can she *think* about it? Those were not the words a man wanted to hear when he asked a woman to marry him. Next to *"It's okay, it happens,"* and *"The cancer's back,"* they were the worst words I had heard in my life. Then, on the other hand, she hadn't said "no." A negative response would have hurt but at least I'd know what to do with it; I'd move on. I didn't know what to do with *"Can I think about it?"*

So I waited. I waited and tried to stay busy with work, family, exercise, and church. I waited as I met with my agent about some last-minute changes to my screenplay prior to production. I waited as I tried to offer some guidance in my clients' otherwise directionless lives. I waited as I attended a men's conference on spiritual restitution to women who had been wronged in the past. I waited as I ran to the lakefront and back, an activity that was beginning to seem futile.

Akil was the only one I had confided in about asking Eva to marry me since Luciano was in the midst of his third divorce and had lost faith in marriage. Akil had started working out with me, stating that he wanted to get into running, so I let him tag along. He was turning out to be a cool brother-in-law; he didn't talk much, which was a great quality when you didn't feel like talking. It didn't even bother me that he called me "brother," which he pronounced phonetically instead of colloquially.

A week before his wedding, Akil brought up the topic of Eva. We were several days into our training session at Lake Shore Beach, sitting on the bench where I had met the college student so long ago.

"So have you asked her yet?" he inquired.

I shook my head, still slightly out of breath. I pulled my collar out and blew puffs of air down my shirt to alleviate the stinging of sweat on my surgical scar, which was still sensitive to any kind of sensation.

"Why not?"

I shook my head again. "You don't know her. She's . . ."

"Tough? Oh, I know." He chuckled. "I remember when she first came to TCCC. A couple of the church brothers wanted to ask her out but they were scared to approach her. She had this aura about her that said 'Don't talk to me.'"

I nodded in total understanding and we both laughed.

"But when you get to know her, she's not like that at all," Akil continued. "I think she's changed. She doesn't seem as hard since her son's death."

I began to feel more comfortable speaking to him about her. "She's just not the kind who buys romance and 'I love you' declarations. I'm not sure how to propose. She's not into jewelry. I mean, the woman buys her own flowers. Man, she grows her own flowers."

Akil laughed. "Well, do you want her?"

"Do I want her?" I repeated. What kind of question was that? *Of course, I wanted her.* "Like you wouldn't believe."

"Then you have to let the Man upstairs know, brother. *'You do not have, because you do not ask God,'*" Akil quoted effortlessly. "*'When you ask, you do not receive, because you ask with wrong motives, that you may spend what you get on your pleasures.'* James four, verses two and three. Ask, and you shall receive."

Though I had heard the phrase before, I did not know it was a biblical reference. I had always believed that God only listened to prayers of significance, prayers from people who were really in need, in trouble, or in pain. Somehow asking Him for a woman didn't seem worthy of His valuable time. Unconvinced, I said, "I've always heard God gives you what you need, not what you want."

"This is true. Do you need her?"

I thought about that. Did I need her like I needed air, water, and food to live? The logical answer would be "no." But the idealistic, personal response would be *yes, God, yes, I need her.* "I do," I answered.

"Fast and pray, my brother, fast and pray."

One of the things I had learned at the men's conference was that prayer is a dialogue, not a monologue. One has to initiate a conversation with God, one on One, not only asking, but waiting for His response. Prayers are best answered through total sacrifice, and abstaining from a basic necessity such as food is one way to achieve spiritual sustenance. Not eating had been part of my cancer period, but loss of appetite and self-denial were two very different things.

For a week prior to Jade and Akil's wedding, I fasted and prayed, drinking only water and Gatorade. It wasn't too hard turning down lunch with Derek since he was used to my funky appetite, but not eating at the wedding was tricky. I was looking peaked and my family was getting suspicious. One by one, they tried to force me to eat. I had to use my pain medication as an excuse for not eating. Akil, the only one who knew what I was contemplating, stuck to his guns and didn't break our confidence.

Before proposing to Eva, I thought of our past conversations about marriage. Our dialogues were always brief, a comment here and there, or in the heat of an argument. Back then, her adamant assertions against remarriage seemed out of competition, to one-up me. We had never really had a serious discussion about the matter. Although I had never been married, I knew marriage was difficult, which was why many people, myself included, delayed the ritual. Experience was not the only teacher; sometimes learning from the examples of others, like my parents' and my sister's, worked wonders. I remembered the night I had suggested out of anger that we tie the knot and Eva almost chopped my head off. I just knew there was no way her reluctance toward marriage was stronger than mine, or even the worst commitment-phobic man. *Most women want to get married, don't they?* I tried to rationalize. *Most women are afraid of being alone, aren't they?* I knew those assumptions came from years of cultural conditioning. And then the obvious answer came to me: Eva was not, and had never been, "most women."

It was hard to believe that housework and the name change were her biggest concerns about marriage. Maybe she didn't want to be stuck with a sickly man, which was understandable since it was not my intention to be a burden to anyone.

Perhaps she was afraid I would be unfaithful like her ex-husband and her ex-fiancé. And how could I convince her that I would never cheat on her because I knew what it was like, and I never wanted her to feel that way.

I thought back on the image I had always had of my future wife, how I thought I would know the woman I was going to marry at first sight. I didn't have that intuition with Eva in the beginning; that sentiment came later. Or how it had always been my intention to marry a Black woman. Even if Eva wasn't "Black" in the ethnic sense of the word, she had the qualities of the Black women I had known all my life: my grandmother, my aunts, my mother and sister. She was resilient and a fighter, a survivor; the kind of woman who held on to her principles no matter what. If she had been Asian, White, or whatever, I would've felt the same way. I fell in love with Eva for who she was, not *what* she was.

What I couldn't understand was, now that I was "Mr. Righteous" personified, the kind of man she had initially wanted, why was her decision difficult? I had come to God of my own accord; she had been the secondary reason.

These were the words that came to me during my fasting prayers, in my discourse with God: all my thoughts, my fears. Prior to my rebirth I would have thought I was losing my mind, but now I knew it was part of an ongoing dialogue with God.

For eight days after the wedding, and Eva's ambiguous answer to my proposal, I waited for her call. Every time the phone rang, I thought it was her. I felt like the goofy ostracized boy waiting for the call from the pretty popular girl, a call that would never come. I felt like a chump. Sitting at home, I wondered if Eva was really "thinking" about her decision or if she already knew what her answer was going to be. No, she wouldn't play games at this late stage. Not after what she had been through, after what I had been through. I didn't know many things but that much I knew. A part of me was prepared for the possibility that she would turn me down because she had been a challenge from day one, high maintenance. So why had I expected her response to a marriage proposal to be any different?

One evening, after returning from movie night with Justin and Ricky, the phone was ringing as I walked in. I didn't bother to check the caller ID and went straight to the shower. The phone rang on two more occasions as I was relaxing and reading on the balcony and, reluctantly, I got up to check the number. Recognizing Jade and Akil's new phone number in Oak Park, I picked up.

"Have you asked her yet?" Akil asked. "I can't keep lying to my wife. And your mom, she's something else. She won't let up. They think you're sick again and you're keeping it to yourself."

I started to lie but I found myself telling him the truth. "Yeah, I did."

There was silence as he waited for details and I waited for further questions. In the interim, I walked into the kitchen and looked in the refrigerator even though I wasn't hungry or thirsty. The inside of the fridge looked like the store floor models, spick and span and empty except for some Gatorade, two eggs, and an apple.

Finally, picking up on the silence on my end, Akil said questionably, "She said 'no'?"

"She didn't say yes."

"Oh. Sorry about that, brother."

"She said she'd think about it."

"Maybe she'll say 'yes' after she thinks about it."

"I don't know." I reached for the apple. "At this point, I really don't care, brother."

*   *   *

On the ninth day, an early Saturday morning, she called. I was ready to be sarcastic, to tell her it only took God six days to create the world, a bigger feat than the decision to get married.

"Hey, babe," she said.

Her voice caught me unprepared and I didn't answer right away. "'Sup?" I then said, unintentionally adopting Justin's customary greeting.

"Can you meet me at the café?"

"I'm not in the mood for coffee right now." I was amazed at how cold I could still be, how quickly I could digress in spite of my renewed spirit. But after all the waiting, I was feeling mean and unsociable. The former me would have begun doubting my conversion but the reborn me was well aware that I was allowing the enemy to get the best of me. I was beginning to learn that being saved didn't mean you are perfect, but a constant work-in-progress.

"Please," she said. "It's on me."

Her voice sounded like a little girl's, begging for the latest televised toy during the holiday season. But still, I hesitated, stalling because I was nonetheless feeling slightly insignificant. "If you're going to say 'no,' I'd rather you spare me the humiliation and tell me now."

"Adam."

Even before I consented, I knew I was going to meet her wherever, whenever she said.

By the time I got to the café, I was sweating profusely from the hot, muggy weather and because the air-conditioning was broken in my car. When I walked up to the door, there was a sign that said "Closed for Inventory." But the door was unlocked. The place was dark and deserted, strange because even early in the morning, there were always customers. There was no one at the counter, no one browsing in the aisles or sitting at the tables, and Caswanna and Hassan were nowhere in sight. Directly in front of the stage was one table with a rose-shaped candleholder that was lit. The place was bare aside from the classic votive candles and the stool that the performers used. To make my temperament worse, the air-conditioning was off. Something wasn't right.

"Hello?" I called out, standing in the doorway wondering if I was walking into a robbery or something. Then I thought, if there was a robbery in progress, then Caswanna and Hassan could be hurt. Or Eva. My street-smart instincts kicked into overdrive as my eyes searched frantically for a weapon.

"Caswanna! Hassan!" I yelled, grabbing the nearest candle-holder. It was made of pewter and weighed a good three pounds, and could probably knock a person out, provided I could get close enough and he wasn't carrying a gun. "Eva—"

And then from stage left she appeared, wearing Simone's orange blouse, scarf, and flared jeans—the outfit she wore when we first met for coffee, our "non-date." Her hair was responding to the discontinuation of relaxers so that her natural kinky-curl was coming through and tumbling from the scarf in a crowning glory. She walked onto the stage very slowly, like a bride or like she didn't know what to expect, carrying a bouquet of flowers like it was a baby. They were orchids, long-stemmed and overwhelming, filling the expanse of both her arms. I began to relax as everything started making sense.

Secretly, I was impressed with her ability to get Caswanna and Hassan to close the coffeehouse for us. I wished I had thought of it. Nevertheless, I kept a straight face, still unsure of her intent. Was she preparing to let me down easy, the offering of flowers to soften the blow—a requiem for a dead man? Or could she be making a big production out of saying "yes"? Either way, I wasn't going to make it easy for her. I knew it was juvenile but after waiting eight days, I wasn't feeling very mature.

Assuming that I was supposed to sit at the reserved table, I took my time walking to the front, slumping into the chair.

She leaned against the stool, not quite sitting, and cleared her throat a couple of times. I wondered what I was in for: a poem, a song, an apology.

"I never told you this but when my boys were shot, I made a vow to God that I would never let another man come before Him," she started, then cleared her throat again.

"I thought the shooting was punishment for going to bed with you. But I know God's not vengeful. I know He allows things to happen in order to test our faith, to make us see that He is supreme. It was something I believed easily enough until it happened to me.

"After you proposed, I had some reservations. Some of them had to do with the reality of being a wife, not wanting to change my name again, all those superficial things. So I went to Pastor Zeke. He made me see that I was letting the enemy steal my joy, get the victory when I should have been happy. He said I was looking at marriage in its worldly context instead of the covenant that it was meant to be. I also talked to Maya since she's been through so much in her marriage. They both told me I needed to ask God for direction.

"Part of me was afraid of getting married again because of my first marriage. But I know you're not Anthony; you're nothing like him. You have a good heart, you're a good man; I've always known that. I saw it in the way you're with Jade, Kia, and Daelen, and your mom. But the problem was you weren't a man of God, and now you are. Anthony and I didn't have God in our marriage. If *we* get married, we'll be one step ahead because we *have* God. And even if we get married, it won't be perfect because nothing is perfect. I know there're going to be good and bad times. I know there are things I'll—we'll both have to compromise on."

I listened intently, my hands folded on the candlestick I had grabbed as a weapon, dissecting her words into affirmative and negative. Most of what she was saying was all good, but my attention focused on her repetitive statement, *"if we get married."* Was she saying she wasn't ready? Or that it might not happen?

"I'm sorry if I embarrassed you at the beach, but you caught me by surprise," she continued. "I'm sorry for making you wait, but I had to wait on God's answer. Before, when I asked Him for direction, if you were the man for me, I didn't wait. I heard the answer I wanted to hear. I thought I had waited for a man long enough so He couldn't say 'no.' I've always believed God answered prayers in His own time, whether in our favor or not.

"Then last night, I told God directly, 'if this is the man I am to marry, then so be it; if not, I'm ready to wait another five years.'

When I woke up, I didn't think about what my first marriage was like, I didn't think about cooking and cleaning, I didn't think about my fears or doubts. I thought about you, about that day in the hospital when you prayed for me. That was my confirmation. With all you had been through, you still thought of me. I do want to marry you. So now I'm asking *you*, Adam. Do you still want to marry *me*?"

I was touched and humbled by her speech, but I couldn't let her off the hook just yet as my stubborn male ego re-emerged. Slowly, I started clapping unenthusiastically. I saw her face drop as she bit her bottom lip.

"Nice speech," I said wryly. "Let me get back to you."

She stepped off the stage and walked up to me, looking down at me with those huge brown eyes as I tried to maintain eye contact, but she stared me down. *Fierce,* I thought.

"Where's Hassan and Caswanna?" I asked.

"In the back, doing inventory."

I broke the ice. "Where's my ring?"

"You want a ring?" she asked, her face breaking into a smile.

She laid the flowers in front of me and sat down, sliding her chair closer to mine. I dug through the foliage. "Is the ring in here somewhere?"

"I'm sorry, Adam."

Worn out from the days of waiting and wanting, of feeling hurt, angry, and tense, I finally relaxed, leaning back in my chair as I twirled the candleholder on the table.

"I wanted to propose to you the old-fashioned way, down on one knee and all that," I explained. "But I thought that was so passé and I wanted the proposal to be unique. I don't know what happened. Something told me to propose that day. Maybe it was seeing Jade so happy. Perhaps it was God. I guess when you're sitting around with all the other little old ladies talking about how your husband proposed, you can tell them how you turned me down—"

She moved the candlestick out of reach and put her hands over mine to stop my nervous twirling. "I didn't turn you down. I said—"

"I wanted my proposal to be memorable," I persisted. "At the

beach, where I first told you 'I love you' in Spanish?" I paused. "I even wrote you a poem—"

"You wrote me a poem?" she asked, perking up like a kid. "Where is it?"

I tapped my chest to indicate I knew it by heart. She swallowed and whispered, "Recite it."

I shook my head, suddenly feeling inhibited. "Too late. You up-staged me."

She reached out and brushed back the sweaty, sticky hairs from my forehead. "*Recítalo*, now."

With our elbows on the table, we interlocked hands and looked into each other's eyes as I recited the poem:

> *Dear Eva,*
> *Who are thee to me?*
> *let me see*
> *you are the woman I hoped for*
> *before you came into my life*
> *who opened my eyes*
> *and opened my mind*
> *time and time again*
>
> *Who are thee to me?*
> *let me see*
> *you are the woman I wished for*
> *before my wish came true*
> *and took over my thoughts*
> *and helped me see God*
> *once again*
>
> *Who are thee to me?*
> *let me see*
> *you are the woman I prayed for*
> *before my prayers were answered*
> *the woman I will love*
> *as I love my own body*

like Christ loved the church
over and over again

Who are thee to me?
You ask?
You are
the Eve to my Adam
whom God made from him
as I am
the Adam to your Eve
made of God's breath and dust
You are
who You are
the woman I will love
forever and ever
until the end of time
Love, Adam

Before I could finish, she was pulling away one hand to wipe the silent tears that were sliding down her face. "Thank you. It's beautiful," she mumbled, her head lowered as she fumbled for a napkin at the next table. I cupped her face in my hands as she tried to wipe her eyes. Seeing her so emotional moved me and I felt my own eyes clouding over.

"*You're* beautiful."

"Right. With snot running down my face," she said, sniffling and laughing at the same time. I kissed her palms, the aroma from the orchids soaked in the veins. "So is that a yes?" she asked.

"Not until you get down on your knee," I joked. When she started to slide down to the floor, I pulled her up. "You know, you're the only woman I've ever brought here."

"That's nice. What's your answer?" she asked, cutting me off.

I laughed. "How do you say 'kiss me' again?"

She sucked her teeth. "You know how."

"*Besame,* Eva, *besame,*" I beseeched her.

But she had already anticipated my move and was leaning over to meet my lips. "We *really* have to work on expanding your Spanish vocabulary."

It was a simple kiss, hesitant and adolescent, our lips barely touching, as if we were afraid of getting carried away, but in its simplicity was a myriad of emotions, desire being the least of them. When we came apart, I expressed my gratitude to the One responsible, "Thank you, God."

I smiled at her, and by the look on her face, I could tell she wasn't finished.

"What?"

"Adam, you know, we don't have to rush into this," she then said. "Pastor suggested we join the couples' ministry." She paused as my smile slowly faded. "For premarital counseling. Maya said it's helping her marriage. And we're going to have to be engaged for a while, *no*?"

The Spanish "no" didn't do anything for me this time. "For how long?" I asked sullenly.

"I don't know. A couple of months. A year?"

I shook my head. "Uh-uh. I'm not waiting a year. If you don't know by now that you want to marry me, you'll never know."

She grabbed my hands. "I already know I want to marry you, you nut."

I groaned, thinking about sitting around in a group discussing my personal business with members of the congregation. I didn't mind God being in the midst of my life, but I had never been a "purging my soul in public" kind of guy. Still, the important thing remained that Eva said "yes."

"Alright," I finally answered.

"You'll go to counseling?"

"*Si*, 'Meesees' Black," I joked with an exaggerated Spanish accent.

"About that . . ." she started.

"I don't even want to hear it."

Laughing, she pulled me to her so hastily she almost tipped over with her chair. We kissed eagerly as if we weren't going to be spending the rest of our lives together.

ACKNOWLEDGMENTS

FIRST AND ALWAYS, thank you to the true Father in my life, who endowed me with my creativity, taught me the real meaning of love, and showed me that death is nothing to fear. Thank You for being my rock, for training my hands for war, and my fingers for battle.

In addition, I would like to thank the following:

My mother, Sylvia Rodriguez Benitez, who in her tranquil belief in God demonstrated the fervor and immensity of His truth.

My younger sister (by one year), L. Marie Ruíz Johnson, who has always inspired and encouraged me, who never fails to make me laugh, and whose strength, determination, and faith to save her twenty-plus-year marriage has been a motivating force, as well as a humbling example.

My little babysister, Madeleine Benitez, whom I wished for and got, and who is a part of the new women of the millennium with the education and ability to change the world and men's views toward them.

My sisterfriend T'Resay (Theresa) Drape-Jones, the inspiration for "Simone/S'Monée," who told me to set my book free so that others can get the intended blessings. I hope you receive its blessings as well.

My sisterfriend Pamela Keys, with whom I have had the privilege of sharing the drama that is life, the dreams that have come to fruition, and those that have yet to be realized.

My cousin Elvia Perez, who always told me I should use my *don* to write for God.

To John and Latin Liz Kobel at www.boricua.com, who first published my work on-line and provided me with numerous fans who have fueled my passion to keep writing.

To Lissette Calderon, founder and CEO of *Cuerpo* magazine, who had a vision to present Latinas in a true light. You are truly an awesome little woman with a huge heart.

To Marcela Landres, for creating *Latinidad* and helping a new generation of Latino writers achieve publishing success.

My former agent, Denise Stinson, for believing in me. Who would have thought, when we first met in 1997, our paths would cross again? Some people call it coincidence; I call it fate.

Many thanks to Walk Worthy Press and Warner Books for creating a venue where this genre of fiction can be shared with the rest of the world.

A special thanks to my editors, Karen Kosztolnyik, Robert Castillo, and Susan Higgins, for their most diligent work and kind words.

Para Arsenia Morales Rodriguez, my grandmother and family matriarch: *aunque no entiendas las palabras en este libro, te doy las gracias por aser el primer ejemplo de una mujer independiente.*

To all who read early drafts and/or influenced my life in one way or another: Delwin "DJ" Johnson, Enjoli Johnson, Daelen Johnson Wideman, Delwin L. "Diel" Johnson, Aurelio Benitez, Luis and Kimberley Quiñones, Lauren Quiñones, Meghan Quiñones, Gabriella Quiñones, Ruben and Marianne Benitez, Krystalyn Benitez, Jazmin Benitez, Hector Perez, Elisa Perez, Amaris Perez, Alyssia Perez, Diane and Alfredo "Punkin" Correa, Siahn Correa, Sofie Sierra-Alise Correa, William "Chany" and Dominga Quiles, Martha Padilla, Ramon Jamil Padilla, Miguel Ruiz, Ryan Cawthorne, Katie Mae Keys, André Taylor, Alexander Ruben Dunbar, Casey and Corey Keys, Benito and Ana "Tata" Benitez, Juan "Pichy" Rodríguez, Genaro and Delia "Nany" Benitez, Wilfredo Benitez, Yolanda Falcón, Alyson Benitez, Jannise Benitez, Vladimir "Blah" Benitez, Sonia Nieves, Sylvia Rosario, Arleen Rivera, Janet Ruiz Nieves, Carlos Rivera, Lindsay Demidovich, Lizzette Pellót, Evelyn Rocha, Jacqueline Rollins, Sylvia Buyco, Beatriz Moreno, Sofia Carrera, Joanne Prinzevalle, Linda Robinson, JoAnn Reed, Shannon Miller, Cynthia Escobedo, and Jan Forsline.

To Dr. Richard Davison, whom I consider the surrogate "earthly father" I never had, who taught me so much in our almost twenty-year acquaintance. Thanks for all the Spanish lessons, jokes, gossip, and stories, and for making my day job tolerable.

To Dr. Dan Fintel, one of the best "bosses" I have had the privilege of working for, and an overall great guy.

My extended family of cousins—first, second, and third, cousins' wives and husbands, and nieces and nephews, and anyone else whom I failed to mention specifically by name. Your lack of mention in these pages has nothing to do with disregard. There will be future books, and I will remember to thank you all—eventually. So stop trying to make me feel guilty!

Finally, and most important of all, I want to thank my children, the loves of my life: Zena-Maria Sylvia and Jameson Roberto, who have provided me with plenty of material over the years and whom I pray for always. My hope for you is that you love yourselves and love each other as God loves you—unconditionally. And remember, with God, all things are possible.